THE QUEEN OF SOUTH BEACH

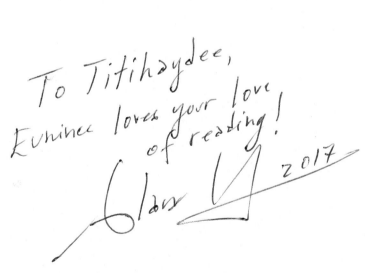

To Titihaydee,
Eunice loves your love
of reading!
Alan W 2017

Alan Wolford

Though they go mad they shall be sane,
Though they sink through the sea they shall rise again;
Though lovers be lost love shall not;
And death shall have no dominion.

—DYLAN THOMAS

CHAPTER ONE

The big rig with the California plates and Baja Grill trailer entered the rugged desert of southwest Texas about fifty miles from the Mexican border, heading northwest at ninety miles an hour. Though the summer sun had set nine hours ago, it was still 100 degrees outside the cab. The two heavily-armed men in the dimly-lit Kenworth were behind schedule after waiting an hour to clear the border crossing into Texas. The fifteen hundred dollar bribe they paid the U.S. Customs and Border Patrol at Laredo saved two hours of waiting in the mile-long line of vehicles, ensuring them a substantial head start on the Los Zetas cartel. With a $100,000 on-time delivery bonus waiting in L.A., the men wanted to get as far from Mexico as fast as they could on their freight train to hell.

In the barren and unforgiving lands of the Texas desert, speed limits usually went unenforced by the Texas Highway Patrol. In accordance with the new directives from the governor and DEA, troopers would be more focused on the illegal flow of drugs and immigrants north from the Mexican border and far less concerned with the Baja Grille eighteen wheeler delivering supplies to their restaurants.

"Pedal to the metal," said Gonz as he leaned on the accelerator, the big Cummins turbo diesel groaning in protest. They needed to make up for lost time.

"Gauges look good, Gonz. Let's get out ahead of them," replied Chico, surveying the instrument panel. Both former soldiers of the Especiale Fuerzas de Mexico were counting heavily on the six-figure bonus, though their plans differed on how they planned to spend the cash.

With the familiar logo of one of the most-recognized fast food restaurants painted in big letters on the trailer, Chico figured they could stay under the radar of law enforcement. The man riding shotgun thought about the promise he'd made to his pregnant wife to get them into a home in time for their first child's delivery. The added responsibilities of becoming a father were weighing on him, and even a modest three bedroom two bath in L.A.'s gang-ridden eastside neighborhoods seemed beyond his reach until he was offered the lucrative job by one of Rosa's lieutenants.

Undaunted by the high stakes, his paycheck for the hazardous haul was ten times what he'd normally make for a similar run across the southwest as a civilian, but the thought of qualifying for a mortgage seemed intimidating. Still, a hundred grand apiece for the run from Mexico to Southern California seemed paltry in comparison to the extra income needed to support a family these days. Uneasy about his $75 million cargo, he checked his mirrors and gauges again as the semi rumbled over the hot rolling desert under the light of a full moon. The dash clock read 5:40 a.m.

Central time, an hour to sunrise. Less than 200 miles southeast of El Paso, Gonz figured their chances of making it to east L.A. in one piece were pretty good, but he still couldn't shake the feeling they had a bullseye painted on their back.

Twenty miles of uninhabited desert separated most of the towns along this desolate section of SR 285. The barrel cacti, tumbleweeds, rattlesnakes, armadillos and scorpions of the high desert appeared in the halogen headlamps for only a fraction of a second like a strobe light revealing snapshots of a hostile planet. In the desert night, the distant cities dotting the landscape were visible only as a faint glimmer of light on the horizon from ten miles out. As they drew nearer, the light from the towns would spread out on the horizon like a solitary brilliant diamond.

Chico checked their route and the terrain on his tablet, ever on the lookout for possible ambush points, paying particular attention to the intersections and narrow passes that lay ahead. The two men passed the time with a minimum of small talk as they guided the turbodiesel through the hot black desert like a high-speed locomotive.

The veteran soldiers had first met in the Especiale Fuerzas de Mexico years before. A camaraderie developed within the ranks of their new employer after sharing three years of hazardous special ops with the Mexican government. The tenfold increase in pay had been difficult to ignore, and so they signed up for one of the most violent jobs imaginable. The two worked to perfect their English as they rehearsed the logistics of delivering their cargo to the warehouse in east L.A. ahead of schedule, and if they could pull it off, they could pick up more money than they'd seen in all their years working for the military.

Gonz could tell his partner was preoccupied and it had him worried. Focus was key. When they'd met years before, his buddy's indifference to gunfire made him think Chico was a couple of cans short of a six pack. But the more time they spent as a team, the more Gonz realized there were good reasons to stay cool under fire. They could pass for brothers, dressed in camouflage fatigues and body armor, both sporting athletic physiques, commando training, lethal weapons skills, and an ice-cold demeanor that was essential when up against competing cartels and trained mercenaries.

His intuition was nagging him, telling him what he tried to ignore; that this would somehow be their last run together. He'd nursed these trepidations before, only to be disproved time after time by their superior skills-and sometimes just blind luck. A confirmed bachelor all his life, Gonz couldn't fathom his buddy's calm acceptance of pending fatherhood. It seemed totally foreign to him in their line of work, but it made him curious about Chico's commitment to something other than a fat paycheck.

"You still planning on a bigger hacienda with Maria, bro?" asked Gonz.

Without taking his eyes from the road, Chico reached into his top pocket for a cigarette and spoke to the reflection in the windshield. "That's the plan." He lit up and took a long drag before continuing. "She's in her fifth month. We're gonna need more room."

"You're gonna make a great dad, buddy," replied Gonz.

"Yeah, if we make it to L.A. in one piece."

Something out the window caught Gonz's attention. He did a double take of the side mirrors to check on what looked like a pair of headlights trailing far behind. Artistic flashes of heat lightening streaked the desert sky in front of the rig every few minutes, but the faint flashes of light on the road behind them had a different look. He checked his instruments again. With the fuel gauge reading ninety percent full and the tach indicating peak torque, he figured they had enough diesel fuel to get all the way to Phoenix before they had to stop to refuel. He made a face, glancing at the man riding shotgun as a foul odor drifted to his side of the cab.

"Whew! Kinda ripe in here. When's the last time you had a shower, hombre? Gonz wrinkled his nose in mock distaste. "With water, not Dos Equis."

Chico smirked at his partner. "Don't quit your day job, comedi-ante. Did I complain about your burritos?"

Another foul odor assaulted Gonz's nostrils as he exhaled a lungful of smoke, "You gotta lighten up on those burritos, buddy." He flicked his cigarette ash into the ashtray and thought about his girlfriend in L.A. The hottest pole dancer he'd ever set eyes on, she still had no idea what he did for a living. Gonz reflected back on their last weekend together when they argued over quitting her job and moving in with him.

Chico continued to stare straight ahead, unwilling to take ownership of his odious deed. "Just crack your window," then glancing to the side view mirror. There it was again, a faint glim-mer of light on the road on the horizon behind them. He squint-ed into the mirror to see if they were gaining ground. Part of him wanted to believe it was heat lightning, but after several en-counters with Los Zetas, his gut was telling him it was something more sinister.

Gonz grimaced. "It's still 100 degrees out there," rolling his window back up. "Rather deal with your burrito." With 96 crates of Baja Grille's black bean burrito mix, chicken breast and yellow rice onboard, the two drivers had made good use of their cargo, never once having to stop at restaurants.

"Suit yourself." He knew the drill and began to prepare for the worst. Chico opened the storage compartment in front of him to retrieve the four twenty-round clips for his Uzi, and in the bottom of the oversized glove compartment he noticed some documents. Removing an insurance card and vehicle registration papers, he held them up in the dim red interior light of the Kenworth, squinting at the fine print.

"Who the hell's Dellacroix LLC?" he asked, shoving them back into the glove compartment and slamming it shut.

Gonz checked the Mossberg twelve-gauge pump wedged between the armored door and his seat. "Believe me, buddy, you don't wanna know," glancing at his partner. "Hand me the sat phone. I'm gonna check in, see what's up.

Chico checked the schedule before handing him the satellite phone. "Wait. Our next scheduled call isn't for another hour."

"Yeah, I know. Gotta bad feeling about this," replied Gonz.

"Yeah, well, when's the last time you felt good about anything?"

Without replying, Gonz pressed the talk button. "Gorilla, this is Road Runner. We're nineteen miles south of Ft. Stockton heading north on 285. Looks like we got company. Please advise."

The phone squawked, then a long pause ensued. He tried again. "Gorilla, this is Road Runner. You there?"

After a few moments, a deep male voice answered. "Road Runner, Gorilla." There followed several seconds of loud static. "Entiendo. Boss says put the pedal to the metal and stay sharp. Our sources on the ground say your route may be compromised. Sending chopper for backup. Over."

"Copy that, Gorilla. What's our ETA on the chopper?"

Gonz could hear background conversation, a few seconds of static, then the man's voice again. "Less than twenty minutes."

"Entiendo. Who we got on the chopper?"

"Interdiction team with Barretts. Good men, excellent shooters to cover your six."

"If it's Zetas, they'll try to take our rig intact. Pedal to the metal. Road Runner out." Gonz handed the phone back to Chico. "Do *not* like the sound of that, bro. Here we go, man."

Chico placed the satellite phone back inside the glove box and filled the empty munitions pouches of the flak jacket he wore with the extra clips, securing them with the Velcro flaps before checking the mirrors again. "Not certain, but I'm guessin' we got company."

"No merde, Capitan Obvio. Tu crees?" quipped Gonz. The intermittent lights were getting closer and it occurred to him that the rolling hills were the likely reason they appeared to be blinking. He pressed the accelerator to the floor, the big turbo diesel groaning as the semi accelerated to over a hundred miles an hour in a bid to stay ahead of their pursuers.

Chico leaned over to check the gauges and scowled at their speed. "What are these tires rated for, Gonz?"

"Brand new ten-ply steel-belted Michelins. They'll hold up," stubbing out his cigarette in the ashtray as the big rig accelerated to 104 mph. "They'll be the least of our worries." He cocked his ear to a slight change in pitch from the turbo diesel.

Gonz studied his mirrors again. "We missed the last sign. Check the nav screen, will you? Let's see if we can make Fort Stockton and shed some light on these pendejos." Leaning forward, he checked the pressure indicator on the turbocharger.

Chico nodded as he traced his finger across the GPS. "Fort Stockton's twenty-eight miles straight ahead," he said, ejecting the clip from his Uzi to make sure it was full. Reinserting it with a loud smack from the heel of his hand, he chambered a round before scrutinizing the mirrors again. In spite of their increased speed, the blinking lights seemed closer, so close now that they'd stopping blinking. For some strange reason, Baja Grille's world-famous advertising slogan suddenly popped into his head, and it made him grin. *Made with only the freshest ingredients...and always delivered with a friendly smile.*

Chico's heart beat faster. "Sounds like a plan, Gonz." He looked over at his buddy and crossed himself. "Rock and roll will never die, but it sure smells like something did in here."

CHAPTER TWO

Seven hundred miles east of the West Texas desert, Stella Wilde glanced up from her Sudoku puzzle. Momentarily mesmerized by the rain drops pattering on the plants outside her window, she unconsciously smoothed the open pages of *The Tallahassee Democrat* that lay in her lap as she prepared to finish the matrix. Completing the crossword and Sudoku puzzles had become part of her daily routine, helping to keep her wits about her to get through the day. She was amazed at how much hardship she could endure as long as she had a few of life's little luxuries to enjoy.

Lifting her arm, she studied the bandage covering the laceration on her left wrist, annoyed about her inability to remember cutting herself. Staring at the bandage, she hoped with all her heart that her husband was recovering from his wound in spite of his wretched infidelity. Wanting to remember everything that happened instead of just the bits and pieces, her requests for doses of oral Prevagen to help reverse her memory loss were repeatedly met with derisive laughter from the hospital staff.

The Florida State Hospital at Chatahoochee in Florida's panhandle was indeed a far cry from the world of money and mansions she'd grown accustomed to during her ten years of marriage to a prominent South Florida restaurant tycoon. Her world had been turned upside down, so very far from the life of luxury she lived at Villa Dellacroix in Vero Beach.

Stella was a strikingly beautiful woman. At thirty-nine, she was slender and athletic, an absolute knock-out by any standard. With sensual pouty lips, shoulder-length strawberry-blonde hair that was usually perfectly coiffured, she got a lot of attention. But it was her incredibly sensuous catlike green eyes that so captured the hearts of men, and sometimes even women, often causing people to stop in their tracks, always so sure they'd seen her on a billboard or magazine cover. But the attention she received wasn't always welcome.

"Hiyeeee." Startled, Stella looked up. Drooling down his chin and onto his stuffed panda was 75-year-old Crazy Larry, so nicknamed because he resembled Larry from The Three Stooges. Barefoot and dressed in his white hospital gown with half of his rear end hanging out, he was a disturbing mess to lay eyes on as he stood there, tugging on his privates and ogling her. Unfortunately for her, Crazy Larry's less-than-gentlemanly attentions had become a daily routine.

"Beat it, Larry." Her instructions caused him to grope himself with renewed enthusiasm, and she instantly regretted her words. "Better yet, please just go away." She went back to her paper, ignoring him and turned her attention back to her Sudoku puzzle. If she was lucky, Crazy Larry would move on and find someone else to fixate on. Out of the corner of her eye, she watched him shuffle on to his next victim in the day room, unable to provoke an acceptable response from his favorite audience. For most of her life, she'd used her stunning looks and taut body to bend men to her will, but in the hospital she grew to resent the attention it got her.

A toothless woman in her nineties who liked to tell everyone she was Jimmy Hoffa's niece had been sitting on the sofa watching Stella. With her hair done up in little pink curlers, and wearing knee-highs and a checkered dress that was covered in food stains, Jimmy Hoffa's niece sauntered over and sat down next to her. "Can I offer you some advice, dearie?" she asked with a tilt of her head.

Without replying, Stella lowered her newspaper, curious to hear what she had to say. "If you wanna get out of here, dearie, ya gotta keep quiet," making a zipping motion across her lips, "...'cause the big white rabbit's coming back." She pointed out the window at the invisible big white rabbit. "He's four hundred pounds, seven feet tall and mean as a snake." She could see Stella looked unconvinced. Jimmy Hoffa's niece pointed at her curlers and added, "Ya know, this hair don't grow on the inside!"

Stella leaned over and peered outside the window to humor the woman. Seeing nothing that looked like a big white rabbit, she pursed her lips and mimicked the crazy woman's zipping motion. "Mum's the word," she said as the old woman with the curlers made her way over to another elderly patient to share her four-hundred-pound rodent fantasy. Stella returned to her puzzle. *And they thought I was the fruitcake.*

Over the years, Sudoku became a habit for Stella since her days teaching high school English at St. Edwards in Vero Beach. Between classes, she'd used the puzzles to fill in the downtime and keep her mind sharp. The games allowed her to exercise her brain like a computer-generated algorithm, filling in the 9 X 9 grids with digits so each column, row and sub grid contained all of the numbers from one to nine.

When she began to have trouble recalling her South Vero Beach zip code, she realized the heavy doses of institutional meds were taking a toll on her short-term memory. She needed to stay sharp if she was ever going to get out of this Godforsaken place. Though her nightmares were becoming more violent, her greater fear was losing control of her cognitive abilities. There were times when she just wanted to get as far from the world as she could. Raised a Presbyterian, she remembered her father's words urging her to "trust in something stronger than herself." And so she did, often cursing like a sailor but praying on her knees like an altar girl.

Her reflections were interrupted by a familiar voice. "Couvoisier for breakfast, Miss SoBe?" Mocking Stella, the nurse who looked like Nurse Ratched from *One Flew Over the Cuckoo's Nest* was bending at the waist with a towel draped over her forearm again, like a bad joke that wouldn't go away. Stella's first inclination was to give her the finger, but she thought better of it, having already lost too many of her privileges from "unacceptable behavior."

"No thank you," replied Stella curtly.

The nurse gave Stella a tight smile and continued to taunt their well-heeled patient. "Don't be countin' on no Seraquim today either, Miss SoBe-not after what happened to you on *that* stuff. You know, Valiant Pharmaceuticals took it off the market," pausing to see if her patient remembered hearing about this from anyone on the hospital staff.

Stella remembered very little of the episode itself. TV and newspaper accounts described her as "being in a hypnotic, dreamlike trance" when the ambulance and police arrived; "...another Seraquim zombie", they called her. Before that, her memories were still a big blur. One of the few things she remembered is laying restrained on an ambulance gurney in her Victoria's Secret nightie as they sutured her wrist. She remembered one of the paramedics asking, "Can you believe a girl this beautiful wants to kill herself?" It was as if her memory of the gruesome details had been wiped clean of the events that later came to dominate the newspapers and internet media for days afterward.

In the week that followed, she slowly began to recall more details. After her wrist was sutured and bandaged, and before the FBI had intervened, she remembered being thrown into a holding cell with ten other prisoners, most of them male. Fearing she would be assaulted, she crawled into a corner with two other females, curling up into a ball and hoping someone would come to her rescue. When a fight broke out over her between two crack addicts, jailers intervened with Mace. Concerned for her safety, officers finally moved her to a separate cell with the other females, and a day later to a mental hospital "for her own protection."

Nurse Ratched was back. "You ready to make your one phone call for the day, Miss SoBe?"

Looking up expectantly, Stella had grown weary of hearing the nurse recount her bad drug experience. She was particularly anxious to hear from her trust attorney after leaving him over a dozen messages. "Thank you, nurse. Yes, I'm ready."

The nurse gave her a demonic smile. "Right after your meds, Miss SoBe. I'll bring them over in a few minutes," turning on her heel to corral Crazy Larry who was giggling hysterically as he relieved himself in the corner behind the piano.

Stella bowed her head in disgust at the sick circus playing out around her. She'd gotten used to the daily taunting from the staff, but the anxiolytics and hypnotic sedatives she was forced to take were messing with her mind even more. She reminded herself that her intellect was the key to regaining her freedom. Over time, she realized the mind-numbing effects of the daily doses of the phenobarbital and Alprazolam could be partially countered by working the puzzles in the newspaper. After having some success, she added other mental exercises that she learned as a child to her daily routine. Anything to help her get through the dark, dreary days. The nights were another story.

Ordinarily, Stella loved being in motion. She loved doing things that made her feel alive, things that made her heart race. Throughout her life, the secret to her health, fitness and happiness, she will tell you, was her desire to excel. The endorphins that her body manufactured during strenuous running, swimming and bicycling came in a close second. Of all the drugs she'd indulged in over the years, her body's own natural endorphins were at the top of her preferred list.

She thought about Manhattan. Able to stop traffic in the middle of Fifth Avenue, she was used to being treated like a goddess but didn't always expect it. Her attention fixed on the view outside, her eyes were glazing over, losing larger in the less as she watched the rain beading down the window. She fell into a reverie, replaying in her mind the list of hobbies she'd taken up to please her husband over the course of their ten-year marriage.

A classical ballet dancer when she'd first met Daniel Wilde, Stella knew he could be a jerk sometimes when he had the gall to suggest she learn to "pole dance" for him. At first, she dismissed his suggestion as an affront to her classical upbringing. When Dan had workers install the brass pole in a corner of their Louis XIV bedroom, to keep the peace, she swallowed her pride and submitted to his sleazy fantasy, slowly teasing him into a state of near-drooling delirium. Long ago, she'd learned that a man in a state of sexual excitement would divulge a lot of secrets to achieve his release, and it was a lesson she often took advantage of.

During their third year together, Stella discovered she'd confused her husband's relentless urge to mate with his love for her. She realized that his sexual urges had become about as impersonal as an hour of weightlifting.

She'd been okay with his fantasies as long as it gave her more control. There'd been the skydiving, when he'd practically dragged her into the plane after suggesting she update her life insurance. Then there was the trauma of scuba diving with schools of hungry black-tip sharks in Bonaire with nothing to protect her except her husband's 12-gauge bang stick. And who could forget playing "strip bridge" with his underworld buddies in the card room at Costa d'Este. Neither could she forget the nude clarinet solos in their living room, learning later that Dan's desire to relive a sexual fantasy about a girl who sat near him in high school band was the reason for her solos. There was no doubt she'd gone above and beyond in her efforts to satisfy her husband's twisted fantasies.

Stella continued to insist that she was misdiagnosed by the hospital's staff when they labeled her as bipolar and "a danger to herself and others." In fact, her family psychiatrist, Dr. Chris Hirt, had classified her years ago as an extreme version of the Briggs Myers INTP personality, and a sex addict since she was nine years old. Though she had a wonderful and normal relationship with her father, she was often embarrassed to admit that her addiction to masturbation began the day she had her first orgasm while her father bounced her on his knee.

The institution's staff continued to claim that her medical files had been "lost" and her psychiatrist was "on vacation". However, her familiarity with the inner workings of insurance companies convinced her they would likely extend her stay for as long as the coverage would cover the costs of confinement. So far, the FBI had stayed in the background while the staff continued to insist there was no one available that could corroborate her denial of bipolar disorder. They claimed her cell phone had been taken away from her "for her own safety", and it was a classic case of the mushroom treatment as they kept her in the dark and continued to feed her crap. Knowing she'd acted in self-defense, Stella wondered who was really behind her incarceration.

Slowly, she began to recall some of the more recent problems with her husband, including his conflict with the IRS that seemed so fixable at the time. But it was her meeting with the managing director at Barclays five weeks ago that proved to be the tipping point, a $28 million margin call, "The Mother of All Margin Calls," she remembered him saying. If *those* weren't enough reasons to have lost her mind, there was her husband's surreptitious attempt to double her life insurance in the midst of his ongoing sexual fling with their next door neighbor. All of these unpleasant developments came into sharper focus after her chat with Special Agent Dominic Beretto, and it all made her curse the day she met Dan Wilde.

As the dreary days of hospital confinement wore on, her problems escalated. Stella felt like she was losing her grip, at times feeling like she was drowning in a swirling sea of black nothingness. Tortured by the thought of being stuck in this hell hole indefinitely, she began to have hallucinations about an incubus assaulting her on the edge of an abyss. The eerie nightmares were becoming more frequent, and the heavy sedatives were pulling her deeper into psychosis, causing her to vent her frustrations in strange ways.

To take her mind off suicide, it helped Stella to formulate a list of ten things that her husband disliked about her:

1. She and her family had far more money than he did;
2. She liked to masturbate at red lights (she noted #1 and #2 were not related);
3. She refused to go down on him when she masturbated (she noted #2 and #3 are related);
4. She had a bad habit of overcooking fish out of her fear of bacterial poisoning;
5. Her birth control cream tasted vaguely like soured milk;
6. She continued to resist his fantasy of a three-way with his masseuse;
7. She fell asleep watching televised golf tournaments, sometimes in his lap;
8. She was better at chess than he was and could beat him whenever she wanted;
9. She would occasionally "misplace" his voice-activated TV remote control;
10. And the thing he hated most was: she was so much better at parallel parking.

Sometimes she thought she'd married a conniving sex maniac, but that was like the pot calling the kettle black. Weary of trying to sort it all out, her dark thoughts were suddenly interrupted by a familiar voice.

"How're we doing, Miss SoBe? You ready to make your call?" teased the youngest of the three duty nurses as she placed her hand on Stella's shoulder. The one who looked like Nurse Ratched had returned.

"You mean, to go with my one snail-mail letter for the day?" replied Stella, staring at the unwelcome hand on her shoulder. "The ones you open and read at will? Have they even been mailed?" Without waiting for an answer, "By the way, it's *Mrs. Wilde.* I'd like to call my trust attorney now. Everyone can't *still* be on vacation at the same time." She was really craving a cup of coffee along with some internet access so she could get the word out and blog about this hell hole. But, of course, coffee was considered addictive and prohibited by hospital rules. Coffee could make you put your baby in the microwave, for God's sake.

"Now, Miss SoBe," removing her hand from Stella's shoulder, "...don't look like you're ready for no privileges yet. Don't go askin' for coffee or Prevagen, or no internet or cell phones, either, 'cause you know ya ain't gonna get it. We need to keep you safe." She gave Stella a stern look of disapproval. "I'll check back when you're more agreeable."

No one on the staff would explain if these were hospital policies or part of her court-ordered incarceration. And where were her buddies, the FBI? She had an urge to talk with Special Agent Beretto. Nonetheless, Stella was doing everything she could to find out what was really going on, but there was still a mountain of information that wasn't being shared with her.

As the nurse shuffled toward her next victim, Stella added, "You do that. With the suit I'm going to file, I'm gonna own this place. You'll be working for about ten seconds until you're fired for abuse and incontinence!"

"Incontinence?" With a twisted smile, the nurse turned toward Stella. "You must mean incompetence." It was obvious she enjoyed holding the trump card in their pissing contest. "Just tryin' to keep the lights on, honey. Ain't nothing wrong with dreamin' a little, Miss SoBe. Ain't it about time for your meds?" Automatically, Stella went to check her watch, her bare wrist reminding her they'd taken her diamond-studded Cartier away when they'd strip-searched her during the admission process.

Ever since she'd been Baker-acted, their trust attorney Damon Morgan had yet to respond to her queries about her release. Her letters and phone calls to him had all gone unanswered, and out of desperation she'd left a message for her favorite author. For weeks now she suspected her calls were being intercepted. Though it was true that Morgan's resemblance to Chris Hemsworth often made her entertain a weekend fling with her trust attorney, so far she'd stayed true to her husband, even though he hadn't returned the courtesy. Still, she was expecting a little more loyalty from her trust attorney.

Even more confusing to her, with assets of well over a billion in her family's Dellacroix Global Trust, she was still Mr. Morgan's biggest client. With Stella as co-trustee, there were plenty of reasons why Mr. Morgan should be answering her calls, though the trust account was only a small part of her family's wealth. The billions her father made from his creation of the next generation 5G programmable GPU was widely used not only in video games and the internet of things, it was quickly becoming the standard chipset globally for artificial intelligence applications. But here at Chatahootchee State Hospital, all that money and success wasn't helping Stella one bit.

Her life in disarray and her sanity hanging by a thread, a plan began to take shape in her mind. Every night before bed, she reviewed her plan as she prayed on her knees, hoping that faith would reach out to her in the darkness as she figured a way to escape the hell hole she was stuck in.

Before sunrise the next morning, she was awakened by the sound of the med cart rambling down the linoleum floor toward her room. After two weeks of confinement, Stella had gotten used to the hospital's frightening nighttime noises. Smiling, she recognized the cart's peculiar thumping, a sound it had mysteriously acquired after she'd stuck a piece of chewing gum to the wheel in an undetected act of subdued rebellion last week. What she wouldn't give to enjoy the sunrise from her Villa Dellacroix terrace overlooking South Beach with a cup of freshly-ground coffee.

Focusing on the thump-thump-thump sound of the cart being pushed down the linoleum floor toward her room, she heard a loud "oomph" as the orderly tripped and fell to the floor, the med cart clattering to the floor on its side along with hundreds of pills and tablets scattering and bouncing over the linoleum hallway. Stella giggled as she listened to the clowns in the hallway scurrying to gather all the bouncing pills before Nurse Ratched showed up to give them an earful.

Then reality set in, her muscles tensing as she pictured the same two perfunctory apes in their ill-fitting white uniforms who enjoyed ogling her as the Alprazolam rendered her helpless. Gripping the edges of her mattress in fear, she craned her neck to see over the tops of her feet at the two goons pushing the cart through the door.

Diondre stood over her menacingly, rattling the meds around in the paper cup. "We gonna do this the easy way or the hard way this morning, Miss SoBe?" his gold tooth gleaming in the overhead lights.

"I've asked you to call me *Mrs. Wilde*," she blurted. "And please don't give me any of the meds that fell on the floor..." glancing at the bedridden patients to her right, "...I don't want what *they* have." Clutching the sheets on her bed, "I want to call my trust attorney now."

Diondre smiled smugly. "Ya gotta work on your attitude, Miss SoBe, if you wanna get outa *here* one day," guiding her head back against the pillow. Knowing the beefy orderly was capable of dispensing unpleasantries far worse than the medication, Stella reluctantly complied.

"Right now, we gotta do the meds." Diondre rattled the pills around in the paper cup again and held up the water. "So, what's it gonna be?" With her head pressed as far back against the pillow as she could, she remained fearful but defiant.

He rattled the pills in the cup once again and leaned closer. "They may make you laugh, they may make you cry, but either way they'll bring tears to your eyes."

CHAPTER THREE

Mark McAllister remembered the first time he'd met Dan Wilde. It was on a sunny Saturday morning back in late April at Abernathy's Beach Shop on Ocean Boulevard. The four month-long season had just ended a week earlier, and business was tapering off as summer approached. Abernathy's of Vero Beach had catered to the island gentry since the 1960s, and ten years ago they added a large gazebo to accommodate the do-it-yourselfers. In the expanded outdoor section, they offered rows of perennials and edible plants along with the customary beach hats and popular cover-ups in the store windows that faced Ocean Boulevard. Mark had always thought it a little touristy, but it was the only place east of the intracoastal that offered live potted flowers, and he was willing to pony up to avoid leaving the island. An admitted "island snob", driving twenty minutes west over the intracoastal bridge to Lowe's or Home Depot was tantamount to leaving civilization as he knew it.

Mark stood at the register with his potted flowers on the checkout counter as a man ambled toward him carrying one of the store's large plastic baskets full of plants. The man who bore an uncanny resemblance to Michael Fassbender wore Levis and a Guy Harvey long sleeved shirt with colorful sport fish all over it. As he unloaded the plants, duct tape and epoxy onto the counter beside Mark, he did a double take.

"Mr. McAllister? Mark McAllister, right?" The man's smiling blue eyes twinkled in admiration as he grinned and extended his hand. Up close, Mark recognized the infamous character from TV newscasts and the local tabloids.

Dan Wilde was a unique Vero Beach celebrity, steeped in controversy that often became scandal. His empire of Baja Grille Mexican restaurants stretched from coast to coast, and he was alleged to have underworld connections and shadowy business partners that sometimes made his appearances at social gatherings in Vero somewhat awkward. Such were the lesser-known secrets of the American Dream. An ostensible philanthropist and a Republican with a checkered past, so far he remained unindicted and unconvicted. A man like Wilde would be celebrated in many third-world countries while shunned by Vero Beach island gentry. Most of the time he was a fairly private man, often seen with his bodyguard, but definitely not the sort of person you'd normally meet by chance at Abernathy's Beach Shoppe on Ocean Boulevard.

As the affable man leaned toward him, Mark could not figure out how they knew each other. Had he autographed a book for him at a signing event? Hesitantly, he shook Mr. Wilde's hand. "Yes, I'm Mark McAllister. Have we met?"

"Dan Wilde. I bought the Villa Dellacroix next door. I'm your new neighbor." The pressure on Mark's hand increased.

Mark wasn't sure what to say but smiled anyway. "That's...ah..."
Bad news.

"I was impressed with your novel," continued Wilde. "Twenty-six weeks on the *New York Times* Bestseller List. Bravo!" With their celebrity status out-of-the-bag, the girl behind the counter began to pay them more attention as she rang up Mark's plants.

"Thank you...pleasure to meet you." Still, he wasn't really sure how he felt about this. Not always comfortable with his own notoriety, Mark's face remained impassive. In the struggle between fame and privacy, he liked to think he'd succeeded in locking his private life deep within a vault, still surprised some-times when he was recognized in public. And so the tug-of-war between his private life and public life as a well-known author continued unresolved, never quite balanced, like a seesaw tilt-ing back and forth. A man like Mr. Wilde moving in next door caught him off guard.

Wilde leaned against the counter while the curious young lady at the register waited to hear more about her celebrity customers. "Mind if I ask you a question about your book?" he asked Mark.

"Not at all," Mark wanting to be gracious but still cautious.

"How much of it is true? Was Tomlinson really a serial killer? C'est vrai?"

Curious to see what effect the truth would have on his new neighbor, Mark smiled and answered Wilde in the vernacular. "C'est tous les verite." The seven months he spent cruising Raiatea, Moorea, Huahine and Bora Bora during his circumnavigation had done wonders to improve his French, and he hoped he wasn't mucking it up too badly.

Not to be upstaged, Wilde answered in kind. "Incroyable!" He paused to size him up. "So the insurance reward, the circumnavigation…"

Mark nodded. "Tous les verite," he repeated.

Impressed, Wilde asked, "Can I buy you a drink at Club Riomar sometime? You're a member there, right?"

It was a rhetorical question. They both knew that Club Riomar membership came with villa ownership, so he focused on the first question. "Oh. That would be…ah…" *Pretty embarrassing.*

"Fine."

"Great then. I look forward to it."

There was a pregnant pause as they regarded each other's purchases before going on to share the customary small talk. The men chatted about a few of the upcoming charitable events where all the island gentry were sure to gather, notably the Vero Beach Wine and Film Festival and the upcoming Art In The Park events. While they chatted, Mark noticed his new neighbor had set on the counter a container of two-part epoxy, duct tape, a bottle of liquid fertilizer, and tomato, pepper and basil plants. *Must have forgot the stool softener, the gloves, and the shovel.* He regarded his geraniums and marigolds, comparing them to his neighbor's items.

"My wife prefers we plant things to eat," explained Mr. Wilde. "She likes to spice things up." *The understatement of the decade.*

Mark gestured toward his floral selections and lightened the mood. "Well, my wife eats the geraniums, and I like the marigolds sautéed in butter and garlic."

Mr. Wilde laughed. "I draw the line at edible hibiscus, with a side of basil, peppers and tomato," he added with a wry smile.

Mark wanted to test his sense of humor. The guy wasn't exactly balls deep in joy today and looked like he might need some cheering up. Gathering his plants together, he grew mock serious. "Well, my wife and I have a wake to prepare for."

"Oh, ah…sorry."

Mark's eyes twinkled. "Don't be. We told them not to play on the tracks."

Wilde chuckled with fingers pointed like a handgun. "Ah…ya got me with that one. Sounds like you never stop writing."

"Artistic license is always lurking in the background," explained Mark. "Well, can't be late for the flower tasting. Let me leave you with this; it is said that while books may not change people, paragraphs will, and sometimes even sentences. Agree?"

Mr. Wilde struck a thoughtful pose before answering. "Very profound."

"Saw it on a bumper sticker," joked Mark. "Au revoir, Mr. Wilde," shaking hands again.

"Enchante."

Mark thought about the goods his neighbor had purchased again as he headed out the door with his arms full of marigolds and geraniums. By themselves, he thought, Mr. Wilde's items seemed innocuous enough, but more apropos to his reputation perhaps, was adding a shovel, some gloves and visqueen to his purchases. That might raise a few eyebrows.

As they went their separate ways, Mark loaded the plants into his Panamera S, having made no definite plans to see Mr. Wilde again. He did wonder what an encounter with Mrs. Wilde would be like. In his mind, he pictured him with a trophy wife to match his huge ego. Leaving Abernathy's parking lot, he hit the gas and headed south on Ocean Boulevard toward Villa Riomar, hoping to surprise Carol with the flowers. Though he was certain she would enjoy tending the flowers *au naturel* in her usual gardening attire, he was far less certain of what the future might look like with his new neighbors next door.

Two more miles up Ocean Boulevard, Mark downshifted and turned to enter the Mediterranean villa's wrought iron gates and the estate's outer wall. He liked the sound of Michelins rolling over textured pavers, imparting the feeling that you've arrived before you got there. Slowing to admire the hundreds of brick pavers, he was proud of the fact that he decided to separate the joints with synthetic Bermuda grass. Along with the solar-powered barrel-tile roof, it was one of the many ecological features that distinguished Villa Riomar from the other estate homes. His landscape architect had been right; happiness was not having to edge or water the synthetic grass that helped define his five-hundred-foot driveway.

Spotting his landscaper busy trimming hedges along the drive-way, he lowered his window before Hector could hide the half pint of Myers rum stuck in his back pocket. "Looks good, Hector. You're going to save that Myers 'til after you're through, right? We need those hedges nice and straight."

"Si, Senor McAllister. Entiendo. Mas tarde," patting his pocket in agreement. Mark had a soft spot for the man ever since learning of his wife's Alzheimer's disability and often tipped him with a C-note on Fridays.

He continued up the driveway, reflecting on the day's events. The expansive three-acre beachfront estate lots along Ocean Boulevard normally afforded ample privacy for seven fortunate families of the island gentry. But today, for the first time since moving to Villa Riomar, he felt crowded by the presence of his new neighbor. Part of him wanted to blame the media circus that babbled constantly on how Mr. Wilde had come to make his fortune. Knowing how hungry reporters usually pushed to spin new headlines, he couldn't help wondering if Mr. Wilde really was as gruesome as the tabloids made him out to be. Or was it just more pieces of fake news flying around in cyberspace?

His crystal ball gave him a rare glimpse of what was to come, and he wasn't completely sure he liked what he saw.

CHAPTER FOUR

Wilde left Abernathy's and headed south on Ocean Boulevard to Villa Dellacroix, smiling up at the sun in his Givenchy sunglasses as he drove with the top down in his new blue-grey Bentley. Life was good. Hoping the intoxicating aroma of the soft beige Corinthian leather would never end, he was glad he'd left the model and color selection to Stella. She was right-the Navy blue would have been too hot for the intense Vero Beach sun. Arm up on the adjoining seat as he drove, the sweet scent of ocean breeze was his to enjoy as he thought about his chance meeting with Mark McAllister. McAllister had been a hero of his ever since hearing about the capture of the serial killer and treasure salvage fugitive in South Boca four years ago. Just his luck he'd landed right next door to one of his heroes at Villa Riomar. *Thank you, Damon Morgan.*

He thought about choosing Vero Beach as their next home after waiting two years to make their escape from Boca Raton, an escape made necessary as Boca had morphed into the proverbial sixth borough of New York. Just before one of the prime oceanfront estates was set to come on the market, his trust attorney Damon Morgan had called him. Moving quickly, Wilde made a full-price cash offer twenty-four hours before it was due to be listed. When it was accepted, Stella was so thrilled she had made passionate love to him on the spot.

To understand the neighborhood into which Mr. and Mrs. Dan Wilde had chosen to place themselves, one would need to understand that Riomar was simply one of the finest oceanfront estate locales in America. It was not a neighborhood in an urban or suburban sense, but actually an exquisite collection of some of the grandest beachfront estates available in the United States.

Predominated by landed gentry and bluebloods holding old money and traditional social graces, The Ocean Estates at Riomar was defined by a gentile quality of life unavailable almost anywhere else. It was seen as the quintessential triumph of substance over style, having become a mecca and a sanctuary for billionaires and Fortune 500 CEOs that sought to escape the mundane and nouveau riche further south on the Florida coast. It was the kind of place where Wilde could look forward to borrowing a cup of Larressingle XO or glass of Johnny Walker Black from the folks residing in the mansion next door. Thinking about his new neighbors, his late father's advice came to mind; "build your castles high, and dream, dream, dream".

As the wrought iron gates opened, Wilde eased the Bentley up the weathered Chicago brick driveway where his daydream was interrupted by the sight of a red Toyota Prius parked in the turn-around. Someone had thoughtfully positioned it to give him just enough room to make the turn into the first bay of the five-car garage. Stella's white Range Rover was parked just behind the Prius, while the car her father gave her, a restored silver-blue 1949 Jaguar XK 120 Alloy convertible, sat safely in the second bay. The island aristocracy tended to be a bit on the Anglophile side, and the Jaguar was a popular car with the locals. Making his way toward the teak double-door entry with his arms full of bagged plants, Wilde stopped to shade his eyes from the sun and take a peek inside the Prius, but the window tint prevented him from gaining any clues about the owner.

Tossing his keys into the Chihuly turquoise glass bowl on the credenza, he set the plants down and called out; "I'm home, Mrs. Wilde. Where are you, honey?"

Her melodic voice drifted through the foyer. "I'm in the orchid garden, Dan."

He made his way through the French doors to the courtyard where he found Stella seated on a carved mahogany chair, dressed in beige short-shorts and a coral-colored halter top with matching slip-ons. Taking a sip of her favorite iced green tea, she pulled her hair back as she studied the Royal Organic label on the bottle before looking up at him. The blooming yellow roses and lavender orchids surrounding her were proof that the many hours spent in the garden courtyard were paying some colorful dividends. With her white cockatiel Perry perched on the birdbath's rim, it was a storybook setting, fit for a queen.

Wilde slid atop a mahogany sidebar to face her and took a moment to appreciate his stunning wife among the colorful surroundings of the orchid garden. He breathed in the fragrances of her regal setting and imagined for a moment his wife's incongruous habit of pleasuring herself at stoplights. Perry turned and raised his crest as if reading his thoughts.

"You'll never guess who I met at Abernathy's this morning," he ventured.

"I probably won't." She would often disguise a randy mood with a frisky wit, so he played along.

"I met our neighbor."

"Justin Bieber?"

"Mark McAllister," said Wilde, watching her reaction for clues about her feelings.

"The novelist?"

"None other."

She looked up with her striking green eyes and alluring smile, making his heart skip a beat. "I was so hoping for a boy toy, honey, but I'll settle for a good-looking author. I'd like to meet him. His last novel blew me away," shaping her lips to form a playful kiss.

"Don't worry, you'll meet him," he assured her. Stella collected her authors and artists like a kid collected video games and comic books. Her personal library was full of autographed novels, from Nelson DeMille to Carl Hiaasen, from Peter Benchley to Tom Clancy.

She cocked her head. "By the way, you have a guest from the IRS. A Wiley S. Peabody. I had a feeling you were on your way back so I parked him in your office." She took another sip of iced tea before looking up to meet his eye. "Should I be worried, Dan?"

"What? No, of course not. He drives a Prius, for God's sake. How dangerous can he be? Just picking up some documents." He glanced at his diamond-encrusted Tag Heuer. "He's a little early." Hoping she wouldn't detect his half-truth, Wilde shifted his weight uneasily.

She pulled a business card out of her pocket and read it before handing it to him. "Says he's a Special Agent, Dan. Wouldn't they normally just send a courier for documents?" Stella knew he wasn't above skirting the truth, especially when it came to his shady deals.

He stood to take control. "You worry too much. I'll take care of it." He started for the garden's entrance, but Stella reached for his forearm. "Wait. What about our author? Do we have any plans?"

After ten years of marriage, he knew when his wife was intrigued by another man. He was detecting more than just a neighborly interest in her eyes and voice, which he would normally be okay with if McAllister didn't look so much like a *GQ* model. *Trivialize it.*

He gave her a smirk and said, "Let's let him come to us. Maybe he'll bring us over a Welcome Wagon fruit and wine basket or something."

"One can only hope." She winked seductively as her hand moved down to his groin. "Don't be too long with Mr. Peabody. I need a visit from Dr. Fitzwell." As if on cue, he reached down the front of her shorts, unable to resist caressing her and kissing the nape of her neck. Being married to an intelligent beautiful woman who was hyper sexual was a man's dream among dreams. It made him recall the first words he'd said to her when they met twenty-one years ago at the Sandals in Barbados; "What gives a beautiful girl like you pleasure?" Discovering her insatiable amorous talents on the beach that same night, he was hooked for life. She'd been all too willing to allow him to show her the value of his peerlessly-durable erection.

"Honey, I'll be back to take care of this," holding her face up to his and kissing her promisingly on her pouty lips. When Stella moaned and pulled their hips together, he knew he'd been right on the money about her frisky mood.

"Don't be too long, dear," she intimated.

"Don't worry. He'll be as long as you need him to be," giving her a randy wink.

Reluctantly, she watched him swagger through the French doors and down the marble hall, leaving her to her orchids, her tea, and her pet cockatiel. With her motor humming in high gear, she expected her husband to dispense with Mr. Peabody in short order and return to address her more primeval needs.

***

Wilde guessed by Peabody's arrogant tone on the phone days earlier that it must be a criminal matter. He'd already decided to be as uncooperative as he could, wondering which of his underworld cohorts was in hot water this time. His trust attorney had done well to insulate him from the nasty brouhaha with Madoff, and he was lucky to have survived the witch hunt unscathed. In spite of the ensuing scandal, Wilde managed to slip out of the hangman's noose and pocket a cool nine million bucks in profits from the commodities trades that the State Attorney had labeled "a pyramid scheme." His father-in-law wasn't so lucky, having close to ten million still tied up in the silver bullion chicanery.

His attorney, Damon Morgan, had more than earned his six-figure fee building an extraordinary defense and managed to pull some strings here and there, successfully painting Wilde as an innocent victim of the Ponzi scheme. Even though the media had a field day with it, in the final analysis the jury was instructed to ignore the sensationalism and sided with the defendant. But that was all behind him now, so what did this power-hungry IRS paper shuffler want from him? Peabody would not have been so haughty with him had he been seeking his cooperation, and that had him worried.

Unfortunately, over the years Wilde had developed a testy relationship with the IRS, a state of affairs further aggravated by his arrogance and loathing of government bureaucrats. When he had his own office on Wall Street, he enjoyed looking down on the bustling crowd thirty floors below, his mind adrift with delusions of power, money and prestige. The lust for corporate grandeur ruled his ego like a maniac on crack, often clouding his judgement in critical decisions. Habitually entertaining Wall Street heavyweights and cavorting with hedge fund managers at Seaport Plaza and New York Yacht Club just made him feel even more invincible. "Dan the Man", they called him, his bar bills often exceeding four figures, egregious excesses that he kept from his wife.

He had a knack for making money in the worst of times, but wasn't always adept at keeping it out of the hands of the government in the best of times. As he watched the IRS continue to chip away an ever increasing amount of his family's income, his tax bracket crept from 40% to over 50%, and he found himself drawn into what seemed like a life-or-death struggle between himself and the Internal Revenue Service. Encouraged by the success of his underworld partners at hiding income from the government, he knew he wasn't alone. Many of his associates, even sophisticated bluebloods and island gentry, were facing tax brackets as high as 80%. For his family, it was a contest that began as early as the passage of the Income Tax Act all the way back in 1913, and about as much fun for him as a bad outbreak of shingles.

For more than a century, the Wilde family regarded tax avoidance as not only necessary for their very survival, but a civil right and moral obligation. When the mantle of Conservator of the Wilde Family Trust passed to him, Stella had urged him to enroll in the Certified Financial Planner program at Florida Atlantic University in Boca Raton. She insisted it was his duty to keep their hard earned money to provide for future heirs and out of the greedy hands of contemptible IRS agents. The government had enough of their money, she reminded him.

The CFP program taught him the difference between tax *evasion*, which was, of course, illegal, and tax avoidance, which was legal. With the new found tools of generation-skipping trusts and eminently more creative tax deductions to bring into the contest, Wilde felt emboldened to file more aggressive returns. In the only audit since completing his CFP designation, he had miraculously won an additional seven figure deduction, which put him squarely on the IRS radar screen for the duration. IRS revenue agents were notoriously poor losers, and as their inequitable and insensitive bureaucratic ranks grew in numbers, so did their vengeful nature. Now, Mr. Dan Wilde could count on an audit every year.

As Wilde entered his sumptuous office at Villa Dellacroix and shut the mahogany door loudly behind him, Mr. Peabody stood to deliver the obligatory limp handshake and display his credentials as a Special Agent. With an arrogant albeit milquetoast air, the IRS agent seemed unimpressed by the fine appointments of his surroundings. Peabody had refused to discuss the nature of his visit with Wilde over the phone, and Wilde's instincts told him this was likely going to be unpleasant.

"Please, sit down Mr. Peabody." The IRS agent did as requested. "To what do I owe the pleasure of your visit?" Making no attempt to mask his sarcasm, Wilde had found Peabody's personality annoying on the phone and resisted the urge to throw him out, keeping his cool while he evaluated the man's appearance.

A slender man in his late 40s with coffee-stained teeth, Peabody wore a black polyester suit that must have set him back sixty bucks if he bought it new; the kind you often see filling the racks of consignment shops on the wrong side of town. He had on black patent leather shoes that displayed an odd sheen as if shined with a scouring pad, and his shirt, tie, socks and watch all looked to be from the same consignment shop. In Wilde's eyes, the frugality was unforgivable. Professional men, or those who portend to be professional and who place little value on a nice suit had no business being surrounded by such accoutrements. How this unwelcomed pencil pusher was able to insinuate himself into a pricey sanctuary like Villa Dellacroix mystified him. But there he was, comfortably ensconced in Wilde's hallowed halls, about to piss all over their lives. Peabody was casually scrolling through a small spiral-bound notebook as if reviewing notes from his last shopping trip at KMart.

He looked up at Wilde. "I'll get right to the point."

Wilde gave him a condescending smile. "I can't wait."

"Mr. Wilde, last year you claimed an itemized deduction for $2,465,850 in margin loan interest in your Barclay's trust account, yet you did not show any capital gains." Peabody checked his notes. "As a matter of fact, quite the contrary. You claimed an additional deduction of $9,112,756 in short-term capital losses." Peabody was smug, like a cop who was already in possession of a signed confession. "How would you explain this?" He tapped his pen on the notebook as if it were a ticking clock, clueless as to just how annoying he was.

It was not a question that Wilde was prepared to answer. "Simple, really. The law, in case you are aware, in the *real* world of private enterprise, provides for the deductible expense of margin loan interest incurred in the pursuit of lawful gains in an investment margin account. Would you like me to show you the code provision? Or did they not teach you that at the IRS?"

Peabody uncrossed his legs and leaned forward in the tufted brown leather chair to make his point. "Perhaps you can show me the section of IRS Code that allows margin loan interest to be deducted *in the absence of capital gains*. I may have missed that part." Unflappable and irritating as his sarcasm was, Peabody cocked his head and smirked as he continued to tap on the notebook with his pen. While the agent's passive-aggressive behavior came as no surprise, for some reason the sarcasm did. Wilde's hopes of winning this particular pissing contest were fading, and he began to look for a graceful way out.

"So, Mr. Wilde, unless you can show the government"-

"You mean show you, don't you, Mr. Peabody?"

"Well, as far as *you're* concerned, in this particular case, *I am* the government." And there it was, out in the open, all the unabashed pomp and arrogance that IRS agents are famous for.

"I owe the government nothing," insisted Wilde, squaring off with him.

Now very annoyed, Peabody was finally showing some real emotion but so far kept his cool and had not raised his voice. He stood up as if to face the jury in a summary address. "So, unless you can show capital gains for the year of your margin interest deduction, I'm afraid we'll have to disallow your $2,465,850 deduction." He removed a slip of paper from his top pocket, adjusted his glasses and reeled off some figures.

"According to my calculations, with back interest, penalties and possible additional fines for fraud, you owe the United States $2,501,735 in unpaid funds." This was the moment Peabody had been waiting for today, perhaps even for weeks or months. All the power to ruin people's lives was his to wield, and it went straight to his bald, bespectacled head. Enjoying the damage his words inflicted, he added, "This was a taxable event, and you've broken the law, Mr. Wilde." He smirked openly. "And *criminal* charges are being considered against you once again." Wilde supposed that was a thinly-veiled reference to his former conviction for tax evasion twenty years earlier.

No matter who you might be, or how much money you may have, those were terrifying words from a Federal law enforcement officer. For more than a century, the Wilde family, with all their diplomas, credentials and special awards hanging on their walls, had been free of scandal and crime-until his conviction. It was a huge mantle to bear.

Wilde remained implacable. "Criminal charges? Maybe you'd better explain."

Peabody looked over the top of his glasses at Wilde like he was an insect. "You hold a Certified Financial Planner designation. Correct?"

"From FAU in Boca. I don't see how that has"-

"You are obviously well-versed in tax law, Mr. Wilde. Therefore, we must assume that this is more than a mere oversight. This egregious deduction goes well beyond tax avoidance. It has the appearance of tax evasion, sir." Finally, he'd heard the word "sir" in their conversation, but only after Peabody and unloaded his full broadside, reducing the normally respectful use of the term to mockery.

There was an awkward moment of silence as the two men faced off, toe to toe, their faces only inches apart, Peabody in his black polyester suit and scuffed patent leather shoes, Dan Wilde in his colorful Guy Harvey shirt, Levis and Sperry Topsiders. In Wilde's mind, it was the quintessential confrontation of private enterprise and government intrusion.

Wilde needed that deduction. He was fairly certain that his trust attorney had the sway to pull some strings and submit a revised return showing a capital gain to legitimize the interest deduction. Having such a large deduction disallowed by these pinheads would put him in a serious bind. And since Stella was co-trustee, it was half her bind, even though they filed separate returns due to the way her family limited partnership income was structured. Wilde began to feel like he was being mugged.

He tried harder to bait the IRS agent, wanting to be able to reference a shouting match for the record. At full volume, he stated, "I'm fairly certain that this is a deductible expense. I owe nothing." Peabody was proving to be a pro and resisted being pulled into a screaming match. Annoyed with the agent's cool demeanor, Wilde was doing his best to restrain himself, but the need for one last insult prevailed. As he reached to open the door, derision reared its ugly head once again.

"By the way, professional men do not wear polyester suits and patent leather shoes, Mr. Peabody. Especially when calling on successful businessmen in Vero Beach. Get it together, man."

Wilde could see that the man was about to explode but managed to get his temper under control. "Prepare yourself for a full audit of the last ten years of returns, Mr. Wilde, including this year," responded Peabody with clenched teeth. "You will please have all your tax records and pertinent documents available for our auditor who will inform you of your appointment before five p.m. tonight." Turning curtly to leave, he stopped, adjusted his glasses, and faced his quarry one last time. "If you withhold any documents, we will issue subpoenas as necessary to complete our audit. Good day, sir." The show of testosterone and muscle flexing finished, Mr. Peabody exited the arena with a smirk, wondering if the man with his finger on the nuclear button would ever truly feel as much joy.

Wilde slammed the door behind him, walked to his desk and pressed his palms down on the cold marble top, wondering what he would tell his wife. Confident that he still had the upper hand, he hoped he wasn't being overly optimistic in his attorney's ability to pull him from the grisly jaws of the IRS.

He stared out the window, indulging himself in a momentary pity party. He could find no solace in the manicured grounds and standing bronze dolphin spewing a stream of water into the reflecting pond outside his window. It all seemed so ironic. Why was he busting his ass to build his family's wealth if the IRS was going to swoop down and take it from him? His pity party turned to anger as he thought about all the injustices in the world and all the criminals like Pablo Escobar and Al Capone, and the thousands of real criminals who went free every day. Why were they picking on him? He spent his entire life championing his country, upholding law and order, when it was convenient, only to be mugged by the same bastions of society that he'd been propping up all these years. It was depressing. In the morning, he would call the man with all the shadowy underworld connections to make things right. Morgan would be back from Mexico by then.

Only now did he remember her words: "Never go to a fight you're invited to."

He felt very lucky to be married to a stunning hyper sexual woman of great wealth who had more smarts than all the LLMs and JDs he knew. But unless he could bury this thing soon, keeping her on his side was going to be difficult.

CHAPTER FIVE

I t was two years ago, but it seemed like yesterday to him, the typhoon tearing at his sailboat like a wild lioness.

Dream Girl was holding together, submerging all sixty-seven feet of her girth beneath the larger waves, decks awash before rising high enough to expose her winged keel and plunging again into the South Pacific's grasp. It was hell on the high seas, and it seemed like the world was tearing loose from its axis. They had lost all electronic aids to navigation and communications two hundred miles northeast of Hawaii. Mark fought the storm with forty footers breaking above her first spreader, driven over her decks by a one-hundred-twenty-knot wind that had blown off all her masthead instruments by midday.

Without her electronics, she was crippled. Gone were the VHF antenna, SSB booster, anemometer, apparent wind indicator, and Sat/Net array-maybe even the masthead light. Through the clear acrylic panels overhead, he could barely make out the radar and Sat/Net domes sitting up on the first spreader. But neither system was operational, forcing them to rely on charts and dead reckoning for plotting their course to a safe harbor. In the grip of the storm, it was all he could do to keep her from falling off course and rolling over. Under bare poles with her thirty-six foot boom bolted to the boom gallows, she was making way at half throttle directly into the typhoon's teeth. The Yanmar turbo diesel labored to keep her bow pointed into the maelstrom while the sea anchor deployed from her stern worked to control her yaw.

During the Atlantic hurricane last year, Mark learned the key to their survival lay in keeping her water tight and pointed up. At the interior helm, and outfitted in his foul weather gear and safety harness in case he was forced to go topside, he wrestled with the wheel to hold her steady. The weather helm was tremendous, but he couldn't let *Dream Girl* fall off more than twenty degrees or she would roll and likely lose her mast. Systems that weren't essential to their survival had been turned off to conserve power and fuel, including the climate control and auto pilot, which he couldn't trust in such a blow, hard lessons learned from Hurricane Matthew the year before. He and Carol had not stopped retching for two days, amazed at what the storm was forcing from their insides, swearing he'd been forced to puke up a peanut butter sandwich from third grade. But the Tahitian rum was there to warm his insides and calm his nerves.

From under his hood, perspiration rolled into his eyes and down his arms as another thirty footer broke over the cutter. The heavy seas made it impossible to see what lay ahead, and the perspiration made his grip on the stainless wheel and bottle of coconut rum feel slippery. The bottle of liquor he held between his knees was liquid courage, helping him keep the bow pointed into the worst tempest he'd ever seen. Following the weeks of almost idyllic South Pacific weather, he continued to maneuver and avoid what he feared most; a wave so massive it would catapult them over backwards. For a wave such as that, he knew there was no defense. He prayed to God it wouldn't come to that as he tilted the bottle and took another swig to calm his nerves. Above the roar of crashing waves and howling wind, he could hear Carol retching into the bilge as she checked the main batteries in the engine room.

Over the deafening roar of the wind, he cupped his hand and shouted aft to her. "CAROL!" No answer. "CAROL!" he repeated. "HOW'RE THE BATTERIES, BABY?"

***

Mr. McAllister, you okay, sir?" asked John. His mechanic stood beside him in *Dream Girl's* companionway. "You look a little peaked, like you just got off a roller coaster. You feel alright?"

For a moment, he'd lost track of where he was. With a knot in his stomach, Mark found himself still staring at the circuit breaker panels and voltmeters. The flashback was so intense that perspiration covered his forehead and rolled down his cheeks. He looked up at his diesel mechanic, busy wiping his hands on a fresh towel after installing new impellors and injectors in *Dream Girl's* 310 hp diesel. He handed the towel to Mark and waited for a reply.

"Yeah, John. Just a flashback," mopping his face with the towel. Disheveled, it took him a moment to gather his wits and recall his surroundings. He took a couple of deep breaths. "You about finished with the upgrades?"

"As soon as I find my torque wrench and wire cutters." John smiled apologetically and started to head aft toward the engine room, sporting the limp he'd picked up from an exploding IED during his last tour in Iraq.

"Appreciate you, John. Lucky to have you. I'm such a lousy electrician, after the last time I wired something on *Dream Girl*, I hit the switch and, I swear, a toilet flushed in France."

John laughed over his shoulder and turned to face him. "Mr. McAllister, your modesty precedes you. If I'd gone through the typhoon that you described in your circumnavigation, I'd be filing for PTSD benefits, believe me."

Mark returned the compliment. "C'mon, John. After two tours of combat in Iraq, being wounded and receiving two decorations for heroism, you expect me to believe that?" He watched his war hero turned mechanic shrug modestly and head toward the engine room to finish up.

Mark stepped toward the bow and seated himself at the nav/comm station, taking a moment to admire the wall of new electronics that his insurance company had so kindly provided when they limped into Honolulu after the typhoon. Surrounded by the finest of hand-finished teak joiner work, he sat and admired the craftsmanship on his Baltic, artistry that only the masters from the village of Bosund, Finland could produce.

He'd come a long way since jetting around Boca at 120 mph on *Momentum*. Years earlier, when he was still cruising the intracoastal bistros around Boca and Delray Beach on his twin-turbo catamaran, Mark had passed over offers to run drugs on the fastest boat in Boca. Aging a few years, he realized he wanted less risk, less noise and less vibration. Nothing but the tranquil sounds of water slipping over the hull and the wind sweeping across the sails seemed as soothing to the soul.

After years of blazing across the water with his hair on fire, he was ready to move on to a yacht of greater length and girth. When he'd stumbled on Tomlinson's $170 million in stolen cash and gold and exposed a serial killer in Boca Raton years earlier, the $17 million reward money afforded him the opportunity to finally realize his dream and upgrade to a world-class sailboat capable of cruising non-stop for months at a time. For the last four years, it was the 67-foot Baltic cutter rig *Dream Girl* that connected him to the sea, the yacht that had taken him around the world and allowed him to express his sense of adventure and love for the ocean.

In the middle of his reverie, he heard a bell chime and checked his phone. It was a text message from Carol.

Mark,

    Join me for dinner and party after? Clothing optional, just you and me... :)

Typical Carol. What a minx.

Lucky for him, his wife was fun-loving, adventurous, and stunning beyond words. She loved teasing and acting out different sexual roles with him, especially those from famous novels. Elusive and unpredictable at times, she craved his teasing, and teasing was his forte.

Now, it was his turn to have some fun. He texted her back;

Carol,

    It's John. Mark lent me his phone when my battery went dead. I'll give him your message as soon as I see him. Your husband is, indeed, a lucky man.

A few moments passed as he wondered if Carol would fall for his playful tease. Being the minx that she was, she texted back;

John, why don't you come too? Our French maid is here, and I'm sure Mark wouldn't mind :)

When he read her message, he knew the jig was up. Carol must have figured out his ploy, so he texted her back;

Carol,

Looking forward to having you for dessert. Be there in twenty. ~M

***

The blue-grey Panamera S headed north toward Vero Beach on A1A. Berthing *Dream Girl* at the Pelican Yacht Club in Port Fierce, as he referred to the city, put his yacht ninety minutes closer to the open ocean, and he didn't mind the drive. Mark peered through the open sunroof of his Porsche at the changing sky, inhaling the sea breeze as new weather moved in. Darker clouds were turning into lighter cirrus clouds higher up, indicating fairer weather approaching. The ride along the ocean was pleasant, and he found himself tracing out the shapes of animals in the clouds, something he hadn't done for a long time.

His euphoric mood was inspired by the expectation of Carol feeding him dinner in the nude, something she liked doing when feeling exceptionally randy. He felt the unmistakable stirring in his groin as he waited for the wrought iron gate to slide open. Turning the Porsche into Villa Riomar's driveway, he parked and ambled up the fossil stone entryway as he felt himself getting aroused at the thought of seeing his wife in her sheer white French maid lingerie.

He was surprised when Carol appeared in the open doorway completely nude. "John!" she exclaimed, smiling and demurely placing one palm over her mons, her other hand covering her mouth. "I thought...!"

He smiled at his wife, delighted with her game. "Very entertaining, Carol." Standing together in the marble foyer, he grasped her tightly around her waist, teasing her as he pressed his manhood playfully against her belly. "I can see you're going to make this really hard, aren't you."

She touched him briefly through his Dockers with the tips of her fingers. "My goodness...I better put dinner on the table," she said in mock surprise. "Looks like someone's working up an appetite!" Her bare heart-shaped derriere taunting him, she sashayed down the hall toward the kitchen. "Did you want to close the front door, honey?" she asked over her shoulder.

Carol's entrée of ice cold shrimp with cocktail sauce was served with a crisp garden salad, fried plantains, and a sumptuous 2013 Hanzell Sonoma Valley chardonnay, all delicately fed to him as she sat in his lap at the dinner table. There was little conversation, but lots of sizzling body language. A gourmet cook, and an outstanding wine aficionado, she knew what he liked. But her most endearing talents were best displayed in the bedroom, not the kitchen, and though the dinner was a little light in quantity, it was served in the nude by his ravishing blonde-haired blue-eyed femme fatale. So, how could he possibly be dissatisfied?

She poured a sip of wine into his mouth from the bottle as he slurped down the final shrimp cocktail. In her coup d'etat, Carol leaned in and lovingly cupped her bare breast to dab a drop of cocktail sauce from the corner of his mouth. Offering it to him, Mark took this as an imminent sign that dessert was about to be served.

"Very tasty dinner, darling. What's for dessert?"

"What would you like?" she asked coyly, tossing her blonde hair back with a grin.

"You know what I like. Something sweet?" Without another word, she laid down with her back against the cool granite table top, offering her body to him like a goddess, smiling and giving him a look that said she was ready for her trip to the moon. Like a bee irresistibly drawn to a flower's nectar, he indulged himself.

There was something about her nectar that drove him wild.

***

Two hours and many momentous moments later, Mark slipped on a silk bathrobe and walked to the master veranda with a Cohiba. Carol watched him from the California king-size bed, stalking him with her eyes, still breathing heavily. He poured himself two fingers of Larressingle XO Armagnac from the side bar, clipped and lit the cigar, making himself comfortable in the overstuffed leather chair. In a quiet mood, they were both enjoying the ocean view from the second floor, tuning into the sights and sounds of approaching darkness. He watched the offshore buoys begin blinking their intermittent message, and the gulls taking refuge for the night. The sun had just set, and it was getting to that sulky twilight time when long shadows were casting an unfamiliar look over their comfortable world.

Propping her head up on a pillow, Carol said, "Honey, let's take a drive when you finish your cigar." He blew a smoke ring into the air and looked over to her, wanting to hear more. "Cobalt has that jazz band you like. Stellar Weather." The last time they'd seen the jazz group perform was at Mezzanote in Boca several months ago. Not quite ready to leave their love nest, she pulled the sheet down just enough to reveal her breasts and legs, wanting to tease him back into bed, sure that she could read her husband's moods as well as any nautical chart.

"Stellar Weather's playing at Cobalt, huh?" catching her eye. She looked remarkably hungry for a woman who'd just climaxed twenty-seven times. "Think we ought to put some clothes on first?"

As if on que, Carol stood up with her hand on her hip like a Vegas showgirl onstage. "How do you like my outfit, darling?"

He blew another smoke ring into the air as he regarded her alluring act, and Carol noticed something stir under his bathrobe as he spoke. "Actually, I think you could be the *real* reason for global warming, honey." With a big grin, Carol licked her lips and settled back into the bed expectantly as she watched him park his Cohiba and undo the belt to his bathrobe.

***

After an encore performance, they left Carol's red M5 in the garage and drove down Ocean Boulevard toward Cobalt in the silver Panamera. Mark opened the sunroof to let the spring sea breeze in as they drove south along the ocean. Passing by the few remaining vacant oceanfront lots, they were treated to intermittent peeks of the surf reflecting the light of a waxing moon.

As their companionable silence deepened, Mark took advantage of Carol's peaceful mood to sort the events of the past few weeks as he drove. He recalled one of his favorite quotes from Baba Ram Dass; 'The quieter you become, the more you can hear.' *So very true*, glancing at Carol who lay with her head against the leather bolster, staring out the window with a satisfied look on her face, her long blonde hair spilling over the back of her seat. She looked as happy as she'd been in years.

He thought about this bastion of gentile culture on the Treasure Coast, bordered on the south by the inlets, bays and beaches of South Florida where the mannerisms and attitudes more resembled those of New York south with palm trees. To the north were the white sand beaches of Brevard County, the Space Coast, providing refuge to many of the elite survivors of a once-burgeoning, four decade-long NASA-based space race and the new subdivisions that gave the those same engineers sanctuary.

But here on the Treasure Coast, development had not been as welcomed, coming more slowly, with tighter controls over land use planning and those who controlled waterfront growth. A blue-blood background would typically ensure an avenue of smoother pavement, leaving the rougher goings to those less privileged.

The chance meeting of Mr. Dan Wilde at Abernathy's had him wondering what kind of neighbors they would make. More to the point, following two hours of incendiary sex with his wife, he wondered what kind of woman Mrs. Wilde would prove to be. Probably quite attractive, intelligent, and apparently quite forgiving to overlook so many of her husband's nefarious habits.

"A penny for your thoughts, Marky Mark." Carol rarely used his nickname, and only when she was extremely content. Or in the mood to patronize him. Women had an uncanny knack for knowing when their man was thinking of another woman, in this case, one that he'd yet to meet. When confronted with the subject of jealousy, she would often ignore him, or just act like he was crazy.

"You surprise and challenge me, darling, and you have world-class sex talents."

"Too sweet, honey." She shifted closer to him, leaning on the walnut console. "Now tell me what you were really thinking about." Looking into her deep blue eyes, any further deception was out of the question.

"Last Saturday, I met our infamous new neighbor, Mr. Dan Wilde."

"That gangster guy from Boca?" Sometimes she could be a little indelicate. "We have a gangster living next door to us?"

Mark offered her a softer spin. "Well, certainly steeped in controversy, maybe a little scandal here and there, but beyond that, I"-

"I remember that awful story about him in *The Sun Sentinel*. Why next door to us?" Indignant, she acted like there was a crack in one of the windows of her stained glass American dream.

Amused, he was unable to resist the urge to tease her. "Ah… maybe to save us from a life of boredom?" he asked with a grin.

"Baby, you know I have my Glock and I was Best Pistol Marksman at the Boca Gun Club before you met me," she said jokingly. It even said so on the black gun club cap she liked wearing to the beach. "Don't worry, I'll protect us."

Suppressing a laugh, he said, "Let me know before your mood turns hostile, honey. You know I'm kinda shy about random public gunfire. Let me step out of the crossfire before you empty your clip, okay Annie?"

Entertained by his humor, she reached over and playfully grabbed his privates. As she planted her tongue in his ear, Mark almost drove over a mailbox. "You're lucky I'm in a good mood, buddy," as if this explained her behavior.

"You're insatiable," he replied. Come to think of it, that's what he almost named *Dream Girl*. After his frisky wife.

She continued to caress him to camouflage her next question. Mark wasn't complaining. "What's his wife like?" she asked.

She was getting catty on him. "Never met her. Just know she likes garden edibles," he answered.

She tightened her grip on his groin. "I'm sure we'll get along fine, just as long as she doesn't make a play for your cucumber. This one's mine!"

He laughed, veering into the edge of the swale before composing himself and bringing the Panamera back onto the pavement.

"I'm sure you'll get along fine," he replied. "Like Oscar Wilde says, 'Just be yourself. Everyone else is taken.'"

CHAPTER SIX

D an Wilde sat on the barstool with his back to the bar, letting the nebulous sounds of Stellar Weather flow over him like a river of dissonant notes flowing past him in syncopated rhythm. The crowded interior of Cobalt was dark and smoky, the soft clinking of glasses blending with the approving sounds of admiring patrons and soft laughter. Stella sat next to him, relishing the euphoria created by the combination of her third Johnny Walker Black and the live performance of the popular jazz quartet. Wilde had turned a thicker skin to the occasional reproachful looks and disapproving twitters when they'd made their appearance at Cobalt a half hour earlier. Choosing to ignore their judgement, he was preferring instead to watch his alluring wife enjoy herself on the barstool as she twisted her body in rhythm to the sensuous beats of their favorite jazz group.

Absorbed by his wife's feminine movements, the jazz vibes created the perfect accompaniment to his study of her shapely torso. Stella's gyrations reminded him of the many times he watched her get herself off as she sat in the car seat beside him. Watching her in the dimly-lit bar as he nursed his margarita, Wilde licked the salt from the glass's rim and, with his peripheral vision, checked for others who might be admiring his wife's sexy moves.

He thought about the extroverted young femme fatale he'd met twenty years ago. She'd changed over the years, becoming increasingly withdrawn and moody. Living more in a world of her own creation, separate from things they once shared, it seemed that the world was closing in on her as she increasingly expressed her unhappiness with his choice of business associates. He wanted to believe that she wasn't unhappy with him, that perhaps they were even still good for each other. But lately, they lived in the ruins of a marriage that was once far more elegant and transparent, one that Wilde ached to go back to. But, there was no returning to innocence if he wanted to keep Stella out of harm's way. Mesmerized by her salacious gyrations, he wished he could put the genie back in the bottle and turn the clock back twenty years.

Dressed in a black silk vest over long-sleeved white shirt, the congenial young bartender interrupted his muse. "Can I get you another margarita, Mr. Wilde?" He glanced at Stella, gyrating on the barstool to the soft sounds of the jazz group, trying hard not to stare at her as she sipped her Johnny Walker Black.

"Sure." Wilde placed his empty on the bar. "Like your vest there, bartender. Brioni, right?"

He smiled. "Yes it is. My first night here, they sent me home to change."

"Oh? Why's that?" asked Wilde, feeling like he was being set up for a punch line.

"They told me to dress to kill. Apparently, a turban, beard, and a backpack wasn't what they had in mind, so they-"

"Funny. And so you gave up on a career in comedy to tend bar." Before the bartender could answer, "Can you throw an extra lime wedge on that margarita for me?"

"You got it, boss," doing a double take of Wilde. He looked familiar, but was unsure of where he'd seen him before.

They both noticed Carol and Mark McAllister enter through the brass doors as they made their appearance at the hostess desk. The couple eased their way into the crowded bar, Carol in her semi-sheer open-sided short skirt and lace top, Mark in his black man-hugging outfit. A popular pair at Cobalt, the attractive couple searched for a place to perch.

"Who's that?" asked Stella, captivated by the couple's appearance.

"Our new neighbors. The author you wanted to meet," he replied, watching his wife's pupils dilate with pleasure.

"That's his wife? She looks like a super model," said Stella with a disappointed lilt in her voice.

"Were you expecting a Bulgarian weightlifter with hair under her arms?" She frowned at her husband's remark. In a softer tone he asked, "Shall I wave them over?" He had a feeling this was the quintessential rhetorical question.

Stella pretended she didn't care, but he wasn't fooled. "Sure. Why not?" she asked. "We may need to borrow a cup of Johnny

Walker Black one day." *In the nude would be nice.* She was jolted into thinking about some of the techniques she and Dan used to jump-start the juices when they were in a frisky mood. Sometimes their foreplay in bed would include a description of a pre-marital lover, and it was all within the confines of their unconventional relationship. Unable to take her eyes from Mark, in Stella's mind, she was still playing within her marital guidelines.

Stellar Weather had just finished their first set to an enthusiastic round of applause as Mark and Carol made their way toward the bar. Mark said, "Honey, that's the guy I was telling you about. We should probably at least stop and say hi." With a twinge of jealousy, he noticed Carol had her gaze fixed on Wilde and looked to break her spell. "Think he looks like a gangster?" he asked her.

"Not at all. As a matter of fact, you were right. He does look a lot like Michael Fassbender. Not at all bad looking, deliciously sinister, an intriguing man I would say." She waited for Mark to respond with a bit of testosterone, but he knew her tricks. Refusing to be baited, he looked around at the throng of night clubbers as if it didn't matter. Surveying the bar for familiar faces, Carol added, "Well, now that we've been spotted, it would be rude not to say hello. We can always say we're meeting someone for dinner if we want to keep moving."

They made their way to the bar as Wilde looked to make them feel welcome by standing and extending his hand. "Mr. McAllister, last time we met, you were up to your neck in geraniums and marigolds. Didn't know you were a jazz fan."

Mark shook his outstretched hand. "Since we're neighbors now, you might as well call me Mark." With his arm around her waist, he added, "And this is my wife Carol." Wilde reached for her hand and bowed to kiss it, the fan fair prompting a new round of twittering from a few onlookers. Carol was curious about the ruggedly handsome man who seemed to carry so many warning labels.

Envious of his neighbor's attention to Carol, Mark tried to ignore his visceral instincts, all too mindful that his wife seemed to have forgotten all about her earlier concerns about a gangster living next door. "And this beautiful lady must be Mrs. Wilde," said Mark, totally captivated by her striking green eyes.

"Call me Stella," with a lingering handshake. "I'm a big fan. Loved your last novel." Not to be outdone by her husband's theatrics, Mark pressed his lips delicately against the top of her hand. Stella reacted with pleasure, running her fingertips over her black pearl necklace expectantly as she leaned across the bar and displayed her pendulous charms. The young well-dressed bartender stood by patiently, pen in hand and pleasantly amused, ready to take their order, but his pen had stopped working.

Amused with the bartender's efforts to get his pen to write, Mark commented; "Made in China with one of those all-day warranties?"

The bartender smiled at Mark. "I guess. What would you like, sir?"

"Larressingle XO Armagnac in a large snifter," said Mark.

"And for you, ma'am?"

Stella said, "I'll have whatever he's having," nodding in Mark's direction. As the bartender prepared their Armagnacs, she turned her attention back to Mark. "You still have your sailboat, Captain McAllister?" she asked flirtatiously.

"All sixty-seven feet of her, refurbished with new electronics, compliments of Typhoon Betty and our trusty insurance company," pretending that he wasn't distracted by her charms. He was watching her admire two couples grinding slowly against each other on the dance floor. Catching her eye, he nodded toward the couple with the provocative moves. "Vertical expression of horizontal desire?"

She nodded and smiled at the author. Taking advantage of her husband's infatuation with Mrs. McAllister, Stella leaned closer. "So, Mark, I'm curious about your hobbies. What do you do for fun?" she asked in a sultry voice, her eyes sparkling with desire. "I mean, besides sailing around the world and writing best sellers?"

Unable to resist the gravitational pull of her striking green eyes, he felt like he was being drawn into unchartered territory, like the astronaut's voyage into the star-filled monolith in *2001: A Space Odyssey*. Though respectful of marriage, he found himself uncharacteristically entranced and gave her an equally enticing answer;

"I enjoy kegeling, collecting handcuffs, and imitating erotic bird calls," he said with a deadpan look.

Stella laughed politely and leaned closer as she continued to run her fingers expectantly over her ebony pearl necklace. "You'll have to show me your collection sometime," she said. "And the kegeling? What does that do for you?"

How bad you want to know?

There followed a pause in their conversation as the author was temporarily at a loss for words. A little jealous over the attention her husband was paying their new neighbor, Carol found the perfect segue to end the flirtation as she spotted the Bondini couple at a table in the restaurant's reserved patio area.

"Honey, look," she said. "It's Diane and Darius Bondini," smiling and waving. The husband and wife restauranteurs were the Vero Beach owners of Celsius, Club Liquid, and Trattoria Darius, the famous Italian bistro in South Beach where Mark held his last sponsored book signing a few weeks earlier.

To the Wildes he said, "Some of my marketing partners. We have some business to discuss," waiting for Carol to follow his lead. "Very nice seeing the two of you. We're gonna say hi before the group starts up again." Lady-like and cordial, Stella shook hands with her favorite author once more before he turned to leave. As the encounter with the Wildes came to a close, Mark couldn't escape the sinking feeling that he'd just stepped up to his neck into a giant pit of quicksand.

Leaving the Wildes at the bar, Mark and Carol made their way across the black slate floor to the patio bar where the Bondinis waited to greet them. There they had a reserved table with panoramic ocean views in addition to the jazz band inside. The posh patio bar was normally reserved for celebrities and private guests of the resort, and the island-gentry couple were eager to invite the author and his wife to share their table. After making sure their guests were comfortable, the restauranteurs wasted no time in launching into an enthusiastic description of what the next champagne and lobster signing event would entail. The foursome toasted the encore event, having come to an agreement on many of the details, their enthusiasm driven by the success of the last book signing bash at Trattoria Darius.

The Bondinis shared a few minutes of chit-chat describing their daughter's success as an interior designer before Mark glanced over at the Wildes. They were busy chatting with a well-dressed middle-aged man whom they later learned was one of Wilde's security men. More comfortable sitting with the Bondinis, Mark felt relieved to have found a way to distance themselves from their new neighbors in such a public place as Cobalt. The social fallout from their encounter with the notorious Dan Wilde would be difficult to quantify, and Mark was anticipating the gossip that would likely follow.

Under the table, Carol put her hand on his thigh. "Join me for some fresh air on the terrace?" He could tell when something was bothering her. They excused themselves, hand in hand, and strolled to the terrace railing for some sea breeze and quiet conversation. Moonlight sparkled off the ocean as a distant cruise ship headed north on the horizon. The ambient sounds of the bar laughter and tinkling of glasses drifted outside to them as they embraced the cool ocean breeze.

He turned to her and softly asked, "So, what's on your mind?"

"*This* situation," looking at him sternly. Mark felt a headache coming on, returning her gaze with a questioning look.

In a warmer tone, she went on. "I really do understand your misgivings about Mr. Wilde, and your reluctance about having any social interactions with him, Mark, but he is our neighbor. It's not like we planned for this to happen."

"Lotta milleniums don't ever plan on gaining 40 pounds and driving a minivan, either," quipped Mark. He took a long look at her. "Why are you defending him? Are you enamored with him?"

There was a long silence, filled only by the sounds of waves breaking on the beach, the clinking of glasses and muted laughter from inside the bar. "I'm your wife, Mark," she answered. "I don't dislike him. Doesn't seem like a bad man. Maybe we could get to know them better over dinner and drinks."

"He's a criminal, Carol."

She shrugged. "So say the tabloids. If he wasn't really a crime boss, would *you* like him?"

"Possibly." Mark wasn't racist, or a bigot. Many of his friends were Catholics, some were of minority races, Italians, some were Jewish, Slavs, Hispanic, Asians, blacks. He didn't normally pre-judge people, preferring to wait and see how they behaved. If they refrained from necrophilia and decapitating people, maybe they were okay.

But what he did know was that Mr. Dan Wilde of Villa Dellacroix was definitely not okay. "Honey, keeping him at arms-length isn't personal, just prudent." He looked at her with a sideways glance. "Best to leave sleeping dragons alone, agree?"

Carol exchanged looks with Wilde across the bar. "Well, he doesn't look very sleepy to me. You know what Tolkien said about dragons, right?"

"What did he say?"

"J.R.R. Tolkien said, 'It doesn't due to leave a live dragon out of your calculations if you live near him.'"

"Uh-huh. I'm just saying it's advisable to keep our distance."

Carol gave him a skeptical look. "You sure? You seem a little… well, maybe a tad jealous," tapping her fingernails on her wine glass. She liked it when he was jealous. It made her feel more like a woman.

He knew she enjoyed stirring the pot a bit to drum up some drama. "Not a bit," he denied. Still, she wasn't convinced.

"Well, everyone in Vero Beach seems to know who he is. It's like we have a celebrity living next door," she mused.

"Aren't we the lucky ones?" Mark finished his Armagnac, savoring the rich flavor of the Laressingle XO, wishing the encounter with the Wildes was just as satisfying. "So, what shall we do, Carol? Take him public in an I.P.O.? Time share them?"

She snuggled up to him. "C'mon, baby, don't be like that."

"Just when I thought I'd discovered the quiet, peaceful life of a writer, we get Mr. Wilde moving in next door."

"Aren't you being a little dramatic, Mark?"

"Well, aren't you being naïve? We've got a barbarian chief, a regular mobster-to-the-stars moving in on our Mayberry-By-The-Sea." She grew quiet as she considered his spin on the whole thing, always entertained by his unique ability for colorful irony.

Slowly, he could see her coming around to his perspective. He remembered a conversation with a reporter at *32963 Magazine* and checked first to make sure no one was eavesdropping before placing his mouth closer to her ear. "By the way, if you ever speak on the phone with him, Carol, be careful what you say. You may be on tape with the FBI," knowing his wife loved drama.

Carol acted surprised. "How do you know his phones are"-

"Not certain, but an educated guess." He'd hoped to discourage her interest in Wilde, knowing she had always liked flying close to the flame. He thought back to one of their first dates when she'd agreed to go skydiving in the nude with him on a dare. Mark knew then he had his hands full. The videographer had waived his $200 fee to film the episode when she agreed to jump in the nude. After the jump, everyone went home happy after Carol talked Mark into buying the original copy for $300 so they could enjoy it on their big screen.

On the subject of Mr. Wilde, he could tell she needed more convincing, so he proceeded to share his sullied stories. "I did a little homework on Mr. Wilde. Some things you should know. He actually did do some time back in '97 when he did a year for tax evasion. Charges for felony assault were later dropped when the witness changed his testimony. Last year, the U.S. Department of Justice charged him with five felony counts of mortgage fraud involving the sale of Baja Grille franchises right here in Vero and Palm Beach, and those are ongoing investigations."

"That's it?" she asked. "So, would you say he's paid his debt to society?" Carol suppressed a smile. Mark could tell she was joking.

"Not exactly," he continued. "According to the U.S. Attorney's Office, Mr. Daniel Wilde is alleged to be involved in intrastate money laundering, racketeering, extortion, securities law violations, mortgage fraud and bribery, but so far they haven't been able to prove any of it. Shall I go on?" Amused with what still appeared to be her husband's jealousy, she continued to smile. "You still want to have dinner and drinks at our 'celeb' neighbor's estate?" he asked.

She launched into her best sketch of, as she would say, an inferior desecrator. "Oh, Mark, I simply *have* to see what they've done to Villa Dellacroix's interior."

"This is not a game, Carol. Be serious for a moment."

Finally, she grew solemn. "So, what do you think the dragon wants from us?"

"Not sure. Social standing, respectability, acceptance, who knows? There's always gonna be people trying to fix us so we fit into their world, but they may not be able to." Carol listened intently to his insights. "Or, like I said on the drive, maybe he thinks he's saving us from a life of boredom."

"Baby..." relinquishing her solemn mood, she put her hand on his chest. "I'm anything but bored! Let's go home, forget about our neighbor's at Villa Dellacroix. Maybe play some Grand Theft Auto?" Snuggling up to him and sliding her hands down inside his pockets. "Better yet, drop some acid and play Twister in the nude," giving him her best Hollywood smile. Mark was enjoying her new direction.

"You mean, with each other this time?" he asked. That earned him the playful slap he was waiting for, followed by a kiss. Maybe Carol *was* finally beginning to understand his genuine concern for her safety. Still, he was a little ticked over her exchanging unrestrained goo-goo eyes with Wilde earlier at the bar. By now, he should be used to it, but he wasn't.

"You told me once that I'm the only one you want to sleep with," she said, playfully pulling him closer.

"I only said that because all the others kept me awake all night," he said with a huge smile.

With her hands still on his hips, she took a step back in mock admonishment. "Well, screw *me* sideways on a pogo stick."

"Careful, girl. I'm pretty good on a pogo stick."

Playfully, she grabbed him by the hand. "All right, Mr. McAllister, looks like we're gonna hafta get into your handcuff collection tonight. C'mon then," leading him toward the door.

On his way out, he thought of what his college roommate was always so fond of saying; "Always be sincere, whether you mean it or not."

CHAPTER SEVEN

I t was the first Monday in May, and the restaurant bustled with waiters and bartenders preparing for a busy lunch hour. The Wave at Costa d'Este Beach Resort in Vero offered a variety of dining options and a unique waterfront ambiance with a panoramic view of the Vero beachfront. Seated at a four-top on the patio, Dr. Hirt sipped his pina colada as he kept an eye out for his attractive lunch date. The balding sixty-year-old psychiatrist was waiting patiently for Dr. Katherine Tremelle to make her appearance.

Surveying the restaurant, the well-known Vero Beach shrink adjusted his black-rimmed glasses, enjoying the vibrant underwater images of oceanic reef life displayed on TV screens behind the bar. The images echoed the brilliant beauty of the vibrant salt water aquarium just inside the restaurant's entrance that captured his attention earlier. The clownfish, the pygmy sea horses, damsel fish, blue tangs and rainbow wrasses all lined up expectantly in a lively display of energy, with the baby octopus hiding at the bottom. If he had time, he could watch for hours the incredibly beautiful sea anemones waving back and forth, displaying their neon brilliance like city lights aglow in a nocturnal sea.

The beachfront bistro was a favorite with local physicians and professionals who had come to expect a creative approach to the culinary arts along with a refined sense of hospitality. Though familiar with the menu, Dr. Hirt enjoyed perusing it to search for newly-added entrees. Of all the flawlessly-prepared delicacies infused with locally-grown produce and fresh-caught seafood, his favorite was still the pecan-encrusted broiled dolphin stuffed with crabmeat and fried plantains. Professionals, retirees and couples meandered in as he took another sip of his pina colada and watched the bartender perform his magic with the specialties of the house.

He heard the click of high heels on tile and turned to see Dr. Katherine Tremelle saunter up to his table. Standing to greet his vivacious guest, he gave a hug and peck on the cheek to the well-dressed clinical psychiatrist. "Katherine, you look as ravishing as ever! Please," pulling out a chair for her, "…have a seat. Appreciate your meeting me. How was the traffic?"

"C'mon, Chris. Traffic in Vero? Really? When my clinic was in West Palm, now *that* was traffic. Vero's so much more laid back." She took a seat, looking forward to enjoying their lunch. "Did you see that aquarium out front, with everything from neon gobies to clownfish, a baby octopus and sea anemones?"

"Beautiful. Thinking about adding one in my office. How're the kids, Katherine?" The two psychiatrists had been friends for years ever since meeting at the 20th Annual Conference of the American Neuropsychiatric Association in Washington, D.C.

"Jason's just entered his second year of med school at Harvard, and Jessica's finishing up on her PhD. in Marine Biology at FSU," she said. He regarded his forty-two-year-old colleague's tasteful Christian Dior outfit as he took another sip of his pina colada. A clinical psychiatrist with fashion sense-who could have guessed? It was a good match with her black page-boy hair, brown eyes and black-rimmed Warby Parker glasses. She reminded him of the demure librarian that he'd had a crush on during his years at Harvard Med.

Dr. Katherine Tremelle held the enviable position of Director of Clinical Research and Trials at Valiant Pharmaceuticals. Valiant was one of the movers and shakers in the development of new and novel medications for a wide range of oncologic and psychiatric disorders. The company had moved their clinical research facility to Vero Beach to accommodate her when she'd threatened to leave them over lifestyle issues. With a PhD. in Microbiology from McGill, and a M.D. in Clinical Psychiatry from Harvard, Dr. Tremelle was responsible for shepherding twelve innovative pharmaceuticals to market in the last ten years. So far, four of them had become blockbuster drugs, and her research was on the forefront of medicine throughout the world. But it was her research on Seraquim that was of particular interest to him. After the waiter had delivered their appetizers and they'd shared some small talk, the conversation drifted to a review of the latest medications for the psychiatric disorders that funded their lavish lifestyles.

"So, tell me about your latest challenges as the busiest shrink in Vero, Chris." Dr. Tremelle liked to tease him about his bachelor lifestyle. Secretly, she envied his freedom. Living vicariously, she enjoyed hearing about his romantic interludes and often wondered if he'd ever settle down.

"Not much new in 'Heaven's Waiting Room' really." Obsessed with comparing incomes, he added, "I heard you were making seven figures over there."

Dr. Tremelle smiled. "Well, with stock options, I suppose so," staring at her wine glass. "I've made them a lot of money, Chris."

"And you deserve every success. Tell me something. I'm keenly interested in Valiant's latest new FDA-approval of Seraquim for acute clinical depression and bi-polar anxiety. Your pet project as I recall. How's the roll-out going?"

Taking a sip of wine, she set her glass down on the table, resigning herself to a peer-to-peer interlude. "Rollout's ahead of schedule, which is what we expected after the drug met the efficacy and safety issues, and all endpoints were achieved. We're hoping sales will be a class leader among the SSNRIs." Dr. Hirt listened attentively. "All responses were assessed by independent blind central review using the iwCLL guidelines."

"Okay, you're giving me the company line. What about contra-indications?"

"From a safety standpoint, combinations with other SSNRIs and some hypnotics were well tolerated with a safety profile consistent with the Phase II study, except…"

"Except for…what?" He could tell she was reluctant to part with the details and needed some coaxing. "If there are safety issues, shouldn't I know, for the benefit of my patients?" he asked.

She looked around and leaned forward. "We're trying to keep this off the label, so we never had this conversation, Chris."

She waited for an affirmative nod from him before continuing. "There were some unsafe contraindications with specific personality traits in combination with certain hypnotics. Because the incidence of correlation with targeted patients were so low-less than half a percent-we were able to deem it irrelevant. The FDA agreed with our stance because the overall profile was so effective."

Hirt wanted more details and leaned forward. "Just in case I do encounter this 'less than half percent', can you be more specific?"

"We learned that Seraquim should not be prescribed for patients diagnosed INTP Briggs, and should not be dosed with Ambienna and similar hypnotics."

"Why?"

"We had one ugly incident. Causal external events were questionable, so we were able to have the results discarded."

Hirt raised his eyebrows and leaned even closer. "What do you mean ugly, Katherine?"

Dr. Tremelle looked around to see if anyone could hear. "Chris, I'm not sure I should…I mean, I could lose my job if"-

Hirt pressed her further. "Strictly between you and me, Katherine." He softened his voice. "Please, from one physician to another, tell me what happened. Define ugly."

She gulped the last of her wine and held the glass up to be refilled, letting a meaningful few seconds pass before answering.

"While under the influence of Seraquim, one of the male patients in the Phase III trial who had a script for Ambienna tried to strangle his girlfriend. He almost asphyxiated her. We dropped the patient from our trial and our staff was able to suppress the documentation and classify it as 'incidental external event.'"

"And the FDA agreed?"

She gave him a stern look. "The FDA doesn't know the whole story. I heard there was a payoff involved, which I did not agree with, nor do I have any knowledge of, if this ever comes up again."

"No worries, Katherine," reassuring his friend as he took a sip of his pina colada. "I'd heard about patients gobbling buttered cigarettes and eating raw eggs, shells and all, in an Ambienna-induced haze. Ambienna zombies, they called them, but nothing like this. Did the patient have a record of prior violent acts?"

"None." They went silent as the waiter poured her another glass of chardonnay before leaving. "We think it was the combination of Ambienna with Seraquim and specific INTP personality traits that induced the aberration."

"Aberration? Katherine, let's be clear here. You're saying, according to your research, that there is a high correlation of potential violence with INTP Briggs patients on Seraquim while in an Ambienna-induced hypnotic state?"

Feeling cornered, she responded hesitantly. "Yes." She removed her glasses, set them on the table and became deadly serious. "Chris, only a small handful of physicians know about this. If this were to get out, our stock would take a *huge* hit and Effexxor and Abillify would probably take substantial market share from us. And, I could lose my job. So, mum's the word." She waited for some sign he understood. "If you'd like to read about the entire series of clinical trials, I'll share our corporate website password, but you can never tell anyone where you got it. Hirt nodded. "Write this password down." Hirt took a pen out and grabbed a napkin. "At Valiant's website, click on TRIALS, and in the drop-down menu where it says STAFF, enter this password: cerebellum911."

"Cerebellum911," he repeated, printing it neatly on the napkin.

"Whatever you do, Chris, it's a restricted site, so don't stay on it for more than ten minutes. They have an anti-hacking software that is *very* efficient."

He covered her forearm with his hand to reassure her. "You have my promise, Katherine. We never had this conversation. No worries. This will help me avoid any land mines with my own patients. Thanks."

The waiter returned with their entrees and Hirt ordered another round of drinks. It became clear to him there was only one course of action, and it was brilliant. Hirt said, "I only have two rules for success, Katherine; one, never tell everything you know." Then he stopped.

A few moments went by before she asked, "And two?" He cocked his head expectantly before it dawned on her. "Very clever, Chris," raising her glass for a toast. "To rule number one."

As they toasted, Hirt asked, "What else is going on at Valiant these days? Anything else of interest taking us to new heights in medicine?"

She went with the flow, as if making light of her story would somehow make it seem like it never happened. She put her hand on his forearm and smiled. "You have got to hear this one, Chris. Did you hear about the fake South Florida doctor who 'enhanced' his patient's buttocks with a mixture of cement, mineral oil, bathroom caulking and Fix-A-Flat tire sealant? They gave him ten years for manslaughter."

Dumbfounded, Hirt set his drink on the table. "This has to be a joke, right?"

"No, this really happened. He was charging $2,000 per injection to enhance the buttocks of patients he found on the web. The side effects created by the materials led to three patients' death by respiratory failure."

"Victoria Secret models wanting a butt to die for, huh?" joked Hirt. "So, is *this* the butt of all jokes?"

Dr. Tremelle laughed politely. "Uh-huh. I mean, you can't make this stuff up. This fake doctor apparently poked her in the buttocks with an eighteen-gauge needle and used Fix-A-Flat and superglue to fill the holes. By the time *rigor mortis* set in, her glutes were the hardest part of her body."

"So, who needs Viagra, right?" Hirt suppressed a desire to laugh out loud. He had a fleeting recollection about swearing to the Hippocratic Oath when he graduated from med school thirty-two years ago. "How could any doctor be so insensitive to a patient's welfare?" he chided.

She shrugged. "Beats me, Chris. Let's eat before our entrees get cold."

Hirt raised his glass for another toast, elated with the information. "Bona petit, Katherine."

***

An hour later, Hirt was mulling over his conversation with the Director of Research at Valiant as he drove back to his office near the Indian River Medical Center. Now it was his chance to even the score, his turn to game the system. Parking his Porsche Turbo, a plan began to take shape. Tired of bowing to the Mc*Whatevers* and the *Something*fields that ran the show in Vero Beach, his plan was a risky course of action, but he was certain the outcome would reinforce his retirement plan enormously. He figured his trading scheme would make the difference between settling for a fourth floor condo at Sea Quay or an opulent southeast exposure on the penthouse-level 13th floor at Village Spires. Entering his office, Hirt pushed open the glass door with his name painted in gold lame and locked eyes with the elderly patient sitting in the waiting room. The seventy-seven- year-old woman was delighted to see him.

"Mrs. Landes, good to see you," grasping her hand. "I have an urgent call to make, after which I'll be right with you."

"Oh, thank you, Dr. Hirt," said the grey-haired lady. "I'm still having those headaches," she complained. We'll hit the easy button and simply double the dosage, he thought.

"Teresa," he said to his nurse assistant, "...hold my calls and take Mrs. Landes to my examination room. Tell her I'll be with her in a few minutes," closing the door to his office.

The psychiatrist seated himself behind his laptop and brought up Valiant's website, entering the passcode Tremelle had given him. He was in, and within minutes, able to confirm the new drug's trial effects in black and white, just as Tremelle had described, all laid out in official bureaucratic medspeak, a language he understood all too well. He was able to exit the website without setting off any alarms and thumbed through his cell phone to find the number for his financial adviser at Morgan Stanley Wealth Management. The phone rang twice before numb nuts answered.

"Perry, how are you? Listen, bring up my revocable trust account and tell me how much cash I have in my account right now."

"Dr. Hirt, always good to hear from you. I can tell you're in a hurry. You have…uh, exactly $653,546 available. Without using any margin. You have something in mind? You gonna add to your Pfizer or Allergan positions?"

"No, Perry. Think I've got enough of the big pharmas. I'm gonna take a flyer on Valiant Pharmaceutical."

"Great. We have a buy rating"-

"Never mind that, Perry. What's it selling for?"

"Last trade was at one-hundred-twenty-five and fifty, down twenty cents in today's action."

"Okay. Perry. Listen carefully. I want you to buy me as many June one-hundred-twenty-five *put* options as you can for five hundred grand, market order. Round it off to the nearest ten contracts." Hirt smiled to himself, unable to resist using his favorite cliché, "Now, how do you feel about that, Perry?"

The Morgan Stanley broker was mystified by what seemed like a reckless, high-risk trade in short-dated put options on a buy-rated stock. "Well, a little awkward"-

"Forget it, Perry. It was a rhetorical question." Hirt waited for him to repeat the order to make sure he had it right.

"Okay. We are buying 400 Valiant June one-hundred-twenty-five strike *put* options at the market, unsolicited. That's a big order. I'll need an email from you saying the order was unsol"-

"*Just do it*, Perry. Market order."

"Got it." A few moments passed as the order was filled. "You're done at an average price of a buck and a quarter a share."

"Good. I'll fax, email or text you anything you need for authorization." Unable to avoid the temptation to gloat, he muttered to himself, "Options on forty-thousand shares. If I'm right, I could make a coupla million." *Come on, doctor needs a new penthouse!*

"What was that, Dr. Hirt? Couldn't quite hear you."

"Never mind, Perry. Are we good?"

"Yes sir, Dr. Hirt. Please don't forget the"-

Hirt had already hung up. Overhearing the conversation, Perry's manager stood over him, ready to grill him about the risky, unsolicited half-million-dollar put option trade on a buy-rated stock. For appearances, Perry continued as if his client were still on the line. "As always, thanks for the opportunity to be of service, Dr. Hirt. Don't forget to return the 'unsolicited' authorization form."

Perry cradled the phone and looked up at his boss, preparing for the third degree he knew was coming.

CHAPTER EIGHT

With the beginning of summer in Florida, afternoon weather became more unpredictable as the days grew hotter. It was Tuesday, and another day had passed uneventfully, unless one were to count the flying drones Stella was attracting by tending her garden in the nude at Villa Dellacroix. Today, to the disappointment of those hi-tech voyeurs who operated the drones, she had reluctantly acquiesced to her husband's plea for more modesty outside and went about her gardening in a black Brazilian-cut bikini. Dan was away, attending a meeting at Bahia Mar Yacht Club in Ft. Lauderdale with their trust attorney, Damon Morgan.

The lush landscaping at Villa Dellacroix was in full bloom, and since it's planting, Stella's vegetable garden had survived two gale-force thunderstorms, along with a host of creepy caterpillar pests that were bent on turning her garden into a month-long smorgasbord. The basil, the green pepper plants, even the eggplant looked healthy. After spending most of her morning at the gym, she busied herself with pulling the weeds from between a row of pepper plants when she looked up to see a Federal Express delivery truck parked at the entrance to their beachfront estate. She stood and brushed herself off, noticing their deliveryman waving to her from the security gate as he held a package.

Stella waved back and, in a modest mood, gathered her sheer black wrap from the patio chaise lounge before making her way down the five-hundred-foot Chicago brick driveway, curious to know why the deliveryman couldn't have left it in their mailbox. Clip-clopping her way over the weathered brick in her Jimmy Choo wedges, she recognized the young man standing at the wrought-iron gate from his many slow passes by the villa during her gardening.

"Hello, Anthony. Watcha got for me today?" Stella was in a good mood and sang out to him in a melodic voice that complimented the mild spring weather.

"Hi Mrs. Wilde. You're looking lovely today," tipping his cap. "Got an urgent overnight package that needs a signature." Anthony adjusted his cap again as he looked her up and down with unbridled infatuation. "It's addressed to your husband, but I guess it's okay if you sign for him."

Though he bragged openly about his success in the markets, her husband shared so little of his secret dealings with her that she was curious why it wasn't sent to his office at the PNC Bank building on Ocean Boulevard. "Who's it from?" she asked, squinting through her sunglasses at the young man wearing the familiar blue uniform. She noticed he was a good-looking man, and the shorts he wore did little to hide his well-defined quads. Stella always had an easygoing way with young working men, quite different from the more formal attitude she shared with men her age. Whenever craftsmen and laborers were present, she enjoyed flirting and moving around the jobsite, especially if they were bare chested, the men often looking at her as if she were a fresh double-cheese pepperoni pizza.

Anthony flipped the letter-sized package over to check the sender's name. "Uh, Barclays Wealth Management, ma'am. It's, uh…addressed to Mr. Daniel Wilde, Co-Trustee, D/B/A The Dellacroix Global Trust." After scanning it, he slipped the electronic pad through the gate with the stylus. Stella signed it with a flourish and took the package.

"Thanks, Anthony," brushing her hair back as she handed him the pad.

Anthony grinned and tipped his hat again, giving her one last flirty sweep of her body with his eyes. "Thank *you*, Mrs. Wilde!" Hopping back into his truck he shouted, "And good luck with your basil and peppers."

Holding her package, she looked back toward the garden several hundred feet away, wondering how he could see such detail all the way from the street before she noticed the binoculars on the truck's dashboard. Feeling totally objectified by the young man's fantasies, Stella was flattered that she'd been commanding so much of his attention. Clip-clopping back up the driveway, she stopped halfway up to unzip the package and read the letter inside.

The letter stopped her in her tracks. It was an urgent notification from Barclays International PLC notifying the trustees of a $28 million margin call in the account due in three days. The letter went on to request that the trustees immediately contact Mr. Robert Abernathy as to how the call was to be met; depositing cash or securities in the amount of $28 million, or a full liquidation of the account.

"What the...?" she asked out loud. Outraged, she glared up at the sky, appealing to a higher power. "Dan, I swear as God is my witness, I AM GOING TO KILL YOU!" She looked again in disbelief at the letter in her hands before reading it for a second time. "Refried bean futures go south on you, Dan? A $28 million margin call? Are you FREAKING FOR REAL?" She felt like a steel door had slammed on her soul. Now she *really* regretted entrusting him with a good chunk of her inheritance. When she made the decision to fund his trading account, she felt guilty about forcing him to sign a pre-nup at her father's insistence. *So this is how you repay my trust, Dan?*

She suppressed her first instinct, which was to call him and demand an immediate explanation, but she knew it was unlikely the philandering SOB would tell her the truth. She checked her watch. It was early, only ten-thirty. Deciding she wouldn't take no for an answer, she planned to be sitting in Mr. Abernathy's office before noon, vowing to plant herself there until she'd heard the whole truth, and nothing but the truth.

***

The motorists and pedestrians crossing the 17th Street Causeway Bridge had a grand view of Emilio Rosa's ninety-meter Feadship moored a few hundred yards north of the bridge at the Bahia Mar Resort and Yacht Club. *Bella Rosa* was the largest and most luxurious vessel quartered at the upscale marina, her top deck reaching as high as the 17th Street Bridge itself. For those standing on the T-dock, her gleaming five stories of white aluminum and polished stainless steel presented an impressive example of unsurpassed opulence on the high seas.

The true owner of the vessel was a carefully guarded secret, the title buried in layers of offshore shell corporations and American-based LLCs that were almost impossible to trace. Very few knew *Bella Rosa* was owned by one of the world's most powerful drug lords, the undisputed king of the Mexican cartel. Following a murderous climb to the top, Emilio Rosa had emerged as the successor to Pablo Escobar, and his Juarez cartel was responsible for supplying 50% of the cocaine smuggled into the United States, bringing over $3 billion a year into his personal coffers.

On the way to Bahia Mar, Wilde paid a visit to Citi Bank on the corner of Federal Highway and Spanish River Boulevard in Boca while Morgan waited in the car. He remembered that Stella kept a safe deposit box in joint name at the big bank and, lucky for him, in the last few years since learning of the box's existence, Stella hadn't changed any of the authorization pass codes. There, underneath a pile of diamond heirlooms, trust documents and deeds, he found what he was looking for in the bottom of the stainless steel box; the master mini-USB flash drive that contained the account number and passcode for her trust fund. Smiling to himself, he removed the flash drive from its clear plastic case and slipped the USB-drive onto his keychain before locking the box and exiting the vault. Now, he could only hope she hadn't changed the passcodes. Holding his keys up to the lights of the bank vault, he marveled at how access to a fund of $1.75 billion could fit so conveniently on a flash drive the size of a small grape.

***

Thirty minutes later, Damon Morgan and Dan Wilde stood on the marina dock watching the parade of boats passing on the waterway as a pleasant breeze blew over Bahia Mar Resort. Scores of Scarabs, Hinckleys, Donzis, Bertrams, and a few smaller Boston Whalers made their way along the crowded approach to the 17th Street Causeway Bridge, the busiest section of the intracoastal waterway in Ft. Lauderdale. It was a nice day in Lauderdale Beach, with the mild 83-degree weather drawing out boaters and beachgoers everywhere. The two men had purposely arrived a half hour early to scope out the area before their much-anticipated meeting with the man who had such a ruthless reputation.

After paying a visit to the posh marina clubhouse, they stood outside the dockmaster's office in their pin-striped Navy blue Brooks Brothers suits, about to undertake of the biggest deals of their lives aboard the 90-meter mega yacht. Admiring *Bella Rosa* at a distance from the far end of the dock, Morgan began to narrate the ship's luxurious features to his client from the brochure he held, including a "40-meter dance floor with state-of-the-art sound system." As he scanned the brochure, it occurred to him that there was no mention of the ship's armory or advanced automated security systems. He handed the charter brochure to his client as a young man dressed in a white steward's uniform passed them pushing a large hand truck full of liquor. Wilde studied it for more clues about Rosa as more casually-dressed yacht owners and passengers sauntered past them on the concrete dock.

Wilde read the brochure's highlights back to Morgan who was busy watching three topless playmates toasting each other on the yacht's sundeck. "Says here she was launched by Feadship five years ago, and *Bella Rosa* was designed to deliver the complete luxury yacht experience for the most discerning owner." He looked up to see what had caught his attorney's attention.

"Pay attention, Damon," chided Wilde. "Maybe we can impress him with our knowledge of *Bella Rosa's* features."

Without taking his eyes from the girls, the attorney said, "You think memorizing brochures are gonna impress a blood-thirsty ego-maniac like Rosa? What impresses Mr. Rosa are the opportunities we bring to the table. It's all about the power and money, buddy."

"Uh-huh." He continued to read the brochure. "Says here 'She was originally designed for the ultimate in charter yachting' before Mr. Rosa pulled her from charter duty. I'm guessing now he only uses the yacht for his personal pleasure." He glanced at Morgan, who was watching two security guards at the bottom of *Bella Rosa's* gangway before continuing. "Hey, I've heard of this guy. 'Her elegant, interior is designed by Laurent Giles who created an elegant layout in a sophisticated yet contemporary style, including a movie theatre and a dedicated medical area. She sleeps 14 charter guests in a split-level upper deck, master suite with a private study, two VIP suites and three additional guest staterooms.' Man, this guy knows how to live!"

"Yeah, and he knows how to make people die, too," quipped Morgan, "...so let's watch our Ps and Qs. Be respectful, but also confident." Their attention was drawn by two giggling bikini-clad girls stacking fiberglass coolers with price tags still attached on the deck of a nearby 51' Morgan ketch. Wilde noticed the girls were wearing rhinestone-studded high heels as they stepped onto the concrete dock. Definitely party girls or strippers from the nearby topless joints along A1A, thought Morgan. The girls smiled flirtatiously at the two well-dressed men before turning and sashaying toward the clubhouse.

Wilde read the last paragraph from the brochure as he stood next to the piling. "'A professional staff of eighteen crew are available to guests 24/7.' Unbelievable."

"24/7 huh? I wonder if those beauties on the sundeck are part of the crew."

Wilde checked his watch. "In fifteen minutes, we're going to find out," brushing off his lapels before squaring off with his attorney. "I really hope you're right about Rosa."

Morgan couldn't resist the urge to tease his nervous client. "I heard Rosa's got a bumper sticker that says, 'SAVE BAJA GRILLE.'"

"Don't be a wise guy, Damon. I'm not in the mood."

"You worry too much. I've been their attorney for two years now, and I've earned their trust. In the cartel's move into legitimate business," he lowered his sunglasses to emphasize his point, "...I've made myself indispensable to Rosa by making him money and controlling risk. As long as I can do that, I can keep him happy. I know what we're dealing with, Dan. Hell, I've played *Grand Theft Auto* with his two nephews for God's sake."

"Who won?"

"C'mon. They're nine and eleven, with thumbs twice the size of mine. Besides, better to let the kids of a drug lord beat you at a video game. Yes?"

Wilde was still skeptical. On edge about the deal, he needed reassuring. With his back against the wall on an unavoidable $28 million margin call and the IRS pressing him in their audit, he faced some unpleasant choices. Moreover, he knew Stella would never agree to bail him out by invading her billion-dollar family limited partnership-at least, not without some help from her psychiatrist.

Morgan must have been reading his mind. "So, how are you and Stella getting along these days? You two on an even keel?"

Complicating matters, Wilde knew Morgan's interest in Stella extended beyond a professional relationship. Uneasy about his liberal ideas of attorney/client privileges, he looked for ways to discourage his attorney's interest in his wife. His last display of inappropriate behavior came when his hands had dallied a little too long massaging sunscreen on Stella on a friend's yacht on Lake Boca. "Stella is all about Stella, self-absorbed and increasingly distant," said Wilde. "She's become even more aloof and moody since our move to Villa Dellacroix."

Morgan was surprised at his candor. "*But,* she's your beloved wife and in love with you, right? I thought you bought the place to make her happy."

Wilde lowered his sunglasses to correct his smiling attorney's rose-colored view. "You're kidding me, right? Stella's only devoted to Stella. She knows her way around men better than any woman I've ever known."

Morgan winked. "Thank God you have your playthings, huh?"

Ignoring his taunt, Wilde said, "Let's talk about Dr. Hirt. What makes you so sure he's on board with us?"

"Hirt's ready to retire and wants to nail down a nice chunk of cash to pad his nest egg. He wants to cash out entirely."

"I trust his loyalty wasn't too expensive."

"Two hundred grand in untraceable tax-free bearer bonds," said Damon. Wilde looked surprised.

"He wanted three hundred until I told him they were seven percent tax-free coupons," explained Damon, "… equivalent to twelve percent in his tax bracket."

"Okay, counselor. If it works, it'll be money well spent." He was still concerned about some of the barbaric stories he'd heard about Rosa. "With the money I'm paying you, you better be right about this guy. I've heard about all the headless bodies buried in Texas and Mexico. My head's worth more than $110 million to me, Damon."

The counselor patted his buddy's shoulder reassuringly. "He's a businessman, Dan. First and foremost."

Morgan had done extensive homework on Rosa after being warned by his friends at the DEA about becoming involved in any kind of business deal. In contrast to the DEA's characterization, from his underworld contacts Morgan learned that Rosa treated his partners and captains with a certain amount of respect but could be ruthless and utterly barbaric if crossed. The stories about the snuff films they made with the headless bodies of their victims were particularly disturbing.

This would be Morgan's first drug deal, and he had no intention of losing his head as others had. He was sure he was smarter than that. It was another business deal, and as long as he treated his partners reasonably and fairly, he felt certain about keeping his head.

Morgan had resigned himself to the choices he made long beforehand, fully accepting all their possible outcomes. With his fees and the egregious return on his investment, his deal with Wilde to buy the Boca Resort and Beach Club would be within reach. By then, he'd be permanently ensconced in the privileged life with all the wine, women and runway models that he could handle.

Approaching the *Bella Rosa* from the main T-dock, it was obvious that Mr. Emilio Rosa had plenty of technology and security at his disposal. The four heavily armed guards standing watch over the gangway all wore matching blue uniforms with the embroidered yacht's name on the front pocket, uniforms that almost covered the bulge of Kevlar vests. Two burly men with Uzis dangling at their sides stood on the second deck at the top of the gangway, and two with side arms and an assortment of electronic gear stood at the bottom to greet them. As Wilde and Morgan approached, a guard with a pock-marked face stepped forward holding an electronic pad as he spoke something unintelligible into his shoulder radio.

"Gentlemen, can I help you?" he asked the two men in a heavy Spanish accent. Wilde wondered if the Neanderthal was paper trained.

"Damon Morgan and Dan Wilde, here to see Mr. Rosa," checking his watch. "I'm one of Mr. Rosa's attorneys," flashing his ID, "... and we have an appointment."

The guard checked his pad for confirmation and spoke again into his shoulder radio. "El abogado esta aqui con Senor Wilde." He pulled a hand-held metal detector from his holster and gestured for them to approach with their arms raised. After making two passes followed by a pat down, he turned and nodded to the guard at the top of the gangway.

Two more guards dressed in suits appeared at the top of the gangway and escorted them up one more deck and through the companionway to the main salon. On the way, they passed a locked cabin where they caught a glimpse through a porthole of money counters and what appeared to be stacks of cocaine wrapped neatly in white plastic bricks.

The two visitors knew there was no turning back now. Ensconced in the yacht's ornate main salon, Mr. Emilio Rosa presided over his world in a plush tan-colored suede armchair. A burly muscle-bound man stood guard next to a more slender man with dark hair and beady eyes, protruding face and quick movements, like an attractive rat sniffing out the cheese. The drug lord's entourage stood to greet their guests.

Wilde took a moment to evaluate the man who was about to become his next business partner. Rosa appeared to be in his sixties, a big man with a weathered, deeply-lined face and crows' feet accenting cold, inky-black eyes that reminded Wilde of the primitive look of a great white shark. Though his nails appeared to be carefully manicured, the plugs forming his hairline stood out, as if the drug lord had paid a hasty visit to the Hair Club For Men emergency glue booth. Meeting Rosa face-to-face for the first time, Wilde and Morgan had already heard all the stories of how a life of adversity had miraculously become one of charm and privilege after he'd separated the heads from the bodies of many of his adversaries.

"Bienvenida, counselor." Mr. Rosa smiled cordially. Extending his hand to both men, his handshake was firm and formal. "And you must be Mr. Wilde." After surveying his two guests, he said to Morgan, "You're all dressed up, counselor." Though he'd spoken on the phone many times with most of Rosa's top brass, Morgan had never before met the drug lord in person.

"Out of respect for your time, I came directly from my office in Vero Beach for our meeting, Mr. Rosa," bowing slightly.

He smiled. "Ah. I see." In light blue slacks, tan Topsiders and a cream-colored polo shirt, Rosa was dressed more casually, and the light-colored polo emphasized his deep tan which served to enhance the impression he'd just stepped off the golf course. The drug lord glared openly at Wilde, sizing him up. "And you will vouch for this man, counselor?"

"Of course, Mr. Rosa," nodding subserviently. Rosa turned to the two men that flanked him, introducing them as Javier and Ramone. Javier, the larger man of about forty, was dressed in a black silk shirt and black sport coat, which did little to hide his bulging shoulder holster. Wilde figured him to be Rosa's bodyguard. Ramone, the more affable of the two, was the younger, slender man who reminded him of a handsome rat, and his quick-witted demeanor suggested that the two visitors proceed with caution.

Rosa gestured toward Morgan. "My men tell me you've been doing a good job for us," he said. "Please," motioning toward the two empty suede armchairs, "...make yourselves comfortable, gentlemen. We have much to discuss. Can I get you a drink?" Immediately, an attractive young woman wearing a white steward uniform appeared to take their order as Wilde discretely regarded the yacht's interior. The décor was a blend of very ornate gold lame panel molding crafted to accent the off-white marble bulkheads with a bleached teak and holly sole decorated with extravagant Persian carpets. To the two visitors, it seemed a little over the top.

In honor of the tequila distillery owned by their host, the two VIP guests each ordered double shots of chilled Padron with lime wedges. Moments later, the steward returned with an entire tray of chilled tequila served in Baccarat crystal shot glasses.

"Gentlemen, help yourselves. Don't be shy," urged their host. As he reached for a drink, Wilde noticed the bulge of his ankle holster, and Rosa took note of his observation. "Don't worry, we're all licensed," he said.

Feeling some camaraderie, "Me too," said Wilde.

"You're licensed to carry firearms?" queried Rosa.

He allowed a few seconds to pass before responding. "No, to trade commodities." Rosa snickered at his offbeat sense of humor.

Raising his glass, Morgan said, "A votre sante, Mr. Rosa," immediately wishing he'd offered the toast in Spanish instead. Recognizing the faux pas, Wilde followed with another tribute; "Salude! To your beautiful yacht, and to your success, Mr. Rosa." After the group of five finished their double shots, Mr. Rosa gave instructions in Spanish to the two stewards. A moment later they were presented with two trays of freshly-prepared crab and lobster hors d'oeuvres fresh from the yacht's gourmet galley. After a few polite nibbles, the men settled down to the business at hand. To his guests, Rosa seemed like a man who knew how to enjoy life, which seemed completely understandable for a man who also knew how to take it.

Using the 50-inch video monitor that hung on the bulkhead, Ramone launched into a story-book account of Mr. Rosa's rise to power in the cartel, from his humble beginnings ransoming kidnapped executives to his later exploits of smuggling stolen art and luxury autos, his group becoming known as the Juarez Cartel. Proud of the fact that his boss held an M.B.A from Notre Dame and a B.A in Marketing from The University of Guadalajara, Ramone emphasized that the cartel was seeking legitimate businesses in which to invest long term to launder their drug profits, particularly in the U.S. Rosa's lieutenant purposely avoided any mention of competing cartels, as well as the many massacres and murders of police officers, judges, locals, and prominent politicians that characterized the drug lord's rise to power. In a nod to the accomplishments of their guests, mention was made of the impressive growth and success of Mr. Wilde's wholly-owned Baja Grille, as well as Morgan's impressive background as lead counsel at Barclays. Ramone ended his presentation with heady projections of rising U.S. cocaine demand, giving Wilde the perfect segue to present the details of his proposal.

Wilde leaned forward on the edge of his seat, anxious to lay-out his deal. "Allow me to get right to the point of my visit, Mr. Rosa," he began. "I'm expanding into Mexico and Canada with Baja Grille, and we did $195 million in revenue last quarter and growing at nine percent. I'm prepared to offer you a 25% interest in my U.S. franchise, and a 49% interest in my Canadian and Mexican franchises in exchange for what I want." He paused as Mr. Rosa listened quietly with his chin in hand. "This, in exchange for financing my expansion, and giving me a 50/50 partnership in future cocaine deals that we distribute through Baja Grille based on a price of $8,000 a kilo, our cost. I propose that my, uh...*our* company, will guarantee delivery of the product anywhere in North America on our trucks with your men providing security."

"And what is the cost of your proposed expansion, Mr. Wilde?" asked Rosa.

"$70 million for the first year, then about $30 million a year over the next four years."

His face impassive, Rosa listened attentively, then smirked as he tossed back his second shot of tequila before slowly setting his glass down on the teak side bar. In a voice absent of any emotion, he said, "And then, Mr. Wilde, you will be able to make your $28 million margin call at Barclays, yes?" Caught off guard, Wilde glanced at Morgan, alarmed that Rosa knew so much about his personal affairs. "Come now, Mr. Wilde, why are you surprised? Would you have come to me if you had other sources of financing…banks, perhaps?" asked Rosa, pushing out his lip like a belligerent school yard bully.

Recovering his composure, Wilde regarded the drug lord carefully before continuing, deciding to avoid crossing swords as he laid his cards on the table. "You are correct, Mr. Rosa. I've been looking for an entry into the drug trade, and Damon suggested that you were the man to come to for our expansion plans," hoping the ego boost would help float his agenda.

Chin in hand, Rosa studied the restauranteur intently. "And your *other* plans, Mr. Wilde?"

Glancing at Morgan for approval to elaborate on their investment plans, the counselor nodded. "We'd like to invest in a piece of blue-chip real estate with our profits. Form a partnership."

"So I heard. The Boca Raton Resort and Beach Club. Very ambitious." Rosa held up his glass for a refill as the steward filled it again. Interlacing his fingers, he slowly folded his hands in his lap as if conducting a prayer meeting. "And your wife's family limited partnership? Are those funds available for our business ventures, Mr. Wilde?"

Sonofabitch. This guy had really done his homework, thought Wilde. Again, he looked at Damon, who nodded for permission to elaborate. "We would have to kind of...well, move her to the sidelines to gain access"-

"Mr. Morgan tells me he has a plan," interrupted the drug lord. "I can think of one point seven billion reasons for it to work, Mr. Wilde," he said, smiling at Morgan through cold black eyes that revealed nothing of his true intentions.

Morgan's thoughts were of Stella. "Well, we don't want to harm her, just put her"-

Rosa quickly dismissed the thought that any harm should come to Stella. "Such a beautiful woman is not to be harmed, wasted, or spend time in prison," gesturing toward Wilde, choosing to avoid mentioning the video footage taken by his drones of Stella gardening in the nude. "You gotta think with your big head, not your small head," tapping his forehead. "That's how men ruin their lives, by following their cocks instead of their brains."

Wilde looked askance at Rosa for an instant. What sort of primitive culture would cause a man to lead his life with such stone-age values? He thought about all the dead men that had defied Rosa in past years. Before him was a person who didn't need hard evidence before he ordered the killing of a man he suspected of being disloyal. Hearing no disagreement from his guests, Rosa sat back in his chair as he motioned for the steward to bring a round of cigars for his guests. Putting aside his rose-colored glasses, Wilde knew he was seeing the drug lord accurately, if for only an instant, and knew he'd have to think like him if he wanted to move up the food chain.

As Rosa continued to hold court, he'd noticed Wilde swallow hard at the mention of Stella and her family trust, pleased that he was able to intimidate his guest. "As you can see, Mr. Wilde, I'm a man who believes in doing my homework. I want to know *who* my partners are, and what *motivates* them." Ramone leaned over and whispered something in his boss's ear. Rosa looked up at Wilde, giving him a taut smile. "That little jaunt you did in Federal lock-up for tax evasion in the nineties was nothing. By now you know that prison is no place for an educated man with a naturally-tight sphincter, Mr. Wilde. Agreed?"

Surprised by his tasteless remark, Wilde sat forward in his chair to explain. "A U.S. prison"-

"Is the least of your worries if I find I can't trust you," interrupted Rosa with a raised finger, taking the man's silence as his unspoken oath of loyalty. The drug lord was living up to his billing as intelligent, charming, and completely ruthless, making Wilde's fraud, extortion and bid-rigging ventures seem like child's play in comparison. He nodded in agreement to Rosa's warning just as a male steward appeared and presented a polished walnut humidor to the men.

"Let's have a smoke to usher in our new understanding. Gentlemen, how about a Cohiba?" Rosa asked. Though Morgan didn't smoke, both VIP guests took a Cohiba from the humidor. Lawyers traveling in certain circles knew when ritual called for a cigar, and both men had a feeling that declining such an offer would likely leave them outside the circle of trust, maybe even swimming home. After lighting up for all five men with a gold table lighter, the steward dismissed himself as the group of five proceeded to puff clouds of smoke into the air. Puffing away, the men exchanged glances with each other as if congratulating themselves on being masters of the universe, yet wanting to make the manner of the conquest seem irrelevant. Rosa took a few labored puffs on his high-dollar cigar, smiled and pointed it toward Wilde. *Here it comes.*

"Mr. Wilde, here is what I'm prepared to offer. In exchange for financing all the costs of your expansion into Mexico and Canada, and offering you our primo uncut cocaine at *$9,000* a kilo, plus a $40 million advance, I will accept a 51% interest in the entire North American Baja Grille operation, subject to oversight and quarterly review. You will continue running the show as CEO with me as your partner and Chairman of the Board. That's my offer." Rosa sat stone-faced, his cold black eyes devoid of expression.

Morgan wanted the deal, but he knew Wilde was used to running his own show and needed some convincing. There followed an awkward silence before Morgan spoke. "Mr. Rosa, will you excuse us? Dan and I will need to discuss your offer." Rosa nodded, waving them off with a flourish of his cigar as his two guests adjourned to the yacht's fantail.

The men stood with their hands on the polished teak stern rail and surveyed the waterway as a slow parade of boats of all kinds passed in the channel a hundred yards out. Never did such an entertaining procession receive less attention as the American flag fluttered from *Bella Rosa's* stern pole. Morgan turned to face the more agreeable of his two clients.

He was frank. "Dan, I like the deal. I figure at 2,000 kilos a load, times 22 trucks, comes to around $ 20 million a month in positive cash flow. Plus, you still run Baja Grille, meet your margin call, and set yourself up for life. We move forward on our deal with the Boca Resort, and with the added routes in Mexico and Canada, those numbers could double in a year."

He winced at the math, leveling with his attorney. "He's being greedy."

"Don't be pig-headed. You're wanting in on *his* turf. Let's make friends with the man and grow and prosper with him. It's a lifetime opportunity, buddy. You help him launder his money through your Baja Grille, he makes you a partner. You know Stella's not going to let you invade her trust to bail you out. She's already ponied up $30 million to get you started, so neither Barclays nor Stella is going to help. Remember what she said about keeping her family's money sacred?" Feeling confident that he was making an irrefutable argument before his one-man jury, Morgan paused to casually clean his sunglasses with his Hermes tie as he watched a 65-foot Hatteras making its way north up the waterway. The counselor surveyed the sky in his Givenchys before continuing to make his case, casually waving at the three young girls on a Scarab who were ogling *Bella Rosa*. Morgan had always been a pro at pretending things shouldn't be taken so seriously.

"Dr. Hirt's gonna need a week or two with Stella-if that is even possible-and you know Barclays *ain't* gonna give you that much time, Dan."

Gripping the rail tightly with both hands, Wilde felt hemmed in, but he knew Morgan was right. Stella had already slammed the door, and none of the banks would be anywhere as liberal as Barclays with his account losses and overages. The margin call was for real and, without a cash infusion, he would have to liquidate the account to meet it. His two options were to take Rosa's deal now, or move Stella to the sidelines and invade her trust fund immediately, a dicey plan that would likely take more time.

Reluctantly, Wilde extended his hand. "Alright, Damon. I'm counting on you. I'll take Rosa's deal just as long as you've got my back with him. You've done business with him and you know his tactics. Just remember who your friends are, buddy."

Their handshake was followed by a shoulder-to-shoulder man hug. "You know I do. You're making the right choice, Dan. Think about the long game and the Boca Resort. The juice is worth the squeeze, buddy."

After sealing the deal with Rosa, Morgan and Wilde made their way down the companionway and past Rosa's security guards. As they descended *Bella Rosa's* aluminum gangway toward the concrete dock, Wilde was the first to speak. "I just hope we can trust him."

Morgan put his arm on his buddy's shoulder. "He's a business-man, Dan. He needs you to run Baja Grille. What the hell does he know about fast food?" He gave his attorney a skeptical look as Morgan continued. "And he knows he needs you to access Stella's family trust if we go that way. If you don't think he's got his eye on that one point seven billion, think again."

From the corner of his eye, Wilde noticed a reflection coming from a window on the resort's mirrored facade as they stepped from the gangway onto the concrete dock. Thinking it was a re-flection from one of the passing boats, the men continued down the dock, briskly making their way toward valet parking at the front of the resort.

***

FBI Agents Frank Mancuso and Nick Holder stood at the window on the seventh floor of the Bahia Mar Resort reeling off photos of everyone who came and went from *Bella Rosa.* Holder's automatic Nikon was busy clicking off ten frames a second as the laser micro-phone recorded everything. "That's one of the cartel attorneys," said Mancuso pointing toward Morgan as he held his binoculars, "...the one from the photos of the dinner meetings at the New York

Waldorf. Some kinda rock star Wall Street attorney." Holder continued clicking off high-resolution photos through the telephoto lens while Mancuso adjusted the focus of his binoculars to ID the attorney's accomplice. "Don't recognize the other guy. Think we got a new player, Nicky."

After clicking off a succession of exposures with his Nikon, Holder looked over the top of his telephoto lens at the two on the dock below. "Yup," he muttered, "...we'll ID him," he said of Wilde. "Photogenic fella, but if you're gonna hang out in that cesspool, you better be able to swim with cinder blocks tied around your ankles."

Mancuso studied the men through his high-powered binoculars. "He looks familiar. I've seen him before on the internet."

"Well," added Holder, "...whoever he is, I hope he knows he's in for the ride of his life."

After Wilde and Morgan had walked out of surveillance range, Mancuso took a seat and uploaded the photos into the FBI facial recognition database for comparison. "Gotcha!" he exclaimed, gesturing at the portrait image on his monitor. "Nick, meet Mr. Daniel Wilde."

CHAPTER NINE

S tella arrived fifteen minutes early to her mid-day meeting with the Managing Director of Barclays, determined not to leave until Mr. Abernathy could help her understand what sort of hair-brained idiocy had led an experienced trader like her husband into a $28 million margin call.

The well-dressed assistant who greeted her looked like she'd just stepped from the pages of Vogue. "I don't think he was expecting you for another fifteen minutes," said Veronica, glancing at her watch. "Right this way, Mrs. Wilde." Stella followed her into the sumptuous office situated on the third floor of the PNC Bank Building in Vero. Meticulously decorated in traditional décor, the office's panoramic view of the park and beach on the east side of Ocean Boulevard caught her attention.

"I'll let Mr. Abernathy know you're here. His directors' meeting should be adjourning shortly. Please," gesturing to the tufted leather seats facing a large Tudor desk, "…make yourself comfortable. Can I bring you anything? Some Evian, perhaps?"

"Thank you. I'm fine," answered Stella. She remembered Dan pointing out one day that Evian spelled backward was naïve, which described exactly how she felt about believing her husband's deception surrounding their investment accounts. Dan was always saying she looked good in red, so she had dressed fashionably in a shimmering red Christian Dior dress that revealed only a modest amount of anatomy. She made herself comfortable in one of the leather chairs and took a moment to evaluate the décor.

The office reminded her of her father's study, with its ornate dark walnut paneling and wainscoting, matching walnut credenza and bookcases. As she regarded the Persian rug and dual chandeliers, her gaze settled on the wall-mounted equestrian paintings depicting dressage events. The scenes took her back to her teens when she rode in high school. Her eyes swept the bookcases filled with volumes of leather-bound tax and securities law books before noticing the worn antique abacus on the desktop behind the computer screens. Thank God her father never found out she'd used his abacus to count her orgasms the day that scoundrel Pete Goodrich had insisted they do it on her father's desk.

It seemed like her whole life, Stella struggled to reconcile her spiritual beliefs with her sexual addiction. Diagnosed as an INTP personality by her psychiatrist, she often had little understanding of decisions made on the basis of a person's feelings, a personality trait her husband could never understand. Her "bitchy side", he called it. She found herself constantly striving to achieve logical conclusions to issues while ignoring the importance of emotions. And because she was often out of tune with how people were feeling after a disagreement, she found herself relinquishing her own personal boundaries to meet the emotional needs of others. In her twenties, she learned that sexual passion always worked best to close the emotional gulf, particularly with men, and her husband had discovered this early in his relationship with Stella. So their fights would inevitably lead to steamy make-up sex, sometimes even violent savage lovemaking, which explained why her husband was never reluctant to pick a fight with his beautiful wife. Ironically, Dan Wilde's predilection for arrogance and confrontation with her was rewarded in a way uncharacteristic of normal husband and wife relationships. His "steamy hot mess", he liked to call her. For Stella, "rode hard and put up wet" wasn't just a cliché.

Her muse was interrupted when the office door opened, and in walked a distinguished gentleman in a dark blue pin-striped suit. "Sorry to keep you waiting, Mrs. Wilde. Robert Abernathy," extending his hand with a polite smile. "Your husband has been a special client of ours for the last four years. I had no idea he had such an attractive wife." Admiring his guest, the Managing Director took a seat behind the desk and brought up their trust account on his computer screen.

Stella responded with a polite smile, wanting to get down to business. "And I'm hoping that we can continue our relationship, Mr. Abernathy," she said firmly.

"I'm assuming it's the margin call you want to discuss."

She nodded. "As you know, I'm co-trustee on this account, and I've foolishly allowed my husband free rein. This is mostly my family's money. My most immediate concern is understanding what has led to this hideous $28 million margin call."

The Managing Director sat back in his tufted leather chair and folded his hands as he re-evaluated the stunning woman seated in his office. Deciding she deserved to hear the truth, he got right to the point. "Mrs. Wilde, your husband has sustained major losses and a series of horrific margin calls by leveraging a large portfolio of treasury bonds almost twenty to one, against our advice." He paused to see if she was following him. She nodded. "As we've entered a period of Fed rate hikes, your husband has been writing covered calls against the portfolio and selling put options to finance the margin expense, using the option proceeds to buy risky biotech stocks, sometimes even shorting highly-volatile currency futures. Again, against our advice."

Though hearing this made her angry, she nodded in understanding and calmly replied, "Sounds like he's lit a pile of money on fire."

"Yes, you could certainly say that, Mrs. Wilde. Your husband claimed to have thoroughly researched these stocks by first-hand reviews of Phase II and III clinical trials provided by two psychiatrists participating in the trials. Now, I have no idea how he got that information, but the biotechs have been moving against him."

"Are you suggesting my husband is trading on inside information?" He was surprised by her directness and let her awkward question stand. "Mr. Abernathy," she continued, "...this strawberry-blonde hair only grows on the *outside* of my head. Why wasn't I notified of all this as co-trustee?"

"As I recall, about a year ago, your husband submitted a written request to suspend duplicate statements and have them sent only to his office in Boca."

"I don't remember ever signing such a request," she replied, now clearly alarmed. Abernathy leaned forward, reached for his glasses and brought up the date of the request on his screen. "Here it is, on April 1st last year, a request to send all statements to his Sanctuary Center office on Federal Highway in Boca."

Stella rolled her eyes. "That figures. April Fools' Day. How appropriate. I'd like to see a copy of that request, Mr. Abernathy." Stella hoped the easiest way out of this unsettling conundrum would be to find fault with Barclay's due diligence and pin the whole mess on them, but she knew that was a long shot.

Accessing his intercom, Abernathy said, "Veronica, bring me the hard-copy files of the Wilde Global Assets Trust account, please."

"Yes sir, right away Mr. Abernathy," she replied. Moments later, the file contents were spread over his desk. Picking out the notarized L.O.A., he studied it carefully before handing it to Stella.

"Signed by you both, and notarized by Damon Morgan, your attorney-*and* the former General Counsel for Barclays," said Abernathy. Resenting her inference, he gave Stella a stern look over the top of his glasses, trying hard to suppress the sympathy he felt for her earlier.

Stella read the L.O.A. slowly. "That is *not* my signature, Mr. Abernathy," pointing at the signature line as she held the document up to him. "Someone else has signed my name."

Easing back into his chair, Abernathy sensed where she was going and removed his glasses. "Mrs. Wilde, unless we have good reason to suspect subterfuge"-

"You mean forgery, don't you Mr. Abernathy?" *And $28 million is chump change to Barclays.*

"…it is our policy to accept said document as valid." Cocking his head, he added, "Unfortunately, even if the request to suspend duplicate statements *is* a forgery, I'm afraid it does nothing to alter the series of *unsolicited* trades leading up to the margin call." Abernathy paused, sensing that she was likely in the dark about another important detail.

"Mrs. Wilde, are you aware of the IRS's notice of audit?"

Her level of anxiety went up a few notches. Stella had never before being the subject of an IRS audit, but, she'd heard plenty of horror stories. *So, Dan, what haven't you lied to me about?* "How would you know this?" She thought about Special Agent Peabody's visit a week ago.

"We received a subpoena yesterday. Apparently, your husband took a substantial deduction for margin interest which the IRS is now denying him."

"How substantial?"

"Over two-and-a-half million dollars," he said with a look of genuine sympathy.

She was incredulous. Still fuming over the forgery, she stared out the window at the ocean as she struggled to remain composed, momentarily mesmerized by the sunlight reflecting off the water. Feeling bitter over her husband's outrageous deception, she entertained the idea of digging a deep hole in the beach sand with her garden trowel to bury her husband's body in full view of all the retirees sunning themselves on the beach. Dwelling on her fantasy, time seemed to stand still before Abernathy spoke again.

"Mrs. Wilde, you look a little peaked. Would you like some Evian? Or something stronger? Some port, perhaps? I know all this must come as somewhat of a shock"-

Her head in a whirl, and unable to stomach any more of her husband's blunders, she prepared to leave. "Obviously, I need to have a conversation with my husband. Before I go, I'd like a copy of the latest statement and a copy of the audit notice."

"Certainly." He pressed the intercom button. "Veronica, can you make some copies for me?"

Moments later, documents in hand, the painful truth exposed, she stood to leave. "Thank you for your candor, Mr. Abernathy," shaking hands. "Someone will get back to you about a course of action."

Visibly upset, Stella couldn't get to her Range Rover fast enough, not having a clue where she was heading. A total basket case, she felt like the Earth had been pulled from beneath her feet. Abruptly exiting her parking spot in front of the PNC Bank Building, she almost backed into a UPS truck before putting her SUV in drive. Teary-eyed and too upset to drive safely, she abruptly pulled into a parking spot at Humiston Park a block away, almost running over the curbstone before switching off her ignition. Her eyes welling, she fixated on the beach beyond, captivated by the reflections of sunlight and the sound of children playing in the park.

Now, she knew the whole wretched truth, and there remained only one imbecile worthy of her anger. Dan would burn in hell for deceiving her like this. He had turned the last five years of her marriage into a gut-wrenching roller coaster ride, causing her to vacillate between self-improvement and self-annihilation, never knowing at which end of the pendulum's swing she would find herself from one day to the next. She thought of what her father liked to say; "If you want something in life, you have to fight for it." Was her marriage worth fighting for any longer? What would Dr. Hirt say? Her world turned upside down, she buried her face in her hands and broke down.

Giving her spiritual side free reign, she said a short prayer before remembering the Bible in her glovebox. Pulling it from beneath a pile of receipts and manuals, she set it in her lap, flipped to the book of Isaiah and began to read. Feeling better after finishing several verses from Chapter 40, she heard herself say "Amen." She focused her attention on getting a prescription to calm her frayed nerves before bringing her father up to speed on her husband's latest mishaps. Dabbing her eyes with a tissue, she thumbed through the numbers on her phone to find her psychiatrist. The last time Dan had put her through an emotional wringer this bad, it was over an affair with his twenty-five-year-old girlfriend. What did it say about her marriage when she had her shrink on speed dial, she asked herself? Dr. Hirt had prescribed Ambienna the last time, and the drug turned out to be a sanctuary for her, a nice high that put her into a soft euphoric tranquility that embraced her like a snuggly blanket. Once again, she needed that snuggly blanket.

One time when she'd taken Ambienna she remembered waking to see her husband with a Band-Aid on his forehead. Apparently, she'd hit him with a bedside figurine during an hour of rough sex, but she had no memory of it. When she stayed awake on the drug, it made her feel like she was flying blissfully through the sky with her arms spread, dreaming with her eyes open. The last time she took it her appetite went off the rails and she gained six pounds in two weeks, but it didn't matter-the stuff made her feel fantastic. Speed dialing Dr. Hirt's cell phone, she got his recording.

At the beep, she said, "Chris, Stella Wilde. I need a script for Ambienna to sleep, and something stronger for my panic attacks. Dan's driving me nuts, and my nerves are absolutely shredded. Can we skip the interview, or are you gonna make me do the couch thing again? Call me." She hung up, expecting him to call right back.

Dr. Chris Hirt was one of the busiest psychiatrists in Vero Beach. His website prominently displayed his credentials and boasted "The Best Patient Care in Florida." At $400 for ten minutes, it ought to be, she thought. When he wasn't parading through the pages of the Vero Beach shiny sheets with swim suit models and women half his age, he was in his office turning a cool million a year, making a pretty good living pandering to the psychobabble of island gentry rock stars.

It was mid-afternoon on a Tuesday, and Stella was an emotional wreck over the situation with her husband. Parking her Range Rover, she decided to pay her gorgeous girlfriends Cathy, Allison and Angie a visit at Veranda on Ocean Boulevard. Her attitude began to improve after shopping and finding an exquisite white pearl necklace and matching bracelet. As she exited Veranda, a multi-colored merry-go-round at Humiston Park down the street caught her eye. Aching to return to happier times, she headed to the park. Removing her heels, Stella laid back on the flat steel surface, gazing up at the clouds as she dug her feet in the sand and propelled it around in a slow circle. As it turned, the squeaking sound took her back to her childhood when her dad used to spin her around on one in a Dallas playground thirty-five years ago, spinning her slowly until all her troubles seemed to disappear. She laid there, trying to figure things out, imagining the puffy cumulous clouds were actually farm animals in the sky. She traced out a pig, an elephant and a bear until a young girl appeared, standing beside her as she watched Stella slowly spin around on the turnstile.

"My mommie was wondering if you're okay," she said with the innocence of a seven-year old girl waiting for her turn to ride.

Not sure of what time it was, Stella sat up and checked her watch. It was two-thirty. An hour had passed. She must have dozed off listening to the squeaky songs the merry-go-round was singing. "Where's your mommy?" she asked the girl who pointed toward the swing sets. Stella waved at her mom across the playground before deciding a walk on the beach would do her good. Descending the stairs to the sand, she stopped to survey the multitude gathered to share the beautiful weather.

The beachgoers busied themselves with their sunscreen and laying out their towels and chairs as she walked, Jimmy Choo heels and Veranda package in hand. Spotting Vero's mayor holding court with three of her girlfriends on the boardwalk, she shouted a "hello" and waved at T.J., Joanne, Elaine and Mayor Laura, who waved back from a distance as they shared an entertaining moment amongst themselves. What struck her as odd were the beachgoers who had their eyes glued to their cell phones with no interest in the view.

The cell phone zombies meandered about like *The Walking Dead* on one of the nicest days of the spring with their faces buried in their cell phones. Stella couldn't figure out how they managed to avoid colliding with each other as they stumbled around in their perpetual pursuit of a virtual reality. She took a deep breath, asking herself what planet she was on. Offering a few hellos to the few who weren't staring at their cellphones, Stella headed back to the stairway, enjoying the warmth of people actually greeting each other in the present moment. She recalled what Dan's C.I.O. at Baja Grille was so fond of saying; "Yup, there's an app for that."

***

After her walk on the beach among the phone zombies, Stella raced over the Barber Bridge, weaving her way through the traffic on Indian River Boulevard on her way to Dr. Hirt's office. Certain that her shrink was ready to help her rejoin "The Prozac Nation", she was ready to descend into the world of "comfortably numb", in the words of the Moody Blues. Minutes later, she was pushing open the glass door to her shrink's office.

Bustling inside, she locked eyes with Hirt's nurse sitting behind the granite counter. "Theresa, I need to see Dr. Hirt right away. It can't wait."

Surprised to see her so agitated, Theresa studied her over the top of her glasses. "You look upset, Stella." She reached behind her to grab a tissue for her patient. "Your mascara's a little smudged. Is everything okay?"

"Would I be here without an appointment if I was? I'm a wreck. Dan is putting me through the meat grinder again. I *really* need to see him."

"Stella, he's with a patient. I can't"-

She put her hand on her hip and pressed her agenda. "You still dating that hunky delivery guy I set you up with? C'mon, Teresa, you owe me one, girl. All I need is a script for Ambienna," she pleaded, "...and something stronger to stop these panic attacks."

Theresa stuck the pen behind her ear and stood. "I'll tell him you're here and see what I can do," heading down the hall to the examination room.

Finding herself temporarily the sole occupant of the reception area, Stella surveyed the empty room with its six armchairs before her eyes refocused on Theresa's workstation. Curious, she leaned over the counter and swiveled the monitor so she could read from what she thought would be her medical file. The email on the screen addressed from Dr. Hirt to her husband caught her undivided attention;

Mr. Wilde,

This is in answer to your question regarding New York Life's request for an additional physical exam for Stella Louise Wilde in order to qualify her for the additional five million dollars in coverage applied for.

To meet the requirement for a supplemental exam from a qualified M.D., I will provide her exam, attending physician statement and medical records from last month proving that she is, in fact, in excellent health.

I trust that, in doing so, this will satisfy both your request for increased coverage, as co-trustee of The Wilde Global Assets Trust, as well as meeting New York Life's underwriting standards to secure the additional coverage requested.

Sincerely yours,

Christopher Hirt, M.D.

Stella was shocked beyond belief. *WTF, Dan.*

Hearing Theresa's voice from around the corner, she quickly returned the monitor to its original position, two minutes having passed before the nurse returned with a prescription for Ambienna DS CR and Seraquim XR. "I told him you're a mess and needed something strong, so he had his Physician Assistant write you a script." Noticing the email displayed on her monitor, Theresa reached over and turned it off. "Dr. Hirt's P.A. said the Seraquim is something new for depression and panic attacks and should do the trick. Here ya go, girl," handing her the two scripts. "He gave you three refills. That do it?"

Stella read the prescriptions. "Thank you, Theresa. I really needed this." She slipped them in her purse and headed out the door to the Publix pharmacy where she intended to add several bottles of Caymus Napa Valley to supplement her list of medications.

Thirty minutes later, she drove up the weathered brick driveway at Villa Dellacroix with her two bags of wine and prescriptions, parking just outside the entryway. Peeking through the garage door, her husband's Bentley was absent, and she was thankful he was still away at his meeting in Ft. Lauderdale. It would give her the extra time she needed to bolster her state of mind before confronting him with all his lies.

Popping the cork on the Caymus, Stella whistled to Perry who chirped a hello in response as she took a look around at the elegant kitchen that she enjoyed so much, hoping she wouldn't have to leave it all behind. She was already missing the coffered ceilings, triple chandeliers, onyx counters, and the custom arched windows that gave such a beautiful view of the garden courtyard and grounds. Her throat parched, she poured herself a generous glass of the Caymus before reading the warning labels on her meds. The label stated that sedative hypnotics and SSNRIs can cause abnormal thinking, strange behavior and hallucinations, affecting chemicals in the brain that may be unbalanced in people suffering from depression. The label went on to explain Seraquim XR is used to treat major depressive disorder, anxiety and panic disorder, and alcohol was to be avoided. *Whatever.*

Of course, the warning labels conveniently made no mention of the hundreds of reports from users who took the drugs before bed only to later learn that, while in a sort of sleep trance, they'd raided their hotel minibars, ordered thousands of dollars' worth of merchandise online, placed large bets with their bookies, or even committed acts of violence, including armed robbery. The recommended dosage was one pill every six hours. Wanting desperately to numb herself to the anguish she felt, Stella popped two of each and finished her first glass of Caymus before pouring herself a second. Tossing it back, she took another look around the kitchen furnishings before focusing her attention on the countertop Henckels knife set that Dan had given her on their last anniversary. At the time, it seemed like just another way to keep her in the kitchen. Heading upstairs, she set about packing a few bags before the drugs took effect.

Screw you, Dan. On my way to La-La land. Yeah, baby!

***

In retrospect, Stella wished she'd already left for her father's the night before as she awoke several hours later. She laid in bed listening to the sensual sounds of palm fronds rustling in the ocean breeze. Except for the soft vanity lighting in the guest bath and the dim light of the full moon on the horizon, the guest bedroom was dark. Shadows of swaying palms played across the ceiling as she remembered mixing a double dose of sedatives with the two glasses of Caymus. Her watch said seven-twenty, and she could faintly hear the sounds of a woman's laughter coming from the family room downstairs. A little woozy from the drugs, she slipped into a casual blouse, slacks and Topsiders, curious to see who her husband was entertaining. Recognizing the voice of Carol McAllister, she tiptoed down the spiral staircase, preparing to catch the brazen hussy in the act with her philandering husband.

Wineglasses in hand, they were both surprised to see Stella step into the room as Wilde set his glass down on the coffee table and stood to greet his wife. "Honey, you're awake. You remember Carol, our new neighbor? She was just telling me about some of her offshore experiences on their circumnavigation." Stella noticed Carol's halter top was askew and her skirt was up high enough to invite an exam from her gynecologist. Avoiding Stella's glare, she sheepishly pulled her skirt lower and wiggled uncomfortably.

"Stella, how are you?" she said with a forced smile, a little embarrassed. "Dan said you were upstairs resting. I hope we didn't awaken you."

Stella managed a weak smile. "Not at all, Carol." Seeing the two of them together on her favorite leather chaise lounge made her skin crawl. To Carol, she said, "You seem to have a habit of making yourself very comfortable around my husband."

In an effort to remain pleasant, Carol replied, "We were just"-

"Uh-huh," said Stella with her hands on her hips. To her husband, she said, "Dan, I've been waiting to talk with you about an urgent matter," she said coolly. "Carol, not to be rude, but I need some privacy with my husband."

"Sure thing," said Carol, setting her glass down on the end table. To ease the tension as she stood to leave, she said, "Maybe we could all get together at the Riomar Club soon."

Stella was impassive. *When hell freezes over.* "Sure," she said as her husband nodded.

Feeling responsible for the awkward situation, Carol pointed herself toward the entry foyer and slid her Luis Vuitton purse over her shoulder. "I'll see myself out."

Hearing the click of her high heels down the marble foyer and the sound of the front door shutting, Stella turned to her husband. "Dan, I'm going to stay with my father for a while."

"Why?" He put on his best concerned-husband look, but she wasn't falling for it.

"I had a long conversation with Robert Abernathy at Barclays today," she said coldly. "When were you going to tell me about the margin call?"

"I was going to tell you when you came home"-

She was tired of his lying. "What, with Carol sipping wine with us on our chaise lounge? Are you for real? And the IRS audit? Refried bean futures go south on you, Dan? How're things at the Baja Grille?"

He took a step closer. "Honey, I can handle both of"-

"Don't 'honey' me, Dan. This is my family's money. I trusted you," her voice turning angry. "Why, all of a sudden"-

"You sound angry."

"Let me be perfectly clear with you. Anger is transient. Right now, I hate you."

"Stella, please," gesturing toward the chaise, "...let's sit down and talk. I've lined up some financing"-

She shook her head. "That's you trying to handle me, Dan. I'm tired of it," raising her voice.

"Maybe we need a vacation. Why don't we take a cruise?" he asked.

"Why don't *you* take a cruise?"

"We talked about this," he replied.

"*You* talked about this. I listened."

She was in one of her moods, he thought. To keep her off balance, he added, "I may just do that."

"That's the Dan I've come to know lately. Maybe my father was right. Have you asked yourself what it is you're running from? A bitchy wife, your shadowy friends, your dislike of my father, financial insecurity, not enough money to control everyone but always trying anyway? More cognac for breakfast, Dan?"

"Maybe. Maybe you're just over-analyzing everything, Stella. Like the pre-nup you insisted that I sign twelve years ago."

"So, what's all this? Passive-aggressive payback for the pre-nup? *That* was my father's idea. Was he right?"

Angrily, he turned his back to her, unwilling to acknowledge how accurate her intuition could be at times. "No, of course not."

"Or are you so afraid younger women aren't attracted to you anymore that you're hitting on our neighbor's wife? Is it all about money and ego, Dan? Not enough challenges for you? No hope, just death and taxes? *More* cognac for breakfast?"

Now she was starting to piss him off. "Enough with the psycho-babble, Stella."

"Well, let's not forget we have an author living next door whose wife you're looking to court. Make a great story, wouldn't it?" she asked in disgust. Wilde repressed the desire to grab her and shake some sense into her.

Stella continued. "You're like a petulant child. The world doesn't revolve around *you*, Dan. Sometimes there's a part of me that wishes you a slow and painful death."

"Oh, so now you *do* want to stay?" he joked.

Exasperated, Stella turned to go upstairs and grab her bags. Moments later, she descended the stairway, bags in hand, having regained her composure. "Have fun with the author's wife, *honey*. You can go knit yourself a pair of socks for all I care!"

With his back to her, Wilde stood at the sidebar, seemingly unconcerned as he poured himself a generous portion of cognac. She'd left him before, only to come to her senses later after he cancelled all of her credit cards. He was confidant she'd be back soon. "So, what should I tell our friends at Villa Riomar?"

"Tell them I've succumbed to a temporary bout of sanity and I'm spending time with dad."

Left without a snappy comeback, he took a greedy gulp of cognac before he heard the door slam behind her. If anyone was keeping score, he was 0 for 2 with women tonight.

CHAPTER TEN

Fresh from her unsettling confrontation with Dan at Villa Dellacroix, Stella headed in her Range Rover to the family yacht *Seaquel* moored at Pelican Yacht Club. Her father always made her feel comfortable on the luxurious vessel and kept it supplied with all her favorite wines, cheeses, fruits and nuts. Well, maybe not *all* her favorite nuts as she thought about her favorite author. As far as she knew, the four-stateroom sixty-foot Morgan was free of guests, and she looked forward to being alone to sort things out. Hopefully, he wouldn't come looking for her and thought about the irony of taking refuge from him on a yacht named *Seaquel*. Triggered by the rain sensor, her wipers began to sweep the light rain from her windshield, giving her a clearer view of the thirty-five mph zone along dimly-lit Seaway Drive.

Stopped at the red light, she felt an overwhelming need for a release and dimmed the interior lights as low as they would go. As she unzipped and reached down between her thighs, she checked the rear view mirror. With no one watching from behind and her

SUV in park, within minutes she'd climaxed twice to the rhythm of the wipers as she pictured her favorite novelist at the bar in Cobalt. Now more relaxed, she reached into her handbag for her new friends Seraquim and Ambienna, popping two more and chasing them with a mouthful of Caymus from the bottle sitting in the seat beside her. Continuing down Seaway, she still felt a little frisky as she rubbed the bottle up and down her crotch, thinking about her last two orgasms and almost missed the turn in the dark.

Stella stopped and backed-up, almost hitting the "Tow Away Zone" sign before steering toward the guardhouse and pulling the car up a little cockeyed. A sixtyish, pot-bellied guard with an unpleasant face and matching personality slid back the glass window.

"Can I help ya?" Peering into the SUV's interior, the guard's facial expression brightened when he recognized Stella. "Oh, hiya, Mrs. Wilde. Didn't see ya at foist," rising from his chair to see what she was wearing.

She couldn't resist messing with him by mimicking his Bronx accent. "Hiya, Tony. Gettin' in a liddle ovatime, huh?" Smiling, she often wondered if the knuckle-dragging guard was even paper trained. *Fifty-fifty chance.*

"Yeah, I guess. Shoulda recognized da car." He looked up at the rain with a pained expression until a drop hit him squarely in the eye, then back at Stella. "Not da best night ta be out, huh?" Pushing the button to raise the gate, he watched it carefully as it slowly rose until fully vertical.

"Gettin' da boat ready fa tamorra is all, Tony." Tonight, she wasn't feeling particularly gratuitous toward men and wondered if he felt it when he dragged his knuckles on the ground.

Before she rolled her window up, Tony said, "Ya yacht's waitin' fa ya. Gotta walk between da drops, Mrs. Wilde. Okay, see ya."

After her underwhelming Neanderthal encounter, she drove further into the marina. The docks were largely empty since the season had ended weeks earlier, with the scores of trawlers, sport fish and sailboats ending up back in places like Chesapeake Bay, Nantucket and Annapolis. She took advantage of the vacant parking lot and pulled to within a few hundred feet of her family's yacht, her floating sanctuary for the night. The marina's bright security lights illuminated the schooner through the steady drizzle, and her safe haven was a welcome sight with its white nonskid deck and Navy blue boot stripe glistening in the rain. The tide was out, the sixty-footer sitting lower in her berth, making it easier for her to step aboard. She found a plastic Publix bag under her front seat and covered her head with it as she stepped over the shore cables with her packages, swinging her legs over the lifelines onto the deck in her Topsiders.

The steady rain seemed all too fitting given the dismal events of the past few days. During their phone conversation in the car, her father had promised her some quality time to catch up during their day sail tomorrow and mentioned inviting an unnamed guest to sail with them. Of the scant things she could feel remotely optimistic about, her father was always good at laying out options she hadn't considered and she looked forward to hearing his sage advice.

Entering her date of birth on the keypad, the electronic lock flashed green as she slid back the main hatch, climbed down, and dropped her bags onto the teak table before pulling the hatch shut. Looking around the yacht, she recalled her father mentioning the remodeling, and the elegant new interior didn't disappoint with a colorful and rugged appearance. Stella loved the scent of new Sunbrella fabric and took a deep breath as she ran her hands over the factory-fresh textured fabric. Alone at last, she made her way aft to the newly-refurbished owner's cabin and laid back on the queen size berth with her arms stretched out. She could feel the drugs kicking in and the sound of the rain pattering on the hatch cover over her head had a soothing sound. As Stella closed her eyes, she felt herself begin to slip away into a dream.

It was not a night she'd normally choose to be out in. There'd been many other rain storms on stormy passages that proved more of a challenge, even some that delivered clear and present dangers to her, but none seemed quite as dreary. In her dream, she remembered what her father told her when she was a girl learning to sail; "Weather comes and goes, but what you do with it and how you come out of it depends on your skills as a sailor."

How was it that she could be the captain of her fate but never quite the master of it?

***

Saturday morning dawned bright and clear, and Stella was awakened from her slumber by the sounds of water passing over the hull and men shouting in the language of sailors. Groggy from the drugs and wine, she sat up and wiped the sleepy from her eyes as she checked her watch. A little after nine o'clock. She heard her father yelling orders from the cockpit to another man whose voice she didn't recognize. Unsure if it was part of her dream, she thought she remembered her dad shouting "Avast ye maties, lower the yardarms," in his version of a pirate's voice. Planning to join them at the helm, she stepped into the elegant owner's head to freshen up, marveling at the new marble counters, nickel-plated fixtures and the new automatic toilet and bidet. Changing into a pair of cargo shorts and a blue bikini top, she studied the bubble inside the brass inclinometer on the teak bulkhead that registered a comfortable six degrees of heel.

Stella stood on her tiptoes to unscrew the stainless steel dogs on the starboard porthole and shouted through the opening up to her father, "Dad, I'll be up there in a minute. I'm just gonna freshen up." Through the porthole, she could see they were headed south in three-to-four-foot seas along the beachfront condos adorning southern St. Lucie County.

"Okay, honey," he answered. "C'mon up when you're ready. I have someone here I want you to meet."

Her father was a legend in the semiconductor industry and generally regarded as a genius. James Dodge had become a billionaire at the age of fifty-five by inventing a series of state-of-the-art programmable chipsets used in everything from accelerated visual computing to artificial intelligence. The wiry, white-haired sixty-five-year old had risen through the ranks to become the CEO of EnVidia two decades earlier. Her father had guided the company into the 21st century by developing the GPU and Tigra Processor used in 5G personal computing and gaming. Quadra for design professionals working in CAD-CAM was also his brain child, preferred in video aided design, special effects and other creative applications used in highly advanced computing and film animation. DRIVE, his revolutionary chipset for self-driving cars, imparted supercomputing abilities to make driving safer and manageable from satellites and even mobile-cloud devices.

Climbing the main companionway stairs, Stella popped up into the cockpit wearing her Dolce Gabbana sunglasses and embraced her father at the helm. "Hey, dad. You look great," playfully grabbing the rim of his Vero Beach Yacht Club cap. "Where we headed, skipper?"

Dodge turned the spoked stainless wheel a few degrees to port to angle her a bit higher and tugged on his manicured white beard. "Thought we'd run down to Sewall's Point and back." He regarded his daughter. "So, when are you and Dan gonna make me a grand dad, girl?"

"C'mon, dad. If Dan had his way, we'd get our kids out of a vending machine like everything else." Relishing the fresh ocean breeze on her face, she brushed her hair back in a feminine flourish and reached across the cockpit, offering her hand to the man holding the jib and main sheets. "Stella Wilde."

"Special Agent Dominic Beretto," he said. "Federal Bureau of Investigation."

"Oh," she said, taking a deep breath. *Great.* Things were clearly getting out of control in Vero, with $28 million margin calls, IRS audits, philandering husbands scheming to double her life insurance, and now this FBI guy.

"No worries, Stella. He's on our side," said Dodge. "Let him tell you what he told me."

Making herself comfortable on the cockpit cushion, she sat down close to her father and regarded the slender FBI agent of about fifty. Beretto was dressed in a black polo and khaki Dockers, dark Ray Bans and had short-cropped salt-and-pepper hair, sallow face and cheeks. She thought he looked a little like Clint Eastwood in his fifties. She noticed he didn't wear a shoulder holster, then noticed the bulge on his ankle. Eyeing the ankle holster, she said, "Let me guess. Walther PPK."

"You know your firearms. Why didn't you guess a snub nose thirty-eight?"

"PPK has a higher power-to-weight ratio, and a higher muzzle velocity. My preference is my Python .357 Magnum." Now that she had the "my balls are as big as yours" stuff out of the way, she regarded him anew. "So, why are you here with us today, Special Agent Beretto?"

The Barient winch clicked a few times as she noticed him over tighten the jib sheet. Beretto said, "Unfortunately, I'm here to share some aggravation and maybe bring you some distress."

"I already have a husband," she quipped. Beretto smiled, but didn't laugh, even though he seemed to appreciate her wit.

"That was funny," he conceded. Then his smile disappeared. "Mrs. Wilde, I've been an FBI Special Agent for eighteen years."

"You must find your work satisfying."

"Most of those years I've spent in organized-crime chasing major drug traffickers. Sometimes we even get a chance to take down a major Columbian or Mexican drug lord." Beretto paused to make sure he had her attention. "There are some things about your husband that you need to be aware of."

No shit, Sherlock. If Stella heard any more unpleasantries about her husband, she felt like she was ready to scream. Instead, she focused her attention on the novice handling the sheets. "Let me swap places with you, Agent Beretto," holding her hand out for the braided lines, "…maybe I can show you something." Trading places, she eased the jib sheet and watched the sail fill as she pointed at the jib head. "See the telltales flying straight back? Better sail efficiency," she explained. She leaned over the binnacle in front of her dad to confirm her assessment and check their speed on the digital knot meter. She smiled. "We picked up a half knot."

"Stella used to race twelve meters," explained Mr. Dodge. "It's in her blood," he said, giving his daughter a hug. "She's always been competitive, and *always* a good girl."

"So," she said to Beretto, easing the main a notch, "… that's Sewall's Point up there to the south," pointing ahead on the horizon. "Anything you want to tell me about my husband before we reverse course and head back to Pelican Yacht Club?"

Just when Stella thought the news about her husband couldn't get any worse, it did. Beretto leaned closer and lowered his Ray Bans. "You ever hear of a man named Emilio Rosa?"

"The Mexican drug lord? What's he got to do"-

"We have reason to believe your husband's gone into business with Rosa in a cocaine trafficking deal."

Stella's stomach churned, feeling like her life had recently taken more twists and turns than San Francisco's Lombard Street. Of all the possible replies that passed through her head, she couldn't think of one response that was even capable of describing her feelings. *Jesus, Dan.*

"We know about the IRS audit, which, by the way, is now a criminal probe, and, although your husband is the primary focus of the investigation, you could be dragged into it by virtue of the fact that one or more of the accounts in question are in your joint name." Beretto watched Stella for signs that she understood the gravity of what he was saying, but her face remained impassive. He continued to give her the lay of the land. "The $28 million margin call, the insurance scam, the silver futures Ponzi scheme he got your dad into, and some of the other bribery stuff may seem penny-ante, but *this*, Mrs. Wilde...*this* is...well"-

Pretty screwed up. "Honestly, Agent Beretto"-

"Dom."

"Dom." Hearing what sounded like an indictment, her heart pounded and her head was spinning as she pretended to study the condo skyline to the west, searching for a handle on the moment. Still untrusting of Beretto, she thought back to her freshman year at Clemson when an FBI agent had tried to dupe her into sleeping with him on the pretext of collaring a would-be mugger. Not knowing what else to say, she defaulted to what seemed like a cliche. "You and I both know that married couples can't be compelled to testify against each other."

"No one is asking you to testify against anyone."

"But isn't that where this is headed?" This time, he didn't answer her.

Seaquel continued to slice her way effortlessly through light seas with the beauty and grace of a ballet dancer performing *Swan Lake* at Carnegie Hall. As the eastern breeze lightened, she eased the sheets out slightly to keep the sails filled, but her attention drifted. Sailing the big schooner had suddenly become less enjoyable after what she'd just heard. "While I'll admit that my husband's methods can seem *careless* sometimes, I really doubt that Dan is *that* stupid." She looked pointedly at Beretto. "What's your end game here, Dom?"

"*Careless?* I'm not sure if *careless* begins to describe the chaos that major drug trafficking causes. Organized crime syndicates, third world or domestic, are hurting the entire country in insidious ways, Mrs. Wilde. Surely you'll agree with me on that." He waited for a reaction, but Stella remained inscrutable. "We are just beginning to win the war on organized crime." He inflated his chest as if preparing to accept an honorary medal.

"Can we skip the FBI playbook, Dom? If you're as good as you think you are, and you were doing your job…" For the first time, Beretto seemed impatient with her, but all she was doing was blowing smoke to get him to lay his cards on the table.

"If you will admit the truth of what I'm saying here." Beretto continued to extoll the virtues of the Federal bureaucracy that employed him. "Since RICO was enacted in 1984, the Racketeer Influence and Corruption Act has given us the mandate to seize billions of dollars in illegal cash, drugs and property, and we've eliminated almost all of the organized crime families here, and many of their affiliates in third world countries." Pleased with his monologue, he broke it down for her. "In this particular case, we have the opportunity to take down a man responsible for almost half of the cocaine traffic in North America."

"Emilio Rosa."

"Exactly."

It was Stella's first opportunity to turn the tables and question an FBI agent, and she didn't hesitate. "How much money *does* he make?"

Beretto studied her awhile before he answered. "Our sources estimate that he grossed over two billion dollars last year, and this year more likely over three billion"-

"*Billion?*" Stella swallowed hard. "How many men are in his cartel?"

"Well, it's estimated that over a thousand men answer to him."

"That's unbelievable. Dad, are you hearing this?" she asked incredulously.

Dodge removed his cap, smoothing back what was left of his sparse silver mane before securing the cap on his head. "Agent Beretto has been briefing me right along, honey. I'm afraid it looks like Dan has climbed into bed with the wrong partner this time. I've made up my mind to work with the FBI on this, and I urge you to do the same. Dan has screwed up before, but now he's gone off the deep end and I don't want you going down with him." Dodge patted her shoulder reassuringly. "Maybe you *should* get my grand-kids from a vending machine." To Dom he said, "Show her the tape, Dom." He pointed ahead at the horizon. "See that tall condo at the inlet entrance? We're about six miles from Sewall's Point, so we'll come about in a half hour or so. Time enough to watch the tape, Stella."

Beretto nodded and addressed Dodge's daughter, wanting both of them on the same page with him. "For this man, it's not just about the money. This is a man who lives on the edge and doesn't think the way you or I do, Stella. Rosa is the kind of man who thinks his enemies can pay him no higher compliment than to target him for assassination. In his own savage way he actually enjoys being the target of killers and hitmen. Rosa murdered his way to the top of the Juarez cartel, and we can connect him to at least twelve murders that he committed personally. Probably another ninety that he ordered killed. These were men that stood in his way or whom he perceived to be a danger to him. Power is like a drug to him, and the money is secondary. Rosa will stop at nothing to expand his empire. Do you see how dangerous this makes him?"

"I get it, Dom. And you want me to help you take him down."

"To stave off disaster and save the ones you really care about." Beretto smiled, but it was an uneasy smile. He could tell she wasn't quite onboard yet. "Out of the many stories about Rosa, I'll tell you about one that I can personally swear to. Before Rosa became head of the Juarez cartel, he suspected one of his captains, a man named Escondido, of being a DEA informant in order to protect his own family. To deter future informants, Rosa had one of his men make a brutal video of him torturing Escondido until he revealed every one of his contacts as he chopped off fingers and toes one by one with a machete. Rosa even gave the informant smelling salts to keep him from passing out from the pain, but the guy bled to death in about an hour. After having Escondido's wife and three kids murdered, this barbarian passed out DVD copies of the murders to his lieutenants to keep them in line."

Stella had heard stories and seen movies like this about cartel members committing heinous acts of violence, even making snuff films of their victims and performing necrophilia on them. To hear in detail about Rosa cutting off a man's fingers and toes one by one until he bled to death, a man trying to protect his family, was gut-wrenching.

Beretto interrupted her thoughts. "We want this guy." He reached into his pocket and retrieved a flash drive. Holding it up between his thumb and forefinger, he said, "I would hardly call this conversation between Rosa and your husband *careless*. You watch and decide. It's all on this file." Reaching into the backpack beside him, he pulled out his i-Pad, opened it and inserted the drive.

For a moment, she entertained the idea of tossing it overboard. Beretto must have read her mind. "Don't worry," he said, "...we made plenty of copies."

Stella turned to her father, who, in spite of the conversation, was enjoying putting *Seaquel* through her paces. "Dad, have you seen this video?"

Dodge nodded as he corrected course five degrees to starboard. "Looks authentic. I can't believe my son-in-law would be stupid enough to get mixed up with such an utterly primitive thug. Sometimes I ask myself what kind of man you married, Stella."

"I've been asking myself the same question, dad." Stella looked away. Feeling trapped, she gazed out on the horizon for a full sixty seconds before she heard Beretto say, "We know you and your dad aren't part of it, and we're prepared to offer you both complete immunity if you'll work with us."

Beretto waited patiently, and no one spoke for two full minutes as Stella left the starboard winches and gazed out across the ocean. The cumulous clouds drifted across the sky among patches of blue and sunlight as she stood and listened to the sounds of sea water passing over the hull, savoring the feel of the eastern breeze on her face. Pondering her predicament, she felt an inconsolable longing for something more, the scent of a flower yet unfound, the longing for a country not yet visited.

One thing was certain; she had no intention of going to prison for her husband's misdeeds. After twelve years of putting up with his dubious dealings and watching him play in the shadows with his underworld friends, she realized she was at a turning point. An eternity seemed to pass as she mentally checked off the few options that remained before slowly turning to face Beretto.

"What is it you want me to do?" she asked him.

CHAPTER ELEVEN

W aldo's billed itself as the quintessential "Last of the Great American Hangouts", and there was much to be said about one of the most extraordinary structures in the South, the Driftwood Inn. It is the home of Waldo's, where the food is great, and a favorite watering hole for Dan Wilde when he felt like blending into a more anonymous Key-Westy "tropical island" life. It seemed like the stars had aligned for him again when Stella texted him to say that she would be staying at her dad's oceanfront estate for a few days, and he heard Mark was away at the Savannah Book Festival for a three-day signing event. Wilde didn't hesitate to take advantage of the missing players. Like a moth drawn to the heat and light of a flickering candle, he couldn't resist calling the author's wife to have drinks on the ocean at one of his favorite bistros.

Waldo's stands apart as one of the best-loved resorts in Florida, and a favorite destination for many of the island gentry who valued a more laid-back venue with an interesting history. Waldo Sexton, the architect of this famous landmark, arrived in Vero Beach in the 1920s and proceeded to build the Driftwood Inn out of driftwood collected from local beaches, along with cypress logs and pecky-cypress paneling from the swamps around the nearby Blue Cypress Lake. The resort was built completely without blueprints, and townspeople from the era describe Sexton pacing back and forth on the beach shouting instructions to the construction crews who acted solely on voice commands, having no illustrations to reference. The unique quaintness of the structure was the result; a two-story hotel that included balconies surrounded by pole railings with rough-hewn lumber and peeled-log supports that added to its rustic look.

What Dan and Carol liked most about the place was that nothing was built to be perfectly square or level. Folks were amazed that everything looked like it had just grown together with little or no straight lines and symmetry. To add to the historical rustic feel, Sexton had filled it over the years with a potpourri of objects ranging from bells, cannons and ships' wheels to antiques of all kinds, including Italian chests from all over Europe. The Driftwood Inn affectionately called this collection "The Menagerie of Monstrosities", of which the most famous part was the amazing collection of metal bells Sexton procured from Mexican missions and steam locomotives that ran the local line all the way to Key West. Many of the antiques were of museum quality, acquired from luxurious older estates in Palm Beach. Folks sitting nearby amused themselves by ringing the antique bells near their tables whenever the spirit moved them.

On this Saturday night at Waldo's, Dan and Carol were hanging out in their swimsuits and baseball caps at a candle-lit table on the wooden balcony overlooking the beach. Looking to blend in, they feasted on the sounds of the surf, the cacophony of soft voices and the gentle sea breeze blowing off the ocean as they exchanged lustful looks in the candlelight. Except for their subtle, under-the-table game of footsie, the adulterous couple had so far managed to keep their hands to themselves and subdue their foreplay. Wilde was quietly amused that all the hotel suites at Driftwood Inn were named after fish, and found it especially appropriate that the suite he reserved for them was known as the "Wahoo."

Making her way down the row of balcony tables, the attentive waitress promptly refilled their glasses from her pitcher of margaritas for a second time as they flirted with each other on the balcony. Wilde raised his glass to toast Carol in her aqua-colored knit bikini, a suit that left very little to the imagination as Wilde studied the outline of her pert areolae. She wore her blonde hair up, tucked under her white "Dallas Gun Club" cap which reminded him of how skilled her hands were at squeezing off a shot or two.

Dan Wilde was used to getting what he wanted, and he was impatient to explore the rest of her charms in the privacy of their hotel room. He leaned forward so only she could hear. "Honey, let's get out of here and go wahoo!"

Grinning from ear to ear, she held out her hand across the table invitingly. "I thought you'd never ask, Mr. Wilde."

***

That same night, Stella decided to extend her visit and spend the night at her father's six-bedroom estate on Vero's South Beach. It was a crescent moon, and she would have liked to walk on the beach if it weren't for the eerie mood she was in. There, except for a few new McMansions built during the last three decades, the pristine beaches had remained largely untouched. Earlier, her father had invited her to a fundraising dinner for the Vero Beach

Wine and Film Festival at the venerable Ocean Grille, but she declined, convinced she'd only be a drag in her dour mood. After rummaging through her father's wine cellar, she found herself a consolation prize; a 1986 vintage of Beringer Private Reserve. Stella poured herself a glass of the cabernet to chase the Ambienna and Seraquim before making herself comfortable in the soft suede couch in the family room. She caught herself gazing up through the thirty-foot glass windows at the moon and stars in the night sky, wishing she were up there instead.

Just as the euphoria began to sweep over her, her father's housekeeper ambled into the room to check on their houseguest. Celeste was a quiet, middle-aged woman of Columbian descent that her father brought with him from Sunnyvale after his retirement. Incredibly loyal to her father, her English had just a hint of Spanish accent. "Miss Stella, can I get you something from the kitchen?" she asked, wiping her hands on her apron. "I just made some spicy chicken, black beans and plantains-your father's favorite."

"You're sweet, Celeste, but I'm not hungry. I have what I need right here," holding up the bottle of Beringer. She was starting to feel pretty good, well on her way to a euphoric sanctuary.

Celeste persisted in trying to cheer her up. "I've got some coconut flan in the oven."

"Maybe later, Celeste." Celeste nodded her understanding and quietly returned to the kitchen, somewhat worried about the mood of her employer's daughter as she wiped her hands on her apron.

A minute later, Stella found herself descending into a narcotic dream-like state where the lines between fantasy and reality were becoming blurred. Her inhibitions dissolved by the psychotropics, she felt like she was floating in la-la land. What she really wanted to do now was to give her favorite author a call. She'd been resisting the urge to reach out to Mark ever since their meeting at Cobalt, and after a tumultuous few weeks, she needed a friend. The sensitive insights in his novel made her crave a second, more intimate conversation with him as she felt an urge to bask in the warmth of tenderness conveyed in his writings. She remembered jotting down his number on the inside cover of his latest novel which she'd thrown into one of her bags. In her state of euphoria, she set the bottle of Beringer on the coffee table, almost missing the edge as she stood to retrieve his book. Feeling frisky as she flopped into bed with her phone and his book in hand, she proceeded to pleasure herself as she studied his photo until she had three monstrous orgasms. Still not satisfied, she rang him up on her cell, wanting to hear his voice.

The phone rang four times before she heard him answer. "Mark McAllister."

From La-La land she asked, "Can you talk?"

"Stella?"

"Uh-huh. Where are you?"

He pulled the cashmere robe closer around him as a gust of wind blew past him on the fifteenth floor pool deck of the Savannah Grand Hyatt. "At the Savannah Book Festival, relaxing beside the pool in my robe with a double Armagnac and a Cohiba." He could hear her sigh into the phone. "I'm practicing my celestial navigation, tracing out the constellations in the night sky. How 'bout you?"

"Lying here naked, in bed, not enjoying it." She let out a soft moan to emphasize the optics. How'd you like something sweet for dessert on my private dining terrace?"

"Like…," playing along, letting her fill in the blanks.

"Maybe some coffee, maybe some tea, or maybe a little bit of me," she purred. He pictured his drop-dead gorgeous neighbor lying nude in bed as he tried to suppress his visceral instincts to better understand what she was going through, but it wasn't easy trying to focus on her problems as he listened to her sex talk on the phone. What he really wanted was to sift through the clues and dig deeper, recalling what the Dalai Lama liked to say about practicing compassion if you want to make people happy.

He put her invitation aside for a minute. "What's the matter, Stella? You sound a little down."

She relented to share some truth with him. "It's my lunatic husband, screwing everything up."

Wanting to hear her laugh, he offered her a confession. "I'd like to talk with you more about that, but I have a massive erection that needs to go down first."

She gave him a suggestive giggle to entice him. "Jamaican me crazy. Open your robe."

At first, Mark was tempted, but instead, he forced himself to think with his big head. "Maybe we get to that, but for now, let's focus on what's troubling you. Tell me what's going on, Stella."

Content to know she was having her desired effect, she paused to listen to his breathing and opened up. "Between the FBI, the IRS, my husband's new business partner and his conniving ways, I just don't know what I'm doing anymore. I feel like I'm floating...with no solid ground to stand on...like no matter where I step I'm gonna drop off a cliff. Last night I had a nightmare that my sailboat was sinking."

"I understand." He grew thoughtful. "And every winter that ever descended has ended, Stella." Sharing another confession, "I've been there a few times."

From his writings, she knew he had. Having an urge to see him, she grew more curious about his schedule. "How's the book festival? Carol didn't come?" *Like I just did three times.*

"She's not big on book festivals, said she wanted to get some shopping done, maybe spend some time at the gym. So, I, uh... seem to be meeting a lot of women who, well...author groupies, I guess...and adding to a growing collection of hotel pass keys." He could tell she was high on something. "You sound kinda out of it. What are you taking, girl? Fess up."

"You name it."

"That bad, huh?"

"Well, it's like the drugs are the only thing I can do where I'm not feeling like..."

"Like what?"

"Like I'm not...*drowning.*" She took a deep breath. "I'm an accessory."

"To what?"

"You don't wanna know."

He did want to know, but a gentleman wouldn't push too hard. There was a long pause before he replied. "When I feel boxed in like that, I take a seven mile run on the beach. Or a long reef dive...or go skydiving. Puts me in a different world."

"How poetic. Stop giving me all that author crap. I want to talk to Mark McAllister, the man. A different world?" It wasn't just his looks she loved. It was his depth. In a super sexy voice, she asked, "Will you take me there, Mark?"

Her sultry voice wasn't helping reduce the stirring under his robe. "Ever been to Bora Bora?"

"No, but I've always wanted to go. Whenever you're ready," she purred. "I heard it makes the Bahamas look like they're in black and white."

Before confirming her invitation, he replayed their meeting at Cobalt in his mind, picturing her stunning green eyes, strawberry-blonde hair and taut, athletic body. From experience, he knew the fantasy was usually better, but, in her case, probably not. "What about Dan?"

"Screw him. Everybody else does."

He chuckled to himself and took a deep drag on his Cohiba, chasing it with a sip of Larressingle. Orion's belt was brilliantly lit in the night sky over Savannah. He knew what she wanted, but wasn't sure if he could deliver, still hung-up on not violating the holy-sacrament-of-marriage thing. Still, he wanted to know what his chances were. "You gonna patch things up with Dan?"

"That's the billion dollar question." Stella wrestled with trying to decide on how much to tell him and thought about Dan's life insurance scam. "What would you think if you found out Carol was trying to double your life insurance without your knowledge?"

"She would never"-

"Humor me…if she *did*."

He tried to imagine why Carol would do such a thing as he took another pull on his Cohiba. "I would think she was up to no good. What other conclusion *could* there be?"

"Mark, I'm scared," she confessed. "Some crazy stuff going on. We do different things."

"What, like you're from Europe or something?" Refusing to be cheered up by his off-beat humor, she was confusing him about where all this was going. "You know, Stella, I used to think a tropical depression was just a bad weekend in Key West. But with you, well…"

"Mark, will you be serious for a moment?"

"Sorry. Just wanna cheer you up." He heard her sigh. "Look, Stella, the *last* thing I want to be is the *reason* you get divorced."

"Oh, believe me, I don't need any more reasons. Infidelity, bid rigging, mortgage fraud, tax evasion, extortion, drug trafficking. I could go on."

"No need. I get the picture." Mark wasn't sure how much he wanted to hear. Testifying in open court was way down on his bucket list of priorities. "Why, may I ask dear girl, have you stayed with him?"

Stella let out a long sigh. "For so long, I loved him, and over the years he's taken good care of me. But lately, the spark isn't there anymore. His business decisions are increasingly questionable. He's just not the great man I married anymore." She was excited by his breathing as he waited on the phone to hear more. "I want a man who'll really *listen* to me, let me be *free*, let me be *me*."

"And it's not Dan?"

She sighed again and hesitated before saying, "With Dan, I'm never sure if I'm embracing redemption or destruction from one day to the next." *It's you, silly.*

Mark searched for the right words. "Je comprende pas. Who was it? I think it was Milton that said, 'The mind is owned by the self, and can make a heaven of hell or a hell of heaven.'"

She'd always been drawn to deep thinkers, which made her ten-year marriage to Dan all the more of a mystery. "Look, I know you're trying to help with your words of wisdom, but…over the last few days, I'm not even sure of what side of the grass I'm on, much less whether I'm in heaven or hell." But she had come to realize that Mark knew her better than her husband ever could.

"Je te comprends."

His words were making her moist. "I want to see you," said Stella in her bedroom voice.

Both fickle and loyal, he felt like he was being drawn and quartered in two directions by teams of Clydesdales. Torn over his feelings, he thought about his loyalty to Carol after intentionally leaving the hotel bar earlier to avoid the oversexed singles that hadn't yet arrived. For the first few minutes of poolside solitude, he'd enjoyed himself. But, like so many married men, he often fantasized about what it would be like to be with a woman who really craved true intimacy and not just hot sex. Feeling guilty about his flirty banter with Stella, he knew he was on dangerous ground. Over the course of his marriage, his wife had been the only woman who kept his interest, but with Stella, he felt a deeper attraction that defied explanation.

Somebody in a room off the pool was playing *Whiter Shade of Pale*, a song that brought back memories of a time that seemed more virtuous, perhaps less intimidating. It made him want to reach out and rescue her as he recited an amusing quote about dragons for her; "Meddle not in the affairs of dragons, for thou art crunchy and good with ketchup." Stella thought that was funny. He asked himself why he simply couldn't be content with a warm fireplace and a ravishing wife. For most of his life, he labored to inhale courage and exhale fear, but it was one thing to read about dragons and entirely different to provoke one. Glimpsing immortality through the train wreck that lay ahead, he took a deep breath and stepped up and into the dragon's furnace.

"I'll be back in Vero day after tomorrow. Let's have lunch at the Citrus Grille and talk more about how to resolve some of your problems, pretty lady."

He was gratified to finally hear some joy in her voice. "Okay. Will you autograph my book then?" she asked in a melodic voice.

"Of course." *I'll autograph the inside of your thigh if you want me to.*

Their conversation ended, a subliminal warning sounded as Matthew 7:13 popped into his head; "*Wide is the gate, and broad is the way, that leadeth to destruction.*"

***

A year earlier, Stella had been painfully aware of all the articles on the web, gossip columns and newspapers abuzz with the headline story of Daniel L. Wilde facing a possible 40-year prison sentence and millions in Federal fines and restitution payments if convicted of the five felony charges brought against him by the U.S. Justice Department. She'd gotten accustomed to seeing her husband's name in the paper in somewhat unflattering terms, but what the authorities hadn't counted on was the brilliant legal defense put up on behalf of the accused by Mr. Damon Morgan, former lead counsel for Barclays.

At the time, the stories stated that Wilde, one of the better-known developers and business men in Vero Beach, had made false and misleading statements on loan applications for buyers of Baja Grille franchises. Court documents filed alleged those deceptive documents induced five banks to lend over $40 million "based on fraudulent statements, pretenses, promises and material omissions," which they otherwise would not have lent, and that Wilde, as the seller of the franchises, made millions of dollars in illegal profits from the transactions. Reading like an indictment themselves, the articles pointed out it wasn't the first time that Wilde has faced federal charges and public scrutiny.

The U.S. Department of Justice court statements said that, between 2007 and 2009, Wilde and his attorneys "conspired to perpetrate an intricate mortgage fraud scheme involving five Federally-insured lenders by illegally concealing financial incentives paid to buyers after closing the purchases of Baja Grille franchises."

Wilde entered a plea of not guilty and instructed his criminal defense attorneys to ask for a jury trial, claiming that no wrongdoing occurred, and that the transactions involved "additional incentives described in supplemental documents that were overlooked by the five lenders and the SEC." So far, the existence of the "supplemental documents" had yet to be substantiated, and the DOJ requested copies of them during what was sure to be a lengthy discovery process.

The 14-page indictment handed down by the DOJ charged two counts of conspiracy to commit bank fraud, three counts of bank fraud, and one count of indecent exposure. Each of the felony counts carried a maximum penalty of 40 years in a Federal prison plus five years of court-supervised probation. Justice officials later stated they agreed to withdraw the indecent exposure charge based on a witness testifying that there was "insufficient evidence."

Wilde surrendered himself to Federal authorities in West Palm Beach on April 1st subsequent to an arrest warrant issued for his arrest on March 29th. According to documents filed with the court, Wilde posted a $250,000 bond and was required to turn over his passport, firearms and his collection of antique Porta-Pottys, where he allegedly met female staff members for illicit meetings. His trial was due to begin in three weeks, but a request was made by his attorneys to request "a continuance until sometime in late 2018 due to the vast amount of discovery required for defense and complexity of the case."

In early March, Wilde's former C.P.A., 34-year-old Jasmine D. Wilcox, now of Asheville, North Carolina, was added to an earlier indictment of 48-year-old Boca Raton resident Giancarlo Repudiante, who, over the last several years, handled real estate title work and closings for Baja Grille. It was widely rumored that Wilde was involved in an ongoing affair with Miss Wilcox, a former pole dancer who now claims that she "was unfairly manipulated" by Wilde after their arrest for "lewd and lascivious conduct" at the Jaycee Park Beachfront Boardwalk last November. Those charges have since been dismissed due to "inconsistencies" in witness testimony.

According to the media, the additional charges involved the sale of several franchises from Wilde to Miss Wilcox who created several LLCs to facilitate the sales and later resold the properties in question, subsequently dissolving the LLCs to open her own topless bar.

The DOJ also alleged that Miss Wilcox completed the bogus loan applications using the names of fake applicants and signing the names of fictitious buyers to conceal the transactions.

The articles went on to say that Wilde's Baja Grille owns a large portfolio of businesses and projects all over the U.S., and his Florida ventures blanket the entire state as far south as Islamorada in the Florida Keys. Prosecutors are carefully examining closing documents at Wilde's other franchises and project sales to see if he or his co-conspirators used similar alleged illegal tactics to close recent real estate transactions.

In response, Wilde's lead criminal defense attorney, Damon Morgan of Palm Beach, filed a rebuttal stating, "The U.S. Justice Department has obviously been consuming an inordinate amount of Baja Grille's re-fried beans and, in filing the indictments, is obviously suffering from a dreadful case of uncontrollable flatulence. These false allegations are the product of malodorous hot air and will have no effect on the sale of future Baja Grille franchises."

Numerous newspaper articles and internet media websites went on to say Wilde is a well-known socialite and prominent figure in the Vero and Palm Beach business communities and has been the subject of at least three former Federal investigations for money laundering, bribery, extortion and fraud over the past 15 years with only one conviction. In each of those cases, charges were later dropped as key witnesses changed their stories or refused to testify. Convicted of tax evasion in 1997, Wilde served one year in the Atlanta Federal Prison for that crime, paid $275,000 in fines and penalties, and completed three years of parole in 2001.

The articles ended by stating "The Palm Beach headquarters of Wilde's Baja Grille did not respond to numerous requests for comment, leaving a pre-recorded message saying that 'Mr. Wilde was out of town at a fundraiser with his wife in Vero Beach and unavailable for comment.'"

CHAPTER TWELVE

S tella was having a dream. In the dream, it was mid-afternoon on an overcast day in May, two days after her meeting with Special Agent Dominic Beretto and her dad aboard *Seaquel*. Following her memorable drug-induced phone confessions to her favorite author, and against her better judgement, Stella had found her way back to Villa Dellacroix to give her husband one last chance to prove to her their marriage was worth saving. In the dream, during lengthy conversations with her father and her telepathic dragon Seraquim, she realized that she wasn't quite ready to give up on Dan yet. It would be so much easier for her to just walk away if only he wasn't such a hottie.

Deep within her dreamy world, she stood at the onyx kitchen counter in her black sheer Victoria's Secret nightie preparing a special dinner for Dan and hoping she could work things out. She felt wonderful, floating in a fantasy euphoria of her own creation where the lines between make-believe and reality were dangerously blurred. Through the kitchen window she was watching her white cockatiel in his cage in the courtyard whistling *Rock of Ages* and flexing his crest to get her attention. Her throat parched from the drugs, she poured herself another glass of the Caymus, ignoring the warning labels on her meds.

Stella's dreams were unusually detailed. She dreamed that they agreed on the phone to talk things over, so she was hard at work preparing one of his favorite dinners; smoked salmon and fresh tuna sushi rolls with jasmine rice, sliced ginger, avocado and cucumber wrapped in nori with fresh wasabi and low-salt soy. To make sure she was in the best of moods for their reconciliation, she'd taken a triple dose of her two favorite drugs and indulged in a third glass of the 2009 Caymus Conundrum Proprietary Blend. A rare vintage to find at The Village Market on A1A, it was so exceptional she dreamed that she flipped the guy a Benjamin for placing a case of it in the back of her Range Rover. For a garnish, she was busy slicing the ginger into ultra-thin pieces, preparing it for the wasabi and soy just the way Dan liked it. She felt like a famous TV chef on automatic pilot as she watched her razor-sharp Henckels chef knife dancing over the cutting board.

She heard Dan's Bentley drive up and the car door slam. Then the front door opened, and in walked her estranged husband with her favorite wine and a huge bouquet of flowers. "Lucy, I'm home," joked Wilde in an impression of Ricky Ricardo as he stepped into the entrance foyer. In her recurring dreams, Dan was often impersonating TV stars from the 50s, and frequently it was Ricky Ricardo from the same show, but this time her dream was in color.

"I'm in the kitchen, Ricky, making you something special," in her sing-song Lucille Ball voice. She went with the flow, still unsure of how all this was going to play out.

Ricky Ricardo morphed into Michael Fassbender as her husband strode into the kitchen and set the bottle of Beringer on the island counter. He held up the beautiful bouquet of fresh flowers. "For my gorgeous wife. Shall I put them in water for you, honey?"

In her dream, he put the flowers into a large fluted Baccarat vase and set it in front of her on the windowsill. "It's great to have my wife back," he said, reaching for her, but she stepped away, eluding his grasp.

"The flowers are gorgeous, Dan," she said as a sort-of peace offering. Frustrated over his many deceptions, she put the knife down on the counter and turned serious. "Can we talk?" He nodded agreeably. "We've caused each other so much pain. Let's stop lying and trying to control each other and really *talk* to each other," she pleaded.

He took a playful step back, trying to figure out what kind of mood had overtaken his sexy wife. "Okay. Sure. What is it you want to talk about?" he asked flippantly.

Not crazy about his glib tone, she turned her back to him, anticipating another lie and continued to slice more vegetables for the sushi rolls. She wanted to hear the truth this time. "Tell me about your new partner Walter White, or Heisenberg, or Don Corleone, or is it the big white rabbit from Alice in Wonderland?" It felt good to unload the sarcasm. "What's his real name, Dan?" Unsure if she was still dreaming, it was all beginning to seem so life like.

"What makes you think I have a new"-

He wasn't getting it. "What the hell did we *just* agree to do, Dan? Something about being more truthful with each other?"

"Okay, okay." To placate her, he put his arms around her and nestled his nose into her strawberry-blonde hair, kissing the back of her head. "Honey, it's all gonna be okay. We're inseparable partners in a new venture." He loved the scent of her perfume. "By the way, who told you I had a new partner?"

Typical Dan. Still with her back to him, she hesitated, unsure of how he would react to what she had to say. "I had a visit from the FBI. Not only did they tell me about your meeting, they showed me the video." Deciding to drop the bomb, she asked, "Did you know your new partner is under FBI surveillance?" She paused to gauge his reaction. "How much does Rosa know about *me*, Dan?"

"What? Are you saying the FBI has a video of my meeting with Rosa? Are you *kidding* me?" Wanting to confront her with this incendiary little tidbit, he dropped his hands down to her sides and grabbed her to spin her around. Something didn't feel right as his hands traced over the microphone and wire taped to her abdomen. "What's this, Stella?" Wilde was incredulous. "My own wife's wearing a wire, for God's sake?"

Wilde was so upset he was losing control. Never in a billion years could he have imagined his own wife wearing a wire in a conversation with him. Enraged by her betrayal, Wilde lost his temper and spun her around violently. Ripping the microphone from beneath her black nightie, he threw it on the floor, crushing it with the heel of his shoe. Venting his rage, he grabbed her throat forcefully in a chokehold. "I trusted you, Stella! What're you gonna do now? Testify against me?"

She was gasping for air, choking, unable to breathe with his strong hands around her neck, so close to breaking her windpipe, her face turning blue from hypoxia. Then, it just happened so fast. Her survival instincts kicking in, Stella snapped into action. The knife came up, and she jammed it into his abdomen to force him to let go of her windpipe. He staggered back, bleeding profusely from the wound, and with widened glassy eyes, stared at her with a look of utter disbelief as he put his hand over the blood-spattered hole in his shirt as she held the knife. His eyes rolled back as he began to go into shock, his knees buckled and he collapsed on the marble floor, clutching his stomach.

Stella was horrified over what she'd done. "Dan, what did you make me do!!?" She dropped to her knees still holding the bloody knife as he moaned loudly and began to convulse in an expanding pool of blood, losing consciousness, unable to answer.

"Dan! Dan! Please don't leave me! Talk to me!" The last thing he heard before passing out was his wife sobbing uncontrollably as she reached for her phone on the counter. Her hands covered in blood, she grabbed the phone and dialed 911.

"911. What is your emergency?"

"My husband, he's dying!" she sobbed. "Please! Can you send"-

"Ma'am, what's your address there?"

"Villa Dellacroix, on Ocean Boul...Boulevard," she sobbed. "He's dying!" she screamed into the phone. "My husband's dying!"

"Ma'am, are *you* in any danger?"

"Yes, dammit! From me…me! Please send an ambulance now!" Dropping the phone on the floor, she was desperate to end the pain and watched the knife flail back and forth on her wrist before clattering to the floor. Feeling faint, Stella was ready to pass out, horrified at all the blood spurting from her wrist.

In the confusion, she thought she heard Agent Beretto yelling at the front door, "Break it down!!" then a terrible loud pounding, then a crashing sound from the entrance foyer.

Minutes later, she regained consciousness in an ambulance as she lay on a gurney wearing an oxygen mask. With two paramedics restraining her, one held the mask in place while the other was busy suturing her bleeding wrist. Everything was so odd because she couldn't feel a thing.

"Vince, stop with the fantasies and focus on her laceration," said the second paramedic administering the anesthetics. The gas was making her dizzy as she drifted closer to passing out again. With the siren wailing loudly, she thought she heard a second siren wailing in pursuit as they turned onto Indian River Boulevard, on their way to the emergency room at the Medical Center.

"Where's my husband?!" sitting up and screaming into her mask, ignoring her bleeding wrist, remembering him lying in a pool of blood. "Where's Dan?!"

She felt one of the paramedics push her down onto the gurney. "Your husband's right behind us. Calm down and breathe, ma'am. Just breathe, c'mon…deep breaths. That's it."

In a fog, the last thing she remembered was the medic's strong grip on her arms as she heard him say, "Can't let this one get away. I'm guessing they're going to arrest her as soon as she's conscious."

Hearing this, she realized it wasn't a dream.

***

The following day, Dr. Hirt slipped behind his office desk and studied his computer screen to check his patient schedule. On his lunch break, following his fourth patient consultation of the day, the Vero Beach psychiatrist made himself comfortable in the padded leather chair as he flipped open the Styrofoam container of General Tso's spicy chicken that Theresa set on his desk. Having only about a half hour before his next patient, he flipped out of the iPatientCare app and into his browser where he went to check on his Morgan Stanley account. Entering his login and password, he brought up the position screen.

"Holy Mother of God!" he said out loud with a forkful of spicy chicken halfway to his mouth. His 400 Valiant 125-strike put options had risen from $1.23 where they closed yesterday to $56.55 today, giving him a profit of over $2.2 million. Not sure if he could believe his eyes, he double checked the stock and found it was down more than $55 a share. Ready to pee in his pants in excitement, he brought up the news on Valiant. There, he read about an as yet unnamed Vero Beach patient who had stabbed her husband while under the influence of their new drug Seraquim.

So far, the reporters hadn't identified the victim or the perpetrator, but the incident was the lead headline on at least four major video news websites. Reporters covering the story were already suggesting that the victim's family would undoubtedly follow up with a very large lawsuit against Valiant for damages. As Stella's lead psychiatrist, Dr. Hirt knew it was only a matter of time before he would be drawn into the investigation. Craftily, Hirt had maneuvered his physician assistant into writing the script during Stella's visit, and he felt smug about having Ryan Peterson's name on the actual prescription, convinced the arrangement would insulate him from the fallout. The media was already busy raising the possibility of additional multi-million dollar copy-cat suits that would likely follow as the news spread throughout the medical community on the new drug's alleged side effects. Hirt reached for his phone and dialed his broker at Morgan Stanley. The broker's phone rang three times before Perry answered.

"Dr. Hirt, you must be calling about Valiant Pharmaceuticals. That was quite a flyer you took. I guess you heard the news." Perry was completely mystified as to how his client knew that a buy-rated stock like Valiant would fall off a cliff like this.

"Yeah, I just saw the quote, Perry. I want you to sell the 400 Valiant put options at the market." Remembering the extra red tape from last time, he added, "Unsolicited, of course."

Perry was quick to offer his astute professional opinion and cleared his throat before speaking. "With the stock getting clobbered 55 points, I think that's a wise move, doc. On a percentage basis, that's a huge"-

"I know, Perry. I can do the math. Just sell them, please."

Perry repeated the order. A few moments passed before he summarized the trade. "We are done at an average price of $55.35, market order, unsolicited. Nice, Dr. Hirt," as he envied the huge sum of money in the doctor's account. "Now what?"

"Just put the money in my account, Perry. I may have you wire it to an offshore account before the end of the day."

Perry said, "I'd be remiss if I didn't mention a special secondary offering we have on Regeneron. There's no fee and the stock is rated strong buy"-

"Thanks, Perry, but just leave the money where it is. I'll be calling you later with instructions."

"Yes sir, just let me know." With his eyes still glued on the $2.2 million cash balance from the trade, Perry was kissing up, full of ideas on how to generate another huge commission. "And, since you're a Wealth Management client, there would be no charge for that wire."

"Thanks, Perry. Have a nice day." *Gotta find a new broker.*

"You too, sir."

Expecting all kinds of hellfire and brimstone to be unleashed by the media in the next few days, Hirt wasn't going to take any chances with his monster profit. The press would do their best to assign responsibility, and he would offer them Ryan Peterson. Still, there would be hell to pay by someone, but the Vero psychiatrist had no intention of becoming Valiant's scapegoat. He wanted his stash in a safe haven and out of reach of the Federal government. Searching his desktop for the Caymans Banc Suisse account number where he deposited the 500 shares of Apple inherited from his mother, he prepared wire transfer instructions for numb nuts.

***

At the same time Hirt was busy taking profits and making plans to move his ill-gotten gains out of reach of law enforcement, Mark was on his laptop in his office at Villa Riomar. It was slightly past noon, and with the media frenzy going on outside the gates to Villa Dellacroix, it hadn't been too difficult to guess who was all over the news. As usual, the media was trying hard to heighten the headline's impact by coloring everything with the tainted brush of Daniel Wilde's alleged mob connections. Why should anyone be surprised? With reporters, vice was always nice, but everyone knew a really juicy scandal ruled cable TV news and the internet media.

The mob stories on the internet that morning took Mark back to his college years when he was married to the mob and working for his ex-father-in-law. Back then, he was dropping off suitcases full of cash and picking up bolita tickets from men on street corners whose faces looked like they'd been kissing lug nuts off 18 wheelers and whose names all ended in vowels. And for those dubious deeds and other equally-dangerous but respectful considerations, he was promised the hand of Mr. Fiore's beautiful young daughter, Melissa.

His ex-father-in-law was a guy named Tony Fiore, a caporegime or capodecina, usually shortened to just capo, a rank used in both the Sicilian Mafia and the Italian-American Mafia. Mr. Fiore was a made member of the "Teflon Don's" family, who was also remembered as Mr. John Gotti. Fiore lived in an upper-middle class neighborhood in Coral Gables with his wife Lucille and two very pretty and precocious daughters named Melissa and JoAnn before Mark came along and swept Melissa off her feet.

The dark-skinned, slender-built Sicilian man was a card-carrying member of the Teamsters Union who played pool in his home with the mayor of Miami once a week and enjoyed making his own wine. Tony also insisted on importing the hottest Sicilian peppers and took pleasure in making cappuccino four times a day with a beautiful expresso machine custom designed for him in Italy. During the mayor's visits, Mark would witness the transfer of large amounts of neatly-bundled cash and knew not to ask any questions. Tony Fiore was one of the few guys that could probably tell you where they buried his former friend, a guy named Jimmy Hoffa. With the Sicilians, Mark learned to pay attention to the good *and* the evil omens, and to further protect yourself, you best put three coins in the fountain and exactly three coffee beans in the sambuca. His father-in-law would always say "You had to respect it because you never knew for sure." Mark thought it all sounded kind of pagan, but when you're married to the mob, you did what you were told. So, he learned to keep his opinions to himself and lived to tell about it.

His summer jobs with his father-in-law went well until the day one of Tony's lieutenants, a guy named Giancarlo Genovese, was busted with three pounds of cocaine and $247,000 in cash in his pockets on a street corner in downtown Coconut Grove. Then the *Miami Herald* got hold of the story after making a connection between Genovese and Gotti, and the whole thing spiraled out of control, resulting in two murders and four arrests in a matter of days. It was the beginning of the end for Gotti. He remembered his ex-father-in-law's advice; "You gotta be damned careful what you say to reporters. They're always twisting things around, looking for a headline. You think they're looking for the facts, but they really just want a good story. So, make it a funny story. That's what they like-funny." When Tony Fiore went out for a pack of cigarettes one day and never returned, nobody was laughing. After his father-in-law disappeared, Mark decided it was prudent to return to the university and finish his education.

His walk down memory lane was interrupted when he heard Carol come in the front door. The clickity-clack of her stilettos made a distinctive sound as she tossed her keys and purse on the granite island counter top before pouring herself a glass of wine and kicking off her heels. The news of the stabbing had spread through the island community like a raging wildfire, and news vans were crowded up and down Ocean Boulevard filled with a myriad of reporters looking to spin the next headline. To the island gentry, it was a repulsive sight.

"Mark, where are you, honey?" he heard her ask.

"I'm in here, Carol," he yelled from the office. The story with the names of the victims were spread all over the local TV and internet news channels. There were videos and photos of Villa Dellacroix plastered all over YouTube along with partial images of adjoining estate homes. The press were gathered at the Wilde's front security gate like ravenous wolves at a bar-b-que with their videographers and recording equipment as they searched for neighbors and passersby who could verify any of the tragic details in the most dramatic way possible. When the firsthand reports began to surface from first responders, the video accounts managed to implicate Valiant Pharmaceuticals along with the yet unnamed psychiatrist who'd prescribed the drugs. Mark wanted to talk with Stella, but no one knew for sure where she was, and both her phones were going unanswered.

Carol stuck her head in his office door to test his mood. "Can you believe all this...crazy media circus, Mark?" She sipped her wine, trying to avoid the conversation they both wanted to steer clear of. "On the way in, Hector was fending off reporters through the gate with his rake, for God's sake. He pulled out a cattle prod to fend him off."

He looked up from the internet stories on his office computer. "Hector has a cattle prod?" Fiercely loyal, their landscaper's actions came as no surprise to him. "Not to beat a dead horse, but with those two moving in next door, I just had this crazy feeling...that something like this...," his voice trailing off. "Dan's in surgery and no one seems to know where they took Stella. They said she was sleep walking when she...ah...stabbed him. The story is...he tried to strangle her." Carol rolled her eyes, convinced it was all Stella's fault. He recalled the night at Cobalt when she joked about Dan 'paying his debt to society'. Mark took the high road with her and let it go.

Carol sat down on one of the leather office armchairs in front of his desk as she struggled with how much of the truth she would share with her husband. "I may go see Dan," she admitted, waiting for his reaction. Her pronouncement didn't surprise him. His instincts told him they'd become more than just neighbors exchanging quiche recipes. "Look, I know you warned me he's evil, and I tried to stay away from him, I really did. I couldn't control myself, he was different, and...well, I was...infatuated with him. He promised me he would protect us."

Her blue eyes searched his for a measure of understanding with her half-true confession. He forced himself to be patient with her, wanting to hear all of what she had to say as he tried to balance his love for her with the bitterness of her betrayal. Devastated to discover she'd climbed in bed with the gangster next door, a glimmer of dark humor took hold of him as he had a fleeting thought that maybe, if he could bring himself to convert to Islam that evening, he could arrange to have her stoned in the morning.

Carol continued. "Mark...I guess we should talk about this. Let's not keep anything from each other. You know...I would never do anything to intentionally hurt you." He stayed silent, letting her come out with it, or as much of it as she was willing to confess. "You're the special man in my life, and I never want to lose you. I do love you." Quite the actress, Carol put on a good show.

Mark wanted to remind her of the day she jokingly suggested he get one of those penis enlargers by telling her, "Honey, I did; she's 25 and her name is Samantha," but held back and kept his dark humor in check, hoping for less faux mush and more truth. While it wasn't a full confession of her adulterous misdeeds, she seemed headed in the right direction.

His heart pounded and his mouth felt dry. "How serious is it?" he asked, knowing the truth of her affair could destroy their marriage.

"He's in surgery for God's"-

"That's not what I meant, and I think you know it," glaring at his beautiful wife, expecting her to be more forthcoming. Deep down, he still loved her and was prepared to hear his wife confess to her sexual relations with their notorious neighbor, maybe even forgive her and move on, but she had stopped short. Unprepared for what could be an emotional holocaust for them, his intuition told him not to push her. But it was the absurdity of her adultery with an alleged gangster who'd been stabbed by his wife that bothered him.

And so, with her half-assed admission, Mark was in a kind of limbo, the husband knowing the truth intuitively but still swimming in muddy water, unable to ask for a divorce or offer a reconciliation or a pardon in the absence of a full confession from her.

On the other hand, maybe he could just ask his buddy Dan, if he were conscious; "By the way, you screwing my wife over there at Villa Dellacroix, or what, neighbor?"

Misty eyed, she avoided looking at him and gazed at the floor as she smoothed her dress. "This much I will tell you, Mark: I care about him. I don't know where it's going, but right now I need to go and see him." Full of emotion, she stood up, more to dismiss herself than to explain, then stopped on her way out. "By the way, my lieutenant friend at the Vero Beach Police told me the FBI intervened and took Stella to St. Mary's Psyche Ward. He said they Baker-acted her for her own protection. In case you were interested."

"I heard a rumor about that," without looking up. "My guy at the FBI called me today. Something else going on there."

In one painful moment, their eyes met to acknowledge the twist of events born by their disparate directions. "All right then," he said, knowing that giving her some leeway might be the best thing for their marriage, or what was left of it. "We'll talk later and try to sort all this out." Reluctantly, she nodded in agreement.

"Well, I guess that's it, then," he said. "My beautiful wife will go see her beloved gangster, and I'll go visit his crazy wife in West Palm. And we'll see where it all goes."

***

Minutes later, Mark rolled to a stop in his Panamera S, waiting for the wrought-iron security gate to slide open as Hector stood inside the gate guarding the entrance with his rake. Bound and determined to protect his employer's turf, they both found the sensationalist insensitivity of the media circus disgusting and invasive. Mark pulled two Benjamins from his wallet and rolled down his window to offer his thanks to their groundskeeper standing dutifully beside his car.

"Hector, this is so you can take your family out for a nice dinner," slipping him the cash. "Please don't stab or kill any reporters. They're not worth it. We don't need any more headlines-we've got enough to last us a lifetime."

"Chu got it, boss." Hector sheepishly pocketed the 200 bucks. "I make sure they no get inside."

Mark did a double take on Hector's utility belt. "Is that a cattle prod you're wearing, Hector?"

Hector's hand dropped to his side to check the device. "Uh… yeah, but…I no use unless you say"-

"Just be careful with that, okay?"

"Entiendo, Senor McAllister. You come back today?"

"Just heading down to West Palm to visit a friend in the hospital. Don't speak to anyone, okay? And remember, don't kill anyone either. Pinky swear?" Mark extended his pinky out the window. Staring at his finger, Hector had no idea what a pinky swear was.

Ten years before, Hector made the headlines when he defended a girl in a tavern in Immokalee from a would-be rapist who was bent on having his way with her. She was a defenseless 19-year old barmaid from Naples, and Hector wound up serving two years for attempted manslaughter when the rapist almost died from the pummeling he inflicted on her attacker. It was an act of chivalry that forever endeared him to Mark, and one of the biggest reasons the author had added him to the payroll.

"I promise, boss. Gracias por la dinero, Senor McAllister."

Mark rolled up his window and exited Villa Riomar, ignoring the throng of reporters who continued to throw out a barrage of questions like; "Mr. McAllister, did you see what happened next door?" tapping their microphones on his window, and "How well do you know the Wildes?" Then there was his favorite hook they enjoyed hurling his way, "Did you know your neighbor's a gangster, Mr. McAllister?"

Leaving the beehive of reporters behind, Mark headed west on Beachland Boulevard, then over the Merrill P. Barber Bridge. Entering the address for St. Mary's Hospital into his nav system, he headed south on I-95, still his least favorite interstate in the entire country.

He was ecstatic to hear Badfinger's *Baby Blue* play over his XM Sirius Satellite station, and the Bose sound system made him feel like he was right in front of the stage at a live performance. The unexpected timing and irony in the lyrics struck him as oddly fitting as he sang along; "I guess I got what I deserved…," listening to the twang and melody laid down by the lead guitar. The song fed right into his reverie on Wilde, and whether or not *he* got what *he* deserved. Was his surgery successful? If not, would Wilde's demise make his life with Carol any easier?

This wasn't the first time he came to question his wife's fidelity. Knowing she was a hot-blooded woman, he was always giving her allowances for her infatuations. He'd long accepted the fact that she had a wandering eye, but he was no saint either. Though he'd managed to stay loyal to Carol through many temptations, the fantasies that both he and Carol indulged in often led him to doubt that marriage was even a natural state for a man and a woman. Maybe the Arab sheiks, with their multiple concubines, and the Mormons with their many wives, had it right all along. But those views were chauvinistic, and Mark was all about equality of the sexes, except when it came to sharing transgender public restrooms. That kind of creeped him out.

CHAPTER THIRTEEN

I t was four o'clock by the time Mark arrived at the hospital, and there was less than an hour of patient visitation time remaining. His instincts told him he'd be using all of the allotted time to help her climb out of the hole she was in. After signing in, he took a seat facing the glass visitation booths at St. Mary's Psychiatric Ward and waited for Stella to make her appearance. Eyeing the phone hanging in the cradle, he wondered about her frame of mind. He was glad the staff hadn't made a big deal about his appearance. The last thing he needed now was a throng of fruit cakes in their hospital gowns clawing their way through the psyche ward for an autograph.

A few minutes later, Stella Wilde entered the patient visitation area wearing a set of teal hospital scrubs and took a seat in the glassed-in booth in front of him. With a slight smile, she gave him a slow-motion royal wave with her unbandaged hand as a heavy-set male guard with a scarred face eyed him suspiciously before stepping back to give them some privacy. She looked like she'd been put through the wringer but was still every bit the vision of beauty he remembered. Pulling her strawberry-blonde hair back around her ear, she scooted her chair up to the thick glass enclosure and managed an alluring smile as she lifted the phone from the cradle.

"Hey, stranger," she said, placing her hand flat onto the glass, waiting for him to match her move. "You missed my dad. He was here a few hours ago. I see you used your real name." Looking like she'd been up all night, her make-up needed touching up and her stunning green eyes looked tired, but she was still a joy for him to behold. He pressed his hand opposite hers on the glass, matching the pattern her fingers made. Giving her a reassuring smile, he wished they could touch.

"Hey, Shawshank," he joked.

She smiled. "Great movie, but if you were to ask me if I would crawl through three hundred yards of raw sewage to get outa here, I absolutely would!"

"That bad huh? Hopefully it won't come to that. So, how are you feeling, Stella?"

"Well, I had two crack heads get into a fight over me and puke all over my nightie at the police station before they brought me here. They said I'd be safer in this hospital," rolling her eyes toward the ceiling. Giving her a sympathetic look, he waited to hear more about her ordeal.

"Mark, I just want you to know I never meant to hurt anyone. Dan just…" becoming emotional and tearing up, "…he just went *crazy*." Distraught, she looked up at him, her eyes pleading with his. "Do you know how he's doing?"

He could see she was overcome with guilt and still extremely upset. "He's going to be okay," he assured her. "After a more thorough investigation, the police are now saying you were in a drug-induced sleepwalk and acted in self-defense. It wasn't your fault, Stella." His words seemed to calm her, and he wanted her to ease up on herself. "How much do you remember? What was the name of that stuff you were taking?"

"Seraquim. And Ambienna."

"Sounds like two deadly angels from the Old Testament if you ask me."

She gave him a smile as she wiped a tear from her eye. "Of biblical proportions. Is this where you quote me Milton again, about making a hell of heaven or something like that?"

"Looks like you're doing pretty well with that already." Mark looked through the window past Stella for hidden cameras that might be recording their visit. He spotted one in plain view that was pointed in their direction and watched it pan toward him as he spoke. "Tell me about your last visitor. Somebody you know?"

"How did you"-

"I read your visitor sign-in sheet. His name was scribbled-I couldn't make it out."

"After my dad left...said his name was Gary, but...I doubt he"-

"Wait. They told me you've only been here for less than a day. Aside from immediate family, how could anyone know you were transferred here from lockup?"

"Same way *you* found out?"

"What? They have a close friend at FBI headquarters? Rather doubtful." He wiped his forehead and cupped his chin in his hand, determined to figure this thing out. "What did, uh...this *Gary guy*...want?"

"I remember he asked me about my bank passcodes." She watched his eyes widen. "I was still a little drugged up, but remember he was slender, about 5'10", short dark hair, Hispanic accent, protruding face and nose-kind of like a handsome rat. He *knew* things about me, Mark. The night we were on the phone, I didn't tell you everything. I'm not sure you'd believe me if I did."

"Try me."

Fighting to control her emotions, she looked over her shoulder at the video security camera, then back at Mark. "Stella," he reassured her, "...these visitation booths come under attorney-client privilege, so our conversation can't be recorded."

"Uh-huh. Well, you said in your book how 'you can't make this stuff up.' It's like that." He waited for her to tell him more. "I feel I can trust you." She looked behind her to check for anyone eavesdropping and leaned closer to the glass. "I've got a husband with a $28 million margin call, and, on top of that, the IRS is threatening us with a $2 million tax fraud charge."

"That's a lot of millions," he remarked glibly, immediately wishing he hadn't.

"You think? It gets better. An FBI agent told me Dan just signed a huge deal with a Mexican drug lord to sell cocaine through his

Baja Grille franchises, and-on top of all that, he's trying to double my life insurance without my knowledge. And now, *apparently*, he wants to strangle me." With her admission, she covered her face and hung her head for a moment before looking up at him. "Think I'm married to a wacko."

Mark gave her a minute to compose herself, convinced that some of M. Night Shyamalan's bizarre tales were more believable than her own crazy story of late. "But you're safe here, right? Mark asked her. "I saw two armed guards when I came in. Vests, guns, radios-they looked like the real deal."

"Yeah, I think there're here because of me. I saw two FBI guys in the hallway." A single tear rolled down her cheek. "Seems like everyone wants me gone. I can't even count on my own husband anymore. They're all after me and my money."

"Hey, hey, c'mon, girl," wishing he could reach through the glass and hold her. "You can count on me, Stella Wilde. We're going to work through this. We're a team, but I need to know everything. Now, what can I do to help?"

***

Shortly after Mark left Villa Riomar for St. Mary's Psychiatric Ward, Carol called the Indian River Medical Center to check on post-op visitation procedures and was told they were only admitting family members to the ICU. Disappointed at first, she remembered Dan had an unmarried older sister named Claire that lived in Orlando and an idea occurred to her.

She thought about Dan laying in a hospital bed in the ICU and wanted to wear an outfit that would lift his spirits. With the glass sliders open on her beach-front master terrace, she peeked outside to check on the weather. The sky to the north looked threatening, with blue-grey cumulous clouds billowing up on the horizon like giant mushrooms and a strong northwest breeze that would keep the inclement weather more to the southeast. Remembering Dan's favorite colors, she chose an aqua floral summer dress with matching Givenchy hat and sunglasses.

Dreading hospitals, but anxious to see her lover, she drove her red M-5 hard, hitting speeds of 80 mph over the Barber Bridge, then turning north on Indian River Boulevard before pulling into visitor parking at the hospital. Inside, the strong smell of medicinal odors at the third-floor nurses' station made her wince as she stopped to check in and sign the guest register. A male nurse wheeled a moaning elderly man past her who was hooked up to several intravenous bags. The man stopped his moaning as his eyes focused on the eye candy standing at the counter, Carol in her skimpy sundress. Looking back at her as they wheeled him away, he started moaning again.

"Clair Wilde, here to see my brother Dan," she said confidently to the rotund middle-aged nurse sitting behind the desk. The nurse reminded Carol of Mrs. Doubtfire as she looked up from the bank of video monitors to greet her guest. "How's he doing?" she asked the nurse.

Scanning Wilde's latest status report, "He's off the critical list, Miss Wilde, but he's still a little groggy from the anesthetics," looking her up and down as she regarded her outfit. "You're his first visitor. Where'd you say you're from?"

"I just drove over from Orlando," removing her hat and pushing her hair back to make herself more presentable. From the attention she was getting, she wished she'd worn something less flashy. "I just got the news this morning."

The nurse checked her computer screen to see if Claire Wilde's name was on the visitor's list, then stood to deliver the rest of her report. "Well, Miss Wilde, your brother suffered a splenic rupture from the knife wound and spent several hours in surgery, so he's"-

"Is he conscious? Can I talk to him?"

"He just regained consciousness an hour ago and may be a little incoherent. The doctor thinks he may have also suffered a transient ischemic attack that resulted from a traumatic loss of blood. It's too early to tell if the stroke effects are temporary or permanent. We're monitoring his condition very closely." Holding her hat in front of her like the concerned sister that she pretended to be, Carol took in the bad news and nodded her understanding. "Please keep your visit short-he's had some difficulty speaking."

"Promise I won't be long. I just want to see him pull through," said Carol as the nurse led her down the hallway.

They stopped at the door to Room 322, which was propped open to give Wilde's security man a clear view inside from his chair beside the door. Already familiar with Wilde's attending nurses, the beefy well-dressed young man studied Carol appreciatively as they entered and walked to Wilde's bedside. Before he could utter anything to give away her true identity, she grasped his hand. "It's your sister Claire, Dan. How are you feeling?"

At first, he was confused about how to respond. Carol was shocked at his appearance. He looked terrible, like a beaten man. His face was sallow, an oxygen tube taped to his nose as she held his hand and surveyed the maze of intravenous lines and catheters connecting him to the monitors. Though he appeared physically damaged, he looked like his spirit had been crushed, his inner light diminished by his brush with death. She supposed a knife to the spleen could have been a lot worse.

"Behr," was his muddled answer. "Oo ook uvly, Claire," playing along, straining to turn his head. Wilde's eyes widened to take her in, his mouth unable to articulate his feelings.

All along, she realized she'd been drawn to his bad-boy image like a bee to a flower's nectar. But weren't we all somehow rooting for the rebel, the outlaw, maybe even an occasional neighborhood gangster, she reasoned? With his loose living and grand deceptions, it looked like life had finally caught up with Daniel Wilde. A part of her knew it was inevitable, and maybe Dan even knew it himself as he went through the motions of formulating plans for a future that might never happen.

"I'll leave you two alone for a while," said the nurse, "…just push the red button beside his bed if you need me," closing the door behind her. At last, they were alone. Carol surveyed the room and noticed the queen-size bed, private bathroom, big-screen TV, several large bouquets of flowers and a tall stack of get well cards. It was everything she'd come to expect of her favorite bad boy.

Laying her hat on the bed, Carol leaned over and gave him a long passionate hug, careful to avoid crushing his tubes and catheter. "Honey, I thought I'd lost you. Are you feeling any better? Anything I can do for you?"

"So appy you…you good…come, unny." Wilde stretched awkwardly to wrap his free arm around her waist in a show of affection.

Pulling back from their long embrace, she could see the fear in his eyes as he struggled to ask her something. "Arol, ill you da...do sumpin' for meh...me?" She searched his face for clues about what he was about to ask her.

Expecting something morose, she continued to squeeze his hand. "Of course, Dan. Anything you need."

"A man was here...eh I wo up."

"What man?"

"E ran ou...Ra...mo...Ramone."

"Dan, who is he? How did he get past your guard?" Clearly, this was a man that Dan feared, and she was afraid of what new dangers they now faced.

"Ne'er mine...look eh meh pants, back o'bathoom da...door. Take meh keys wi you, arol. Ease, muh...must do dis for meh...me."

Hesitating at first, Carol did as he instructed. Reaching into his pants pocket on the back of the lavatory door, she retrieved his keys with the distinctive Bentley insignia and flash drive, returning to his bedside as she dangled them on her finger. "Okay. Now what?" she asked. Grasping a bedside pen and notepad, Wilde struggled with his free arm to write down the code to his security alarm and floor safe. She watched his face contort in a strange way as he penned the codes.

"Here," handing her the note with two series of numbers. "Pu... put da keys in meh safe in meh 'oset...closet. Pra...omise meh you ill do dis, arol. Buh...erry importan, unny."

Wondering what was so important about his keys, Carol avoided asking him. Tucking the keys and codes into her purse, she leaned over to give him a kiss on his forehead. "Don't worry, I'll take care of it," sliding her purse over her shoulder and gathering her hat. The effects of his stroke and slurred speech bothered her, but still she managed a weak smile. "Now, get some sleep. You need to get your strength back, Daniel Wilde," pressing him back onto his pillow.

"Oh, tank ga...God. Ill I see ya ater?" The damage from the stroke twisted his intended smile into a smirk as he fixated on the sexy outline of her heart-shaped derriere.

"I'll check on you tomorrow, honey," winking at him before exiting his room and heading down the hallway. Waving goodbye to the nurse sitting behind the desk, Carol walked briskly toward the elevator with the passwords to Stella Wilde's $1.7 billion trust account, totally oblivious to what she carried. Her intuition told her something wasn't right. As she stood waiting for the elevator, a middle-aged woman who looked like Dan walked right by her.

Just before she stepped onto the elevator, she heard the woman at the nurse's station say; "Hi. I'm Claire Wilde, here to see my brother Daniel Wilde. How is he? Can I see him?"

As the elevator doors closed, Carol clutched Dan's keys inside her purse and breathed a sigh of relief. *Okay, Dan. What the hell have you got me into now?*

***

Special Agent Dominic Beretto was on his office computer reviewing the digital surveillance file recorded from the visitation rooms at St. Mary's over the last 24 hours. Paging through the scores of color images and unfamiliar faces, he stopped at Stella Wilde's file. Scowling at the image of the person sitting across from her in the visitor's booth, he was alarmed to see the face of Ramone Salamonaca. Beretto studied the man's face in the video, the face of a good-looking rat up to no good. Why would Emilio Rosa send his top captain and right-hand man to scope out his witness? With the cartel showing interest in his imagined new sweetheart, keeping her out of harm's way had just gotten a lot more complicated.

Beretto fast-forwarded past the video of her author friend Mark McAllister, a man he'd already dismissed as any threat to Stella or his investigation. But unlike McAllister, Beretto had to assume Salamonaca was armed and dangerous, a man known to be of purely evil intention. He replayed the video seven or eight times trying to lip read RatMan's words. While the slender man's body language was distinctly sinister, the one word he'd been able to ferret out on the slow-motion playbacks was "passcode". He realized Salamonaca was on the prowl, doing what he was hired to do as a master-of-disguise hit man for the Juarez cartel. How was it that her husband could be so naive in leading the cartel straight to his wife? When you put cheese in front of a rat, the rat will go for it every time. To confirm RatMan's identity, Beretto called in his technical assistant, Lenny Scott. He had to be sure.

"Lenny, take a look at this. You're not gonna believe who just popped up on St. Mary's visitation CCTV. Run the facial scan program and tell me who you think this is." Together, the two FBI agents reviewed the images. Based on Beretto's new findings, Lenny agreed with Beretto's conclusion that Rosa was either after the billions in her trust account, or the cartel considered her a threat. Maybe both. Assuming he knew the account balances, they knew Rosa would stop at nothing to get his hands on that much cash. "Rosa must have one helluva cracker-jack IT guy. How the hell did they find out about her trust account? Morgan?"

Beretto reviewed his options to protect Stella and her family jewels. "I dunno, but that idiot husband of hers sure put her in the crosshairs. Talk about a lame-brain with his head up his ass," giving Lenny a disgusted look. "We gotta figure out their next move if we're gonna keep the Wilde's around long enough to testify. Otherwise, Rosa's gonna cover his tracks," running his finger across his throat to mimic a blade.

Lenny asked, "Dom, where'd they take our Vero racketeer for surgery? Indian River Medical Center, wasn't it?"

Re-checking the EMS report, Beretto leaned over the computers next to his IT officer and confirmed the destination. "Yeah, IRMC. Got a bad feeling about this. Let's pull the images from all the CCTV in the area, focus on the med center."

"You got it, boss." If their hunch was right, RatMan's face would appear in them as well, which would confirm the cartel knew where both their witnesses were located. Five minutes elapsed before the digital images were uploaded and appeared on the FBI's monitors.

"There's our guy again. Man, this guy is slick," observed Lenny. Salamonaca's peculiar face and protruding nose wasn't hard for the FBI tech to spot.

"Does not bode well for the Wilde family tree," said Beretto. "Jesus, who's the hottie that went into Wilde's room after RatMan left in a hurry?" he asked, fast forwarding and replaying the video file.

Standing next to him, Lenny studied the images a few more times. The blonde woman was fashionably dressed, with a skimpy aqua-colored sundress, Jimmy Choo wedges and carried a matching Givenchy hat in her hand. *"That's* McAllister's wife Carol."

"What the hell's she doing in Wilde's room?" Beretto wanted to know. For a moment, he considered sharing the info with Stella, figuring it might give him more leverage in earning her trust, then decided that discretion was the better part of valor.

Lenny checked the visitor manifest that accompanied the videos. "Says here, she's Daniel Wilde's sister Claire from Orlando."

Beretto ran a quick check on the license plate on the red M5 she left in. "Uh-huh. Then tell me why she's driving Carol McAllister's car." Waiting for Lenny to come up with an alternate explanation, he brought up the images of the two women on the FDL website as the State of Florida web page popped up and displayed the photo IDs of the two women.

"Okay, here's what we got so far," said Lenny to his boss. "Wilde's first visitor *was* Ramone Salamonaca, a/k/a RatMan. Looks like something spooked him and he left in a hurry. Then, we get Carol McAllister impersonating Wilde's sister, Claire. Why does she do that? Ten minutes later, Claire Wilde shows up." Lenny raised an index finger, "Unless…*my* guess is Mrs. McAllister and our favorite gangster Danny boy are gettin' a little, ah…extracurricular exercise on the side," raising his eyebrows. He tapped his pen on the top of the PC, waiting for agreement from Beretto.

"You could be right," said Beretto. "They did look a little chummy the last time they were under surveillance." He held up a finger and picked up the phone, speed dialing his boss in Miami.

Covering the mouthpiece as it rang, he said to Lenny, "Hang on. Got an idea." Lenny waited, anxious to hear his boss's idea as Beretto autodialed a number on his desk phone.

Recognizing the number of the West Palm Beach field office on his cell phone in Miami, 55-year old District Manager Hank Greenberg stroked his bald head and leaned back in his leather chair to take the call. He figured it was about time to hear some good news on the Rosa investigation. "Dominic. Talk to me. Watcha got on the Rosa case?"

"Hank, if you want our star witness to live to testify, we're going to have to move her right away. Rosa's men are onto her. I'm thinking Chatahootchee. You know, that old state-run loony bin in the panhandle? We can keep the Baker Act as a cover. Whaddya think?" Beretto was counting on Stella's cooperation, even though she had no idea of the danger she was in. If the cartel knew about her trust account, she would need all of the FBI's protection to stay alive.

Greenberg knew Chattahootchee State Hospital to be a minimum security facility far removed from the prying eyes of South Florida media reporters, and he was weary of the frenzied press coverage their prime witness was getting. "Do it," was the reply. "And keep it quiet. I'm tasking our twin-engine Cessna to West Palm immediately for Mrs. Wilde's trip to Chatahootchee. No way they tail her to the panhandle. Have her at the airport in 35 minutes."

"Sounds like a plan, Hank. Leaving here in five minutes in the chopper to pick her up. The sooner we get her out of St. Mary's, the safer she'll be. Also, got an idea to get a GPS tracker on Rosa's man, Salamonaca. RatMan, as we affectionately call him, also paid her husband a visit today at IRMC, and we're not sure why.

Someone on staff came in and may have interrupted his visit. My guess is he's returning. Either way, it's not good."

District Manager Greenberg thought about an angle. Using one gangster to bait another sounded like a win-win to him. "RatMan's already got two warrants on him, one for first degree homicide, doesn't he?"

"Quashed by his appointment to the Mexican Ambassador's office last week when they extended him diplomatic immunity," answered Beretto.

The District Manager was incredulous. "To a murdering psychopath like him? Who the hell's running that damn country?"

"Juarez Cartel's their new gravy train, sir. Haven't you heard? They gotta pay for Trump's border wall down there."

The political theater of the absurd, thought Greenberg. "All right, Dom. Send your guys, but let's be careful out there. I can't afford to let you use more than two men on your stakeout. I've got a lot on my plate right now with Russian counter-intel and all that bullshit with Trump, and Mar-a-Lago has us spread pretty thin."

"Yes, sir. I understand. It'll be a little tight, but I think I can manage. I'll take Mrs. Wilde to Chattahootchee and assign Scott and Perez for the stakeout on her husband. We'll snag 'em. We get a GPS on RatMan, our job gets a whole lot easier."

"Heard that." Greenberg hesitated before hanging up. "Oh, and Dom…"

"Yes sir?"

"I'm counting on you. I don't need to remind you of how important she is to our case." Greenberg smiled to himself, knowing Beretto had a things for the ladies. "Heard she's a looker."

"Sir, you have no idea. She's a taut version of Scarlett Johansson with stunning eyes the color of Columbian emeralds. Ring your bell without even leaving the station."

"Keep it in your pants, Dom. Remember, she's our *witness*, not *your entertainment.*"

"Yes, sir." Beretto hung up with his boss in Miami, knowing he had to move fast. Next, he dialed dispatch one floor up. "Rody, prep the chopper for a flight to St. Mary's. We'll be picking up a key witness and transporting her to PBIA to hook up with our Cessna for a flight to north Florida. Lives at stake, so let's make it snappy. "

"I'll have her ready for lift-off in four minutes, boss," responded Mike who gathered his gear and headed to the roof-top stairway. The FBI pilot had already started his checklist to initiate the pre-flight for the Honeywell AS 350. With the tanks almost full, he planned to top off the chopper at PBIA after the short flight and initiate a stand-by mode.

"Lenny and Oscar. Need you in here," barked Beretto, sticking his head into the hallway, then grabbing his overnight bag and laptop from the locker. From the staccato rhythm of his words, the two agents could tell their boss was all business.

"I need you two to set up a stakeout at the med center to intercept RatMan." The two younger agents nodded as he handed Agent Perez his keys. "Take two cars in case we need to have one of you double back and cover the field office. I have a hunch he's shaking down Danny-boy for accounts and passwords, and it may get ugly, so go in heavy, but keep it quiet. Let's get there first and set up the laser microphone."

"Okay, boss." Perez took his keys and the men turned to leave before Perez stopped in the doorway. "Dom, we can't detain a Mexican diplomat, can we?"

"No, but we can find out what he's up to, record his conversations and get a GPS tracker on his car. Gather more evidence on Rosa, guys. Remember, it's Rosa we want. All roads lead to Rosa, right?" The two junior agents nodded.

"Okay!" Beretto clapping his hands, "Let's get to it. Daylight's wasting!" Adjusting the straps on his satchel and laptop, he heard the AS 350's turbines start to whine as he climbed the steps to the rooftop. Though the FBI crew boss relished a visit to Chattahootchee about as much as a root canal, the striking features of his star witness came to mind. Sharing a flight to Tallahassee with Mrs. Stella Wilde would provide him with all the entertainment a man could want. That part he wouldn't mind.

***

Carol placed the bottle of Padron onto the center console of her M-5 before climbing into the black leather driver's seat. Closing the door and cranking the engine, she was on a mission, determined to keep her promise and deliver Dan's keys to the safety of his floor safe. Feeling at least partly responsible for what happened, it was the least she could do for the poor guy.

The parking lot at ABC Liquors on Miracle Mile was nearly vacant as she uncapped the tequila and took a giant swig to assuage her nerves. With her air conditioning blasting and car in park, she took a second swig of Padron. Upset about Dan's inability to speak clearly, she was concerned about how long the effects of his stroke would linger. It looked like he'd aged 20 years overnight. It seemed like the more you cared about someone, the more the world found ways to hurt you for it, she thought. She remembered that Dan had blamed his wife for being on the downslope of their marriage as a warm tingle emanated from the tequila in her belly. With the liquor taking effect, she tipped the bottle up for a third generous swig, hoping it would help drown her sorrow. No one coming or going from the parking lot seemed to care as she sipped from the bottle. She sat there with the tequila in her lap and thought about Mark. How was she going to explain all this to him?

Cars came and went from the Publix lot directly across Miracle Mile. She watched a noisy dump truck filled with beach sand heading west as it ground through the gears and spewed a thick plume of diesel fumes in its wake. As she watched the huge truck go by, she remembered it was the third such dump truck full of beach sand she'd seen since leaving Dan at the ICU. Nice of them to finally get around to re-nourishing the beach erosion from the last hurricane. She reached into her purse for Wilde's keys, rubbing the distinctive Bentley medallion affectionately like a rabbit's foot, curious about what the attached flash drive contained, wondering once more why it was so important that she lock the keys in his floor safe at Villa Dellacroix. The fear in his eyes had been real, and it wasn't like him to be afraid. It haunted her to see him like that.

She took another generous gulp from the bottle of Padron as she eased out of her parking spot, running down a list of items that could be on Wilde's mind, careful not to back over the white-haired elderly couple maneuvering their grocery cart full of liquor behind her. The tequila was making her feel tipsy as she nestled the remaining half bottle of Padron between her legs and used both hands on the wheel to make a hard left turn at the traffic light. Turning north onto Indian River Boulevard and heading for the Barber Bridge, a tear rolled down her cheek as she was unable to avoid the image of her lover laying helplessly in the ICU.

Crossing the bridge over the intracoastal, Carol received a text message and waited for a stop light to check her phone. After hitting three green lights in a row, she'd ordinarily be happy, but she ran out of patience to see who'd texted her and fumbled for her phone as she turned south onto Ocean Boulevard on her way to Villa Dellacroix.

With her eyes glued to her phone instead of the road, she studied the text message to formulate a response when she inadvertently swerved into the oncoming lane. Carol never saw the monstrous dump truck. The truck driver hit the truck's horn, blasting a warning loud enough the wake the dead, but Carol responded too late. It was a horrific collision, so violent that the M5 was almost sheared in half. The truck driver was violently thrown through the windshield onto the hood of the Mack diesel where he lay bleeding until the paramedics arrived.

As fate would have it, the dump truck driver survived, but in the terrible collision with a vehicle ten times heavier than her BMW, Carol would never feel anything again.

CHAPTER FOURTEEN

A sorrowful seven days later, heartsick and emotionally drained, Mark attended his wife's memorial service at Holy Cross. It was the most popular of Catholic churches with the island gentry, and Monsignor Monaco held a beautiful service for his beloved wife, Carol Louise Nutter McAllister. The Monsignor spoke quite well of the deceased, thankfully making no mention of the trials, tribulations and affairs that had often colored her life on Earth, so he guessed the check had cleared.

It was a somber affair, as most funerals are, of course, and a month earlier, the McAllisters attended Holy Cross's High Easter Mass. The High Easter Mass proved to be a service filled with rituals and procedures that had confused Mark at times, not having been raised a Catholic, sometimes kneeling when he should have been standing, and standing when he should have been kneeling. The closest he'd gotten to such pomp and circumstance had been the services he attended at an Episcopalian Church in mid-town Manhattan years earlier. Having been raised a Catholic, Carol was a pro, anticipating the many changes in posture correctly in spite of the tight leather skirt she wore, which had drawn more attention than it should have in a church service.

The Easter High Mass had been preceded by a pre-recorded video played on three large big screen TVs placed strategically on the altar, a plea for additional contributions on behalf of an orphanage on the outskirts of Rome. The video presentation had prompted a parishioner in the pew behind them to sardonically suggest that the church install a drive-through window so that parishioners could roll down their car windows to receive a splash of holy water and swipe their credit card before heading for the Sunday All-You-Can-Eat Buffett at Red Robin down the street. Those within earshot struggled to contain their chuckles so as not to attract undo wrath from the clergy.

As it turned out, Carol had been so taken with the Easter ceremony that she'd quipped, "If I don't survive my next death-defying act, I'd like my own service to be held here." *Your wish come true, honey.*

He'd spent the past seven days pouring over photos, blaming himself and wishing with all his heart he could have patched things up with her, thinking that if he had, maybe there wouldn't have been an accident. As her next-of-kin, his trip to the Vero Beach Police station to retrieve her purse and personal effects from the unrecognizable twisted heap of metal that was once her M5 was one of the most gut-wrenching things he'd ever had to do.

When Mark emptied out her purse at home, he was surprised to find Daniel Wilde's key ring, and alongside the keys, a scrap of paper that had two sets of numbers that looked like pass codes. On the Tiffany key ring were the keys to Wilde's house, his Bentley, along with a safe deposit box key and a curious USB Type-C flash drive. Finding the keys hidden in the side pocket of her purse had confirmed his suspicions about their surreptitious affair. An extra set of keys for his mistress? He wondered what was on the flash drive. Tempted to plug and play the drive before returning it to the man he blamed for his wife's death, Mark found that none of his devices had a USB Type-C port to fit the device. Then he remembered his conversation with Stella at St. Mary's about the sinister-looking rat-man who was after her passcodes and decided it was best to lock it up.

When he swung by Northern Trust on A1A later in the afternoon to retrieve some legal documents, he dropped the key ring and the pass codes into his safe deposit box until he could figure out what to do with it. Given Carol's sudden death, Mark's grief was clouding his normally rational judgement, making him procrastinate on major decisions. He might have forgiven her if only she'd asked. God, how he missed her. On the other hand, he was relieved that Wilde's surgery had prevented the man from attending his late wife's service, particularly since he was unsure about his ability to control his anger. Punching a man in a wheelchair seemed a bit ungentlemanly to him, even if the man *was* an infidel and a gangster.

The burial itself took place at an old cemetery in West Vero. It was a very ornate affair with forty or fifty black limousines and enough flowers to cover several other surrounding gravesites. For a woman with no living parents and few surviving family members, the service was remarkably well-attended, especially considering the light rain that was dampening everyone's spirits. Carol's popularity became more obvious to him as he watched the myriad of black umbrellas proliferate with the multitude of mourners gathering around her gravesite to say their last goodbyes.

Many of her OMG shareholders and their entourages were there to pay their respects in appreciation of how fabulously wealthy she'd made them when OMG went public on the New York Stock Exchange five years before. Of course, her largest shareholders hadn't forgotten to bring along their CPAs and attorneys to bid farewell to the woman who had made their exorbitant fees so necessary. One by one, Carol's former friends, associates and shareholders eventually made their way over to Mark to pay their respects and offer condolences. One of them even had the unmitigated gall to ask him what he'd planned to do with the shares now that he owned a controlling interest, and that was something he'd have to think about.

Three local bartenders were there; one from Waldo's, one from Cobalt and one from Citrus Grill, two men and one woman claiming they'd been madly in love with Carol from the moment they'd first met her. She had always treated her servers well, and Mark was certain they were very sorry indeed to see their best tipper forever departed from the Vero Beach restaurant scene. He'd later learned that the bartender from Cobalt had the questionable taste to describe Carol's drunken flash dance on the bar top one evening to a few of Mark's friends at the service. So, okay, she was a hottie, and everyone knew she could get wild and crazy. One more thing that she would always be remembered for.

Hector was there, with his entire tribe of future landscapers who had come over one at a time to express their condolences in broken English.

So too was Carol's only surviving sibling Yvonne, her older sister, accompanied by Carol's three nephews Wyatt, Ryan and Tony, all standing nearby. Mark recognized Wyatt as the oldest, a kind of big Neanderthal-type who looked more benign than threatening. Ryan, the Clemson student, with his handsome, All-American looks, undoubtedly headed for the executive suite of a Fortune 500 company one day soon. Tony was the outlier, the one Mark had met one summer. Clad in his Citadel uniform, he looked every bit the clean-cut stand-up officer, and if you looked past the short haircut, you saw Carol. His sharp blue eyes missed nothing, eyes that appraised everyone, and the resemblance to his aunt was remarkable. At one point, Mark saw Tony staring at Monsignor Monaco as if he were responsible for his aunt's death, and if Daniel Wilde knew what was good for him, he would keep an eye on that kid.

In any event, Special Agent Dominic Beretto was present, standing discreetly some distance from the crowd while his FBI photographer took snapshots and made videos of the proceedings for whatever nebulous or unexplainable government reasons.

Reaching inside his coat pocket to review the service program, he felt the card that he'd received from Stella a week earlier and pulled it out. The postmark was stamped Chatahootchee, Fla., probably the only such-postmarked card he would ever receive. Mark opened the standard Hallmark card and read the personalized note she wrote beneath the pre-printed words of live, laugh and love;

Mark,

You have no idea how many times I think of you, dreaming of the man I can love forever.

Eternally yours,

Stella

He put the card back in his pocket, and one day, when it was appropriate, maybe he would find out if eternally yours was really eternal.

In the meantime, he would never forget what the 70-year-old Monsignor Monaco had said at his wife's graveside, quoting from Phillippians: *"Finally, brothers and sisters, whatever is true, whatever is noble, whatever is right, whatever is pure, whatever is lovely, whatever is admirable-if anything is excellent or praiseworthy-think about such things."*

And so he did, and would continue to until he was ready to move on.

***

The next day, Mark was at Villa Riomar reminiscing about some of the better times he shared with Carol aboard *Dream Girl*. They were on a colorful South Pacific sailing passage almost three years before. He remembered it was spring in the southern hemisphere, and he found it impossible to think of the exotic landscape and waters of Tahiti, Marquesas and French Polynesia without using visually-rich clichés as he let his mind surrender to the flashback.

From the lush, green slopes of the high islands to the pink-sand, palm-lined atolls that surrounded lagoons bluer than the purest of cobalt blues, he thought of French Polynesia as the origin of idyllic, stereotypical descriptions of paradise.

Like many sailors before him, Mark liked reading up on the history and cultures of his destinations. From his research on French Polynesia, he learned the early Polynesians were an adventurous seafaring people who displayed highly-developed navigational skills. Genetic research and archeological findings indicated they colonized previously unsettled islands by making very long passages in dugout canoes, only adding sails to their craft around the thirteenth century. Early Polynesians were also accomplished celestial navigators who steered by the sun and the stars, often able to detect the existence and even the location of new islands by skillful observations of cloud reflections and bird flight patterns. One Polynesian word in particular that kept repeating in his mind was the name given by early native navigators to a star or constellation used as a mark to steer by; *kaweinga*. Over the centuries it was a word that had acquired several meanings among Polynesians, all having to do with either spiritual or maritime direction.

According to his studies on Polynesian culture, by 1280 AD, archeological evidence suggested entire small villages of Polynesian explorers had set sail in their primitive catamarans and succeeded in settling the vast Polynesian triangle. The Polynesian triangle is anchored at its northern corner by the Hawaiian Islands, the eastern corner marked by Rapa Nui, which later became known as Easter Island, and finally the southern corner in New Zealand. By comparison, other better-known archeological timelines indicate the Vikings colonized Iceland about 875 AD and there are suggestions that early Polynesian seafarers even reached the South American mainland.

Around July 13th, following two weeks of blue water sailing due south from Hawaii, Carol and Mark were excited to see the northeastern-most shores of French Polynesia as they approached Hiva Oa, the first island in Marquesas. After being confined aboard for fourteen days of crossing open sea, they were dying to stretch their legs on a good run on their next landfall. The Marquesas is the most remote chain of islands in the Tahitian archipelago and it's the first point of land that every boat crossing the Pacific from the Americas sees. Towering above the deep blue waters of the Pacific, unprotected by any atolls, the Marquesas lifted their stunning peaks from the depths of lush green tropical valleys high into the rarified air.

With Carol sunning herself in the nude on the foredeck, Mark steered the 67-foot Baltic toward the nearest of the six inhabited islands out of twelve in the group, Hiva Oa. The other five occupied islands were Nuku Hiva, Fatu Hiva, Tahauta, Ua Huka, and Ua Pou. Visiting sailors were left with a visual image they could never forget with Fenua Enana, or The Land of Men, as the Marquesans called it. On a beam reach, the melody and lyrics of Crosby, Stills and Nash's song *Southern Cross* filled his head as he looked toward the sky to check the tell tails on their approach to the legendary island chain. They'd run out of fresh fruit ten days ago, and fresh guava, coconut, papaya, grapefruit, mango and pineapple awaited them at their anticipated landfall. Their entry to the archipelago was fortuitous and opportune, arriving just in time to see the celebrations and native dancing for the French National Holiday on July 14th.

On their last dive in Hawaii, Carol had stepped on a sea urchin and the puncture wound on her instep had gotten infected. Lovemaking had only succeeded in taking her mind off it temporarily, and to top it off, they'd run out of antibiotics. Dousing the roller-furling jib and mainsails, together they moored *Dream Girl* in the snug harbor with anchors deployed fore and aft and took the dinghy in to the city dock. There, they found a young native boy who eagerly agreed to look after their dinghy and yacht for twenty francs (about two dollars) until they returned from the hospital in a day or two.

With the only real hospital in Nuku Hiva, the next island over, they took a short flight on a single-engine Piper for $150 and hitched a taxi ride from the airport to the town of Taiohae for another 25 bucks apiece, a discount, they were told by the Marquesan cabbie. The journey through the mountain passes to the hospital was quite breathtaking, with stunning views from the hairpin turns of the winding mountain roads. Carol used her charm to sweet talk the driver into stopping so they could pick some fresh guavas (her favorite), papayas and mangos that grew wild. They had fun on the ride through the most fertile valley, the Valley of Taipivai, and they practiced their rudimentary French with the cabbie who pointed out some historical sites and local landmarks that included some abandoned concrete gun emplacements left over from World War II.

Everyone they met along the way was so genuinely nice, so hospitable and giving that it seemed like a different planet, a stark contrast to the commercial materialism of Hawaii. It was their first exposure to Marquesan hospitality, and they were amazed to discover that the natives often wanted nothing in return. Some were even insulted if they were offered a tip. The locals were very intrigued with the lifestyle of an author and his beautiful wife, and so it was that Mark and Carol generously shared the personal details of their lives, their travels, and other pleasantries in lieu of tipping. It was an arrangement that worked like magic with the congenial locals who were so completely entertained by personal stories from the life of an American author.

After receiving a shot of ceftobiprole and a month supply of 5th generation antibiotics from the native attending physician, Carol was able to comfortably enclose her freshly-dressed wound in her Topsider and leave the hospital with a barely-noticeable limp. Taken by the quaint seaside ambiance of Taiohae, they stopped at a floating restaurant a short walk down the beach for a late lunch and enjoyed the delicious local Marquesan seafood delicacy; crabmeat in lime coconut sauce, together with a couple of Tahitian-style rum daiquiris to kill the pain. In the Marquesas, it didn't matter if it wasn't yet happy hour-they were on island time.

With her wound on the mend, Carol had talked him into taking a sailboat back to Hiva Oa, but the trip was directly upwind and no boats were headed that way for a few days as the captains waited for the wind to shift. A local gendarme they'd met in front of the restaurant told them the *Aranui*-the local cargo ship that delivered all the goods and supplies from the Tahitian capital of Papeete-was arriving later that evening and accommodations could be made for half the price of air fare, or about 6500 Fr ($81).

The overnight voyage turned out to be one of the most romantic passages of their French Polynesian transit. In the night, *Aranui* cruised past Ua Pou, another beautiful volcanic island in Marquesas, world-famous for its archeological sites and uniquely-shaped twelve pinnacles. They enjoyed watching natives dancing and twirling lit torches to drums in the light of giant bonfires to celebrate the French National Holiday as the ship slowly slipped past the island. Emboldened by the privacy afforded them by the crew and the sparsity of passengers, they found themselves making love under the stars while nestled in a secluded section of the cargo ship's fifth-story aft deck. There, following several momentous moments with each other on top of an overturned inflatable dinghy, their passionate sounds were serenaded by several passing pods of porpoise and a gigantic but gentle humpback whale with her calf in tow. As the creatures crested the waters alongside the cargo ship, their eyes seemed to fixate on the amorous couple, their playful antics illuminated only by the light of the stars, a half moon and the phosphorescence created when they repeatedly

broke the surface. An amazing overnight passage, the sea creatures kept them company through most of the night, entertaining
them until the sunrise broke over the bow.

The morning after, the ship was headed to Hanaiapa and
Atuona to deliver fresh food, construction materials, petrol, and
spare parts, but Carol and Mark had disembarked at Puamau,
Hiva Oa, sadly saying their goodbyes to the local crew and the
friends they'd made during the cruise. They'd heard much about
the incredible beauty of Fatu Hiva, the southernmost island in the
Marquesas, and one of the wildest, and so they were anxious to get
Dream Girl underway.

Raising the dinghy up on the davits, it began to pour and the
sea swelled, prompting Mark to set up the big blue canvas deck
awning on *Dream Girl*, tethering it with the main halyard so they
could keep the hatches open to the breeze. Accepting invitations
from three other boat captains on *Vitamin Sea*, *Blew Bayou* and
Legend, they rafted up and partied while waiting in the frothy lagoon for the weather to clear. What better way to pass the time
than to party with the multinational crew and passengers of four
sailboats all sharing wild stories of their French Polynesian island
hopping? The convivial fifteen adventurous seafarers from the
four sailboats were delighted to discover that every single captain
and first mate they met shared their own secret recipe for the
"best Polynesian cocktail", and it would have been impolite if they
hadn't tried them all. Mark was able to barter a spare impellor and
200 feet of braided line for a case of his favorite Charbay Tahitian
vanilla rum, compliments of the captain of *Vitamin Sea*.

The wild four hour rafting party was followed by seven hours
of peaceful sleep, and it was good to be back in the clean and
comfortable main cabin of *Dream Girl*, with her queen-size berth,

electric heads and reverse osmosis water maker. Very few boats enjoyed the luxury of a water maker, which meant passengers could use fresh water for everything, including hot showers. Fresh water to wash dishes and clothes in a washing machine were also a luxury few boat owners enjoyed. The solar panels and wind-generator easily kept up with the desalinator's meager electrical appetite of six amps and, run every day, the freshwater output was sufficient for two people who loved showering together. The beermeisters at Hinano pointed out that potable water created through reverse osmosis doesn't contain the mineral content that our bodies require, while *beer*, he was reliably informed, does. So, they conducted themselves accordingly.

Anxious to set sail for Fatu Hiva, Mark allowed his first mate to talk him into accepting an invitation to a wedding at Taipivei where 900 guests (half the town) were invited. One of the villagers owned a bus, so thirty-some party animals and yachties climbed aboard for the trip past Anaho Bay to Taipivei where they stopped to pick some flowers. One of the pink and yellow tiares he gave to Carol to put in her hair, and on the way, everyone stopped to enjoy fresh mangos and guava. There were plenty of coconuts, but you had to be careful under the coconut trees. Local Marquesans will tell you that more people get killed by falling coconuts than by sharks, but that little factoid didn't mean you could ignore the sharks while in the beautiful blue waters of paradise. You still kept a wary eye out for the hungry predators if you wanted to live to tell your story with all of your limbs intact.

The native wedding in Taipivei was a truly festive occasion, with most of the town laughing, dancing and drinking their way into a state of delirium. Out of several hundred festive partiers, Mark and Carol met some rather interesting people.

In one encounter, while Carol kept track of him from across the coconut-palmed yard, a pudgy woman confronted him, removed her sarong to reveal her naked body and asked, "What turns you on more, my pretty face or my sexy body?" Mark had enough rum in him for an entertaining response when he replied, "Your sense of humor."

With the alcohol kicking in, they returned to *Dream Girl* to say their goodbyes to all their friends in Hiva Oa, and Mark and Carol set sail for Fatu Hiva early the next morning. Sailing in the nude on a beam reach with a rail under, the couple reached their destination in only a few hours with Carol on the staysail and jib winches and Mark beside her at the helm on the main winch. Every few minutes she would lean over to keep her captain smeared with sunscreen everywhere except his manhood because, as she reminded him, she had a fond preference for his *au naturel* flavor.

Famed for its stunning coastal scenery and lushly-landscaped cliffs that looked like they were right out of a dream, Fatu Hiva was an unforgettable stopover. One of the most popular destinations in the Marquesas, they spent the first day exploring the island's coves and waterfalls filled with clear waters ranging in hue from turquoise to the deepest of blues. With the cloudless skies, azure lagoons, kaleidoscopic tropical coral gardens and a mind-blowing array of colorful fish to entertain them, Mark and Carol spent the second day snorkeling all around *Dream Girl*'s anchorage. As with most of the 40 outer Marquesan islands where the townships were all on the larger islands, Fatu Hiva had thankfully escaped major development; it felt like a place where time had stopped altogether.

Finally, after a week in the Marquesan paradise, it was time to leave the archipelago. The simplicity of local island life, the mind-boggling flora and fauna, the friendly people and their generosity all made them want to stay forever, but there was so much of French Polynesia yet to explore. Still, Mark and Carol agreed there was something melancholic, but beautiful, about these remote islands that had forever captured their hearts.

Some days after the riotous wedding on Taipivei and enjoying the amazing awe and wonder of Fatu Hiva, Mark took a break from writing. Their full attention was required for the last two days of sailing as they deftly threaded their way through the labyrinth of shallow atolls called Tuamotus. This group of remote atolls was layered with white sugar sand and dense thatches of coconut palms protected by huge coral reefs. At high tides, these atolls appeared to offer clear passage to the secluded blue-water lagoons but could be particularly treacherous at night, especially if you were without accurate charts or local navigational software.

Manihi, where they'd planned to drop anchor, was quite different from the Marquesas, and the passage to the island was all good sailing until they bumped a coral head with the trailing edge of the rudder. Shortly after clearing the coral heads, another mechanical failure presented itself; the roller-furling headstay jammed until Mark could sprint to the bow to help Carol free the stuck gennaker. Aside from these few minor problems, they sailed on toward Manihi, and if pressed to describe Manihi in one sentence, one would have to say; postcard beach views, crystal azure waters, and plenty of corals and coconuts. He remembered all the island banter about the Black Tahitian pearls, the black gold of Tuamotus, where 90% of the world's black pearl production could be found. The natives called the rainbow-lipped oysters Concha Nacar, and the black pearls from these oysters were the most sought-after in the world. On his bucket list was finding his beautiful wife at least one of these ebony Tahitian treasures that waited for them somewhere at the bottom of the crystal blue lagoons of Manihi.

The tricky passage from the Marquesas to Tuamotus had proved to be strictly daylight sailing, and with GPS and electronic color charts, getting there was not as difficult as winding their way through the atolls without running aground or hitting another coral head. Upon their arrival at the series of atolls the Polynesians called Tuamotus, it was back to the navigational aids most common to the ancient mariners; visual dead reckoning. The atolls usually offered at least one clear channel into the lagoons, and sometimes two passes appeared to be navigable for a yacht the size of *Dream Girl*, but they were tricky. The swift currents could exceed seven knots, and the narrow channels were often too shallow to navigate. With no reliable published information on the currents, Carol and Mark often found them hard to maneuver. After freeing themselves from two soft groundings earlier, they learned to keep their guard up after entering the lagoons. They were often faced with a plethora of coral heads once inside the entrance, and adding to the danger, most of the lagoons in the Tuamotus archipelago were uncharted or often described inaccurately due to shifting sands and tides.

The ability to read water during visual navigation was essential for safe passage, and the bow watch would always hope to have the sun shine through the water over one's back. In clear water, with good sunlight overhead, coral heads were brown, light blue was very shallow, and darker blue usually indicated deeper, safer water. Reading water from the bow watch proved to be an essential skill, a skill the couple had painstakingly acquired along their 37,000 km of seafaring.

Carol had developed exemplary skills as a bow watch, ever on the lookout for coral heads and shoals as she peered into the water from the stainless steel bow rail. The seclusion of these outer islands made sailing in the nude a regular practice, and she loved the feel of fitting her shapely pelvis into the rounded crook of the Baltic's bow rail s she posed against the background of azure skies. With a pink and yellow tiare tucked behind her ear, she would often look aft and smile at the man who carefully steered the cutter rig from behind the wheel. Unable to take his eyes off Carol, Mark couldn't imagine a more alluring or more feminine figurehead to grace the bow of *Dream Girl*. What would a day in paradise be without a tiare behind her ear?

"Mark Twain," she called out to him to identify deeper water. She pointed 30 degrees port toward the channel in the direction of the first large island in the group, which was Manihi. In a randy mood, she gave him a flirty over-the-shoulder salute. "Is thar ta be any friggin' in the riggin' in the King's navy thar, Captain McAllister?" taunting him in a British pirate accent and tossing her blonde hair back provocatively.

She was quite the temptress. He answered her tease, "You betcha, missy," in a matching British pirate's accent, "...prepare fer some foreplay on the foredeck!" he called out to her, raising his bottle of Charbay Tahitian vanilla rum from the teak holding rack and taking a swig. She continued to tease him with the sway of her bare derriere when he announced his true intentions; "I'm a'goin' balls deep into that thar, missy, so get that thar anchor down on me command."

She loved gyrating her hips slowly to peak his interest before indulging in their favorite game of "Fly Me to the Moon." Grinning and looking over her shoulder to make sure she had his full attention, she playfully saluted him again. "Aye aye, skipper!"

Before he could go balls deep, the channel widened and deepened to a depth of 10 meters as they sailed into Manihi Harbor, and they were able to sail right up to within 50 meters of the beach. Picking a spot, they dropped anchor and nestled their yacht among the three boats they'd partied with at the Marquesas days earlier; *Vitamin Sea,* the 45-foot CSY cutter rig, *Legend,* a 51-foot Morgan ketch, and *Blew Bayou,* a 55-foot Hinckley. Receiving no answer on the VHF from any of the three captains, and seeing no one aboard the vessels, Mark and Carol figured the captain and crew were probably on the island scoring some fresh fruit and supplies at the bon marche in the village.

Taking advantage of the privacy, the teasing turned into action and the couple made love on *Dream Girl's* foredeck. Carol loved to feel the sun on her skin as she rode him, wearing nothing but her skipper's hat as she squealed her way through several monstrous climaxes. Mark waited for her to reach her peak four times before allowing himself the pleasure of his release, which sparked yet another huge crescendo from his beautiful wife. She rode his manhood like a young mare in heat until the Irish honeymoon was over, or put another way, "when Peter went to Dublin".

An hour later, with the return of the captains and crew of their two neighboring boats, the three couples spent the rest of the afternoon and the following morning catching up and snorkeling for pearls and fresh seafood. After grilling some fresh-caught mahi mahi and serving it with three bottles of Oak Vineyards California Chardonnay and a case of Hinano from the brewery in Tahiti, the entire group elected to head to the village bon marche.

At the market, Carol found a magnificent hand-sculptured teak mermaid that later became part of *Dream Girl's* master cabin décor, and Mark was lucky enough to stumble upon a box of Pleiades Antares, one of his favorite cigars. At dawn, after saying goodbye to their fellow seafarers aboard *Legend, Vitamin Sea and*

Blew Bayou the night before, Mark and Carol engaged the windlass and weighed anchor. Setting a course for Fakarava, their next destination lay less than a day sail southwest. The island-hopping flotilla had proven to be too much fun and their friends from the three other sailboats all promised to reunite with them before sailing for Rangiroa.

After eight hours of easy sailing, the weather began to look ominous. It was a partly-sunny afternoon with lots of billowing gray-blue cumulous clouds when the couple set eyes on the rectangular-shaped reef crown of Fakarava. They could see the atoll was about 60 km long and 25 km wide, making it the second largest in French Polynesia. Approaching through the Guruoa Pass, the widest such pass in all of Polynesia at two kilometers, the swift current was running against them at five knots, so they hoisted the gennaker to increase their speed over the bottom. With the gennaker fully deployed, they made headway at a net three knots against the current. Their slow progress was made more entertaining by the mind-boggling scenery, with pods of schooling porpoise, manta rays and spotted eagle rays all making it a memorable passage.

Famous for its picturesque panoramas and emerald waters, Fakarava's main attraction, apart from the many pearl farms, is the perfect diving. With legendary visibility of up to 100 meters, everywhere they looked there were hammerheads, gray, lemon and tiger sharks, and spotted sting rays. The sightings of enormous manta rays continued, with barracudas in coral crevasses so tight they waited undetected in darkness for their prey, and once inside the lagoon, usually there was no escape for the hunted. On the horizon, as far in the distance as they could see, were pink sand beaches, huge coconut trees and the most colorful palette of blue lagoon hues they'd ever seen.

In the following days, they made their way to Fakarava's South Pass, where they anchored for the day and night. Late that afternoon, Mark speared a large grouper that was attempting to camouflage itself as it hid among the coral heads of the lagoon. The grouper filet was good for several grilled meals of grouper salad and blackened grouper sandwiches that Carol served on the fresh-baked croissants from the Manihi bakery. Later that night, a thunderstorm reared up with high winds and waves. As *Dream Girl* rode out the swells and howling winds that gusted over 40 knots, Mark was glad he'd watched the weather report and had set double 85-pound Danforths from the bow and the stern.

By seven the next morning, the weather had cleared, and they set sail for their next port o'call, Toau Atoll, only 15 nautical miles from Fakarava. There they recognized several other boats they knew from earlier anchorages and decided to moor within easy swimming distance. Happy to see familiar faces, Mark and Carol caught up on useful yachtie information, exchanging tips and pleasantries on the "coconut telegraph". After catching up with their neighbors in the anchorage, the couple lowered the dinghy and took it through the crystal clear turquoise waters of the Toau atoll to meet the few native inhabitants. On the leeward side of the atoll they found five large and very friendly families grouped together on the highest point of the narrow island. The families spoke both French and broken English, and Mark and Carol were able to strike a dirt-cheap bargain for a three-day supply of fruits and vegetables in exchange for two six packs from their store of Hinano.

Early in their circumnavigation they learned that beer and spirits were always in demand in the outer islands. While in Hawaii, they had stocked both crew cabins with 36 cases of Hinano and 18 cases of Charbay rum and Grey Goose vodka, securing and padding it against the bulkheads with extra cushions and life pre-servers. Using their stores of liquor like an ATM, the stash of alcohol proved to be even more popular than American dollars when it came to procuring needed supplies.

On his last hull inspection while spearfishing, Mark spotted a dislodged lower pivot pin on the rudder. He put it on his list of immediate repairs, probably knocked loose when they'd gotten too close to a coral head days earlier. Having but one rudder, he decided not to wait until their arrival in Tahiti or Raiatea to have it repaired and set his sights on the Apataki Carenage, the only full-service boatyard in the Tuamotus archipelago that was capable of such repairs. From the coconut telegraph, he'd learned it was a brand new boatyard, able to haul out larger boats like *Dream Girl* if needed, so they set sail for Apataki two days later with light repairs in mind.

The busiest boatyard between Hawaii and Tahiti, the Apataki Carenage was a new family-owned business which, in its brief two-year history, had become quite popular with South Pacific cruisers. The yards owners, Pauline and Alfred LaCroixe, provide a superb service to seafarers, and since they were fans of Hollywood and American authors, their wait on the mooring buoy was less than a day. Spending three days in dry dock was a new experience for them, and they were fascinated by the ease of which the gargantuan hauling trailers could be adapted and used for catamarans and multihulls. During their dinner with the LaCroixes the following evening at a rustic seaside restaurant, they discovered the native couple also kept themselves busy with a pearl farm and a copra plantation.

Three days later, *Dream Girl* had completed her needed maintenance, outfitted with new stainless steel rudder fittings, zinc anodes, two new ship's batteries, a few new 12 and 110-volt switches, a fourth automatic bilge pump, and some minor maintenance to her hydraulics and standing rigging. Luckily, the yard was equipped with WIFI, and Mark was able to arrange payment over the internet. Online, he took the opportunity to upload to his publisher the new chapter that he'd written during the three days of repairs.

Cradled by the gargantuan trailer, their cutter rig was carefully slipped back into the lagoon by the pros at Apataki Carenage on a sunny afternoon of the third day of dry dock. The McAllisters were delighted to see that their friends aboard *Vitamin Sea, Legend* and *Blew Bayou* hadn't forgotten about them, all waiting nearby where they stood waving and smiling on deck with raised drinks in hand.

"You guys ready for Rangiroa?" he shouted to the engaging group of island-hoppers.

A French captain's enthusiastic answer rang out across the water. "Nous sont tres faim por le Rangiroa, mon capitain!" shouted back the smiling skipper of *Vitamin Sea,* raising his can of Hinano to salute them from the foredeck of his anchored CSY.

Not to be outdone, *Blew Bayou's* skipper shouted across the water to him in Spanish. "Nosotros vayas con Dios manana, Marky Mark y Carol!" The change-up in language intrigued him, triggering a flashback to the week they spent in Cabo San Lucas. Though the upgrades had cost him more than he anticipated, Mark was gratified that the repairs and maintenance that *Dream Girl* needed to safely continue her voyage were now complete and his peace of mind restored.

Dream Girl was back in the water again as Carol took a deep breath, sighed meaningfully and tugged on his arm to let him know she was happy.

Like most of their passages to faraway places, it was as if the lovers of forgotten beaches had sailed backward into an enchanted time and right up to the pristine shores of paradise.

CHAPTER FIFTEEN

In the twilight just before dawn, Gonz and Chico studied the black Humvee in the eighteen wheeler's side mirrors. For the last hour, they'd been driving at speeds over 115 mph through the desert plains of Texas, staying well ahead of the sinister-looking SUV. Now that the Humvee had pulled to within a hundred feet, it appeared to be a bigger threat and about to make a move. With the sun due to crest the desert horizon behind them in a few minutes, they could now see the para-military vehicle was upgraded with dark green polycarbonate bullet-resistant windows and a curious grouping of advanced antennae unlike any civilian Humvee they'd ever seen before.

"That's a bad-lookin' bogey, Chico. *This* we gotta call in. Hand me the phone," reaching toward the glove box. Chico complied before checking his Uzi and patting his vest to count the six 20-round clips as he stared out his side view mirror at the intruder. *What's on your mind, guys?*

Gonz was nervous. "Gorilla, this is Road Runner. Our bogey's pressing our six. Where the hell are you?"

Several seconds of static followed, then a response over the phone with the screaming whine of an aircraft's turbine engines in the background. "Road Runner, Gorilla. We've got your bogey a thousand feet below us. Texas tags, but if I had to guess, looks like Los Zetas or Beltran Leyva. Waiting on them to make a move. They want you intact."

Rattled by his matter-of-fact attitude, Gonz wanted to hear the pilot's strategy. "So Gorilla, what's your plan?" Before he could answer, as if on cue, the Humvee suddenly pulled out into the passing lane, advancing slowly along the side of the truck at high speed as the four occupants inside the Humvee studied their quarry.

"Road Runner, we got this. If he pulls ahead to try and jack your load, we'll take him. Speed up and stay in your lane. Don't let him get out in front. Find another gear, guys."

The pilot swung the black Huey UH-1B in low over the highway. Descending to a hundred feet, the pilot reduced the Huey's noise signature to stealth mode and lined up on his target. The hunter became the hunted as the two cartel snipers studied the SUV's armaments through their scopes, knowing the acrylic polycarbonate glass and light armor would be no match for their 50-caliber depleted uranium projectile from the Barrett M107A1. Almost simultaneously, the two veteran marksmen chambered a round and leaned the muzzles out the cargo door, steadying them against the wind. Nodding at his partner crouched opposite him on the port-side opening, the starboard sniper watched his partner take aim at the vehicle's hood, intending to put a round through the engine block in case his shot missed the driver.

Over the noise of the turbine, he counted down, took aim, and they both fired simultaneously. They watched as one bullet went through the Humvee's hood and shattered inside the engine block, the other went through the roof and into the driver's torso. The Humvee pitched out of control to the right side of the road, veering in behind the big rig as it swept past. Rolling over repeatedly in a twisted ball of smoke and flames, the spiraling wreck veered off the road and plowed a path through hundreds of feet of barrel cactus, sand and open desert before coming to a stop in a burning heap a hundred yards into the desert.

With a look of relief, Gonz slowed the eighteen wheeler, he and Chico watching the smoldering wreck in their side view mirrors as the gas tank blew and lit up the desert with a giant fireball. With the destruction of the cartel Humvee, the Huey reversed course and circled back to make sure there would be no survivors.

"Jesus!" exclaimed Chico as they continued to pull away from the debris field, "...am I glad those guys are on our side."

Reassured, Gonz breathed a deep sigh into the sat phone before speaking. "Nice shooting, guys. Saved our butts."

The whine of the chopper's turbines could be heard over the phone as it banked and headed northwest toward California. "De nada, senores. Gorilla is history. See you in LA."

Gonz throttled the big rig back but kept the truck running at a brisk 90 mph. They swept past a Walmart eighteen wheeler headed in the opposite direction just as the sun peeked over the desert horizon behind them. In their side view mirrors, the bright sunlight blotted out the plume of smoke from the Humvee's wreckage, and the two mercenaries were grateful to put some distance between themselves and the carnage. Chico reached for the glovebox, restocking it with the extra 9mm clips from his flak jacket as the two men in the Kenworth were bathed in the light of the rising sun. Breathing easier with a new-found appreciation for life, they gazed out over the open desert from their seats high-up in the Kenworth as the cacti, scorpions and tumbleweeds swept past them at 90 mph. The men fervently hoped this would be the greatest obstacle they would have to face.

In a celebratory mood, Gonz spoke over the groan of the turbo diesel; "Nosotros vayas con Dios, hermano," and held up his fist for a bump from Chico, buoyed by the elimination of the Los Zetas threat.

"To our families," replied Chico. The two mercenaries returned to planning on how they would spend their bonus money once back in Los Angeles.

Emilio Rosa was the kind of man who enjoyed cleaning his collection of antique firearms while puffing on his favorite Cuban cigar. Two weeks had passed since visiting his family just outside Tampico, and he was sitting at his hand-carved Laotian teak desk aboard *Bella Rosa* thinking about his pretty young wife and two sons running on the beach and playing soccer. His Columbian-born wife had warned him that he could set himself on fire smoking cigars with all the gun oil and lubricants he used.

Reassembling the pearl-handled Colt .45 Peacemaker laid out on the felt cloth was something he could do in his sleep. Ten years ago, the Peacemaker was a gift from an arms dealer who was still his main supplier of Uzis, Berettas, Glocks, M-48 grenades, MAC-10s and C-4. It was his most cherished antique, having once been the prized possession of Jesse James, and he took exceptional care of it. Fitting the cylinder into the revolver carefully, he held it up and rotated the cylinder with his thumb as he listened to it click into place. Finished with his polishing, he admired the light reflecting off the antique .45 and wondered how many men the outlaw had dispatched with his favorite firearm just as Ramone Salamonaca knocked on the open door holding a satellite phone.

"Boss, its Damon Morgan. Says it's important."

"All right, Ramone," reaching for the phone and setting his cigar into an ashtray, "...let's see what the counselor has to say." Dispensing with Salamonaca, Rosa wanted some privacy for his conversation with the cartel attorney.

Hearing Rosa's voice, Morgan did his best to sound upbeat. "Senor Rosa, como estas?" he asked from Vero Beach. Today, he wished to hell he hadn't vouched for Wilde and hesitated to make the call out of fear of retribution from the drug lord. To save his own skin, he knew he had no choice but to distance himself from his buddy if he wanted to stay in Rosa's good graces.

"Muy bien, counselor. Y tu?"

"Fine, padron," replied Morgan, listening very carefully to Rosa's non-verbals and nuances. "You asked me to keep track of how Mr. Wilde handled your $40 million advance and I have an update on what he's been up to."

"Uh-huh. That's so kind of you, counselor." There was a pause as the tone of Rosa's voice changed. "And, how's our friend doing after his domestic difficulties have put him so prominently in the media limelight?" he asked with a hint of irony.

"The publicity has subsided, and he's able to walk again after some rehabilitation at the med center here in town."

"I am so very happy. And his wife?" Rosa had become so enamored with the drone videos taken of Stella during her nude gardening that he saved the files to his laptop. Once or twice a day, he enjoyed opening the video shortcut to view his favorite fantasy girl.

Morgan continued to pretend to be a fountain of information, hoping to reinstate himself into the drug lord's circle of trust. "Our sources tell us the FBI has her incarcerated at Chatahootchee State Hospital near Tallahassee under the guise of the Baker Act. They have her sequestered, guarded and incommunicado." Morgan listened intently to Rosa's voice for clues as to his future. "And, this information is less than a day old."

"Uh-huh. Well...so much for the charmed lives of the privileged and well-heeled. And my $40 million? Where is *it*, counselor?"

Rosa could hear the rustling of papers as Morgan prepared to give him the rundown from his notes. "Well, sir, that's the disturbing part. After paying off the $28-and-a-half-million margin call at Barclays, it appears that Mr. Wilde has spent ten million with the Columbians for his own supply of uncut cocaine." Realizing the impropriety of Wilde's actions, he added, "I'm truly sorry to be the one to have to tell you this, Mr. Rosa." In sharing this little tidbit, he'd likely signed his friend's death warrant. But after vouching for him, Wilde had given him no choice if he wanted to continue playing poker with all ten fingers.

Morgan could hear a sharp exhale from Rosa that sent a chill up his spine. Clearly, he was not happy to hear the news. Rosa's voice dropped and his tone grew dark. "Let me get this straight, counselor. You bring me this guy, you vouch for him and promise to be responsible, I take him in, give him a partnership, advance him $40 million to pay off his broker, and this is how he repays me? Before the ink is even dry on the stock transfer?"

With Rosa intoning culpability, Morgan desperately needed to get out of the crosshairs. He knew the only way to avoid Wilde's likely fate at the hands of the cartel was to throw him under the bus. "I am sorry, Mr. Rosa," said Morgan sadly. "I thought I knew him better. What is it you want me to do to make things right?"

Rosa reached for his Cohiba, drawing deeply on his cigar and blowing a cloud of smoke into the air before answering. "If you choose to exonerate yourself, counselor, bring Mr. Wilde to me. *Bella Rosa* is back at Bahia Mar on the outside dock. I'll be waiting." Before Morgan could open his mouth to express his desire to comply, he heard a click on the sat phone, then nothing but silence.

Certainly not a man that took betrayal lightly, Rosa thought about the treaty he'd struck with the Columbians fourteen months ago and needed to re-verify its validity. "Ramone," he yelled out into the main salon, "...get me Gustavo Allejandro on the South American sat phone."

"You got it, boss." A moment later, in strode Salamonaca with the second sat phone as he speed dialed Santa Marta, Columbia.

A moment later, a man's voice on the phone answered, "Allejandro Estate."

Salamonaca said, "Luis, I have Emilio Rosa here for Mr. Allejandro," handing the phone to Rosa. Angry over Wilde's betrayal, the drug lord glared at Salamonaca as he took the phone.

"Gustavo," began Rosa with a smile, "...como estas?"

Sitting on his palatial oceanfront veranda on the outskirts of Santa Marta, the head of the Santa Marta cartel was enjoying some vintage Armagnac as he watched over his young son and daughter playing badminton in the yard. "Bien, Emilio."

"Y su familia?"

"They're fine as well. To what do I owe the honor of your call?"

"My friend, allow me to get right to the point. I'm still your biggest customer, agree?"

Allejandro smiled, seeing an opportunity to lighten the mood. "Yes, you are immense."

"Gustavo, don't screw with me. This is serious."

"Of course, Emilio. I appreciate your business, as always," shrugging his shoulders at Luis about his reason for calling. "You are my most important customer." Rarely did Rosa need any hand holding, so Allejandro assumed there was more to come.

Rosa continued. "And our agreement? Is it still intact, Gustavo?"

"Of course. Why do you question our arrangement?"

"My sources tell me someone in your cartel is selling large quantities of cocaine to my customer, Daniel Wilde." There was a meaningful pause before he added, "I need you to put a stop to it immediately." Rosa avoided admitting the part about the purchase being made with his own money for fear he would look weak to the Columbians, something he could ill afford. The last time the Columbians smelled weakness, a turf war broke out and he lost nine good men. It was a painful lesson.

The new leader of the Medellin cartel had worked hard to keep the peace over the years since their last turf war. Concerned, Allejandro stood up and walked across the lawn, away from the sounds of his innocent children playing. "Let me look into this, Emilio, and if it is true, I will put a stop to it immediately. You have my word."

"I'm counting on you, Gustavo." He put his hand over the mouthpiece and shared a word with Salamonaca before continuing. "And Gustavo?"

"Is there something else my friend?"

"What is the ETA on our next shipment?" He heard muted conversation on the other end of the phone and took another pull from his Cohiba, patiently waiting to confirm the timeline.

"Four days," replied Allejandro.

"Can you make it two? We're running a little short."

With a questioning look on his face, Allejandro held up two fingers to Luis, his logistical coordinator. Luis nodded. "For you, Emilio, let's make it two days. I'll have my men expedite the shipment this time, but I can't do this very often. As you know, shipping can be complicated with many moving parts." The Columbian drug lord paced back toward his lounge chair and waved at his son who just scored a goal. "I'm glad to hear your business is doing so well."

"Muchas gracias, mi amigo. Buenos tarde, Gustavo."

***

Alternating between positive feelings of creation and darker ones of destruction, Mark gazed into the fire, surrendering all sense of time, his eyes losing focus within the flames. He was sitting in the family room at Villa Riomar with a snifter of Armagnac, his mind drifting aimlessly between past and present. When he was a child, he couldn't wait to experience the future, but after tasting the bitterness of losing his wife, he wanted to slow the world down, a little less certain about embracing the future, thinking maybe it was somewhere he didn't want to go. Heartsick over his loss, he felt like he'd aged a hundred years as he scanned the photos and letters he'd spread out on the table. It was a lot to go through as he studied the photos of Carol in the light of the fire. Viewing each one separately, he was reminded what a stunning woman she'd been, with her blonde hair, beautiful blue eyes, sensual lips, and the athletic toned body of a woman who'd always been devoted to fitness.

He walked to the sidebar and poured himself another Armagnac, then out into the courtyard where he stood surveying the flowers and vegetables she'd been tending for the past few months. Unsettled, he revisited the courtyard before sitting down again in front of the fireplace. He never thought it would be easy, but neither had he imagined losing her would be so hard.

The split oak logs crackled and popped as he picked up one of his favorite photos of Carol and studied it in the flickering light of the fire. She was standing on the foredeck of *Dream Girl* on a bright sunny day, topless in her G-string, pointing over her shoulder at the unmistakable skyline of Bora Bora in the background. The photo portrayed her cupping one breast in mock surprise and embarrassment as if surprised by the photographer. Mark remembered taking the shot on their approach to Bora Bora while Carol was acting out one of her favorite sexual fantasies as she pretended to be the captain's sex slave. It was a fun day, and after making love on the foredeck they wound up anchoring in front of the famous Sofitel Bora Bora Marara Beach Resort. He remembered that Carol had gone inside and made friends with the receptionist who gave her the password for the WIFI, giving them good internet for their five-day stay. Surveying the rest of her photos, he fell into a reverie of their last trip together.

Recalling the two island stops before Bora Bora, Rangiroa was one of the largest atolls in the entire world, so large you could fit the entire island of Tahiti inside, and it was the best diving they'd experienced on their passage. They'd averaged almost nine knots on the two-day sail to Tahiti, outsailing *Blew Bayou* and *Vitamin Sea* by seven hours before they put into Cook Bay at Tautira where the sea swells and wind were reduced by the bay's protective shape. Most of the larger islands around Tahiti also had a Cook Bay, as Captain Cook had also visited Moorea, Bora Bora, Huahine, and Raiatea. Outside the bay in Tahiti there were heavy eight-foot swells and 35-knot winds, so they were forced to keep *Dream Girl* anchored in Cook Bay during the rainy grey days until the weather improved for their trip around the island of Tahiti.

After two months of sailing the pristine outer island groups of Marquesas and Tuamotus, there were certain aspects of civilization they'd come to miss, including real supermarkets, quaint local arts, crafts and seafood shops, internet, rentable taxis and scooters, and dive shops. Frequenting the dive shops always paid off for the McAllisters, a place where the French-speaking natives might share some tips with you if you showed an interest in their language and culture. And if you paid homage to the father of SCUBA, Jacques Cousteau. All of these remnants of colorful native civilization they discovered a week later in the bustling city of Papeete, which was about as close as you could come to experiencing an actual "tourist trap" in the Society Islands of French Polynesia.

At the anchorage at Point Venice, they rafted up overnight with four other island-hopping boats for a seafood grilling party, then headed to Marina Taina where just about everyone else was anchored. At Marina Taina, they saw several super yachts longer than 50 meters, and after two days of hiking, partying, shopping and snorkeling, they bathed in one of the island's incredibly beautiful cascading waterfalls. Upon their return to Marina Taina, one of the sons of the legendary late actor Marlon Brando dropped anchor within fifty meters of their flotilla, and having run into the 35-meter catamaran *Onetahi* before, Carol and Mark took the dinghy over and shared a few cocktails with the famous heirs and convivial entourage crewing the sailboat.

More photos from the same passage reminded him that the weather had gotten strange the next day. After a three-hour sail to Moorea under grey-blue skies, they decided to drop anchor at Vaiare Bay, Moorea, close to the Sofitel Hotel on the Tahitian side. There were four or five other sailboats anchored close by, and spotting their dinghies parked on the beach next to Sofitel, the couple joined up with five other seafarers after being invited to spend the night at what turned out to be a palatial home (by local standards) just across the Beach Road. There, they grilled snapper, grouper and mahi-mahi, partying and sharing sailing stories and Tahitian drink recipes until the wee hours of the morning.

The next day they sailed to Oponuhu Bay, Moorea and snorkeled around *Dream Girl's* anchorage for mother-of-pearl shells which the locals would carve into beautiful ashtrays and artifacts. In an hour of snorkeling, Mark brought to the surface scores of mother-of-pearl shells which they used to barter for fresh fruit in Huahine, along with a rusty auto tag from California he discovered inside a sunken wooden dory. He remembered Carol quipping, "…now all you need to do is find the Ferrari that was attached to it."

Entering the Leeward Islands of Tahiti, the seafarers were delighted to discover Huahine, which was actually two separate islands connected by a quaint short bridge. Despite the island's perfect untouched beaches, enchanting lagoons, breathtaking reef breaks and many isolated coves, Huahine had managed to escape the touristy overdevelopment of many of the neighboring islands. With only a solitary luxury resort on Huahine, the locals were not in favor of constructing anymore, and most visitors were quite okay with that. Mark and Carol loved picking their own guava, mangos, papaya and pineapples that grew along the road and just about everywhere else. The couple found the locals gracious and generous, though not quite as used to foreigners as in Tahiti, Bora Bora and Moorea.

A three-hour sail from Huahine, Raiatea is considered the sailor's paradise of the Leewards and is the second largest of the Society Islands, after Tahiti. On their bucket list was the exploration of the Faaroa River, the only navigable river in all of French Polynesia, so the couple dropped anchor at Faaroa Valley at the mouth of the river and took *Dream Girl's* dinghy up river. They found the picturesque river fairly calm and the wild vegetation reminded them of their trip through the Amazonian rain forests months earlier. Also in Raiatea, they found one of the largest fleets of charter yachts anywhere in the South Pacific headquartered in the largest lagoon. Folklore and ancient temples could be found everywhere on the pristine island, considered to be the center of the eastern islands of Polynesia, and Captain Mark and his first mate spent their first day on Raiatea exploring several of the ancient temples.

Last on their list of Polynesian islands they visited was the most famous, Bora Bora. Despite being somewhat limited in total area, the Society Island of Bora Bora is home to two mountains that were once parts of a now-extinct volcano. Rising out of the center of the island are Mount Otemanu and the slightly smaller double-peaked Mount Pahia, the famous mountains that created one of the most distinct skylines in the world so often pictured on postcards and travel brochures.

Entering the inner atoll at the wide western channel just south of the Bora Bora Pearl Beach Resort, Carol and Mark were treated to some of the most spectacular unspoiled scenery they'd ever set eyes on. Bora Bora was one of the most developed islands in Polynesia, and it was where most of the upscale hotels were found, including Sofitel, Le Meridien, Four Seasons Bora Bora, InterContinental Resort, St. Regis, Hilton Nui Bora Bora, Pearl Beach and LaMaitai. In spite of the ubiquitous resorts and hotels, Bora Bora still displayed its own exquisite charm and is also known as "The Romantic Island".

A week earlier, they met a couple of honeymooning Manhattan investment bankers and made a promise to visit them at La Meridien Resort on the eastern side of the island atoll. La Meridien was a series of upscale Polynesian bungalows built out over a beautiful reef with some rather unique features. After helping the couple slip down through the retractable glass-topped coffee table in their living room and through the floor opening into *Dream Girl's* dinghy floating directly under the bungalow, Carol and Mark took them to rustic Roulotte Matira at Matira Pointe for a five-star dinner of French cuisine. The scones, seafood and croissants were all fresh made, and it proved to be an unbelievably enjoyable evening with gourmet food, entertaining company and fine French champagne.

The next morning, they sailed *Dream Girl* back to the main channel on the western side of the Bora Bora atoll and anchored just inside the pass where they dove, snorkeled, fished, drank, partied and grilled their fresh catches with their friends. The foursome had so much fun spearing fresh seafood on the incoming tides they stayed anchored at the atoll's main inlet for ten more days. With visibility of 100 meters through aqua-tinted crystal clear water, they were moored among groupings of large coral heads in 10-20 meters on the starboard side, and on the port side a sheer wall of coral dropping to 70 meters where the blue water predators hunted for smaller prey. Off their stern on the main island of Bora Bora, across the lagoon, stood a tropical forest paradise of pineapples, coconut palms, guava, papaya and mango trees that they visited regularly during their stay. Inside the Bora Bora atoll, they swam with dolphins, learned to husk coconuts, fed the sharks and sea turtles, ate fresh seafood every day, and fell in love all over again.

He held up the last photo of Carol in the stack that he remembered taking at their favorite Bora Bora anchorage with the sun setting in the background. It was one of his most cherished photos, the one that captured her looking up into his eyes with the exhilaration only a free woman can feel, the look of a free woman at the beginning of a long sojourn whose ending had proven quite unpredictable.

And so the eloquent F. Scott Fitzgerald must have had it right when he ended *The Great Gatsby* by writing, "So we beat on, boats against the current, borne back ceaselessly into the past."

As he set the photo on the table, he recited the passage again, unable to imagine a better characterization of his Polynesian sailing adventures with his beloved late wife.

CHAPTER SIXTEEN

Ramone Salamonaca slipped inside the ambulance bay at Indian River County Medical Center unnoticed. Wearing the white uniform of an orderly, a sanitation cap, fake mustache and dyed blonde hair, the man known to law enforcement as RatMan pushed the rented wheelchair down the passageway toward the elevator bank. Wilde's rehabilitation was scheduled three days a week, from three to four o'clock. His watch read two-thirty, right on time.

He stepped inside the EMT locker room and snagged a clip-on ID that he found hanging in an open locker before returning to the wheelchair and pressing the elevator call button as a pair of EMS techs scrambled past him toward a waiting ambulance. On the way up, he dabbed a bit of blood from the door and smeared it on the ID making the photo harder to identify.

Salamonaca wrinkled his nose at the strong smell of medicine and disinfectants, the elevator doors opening on the third floor as a patient gurney clattered past him into the open elevator. Rolling past the nurses' station with the empty wheelchair, he smiled and waved at the two RNs on staff at the desk who glanced at him briefly before returning to their monitors. Arriving at Room 322, he noticed the empty chair outside before knocking and, without waiting for an answer, backed the wheelchair into the private suite. His eyes glued to the TV, Wilde lay propped up in bed, unconcerned with the orderly who brought the wheelchair around.

Fearing he'd be recognized from their meeting on *Bella Rosa*, Salamonaca was careful to hide his face from Wilde as he wheeled the chair around to the side of the bed and adjusted the chair's settings. Salamonaca pulled Wilde's patient file from the foot of the bed and flipped through the pages, pretending to read. "Mr. Wilde, you're scheduled for rehab. Let's get you in the chair, sir."

Finally, Wilde diverted his attention from the episode of M.A.S.H. he was watching, trying to focus on the orderly's face, still groggy from the Roxicodone and morphine, unsure if he'd seen the man before. Where was the guy who took him to rehab last time? "Duh uh know ooh?" he slurred.

Fearing he'd been recognized, Salamonaca yanked out the stun gun he had hidden in the back of his pants, whirled around and jammed it forcefully into the center of Wilde's chest. A brief look of surprise and shock was followed quickly by the pain from the voltage as Wilde flailed and screamed before passing out from the huge jolt, tearing loose the leads to his monitor. "Emilio Rosa says 'hi'," said Salamonaca, tucking the stun gun back into his waistband. Before he could load Wilde into the wheelchair, he heard someone calling his victim's name from the hallway outside and quickly positioned himself behind the door as it opened.

A portly middle-aged nurse that looked like Mrs. Doubtfire wearing thick glasses stepped into the room. Seeing Wilde unconscious on the bed, she blurted, "Mr. Wilde, are you"-

The imposter grabbed the nurse from behind and covered her mouth with his free hand, knocking her ID badge to the floor as she struggled to free herself. Closing the door behind her with his foot, he jammed the stun gun into her armpit as she emitted a muffled squeal from the painful jolt. The nurse went limp and dropped to the floor unconscious, her eyeglasses clattering to the floor. Her assailant quickly dragged her by both arms into the corner before turning his attention back to Wilde.

With little time left to make his escape, Salamonaca needed to move fast, surprised to find Wilde unguarded. He wrestled his victim into the wheelchair and propped his head up before exiting the room with his quarry and closing the door behind. The hallway looked clear in both directions and he proceeded quickly with his unconscious patient toward the bank of elevators at the far end, nodding at nurses and doctors he passed along the way. A duty nurse at the nurse's station looked up from behind her computer screen as they passed.

"How's he doing?" she asked.

"A little tired…taking a nap…he's dying to get to rehab today," he replied, smiling at the irony. The nurse nodded and turned her attention back to her paperwork. Salamonaca found the elevator empty as the double doors opened and he quickly wheeled Wilde inside, hoping for a clean getaway. Arriving at the ground floor, he pushed the wheelchair toward the ramp that led down to the waiting van where Javier waited to help him load their hostage for the trip to Bahia Mar.

"Anyone recognize you?" Javier asked, pushing the chair and hostage up the van's side ramp.

"No," he answered tersely. "Guard was on a break. Let's get moving."

Javier eyed the blood stain on his photo ID. "He give you any trouble?"

Salamonaca yanked off the fake ID and tossed it into the center console. "Nope. That's from another patient," he explained. Minutes later, they were rolling south on I-95 toward Ft. Lauderdale in the handicapped-equipped van he rented from Perkins Medical Supply. Speed dialing his boss on his cell phone, Salamonaca glanced at Javier and motioned for him to slow down as they passed a state trooper in the opposite lane. He still couldn't believe how easy it had been to get Wilde in the wheelchair and past his guard.

When his cell phone rang, Rosa was enjoying a massage on the sundeck of *Bella Rosa*. He reached for his phone to see who dared to interrupt his massage. "Diga mi, Ramone," answered Mexico's most-feared drug lord.

"Boss, we got him," looking askance at Javier behind the wheel. Javier glanced in the rearview mirror to check on the still-unconscious Wilde sitting with his arms and legs duct taped to the wheelchair and a black hood draped over his head.

"And how is our friend?" asked Rosa, his pretty Japanese masseuse paying close attention to Rosa's flabby arms.

"Still out from the meds and shock therapy," he quipped. Taking a deep drag from his cigarette, Salamonaca swiveled in his seat to check behind him and see if their guest was regaining consciousness. "He won't remember the trip."

"Bueno. Got a few questions for him. Did you get the QuikKrete like I asked?"

"Si, boss, at the Home Depot in Vero. Five ten-pound buckets, just like you said."

"Bueno. We going to have some fun with Mr. Daniel Wilde in a few hours, mi amigo."

"Yes, boss." After Rosa ended the call, Salamonaca smiled to himself, confident that their guest would soon be spilling his guts to El Padron. "Javier," pointing ahead to the next interchange, "... there's a Baja Grille up ahead. I'm in the mood for some great Mexican. How 'bout you?"

Javier suppressed a chuckle. "Great Mexican for a pair of great Mexicans. Sounds good to me, boss." Checking his blind spot in the side mirror, Javier steered the van into the right-hand lane and prepared to take the Jensen Beach Boulevard exit.

He'd heard the spicy chicken, black beans and rice with extra jalepenos were to die for.

***

Trailing a half mile behind RatMan's van on I-95, Special Agent Epifanio Perez drove the unmarked black Ford Taurus and wondered about the ethics of using one gangster to catch another. Special Tech Agent Leonard Scott sat next to him, keeping track of the moving blip on the tablet with the GPS in his lap. The two agents were used to working stakeouts together and had a pretty good idea where the cartel bad boy was headed. His hip sore from the holstered Glock, Scott shifted his weight and sat up when he noticed the van veer off the interstate at the Jensen Beach Boulevard exit. He leaned forward to double check if it was the same exit that was marked on the map.

"What's up," asked Perez.

"Looks like they're exiting at Jensen Beach, Epi. The next exit ahead. They're slowing, so keep your distance," forgetting for an instant that Perez had twelve more years of experience with the Bureau than he did.

Perez gave him a condescending look. "Don't get your panties in a twist, Lenny," looking over at his younger partner. "Ain't my first rodeo, ya know." Scott thought it sounded odd to hear his forty-year-old Puerto Rican partner trying to imitate a redneck's accent.

"I wonder what they're up to," said Scott. He checked the list of vendors available at the interchange as they turned off. "Well, what'ya know. A Baja Grille ahead to the left."

"Ain't that a kick in the head," said Perez.

"Think they'll give Wilde a bite, since-technically-he's still the CEO?" asked Scott.

"Doubtful. The fox that raids the henhouse doesn't like to share."

Across the street from the Baja Grille, Scott noticed a Burger King. "You feel like a Whopper?"

Perez smiled at his partner. "Sure, sonny. I'm wearing your Whopper."

"Get real." Scott gave him a disgusted look. "Okay then, old timer, have it your way," he quipped as they parked out of sight across the busy intersection. Perez exited the unmarked Ford Taurus to grab their burgers while Scott sat with his binoculars and kept a wary eye on RatMan and his entourage. Double checking the blip on his GPS monitor to make sure it was stationary, he raised his binoculars to get a visual confirmation on the Perkins Medical Supply van as Perez stuck his head back inside the driver's window to take his order.

"Make mine a double cheese Whopper all the way with fries, no onions," said Scott. He looked at Perez still standing beside the car. "Go. I'll call you if there's any movement."

"You do that, Lenny," smacking the side of the car with his hand for emphasis and heading inside for their Whoppers. "We don't wanna lose'em now, partner."

***

On the same day, Damon Morgan stood at the window in his second floor office in the Northern Trust Building on A1A and Beachland in Vero and watched the sparse morning traffic pass below him. Feeling smug about the thirty-minute internet chess game he'd just won with his anonymous opponent, he was congratulating himself on his victory and being such an outstanding chess player. He'd lost only one game in the last year, ironically, to his most affluent client, Stella Wilde. Now, if he could just figure out a way to apply those same kind of moves to his current untenable situation with Rosa and avoid the potential checkmate he envisaged.

Morgan eyed the chess board sitting on the small conference table and thought about his game with Stella in his office, visualizing the minx sitting across from him in her short skirt with her legs confidently crossed. Impressed with her powers of concentration, never once did she look up at him during the entire ten-minute match, her eyes glued to the chess board until she checkmated him. He wondered if the outcome would have been the same if he hadn't allowed his focus to drift to more erotic thoughts about her. Genuinely embarrassed at the brevity of their game, who could have known she was that good?

Now, he was in a chess game with a lot more at stake than just his ego. In his mind, he played back his last conversation with Emilio Rosa again, fearing his life was in jeopardy after angering the most violent drug lord in the Western hemisphere. Although it was never his intention to violate Rosa's trust with his endorsement of Wilde, Morgan concluded that the only way out of his predicament was to find a way to transform himself from someone who was disposable to someone who was indispensable. Attorney/client privilege and Barclays be damned, he thought. From disposable to indispensable-that was the key. Purely in self-defense, he would go public if he had to, fully aware that any proof of what he did for the cartel would result in disbarment anyway.

Racing through the cartel's financial statements on his office laptop, he knew it was only a matter of time before Rosa denied him access to sensitive files. Printing the files as he searched for something particularly incriminating, he found himself copying everything he could get his hands on. The details of the business deals that he arranged for Rosa in the last two years were still at his fingertips, including the convoluted shell corporations he created to title the six-boat trawler fleet, sixteen semis and vans, four fixed-wing aircraft, two helicopters, seventeen paramilitary

Humvees, and over a dozen international bank accounts, as well as GPS coordinates of warehouses, processing labs, safe houses, fuel depots, and delivery points. Morgan transferred all 152 pages onto a separate flash drive and printed off an extra two pages on the offshore accounts as proof of his file before clipping the drive onto his keychain. Holding the key ring up in the light, he smiled at his stroke of genius, admiring his digital "get-out-of-jail-free card" as it dangled like a charm on a charm bracelet. Morgan began to feel a little less disposable as he gathered his laptop and important files for the trip to Chatahootchee.

He stood at his paralegal's desk as the young girl who reminded him so much of Penelope Cruz put her call on hold to hear what her boss was about to say. "Charlotte, I'm heading out of town for two days to see a client. Will you forward any urgent calls to my cell?"

Charlotte smiled up at her boss. "Of course, Mr. Morgan." With a suggestive tilt of her head and lilting voice, she asked, "Can I do anything else for you before you go?"

Reaching for the handle on the glass front door with his name in gold lame, Morgan smiled over his shoulder. "In a hurry, Charlotte, but hold that thought 'til I see you again."

"Anything you say, Mr. Morgan."

Roberto deCespedes had been Rosa's IT guy ever since he'd found a back door into the DEA's personnel files, a move that not only impressed his boss but allowed Rosa to track and identify the DEA's attempts to infiltrate his network. With this new advancement in the cartel's IT capabilities, Rosa conservatively estimated his operational savings at about four million dollars a week by avoiding the DEA's sting operations. With state-of-the-art electronics and software loaded into a room one level below *Bella Rosa's* aft sundeck, deCespedes detected an intrusion into cartel files reserved for only upper level users. Leaning over the eight active monitors on his desk, the Juarez cartel's top IT guy rang his boss as he as he tracked the intruder.

On the upper deck enjoying the morning, Rosa blew a smoke ring from his Oliva Melanio Torpedo and lifted his demitasse for another sip of Kopi luwak. One of the most expensive coffees in the world, Kopi luwak sold for around $600 per pound and was made by collecting coffee beans eaten by wild civets. Rosa didn't care where it came from, he just liked the taste. The pretty stewardess smiled as she offered him the morning news. "Lila, if I'm not in the obituary section of the paper today, will you bring me some fresh melon?" he joked.

Lila nodded and chuckled politely. "Yes, sir, right away." Reaching for his phone, he pushed the talk button. "Diga mi, Roberto."

"Mr. Rosa, we've got a situation."

"I'm listening."

"We have someone in top brass straying into the forbidden zone, sir, and it looks like they're copying files."

"Quien es?"

"Tell you in just a…triangulating the home address…who do we know at 755 Beachland Boulevard, Vero Beach? It's the Northern Trust Office Building, Mr. Rosa."

"Es decir Senor Morgan," said Rosa in a dark tone. In a flash, Rosa decided it was time for a "Come to Jesus" meeting with Mr. Morgan as he took a greedy sip of his Kopi luwak. "Call the counselor and tell him I'd like to see him before noon today. Tell him anything, but get him here today."

"Yes sir, Mr. Rosa." As instructed, deCespedes speed dialed Damon Morgan on his cell phone and listened to it ring nineteen times with no answer.

***

Two hundred miles further north on I-95, Morgan was driving his black Mercedes 550 AMG at high speed until he exited the interstate in West Melbourne on New Haven. Parking away from the horde of cheaper cars and pick-up trucks that sported chewing tobacco stains in the parking lot, he was on his way to the Walmart entrance to pick up a new burner phone when his cell phone rang. Before answering, he eyed the number and realized they were probably tracking him. Paranoid, he popped the cover off and pulled out the batteries and SIM card, crushing them under his heel. Try tracking that, you morons. Wrapped up in destroying his cell phone, he didn't notice the dog poop. The dog nasty that stuck to the heel of his $500 pair of Ballys was completely unsatisfactory, bordering on sacrilegious, he thought, stooping to scrape off the disgusting mess with a squashed paper cup he found. *Merde. Who the hell walks their dog at Walmart?*

***

Aboard *Bella Rosa*, the counselor's phone ID disappeared off the cartel's GPS grid. Not to be denied his electronic eyes, deCespedes reached across his control panel and activated the transponder

234

located under the wheel well of Morgan's Mercedes. He checked the transceiver monitor again to see if the signal was clear. Ah, there you are, in West Melbourne. The head of IT for the Juarez cartel immediately redialed his boss.

"Diga mi, Roberto," answered Rosa who was sitting in the main salon enjoying his expresso.

"Sir, Mr. Morgan is not answering his phone and looks like he's heading north on I-95, away from us."

"Donde esta, Roberto?"

"He's in West Melbourne, parked near the New Haven interchange." Rosa tipped the demitasse up, draining the last sip of Kopi luwak before taking a deep pull on his high-dollar smoke and leaned back in the plush leather chair. "Call Ramone. Tell him to drop what he's doing and bring that pendejo to me immediately."

"Which pendejo, sir?"

"Morgan, you idiot. Tell him to bring me Morgan," he repeated in a lower voice and squinting menacingly.

"Yes, boss," answered deCespedes. The last person in the world that he wanted to be right now was Damon Morgan.

"Forget it, Roberto. I'll call Ramone myself." Rosa decided it was time for an excommunication and permanently remove Morgan from his circle of trust. "What I want you to do now is cancel the counselor's passcodes and all access to our computer files. If we can't trust the counselor, we have to cut him off. And by all means, keep tracking him. I want to know where that pendejo is every minute." He lowered his voice and added, "If he goes rogue on us, we go with Plan B."

"Entiendo, padron."

Rosa blew another smoke ring from his Oliva and sat back in his leather chair, waiting for Ramone to answer his phone.

"Ola, don Rosa," answered Salamonaca.

"What are you doing, Ramone?" Distracted, Rosa squinted at a 54-foot Hatteras with two topless girls sitting up on their chaise lounges and rubbing each other with sunscreen on the sundeck. They waved at the drug lord as the yacht made its way against the incoming tide toward the 17th Street Causeway Bridge.

"Making sure our new guest is comfortable down here in the engine room," replied Ramone. "He whines a lot. The little diva whines louder than the generators. You'd think the man has never been hung by his feet before." Rosa's lieutenant stepped to his hostage and tightened the draw string on Wilde's hood before hitting him hard in the hamstrings with the baton again. Wilde let out a moan. "We ready with the scopolamine, boss?"

The pretty brunette stewardess smiled, setting down his sliced melon on the table in front of him and arranged a place setting. He waited for her to leave before answering. "Hold off on that, amigo. I have another job for you first," taking another pull on his cigar. "The counselor has gone rogue, and I want you to bring him in. If he refuses, or eludes you, you know what to do. Go see Roberto in his office. He'll bring you up to date on Morgan's location."

"Entiendo, padron."

PART II

The queen of the south shall rise up in the judgment with this generation, and shall condemn it: for she came from the uttermost parts of the earth to hear the wisdom of Solomon; and, behold, a greater than Solomon is here.

—Matthew 12:42

CHAPTER SEVENTEEN

I t was the last day of May, and Stella sat at the far end of the brightly-lit rec room trying to look inconspicuous in her sundress as she searched through the magazine rack by her side, wondering when the hell the FBI was going to let her out of this nut house. Pawing through faded older issues of *Modern Alcoholic*, *Shingles Today* and *Transgender Nurse*, she was disappointed to discover that her best choice of entertainment was a fifteen-year-old copy of *Cosmopolitan*. She turned the overstuffed armchair to face out the window with views of blue skies and magnificent oaks before settling into the armchair. Turning the first page, she prepared herself for a look backward in time into the wonderful world of women's fashion as it was a decade-and-a-half earlier.

Every so often the scar on her left wrist tingled, and Stella would massage it as a reminder of how close she'd come to allowing a moment of weakness to end her life. She vowed to grow strong again, knowing now there was no one else she could depend on. Her trusted dominions were falling by the wayside, one by one. She thought about her devious husband and how violent he'd become, wondering if her instincts and intuition would be enough to protect her from making the same mistake with a man again. And she thought about Mark.

Before she could delve into her vintage *Cosmopolitan*, Veola stopped by, the ninety-two-year-old woman who ran around in her pink hair curlers, dirty knee-highs and gingham food-stained dress. Carrying her pink teapot, she paused to pour Stella some invisible tea brewed by her constant companion, the White Rabbit, who was also quite invisible. "Some tea?" she asked. Stella nodded politely. Pouring her make-believe tea, Veola shared her toothless smile and reminded everyone in attendance that she was Jimmy Hoffa's niece and knew "fer sure" where his body was buried.

Then it was Crazy Larry's turn to rock her world. "Hiyeeee!" Drooling down his chin and onto his stuffed panda, Crazy Larry was truly a disturbing mess to lay eyes on. Nicknamed for the obese curly-haired look-alike to one of the Three Stooges, Larry loved to startle his fellow inmates by meandering around barefoot and sneaking up on them while tugging on his privates under his hospital gown. The mentally-challenged head case would always come around dressed in the same stained outfit with the same goofy grin and rear end hanging out. To appease him, Stella had agreed to play one game of checkers with him if he promised to abstain from playing with his privates. Surprisingly, Crazy Larry had kept his promise to her, right up until the very end of the game when his manhood had reared its ugly head and poked out the edge of his gown. Disgusted by his antics, and not interested in any more nude bingo with the other crazy men in her ward, Stella went outside for a walk on the grounds.

Her walk along the barbed-wire perimeter prompted her to think back on her insufferable incarceration at Chatahootchee, a life so far removed from the life of luxury, mansions and exotic cars she was accustomed to. It was five weeks ago today that she'd been introduced to the sick circus that surrounded her, and she bowed her head, recounting the many humiliations she was forced to endure. Over time, the taunting from the staff had diminished, along with reduced amounts of psychotropics, and the security was less restrictive. Unquestionably, Stella had grown stronger from her ordeal and better prepared for what lay ahead.

Following the fiasco with her former psychiatrist Dr. Hirt, she had come to trust the in-house psychiatrist who was assigned her case by the FBI, Dr. Marie Miranda. Stella was delighted that her new shrink brought a welcomed female perspective to her treatment, doctor and patient even agreeing that a gradual reduction in medication and regaining control over her intellect, memory and emotions were the keys to regaining her freedom.

She heard footsteps on the grass behind her and turned to see the woman who looked like Nurse Ratched. "Stella, I need to have you come back inside," she said in a condescending tone. "You have an important visitor," gesturing toward the rec room.

"Who?" Stella wanted to know, fearful that it could be another cleverly-disguised imposter.

"He says he's your attorney. Good lookin', too. Looks like that actor, Michael, ah..."

"Fassbender?"

"Yeah...how'd you know?"

"Like you said, he's my attorney." Accompanying the nurse inside, Stella walked across the room to greet Morgan who stood beside a small round conference table in the rec room.

Dressed in a grey-blue Brioni suit, with a brown Bally leather satchel hanging on his shoulder, Morgan embraced his favorite client and kissed her lightly on both cheeks before gesturing toward the chairs. "Stella, you look ravishing."

With a certain degree of familiarity, they both sat down together. "Cut the crap, Damon," looking sternly at him across the table with her fiery green eyes. "Why did it take you so long to answer my calls? I should fire you."

Morgan smiled confidently. "If you do that, you'll be here for many more months. Is that what you want?"

Still angry with him, she replied, "Go on, counselor. I'm listening."

"It was the FBI's idea to keep you here under the Baker Act, as a cover, for your own protection. I tried to talk them into"-

"Apparently, not very successfully, huh?" Out of the corner of her eye, she saw Crazy Larry watching her from the far corner of the rec room, busy stroking himself under his gown. With a disgusted look, Morgan nodded in his direction.

"Looks like you have a secret admirer there, Stella." He surveyed the room and added, "Never a dull moment around here, huh? I met Veola earlier." He leaned closer to her and whispered in a secretive tone, "She promised to tell me where her uncle Jimmy Hoffa was buried if I French kissed her."

"You'd make a lovely pair, Damon."

"Pardon the cliché, but you *are* beautiful when you're angry, Stella."

"Like I said, cut the crap, counselor." She folded her hands on the table and leaned forward, pulling her strawberry-blonde hair back behind her ear. "How's Dan doing?"

"Not that he deserves you, but look's like he'll make a full recovery." *Unfortunately.*

"I'm glad." For a moment she became emotional, realizing she still had mixed feelings about this. "What's your plan to get me out of here, Damon?"

Morgan held up an index finger before reaching into his pocket and withdrawing his keychain, holding up the attached USB Type-C drive. "This little gem will not only persuade the FBI to let you out of this God-forsaken place, it will make us both indispensable to Rosa. Just in case, I made copies." He pulled it off his key ring and slid it across the desk to her, then reached inside his leather satchel and pulled out an envelope, setting it on the table in front of her. "Open it," he said, looking across the room as two orderlies escorted Crazy Larry into the hallway outside.

Stella eyed the firm's name embossed on the envelope as she opened it. "Morgan, Holloway and Abernathy," she read. "More like Grabbit, Ripitoff and Runn if you ask me," with a hint of sarcasm. She unfolded the two pages, laying them on the table as Morgan surveyed the room to see who might be watching. Reading the documents, Stella scanned through more than fifteen bank account numbers with accompanying balances ranging from $20 million to more than $1 billion.

"Proof of the cartel's holdings, and proof that you hold the remaining files on the USB drive," he explained. He tried harder to get her to understand his plight and placed his palms down on the table. "I had to make some choices, Stella. Now, it's your turn."

She looked up from the documents. "You know they'll come after you, Damon." Despondently, he nodded his understanding. She continued. "No matter how much you change, you still have to pay for the things you've done. We have a long road ahead of us."

"That's why I want you to hold the files, Stella. I trust you. If anything should happen to me, if I slip in my shower, or die from a hang nail; if I succumb to a toothache, I want you to give these files to Special Agent Dominic Beretto, the DEA, the Beltran Leyva and Zetas cartels, and anyone else you can think of on God's green Earth." He met her eyes again. "Now, I've gotta find out if he still wants to kill me."

"Damon, these people are not your friends, and you certainly can't afford to make any more enemies." She studied him for several moments, trying to get a handle on what was motivating him. "I met Beretto. He's a good man, but what makes you think this will work? Couldn't they just retitle the assets and move the accounts?"

Morgan leaned closer to make it impossible to overhear them. "There are *152 pages* of cartel assets," he explained, "...I mean *everything* is listed on those drives. Too many assets to move or retitle, and with this information, we are no longer *disposable*. We are, in fact, *indispensable*."

With all the allure Stella could muster, she looked at Morgan and said, "From your lips to God's ears, counselor." She scooped the USB Type-C drive and folded the paper copies up, stuffing them in her pocket before they adjourned their meeting. "Damon, I have to admit, you're braver than I thought. Nice to see you finally grow a pair," she said not unkindly. She thought how every scheming scumbag in the USA seemed to turn up in Florida sooner or later. But Vero was seen as one of the last bastions of nobility, and maybe it was starting to rub off on him.

"I've gotta know something. Were you doing work for the cartel while representing us, Damon? Be honest with me."

Morgan pursed his lips. "What did you expect, Stella, a full-page ad in the *Wall Street Journal* declaring my new client, Emilio Rosa? I would have alienated all those blue-chip clients I acquired when I was at Barclays. It would have been very unwise to be so candid." He cocked his head inquisitively. "Wouldn't you have left me?"

"Probably not, but you could have been a little more, well... forthcoming with me. Look, I know any attorney familiar with international law could represent Rosa. I think you do it because you like the danger, the high-explosives. It's like most men who enjoy grilling because of the danger of setting themselves on fire. Kind of like sailing in a storm at night. I get it. People with lots of money need something to get their heart pumping. Some gamble, some sky dive or race cars or boats, some climb Mt Everest." She paused and looked him straight in the eye. "And some have affairs, Damon."

Morgan raised his hands as if she were pointing a gun. "Guilty as charged, Your Honor. What can I say? Evil is seductive, and it sure pays a helluva lot better than virtue"-

"Which is its own reward," she interjected, "...and you know that."

"Yes, I do know that because I'm an honest man, Stella. I'm doing nothing dishonest with Emilio Rosa."

"Do you really *believe* that, Damon?" She watched him raise his eyebrows in mock sincerity before she continued. "This...from the man who just handed me a file with evidence of more evil on it than almost any organization in the world...except for ISIS, maybe. How long have you been lying to yourself?" Morgan regarded her impassioned plea with a poker face, having been too caught up in the smoke and mirrors of Wall Street to recognize who he was anymore.

"You've been around Rosa's men, right?" she asked, "...met a few of his top men?" Morgan nodded, letting her continue. Wanting to be her moral project, he was touched that she even cared.

"When I was hospitalized at St. Mary's, there was a man who came to see me. I was still drugged up then, but I do remember. Said his name was Gary, like I was supposed to know him. He wanted something from me"-

"Understandable, a girl with your looks."

Letting his remark slide, "I can't get his face out of my mind... like a good-looking rat."

"Salamonaca."

"Sala who?"

"Ramone Salamonaca. Rosa's right-hand man. He came to visit you? How did he know...unless they're tracking our phones," ventured Morgan.

"They can do that? I thought only the NSA and the CIA could do that."

Morgan took a moment to bring her up to speed on the cartel's capabilities. "On that USB drive are listed the cartel's ownership of 79 cell towers they control in the southern states, and, yes, they can track us on our phones using those towers with frequency triangulation software."

"Does the cartel know you've copied their files?"

"Doubtful."

"Because if they know, maybe they tracked you *here*," reasoned Stella.

Encouraged by her earlier display of emotion, Morgan grasped her hands. "Either way, I'll have you out of this rat hole within two days. I'll call Beretto on my way back to Vero and bring him up to speed, let him know what we have on the cartel."

Conflicted over why she should be holding hands with her morally-challenged trust attorney, she was more than ready for his help in leaving Chatahootchee. The words "trust attorney" echoed in her mind like the oxymoron that it was. "Damon, I know deep down you're a good man. But being involved with Emilio Rosa is immoral and unwise. Very unwise for *all* of us. I've seen it in my dreams. The man is pure evil and may destroy all of us, and it will be *your* fault for bringing him into our lives. Es verdad, escucha."

"What did you say? I didn't know you spoke Spanish," said Morgan in amazement.

"I don't. I have no idea where that came from." Stella almost felt like she was having an out-of-body experience, like a sentient being was speaking through her. A moment later, it was gone.

Morgan snuck a glance at his wristwatch and stood to leave. "You have the file, Stella. It's ground zero for Rosa. Make it count." He bowed elegantly and kissed her hand before heading for the door, his gracious act hiding the fact he felt like a condemned man.

"Keep your head down, counselor."

He turned to look at her one last time and smiled. "That's where I do some of my best work," he quipped, earning him the smile he craved so much. He took one last look around the rec room, convinced he wouldn't miss any of the characters in this place.

Well, maybe with the exception of Veola and Crazy Larry.

***

Once Morgan had left for Vero, Stella took the manila envelope out again and matched it with Beretto's business card, carefully copying the mailing address onto the envelope. Worried that Rosa's men would somehow try to intercept the stolen files, she wrapped the USB-C drive in several layers of folded tissue from the ladies room to cushion it from impact and slipped it inside the envelope, hoping her new-found camaraderie with

Dr. Miranda would make a difference and speed its delivery. Hurriedly, she printed her shrink's name on the Post-It note before sticking it on the envelope and handing it over to the head nurse for snail mailing. Still, she couldn't be sure if it would ever make it to Beretto, but it seemed safer than hanging onto it. How ironic was it that she was trusting the U.S. Postal Service with her life, she thought, affixing two 49-cent stamps, supposing each stamp was the sum of 2 cents for postage and 47 cents for storage. In the office, she handed the envelope over to the nurse behind the counter.

The nurse supervisor turned the package over, eyeing it suspiciously. "What's this?" she asked, reflecting on the long list of lowlifes that had darkened her doorway at Chatahootchee.

"Something very personal," explained Stella, hoping she'd let it go.

The nurse's face was expressionless. "No drugs or harmful chemicals, right, Stella?" she asked sternly, knowing that Stella had been a model patient during the last several weeks.

"No, of course not. Where would I even get them? I've been locked up in *here*."

The nurse hesitated, unable to refute her logic, turning the package over again. "You know it'll have to be inspected."

Stella nodded as the nurse reached across the desk and dropped the envelope in a bin labeled "ATTN: DR. MIRANDA" Behind her back, Stella had her fingers crossed as she returned to the rec room to finish her Sudoku puzzle for the day.

***

Right after he turned off eastbound I-10 onto I-75 south somewhere around Lake City, the newly-paved roadway smoothed out nicely, and the plush driver's seat of Morgan's 550 AMG helped induce his daydream. In his fantasy, he was sitting in the giant Jacuzzi tub at Villa Dellacroix enjoying a Fuente Robusto when Stella showed up wearing only a skimpy black Victoria's Secret nightie.

"Where'd you park?" Stella asked as she removed her emerald earrings and set them on the marble counter beside his folded slacks. In his daydream, the emeralds were an identical match to the stunning green of her eyes.

"I took a cab," he said, guiding the rubber ducky in circles around the tip of his manhood as it poked up through the Jacuzzi bubbles. She smiled at his teasing, and he parked his cigar in a silver ashtray on the edge of the huge tub, anticipating some excitement. In a flash, Stella was out of her nightie and straddling him assertively.

"Donne-moi dur, monsieur," commanded Stella in her sultry bedroom voice, pushing her palms against his hairy pecs. He took a deep breath and pressed his eyes closed, submerging into the bubbles as she began pounding against him with her taut body in a wild froth of motion. With water splashing in every direction, Morgan felt like he'd been tossed into a wood chipper with a female badger. The really weird part was that he was enjoying it.

In his daydream, her high-pitched yelps and howls were loud enough to wake the dead in Utah, her screams getting louder every time he surfaced for a gulp of air. Stella continued to pound against him so hard he thought the tub would surely break apart from her primeval thrusting. In his daydream, Morgan was confident he could stay hard longer than it would take her to reach her crescendo, as long as his eardrums didn't burst or he didn't drown first. She let out a high-pitched feral scream that seemed to last forever as she reached her climax somewhere near the summit of Mt. Everest, he supposed. Morgan pulled out of the stunning goddess, stepping out of the near-empty tub one leg at a time to grab a towel. Stella's legs were strewn in the Jacuzzi like a broken doll, one foot hooked on the tub's edge, the other leaning against the faucet, her dripping strawberry-blonde hair draped across her face in a lopsided tangle.

"Un…believable," she panted between gasps for air. "Damon, that was fantastic."

Morgan played the erotic fantasy of the woman who'd come to dominate his dreams over in his mind one last time before coming to grips with the reality of the moment. The aged concave sections of eastbound I-10 had taken their toll on his sacroiliac, and as he watched the cows, croplands, doublewide trailers and big green tractors zipping past him at 80 mph, he had a new idea of what country living was all about. By the time he hit Gainesville, sunset was nearing and he was ready to gas up, drain his lizard and looked forward to stretching his legs. The computer readout indicated that his big German V-8 had delivered almost 30 mpg on the stretch of interstate between Chatahootchee and Gainesville. Approaching his exit, he wondered if it made any sense to pay 20 cents more for premium gas so he could save 15 percent on mileage, but high-test was what the manufacturer's handbook required. Checking his burner phone for the first time since leaving Chatahootchee, he noticed that no one had called during his visit with Stella.

Spotting a Speedway at the Williston Road 121 interchange, he exited and turned left on Williston Road, pulling into the gas station that offered the cheapest premium grade he could find. A year earlier, Morgan remembered advising the parent company, Marathon Petroleum Corporation, on its planned spinoff of the Speedway chain, as well as other ideas to improve shareholder value through his client Elliott Management. Sporting a doubling of the price he paid on his ten thousand shares, Morgan was tickled pink that he'd hung onto his stock in the independent refiner.

He stepped out of his Benz and surveyed the gathering gloom and the shadowy pastures surrounding him. The sun had just set, and it was getting to that time when the long shadows of mature oak trees were casting an unfamiliar look over the countryside of southwest Gainesville. The Speedway station backed up to a large cow pasture with an old weather-beaten barn that could have used a coat of paint fifty years ago. A small lean herd of cattle looked hungry, mooing and nuzzling up against the wire fence as if readying to gallop across the road and raid the Domino's Pizza joint across the street. Morgan stretched his back and legs, surveying the herd and mooing back playfully as the middle-eastern attendant watched him through the window from inside. Fearful of the credit-card skimmers, Morgan walked inside to prepay as a black Humvee with heavy limousine-tinted windows turned into the station and pulled in behind his AMG to gas up.

"Lemme get fifty bucks wortho' premium on pump #3, there," pointing over his shoulder with his thumb, "...and three of them there jalapeno Slim Jims, podna," said Morgan to the clerk in his cheesy imitation of a redneck twang. When in Hogtown, do as the rednecks do, he figured.

The clerk nodded politely and rang up his purchase as he leaned to one side and peered out at the pumps outside. "That guy's checking out your car," he said with his Indian accent, gesturing toward his black Benz as the man outside climbed back into his Humvee.

Morgan turned in time to see the Humvee drive away, unable to ID the driver through the heavy window tint. Replying with his ego instead of his brain, he said, "Pretty common, actually. It's a 550 AMG with some custom features. Gets a lot of attention." Morgan thought about it again. "By the way, that guy get any gas?" Two years of working inside the cartel made him privy to their techniques, and it made him suspicious but gave him an idea.

The young clerk took a moment to check his cameras and computer screens. "Ah...not sure. Don't think so." Handing Morgan the Slim Jims and credit card receipt, he asked, "Anything else for you today?"

Morgan pulled out a hundred dollar bill and held it up, shifting into his game-show-host routine. "I'll give you a hundred bucks if you can start my AMG on your first try." He pushed the key across the counter, and the college-age clerk eyed the bill before looking up at Morgan with joy-filled eyes, certain it would be the easiest C-note he'd ever make.

"You're on." The young man eagerly plucked the bill out of Morgan's hand and came from behind the counter to demonstrate his knowledge of electronic car keys. Morgan put on his best dumb-blonde act as he watched the clerk take the bait. Bustling his way out the door, over his shoulder, the young clerk confidently added, "My dad's a doctor at Shands and he drives a new Mercedes." Holding the bill up high, the clerk added, "I'll put it toward my med school tuition."

Nervous about the Humvee, Morgan stayed back, watching from inside just in case, hoping his hunch was wrong, hoping his car wouldn't go up in flames. The clerk opened the driver's door and climbed inside, and Morgan held his breath. Within seconds, the nervous attorney heard the big V-8 start up. Relieved beyond words, he watched as the clerk exited his AMG with a big grin as he thumped the top with his outstretched arm. Waving his trophy $100 bill in the air, he gestured for Morgan to come and claim his car. "Piece o'cake," said the gas station clerk.

With his fears now alleviated, Morgan joined the clerk at the pump outside, giving his new-found buddy a celebratory fist bump as he grabbed the hose and pushed the PREMIUM button. What's a C-note when your life's at stake, he asked himself. "Congratulations. I didn't get your name," said Morgan.

"It's Ahirbudhnya, but you may call me *Bob*," he answered with his Indian accent and a big smile.

Morgan shook his head, amused at all the "Bobs", "Jims" and "Bills" of Indian descent he'd spoken to on the phone with companies that outsourced their customer service to the other side of the world. "Bob" smiled, waving the $100 bill again. "Thanks. You made my day."

"So, what area of medicine are you studying, Boberino?"

"Plastic surgery," he answered, "...to keep abreast of the situation," he joked, heading inside to answer the phone.

Morgan laughed and squeezed the pump handle harder to speed things up, weary of slapping the scores of mosquitos that seemed hell bent on giving him an unwanted blood transfusion. Nineteen gallons of 91 octane later, Morgan slid back behind the wheel of his AMG and waved goodbye to "Bob" and all the malcontented cows, heading south again on I-75.

Twenty-eight miles north of Ocala, he rehearsed what he would say to Rosa, confident he could patch things up and make it all about the money. Now he felt a little foolish over being so paranoid about the Humvee earlier. He replayed his earlier fantasy of Stella straddling him in the Jacuzzi, sparking his desire for some rock and roll. Now that her marriage was on the rocks, he was more confident than ever that his fantasy would actually come true. Dan, you really don't deserve her, he thought. He reached for the XM Sirius satellite radio button and dialed up some classic rock, striking it rich as Led Zeppelin's *Stairway to Heaven* filled the interior. Morgan sang along, blissfully thumping the steering wheel in rhythm to the melody, with the lyrics "...and she's buying the stairway...to hea-ven" echoing in his ears.

Glancing in the rear view mirror, he spotted what looked like a black Humvee following a quarter mile behind and did a double take, glaring at the sordid-looking vehicle following him. *Sonofabitch. No way.*

His fantasy and good vibes evaporated, out of fear he stomped on the accelerator. He watched the speedometer climb from 80 to 130 mph in his attempt to leave the Humvee behind as it receded in the rear view mirror. At first he felt giddy about being able to outrun it, then his heart filled with dread as the sinister-looking Humvee followed suit, speeding up and matching his speed, even closing the distance between them slightly. Obviously, it was no ordinary Humvee.

Suddenly, he saw a flash of light in the rear view mirror and sparks filled the interior as his rear window and instrument panel exploded. Morgan felt a massive concussion from under the car, and he was thrown violently into the roof like a rag doll, the windows shattering, his AMG bursting into flames. The last thing he heard were the final lyrics to *Stairway to Heaven*.

A hundred yards behind Morgan's AMG, the Humvee driver handed the remote detonator to the man seated next to him as the four men in black suits watched the car veer out of control and roll over five or six times as it crashed over the guardrail. The men continued to watch as the AMG plowed through a barbed-wire fence and came to a rest in a cow pasture, a flaming pile of twisted metal. Slowing to 60 mph, the Humvee driver veered to avoid a slower vehicle as several pieces of wreckage scattered over the roadway and came to a rest in the southbound lanes of I-75. A hundred yards further south, the black Humvee suddenly braked and did a U-turn across the median before joining a parade of three other cars and a pick-up truck that had slowed to a crawl to rubber-neck the flaming wreckage.

A middle-aged man in an older red pick-up truck with gun racks in the back window swerved and stopped his F-150 to render aid. Wearing a Roy Rodgers pearl-button flannel shirt, the tattooed pick-up truck driver jumped out with a cell phone to his ear as a pile of empty beer cans tumbled out of the truck and into the swale at his feet. A little unsteady on his feet, the man continued to shout into the phone, then sniffed the air like a bloodhound as he carried on a frantic conversation with authorities.

Redneck: "Yeah, I'm tellin' ya it just blew up!"

911 dispatcher: "Sir, can you see any survivors?"

Redneck: "Ya jerkin' me? The car was doing 'bout a hundred forty...and it jus' exploded in a balla flame"-

911 dispatcher: "Sir, can you give me your location?"

Redneck: "Yeah, c'mon southa Hogtown 'bout five clicks, jus' sniff 'til ya smell burnin' flesh, then ya turn right at the plume'o black smoke."

911 dispatcher: "Sir, no reason to be a wise guy. Can you tell me what you see?"

Redneck: "Yeah, burnin' car in a cow pasture, and 'bout twenny head'a cattle scared outa their minds, ready ta bolt out onnta the highway. Better get here quick or Farmer John's gonna loose some prime beefsteaks."

911 dispatcher: "Sir, yeah...well we don't want that mess."

Redneck: "Well, if'n it ain't a mess awready, it'll sure do 'til the mess gets here!"

911 dispatcher: "Sir, I need your name."

Redneck: "Virgil...ah..." Virgil was feeling a little tipsy, maybe even drunk. Headed north from a nude dance club in Ocala called The Pink Pussycat, he'd just pounded down a six-pack of Old Milwaukee on top of imbibing in five or six shots of Wild Turkey. With an outstanding warrant for skipping out on his bail after driving drunk on a John Deere lawnmower down the middle of State Road 441 last month, he was in no hurry to divulge his identity. A truck pulling a backhoe zipped passed him heading in the opposite direction. "Ah...Virgil Backhoe."

911 dispatcher: "Virgil Backhoe?" The 911 operator thought it might have been an Indian name. "Sir, did you say 'Backhoe'?"

Virgil jumped back in his F-150 and slammed the door, still on his phone. "Yeah, Backhoe. Tell the highway patrol it's the same spot where the cops arrested that woman doin' yoga poses in her panties las' week." Virgil thought he'd given them enough information and thought it best to hang up, tossing the phone into the seat next to him as he hit the truck's accelerator.

Moments after Virgil had peeled out and headed north on his way back to his doublewide in Gainesville, Salamonaca and three other well-dressed men in the Humvee pulled up to a pile of empty Old Milwaukee cans in the swale as they studied the flaming wreckage in the twilight. The four men leaned forward to scan the wreck for signs of life as a plume of black smoke rose a hundred feet in the air. The four men stayed put inside the vehicle, craning their necks for any hint of movement as they watched the gas tank catch fire and the tires begin to burn.

Satisfied there were no survivors, the black Humvee drove back onto the pavement and resumed its drive north on I-75 at a modest speed, on its way to the Florida panhandle to pick up an important package.

CHAPTER EIGHTEEN

I nside *Bella Rosa's* engine room, Rosa's chief interrogator stood over Wilde with a 20-pound pipe wrench in his hand, a man they called Troll. While the yacht's mechanical systems whirred and hummed around them, Rosa, his lieutenant Vasquez, and the big man who resembled a bear wanted some answers. Still hooded, Wilde was propped against the bulkhead, his arms raised over his head by steel cuffs and chains while Troll continued to tap his survival knife menacingly against Wilde's bare knee as he towered over his victim with his six-foot-seven, 385-pound woolly body. With the drugs wearing off, the welts on Wilde's face and bruises on his head began to throb painfully. Several hours earlier, Vasquez had shot him full of fentanyl and scopolamine to soften him up and loosen his tongue, and the man who was once on his way to becoming Rosa's partner was beginning to regain a painful state of consciousness.

Not the best looking man to lay eyes on, Troll had a head like a dinosaur, his body matted with hair so thick he perspired even in mild weather. Standing in front of Wilde, he closed his fists and studied his skinned knuckles, still ticked off about a hunter mistaking him for a wild boar a month earlier and shooting him with a 30-caliber rifle somewhere up in the hills of Juarez. The heat from the engine room was causing him to perspire so profusely he dripped like a giant tree after a rainstorm. Sweat dripped off his nose and onto the knife blade as he entertained the thought of shredding Wilde's hospital gown but held back and waited for further instructions from his boss.

The pain from the bullet lodged in his right buttock was still so uncomfortable that he'd been forced to give up his job as a rough neck on the only working oil rig in Juarez. A crack-head friend suggested he try propofol, a powerful liquid painkiller used during major surgery, which also came in convenient easy-to-use topical skin patches normally prescribed for use by terminally-ill cancer patients. One way or another, Troll was determined to acquire the narcotics that had the power to put a stop to the constant pain in his ass, and he couldn't care less how he did it.

Unable to afford health insurance or a doctor's prescription, one of the few skills Troll *was* adept at was the art of breaking and entering, which he practiced weekly at poorly-secured nursing homes in the Margate and Tamarac area. During the wee hours of the morning, when security was lax, Troll would sneak in and routinely remove the propofol patches from sedated cancer patients in the hospice wards and apply them generously to his own shaggy torso. Within a week he became so addicted that he had to increase the dosage to levels that would ordinarily have killed a more highly evolved *homo sapien*. Unfortunately, Troll was so hopelessly addicted to the painkillers that he would often become delirious, drooling and passing out behind his trailer park's trash receptacles while dumpster diving, which is where Rosa's men found the hairy beast one day. Before becoming employed by the Juarez cartel as an enforcer, dumpster diving had been his favorite hobby. One of the fringe benefits of being on the cartel's payroll was a plentiful supply of narcotics, which suited him even better than having health insurance. With his new all-cash pay plan, unlimited supply of powerful painkillers and other advantages of working for the cartel, Troll no longer missed his old job in the oil fields or the 401-K that went with it.

Fresh from a round of golf at Ft. Lauderdale Country Club, Rosa entered the engine room still clad in his colorful golf attire. To Troll he said, "Take his hood off. I want to look him in the eye." Heeding his master's voice, Troll jerked his hood off while Vasquez tried to revive him as he held a pocket flashlight up to his eyes. Gradually coming around from the heavy doses of scopolamine and fentanyl, a woozy Daniel Wilde slowly focused on Rosa's face as the big Mexican drug lord leaned over him menacingly.

"Hey, buddy," began Rosa, "...the *plan* was to have your wife committed so you and Morgan could take control of her family trust account-*not* to use my money to rip me off. What went wrong, buddy?" With the cold black eyes of a great white shark, Rosa glared at his hostage. "What was it about loyalty didn't you understand?"

As he came around, a remorseful Wilde struggled to enunciate his response, his speech still slurred by the stroke he suffered. "Emilio, eh"-

Angry over his lack of respect, Vasquez grabbed him by the hair and pointed to his boss. "It's *don Rosa*, gringo. SAY HIS NAME!"

Wilde struggled to placate their anger. "Eh Da...Don Rosa... eh"-

Rosa grasped Vasquez's arm and pulled him back. "Let him talk, Javier. I want to hear how he screwed this up." Vasquez took a step back, shaking the chains to make sure they were still securely bolted to the generator bulkhead. Troll stood behind them menacingly with the knife in one hand while he scratched an itch between his shoulder blades with the 20-pound pipe wrench.

Wilde had heard all the grotesque stories of cartel interrogations and knew his life was on the line. Fearful that he was past the point of any reconciliation, and fearing the loss of his fingers and teeth one by one, he forced himself to try and articulate his words to express his regret. With the scopolamine in his system, the truth of his actions began to emerge, but the reasons for them remained ambiguous to his three captors. "Meh wife wah wearing a wire, don Rosa, knew 'bout you fra FBI." His expression was one of deep regret. "Eh ha no ch...choice. No choice, en I pray f...fer yer...divine justice," shaking his head.

Rosa looked at him in disgust. "Danny boy, there *is* no divine justice. If there was, you'd already be dead, buddy." Wilde had no reply. "And the 500 kilos of coke you bought from the Columbians with my money? I suppose you had no choice in that either, huh buddy? Tell me why I shouldn't put a bullet in your head right now." His eyes pleading for mercy, Wilde was at a loss for words.

Rosa nodded at Vasquez and reached for the Band-Aid tin full of teeth, shaking it in Wilde's face before he opened it and poured the contents onto the floor. Horrified, Wilde watched them bounce and scatter around his feet. "You know what these are, right, Danny boy?" pointing at the teeth littering the floor. "Now, I want to know where the flash drive is with your wife's bank passcodes. I know you have it." He reached for the vise grips from

Vasquez and held them in Wilde's face. "Don't make me do this, Danny boy."

With few cards to play, Wilde looked up at his tormentor with as much genuine sorrow and regret that he could muster, unsure if giving Rosa the information he wanted would save his life. "Ca… Carol took eh…ah ma keych…chain," he stuttered. "Ah da 'ospital."

"Carol McAllister?" asked Rosa, squinting at his victim. "You know she's no longer on the right side of the grass, so to speak, right Danny boy?" Troll continued to swing the serrated survival knife in his direction. "Your girlfriend had a *lee-tle* problem with a dump truck," he added.

Wilde nodded and hung his head, his eyes tearing as he thought about Carol. "Sha put dem in meh floor sef. Ah meh beach house."

Vasquez turned to his boss. "*That's* why Ramone didn't find them in his hospital room."

"You think he's lying?" asked Rosa under his breath.

Vasquez clarified the effects of scopolamine. "The truth drug works 90% of the time." He nodded toward Wilde. "He's not resisting. He's trying to save his skin." Behind them, the huge generator shuddered and went into a quieter standby mode, and suddenly it was easier for the three men to hear.

Rosa nodded in agreement with Vasquez and glanced at Wilde, rubbing his hand over his two-day stubble before reaching a decision on what to do with the traitor. An idea emerged on how he could use Wilde to give him more leverage. "Give him another shot of fentanyl, and keep him on ice until I decide what to do with him," handing Vasquez back the vise grips. "He may be of further use to us."

Rosa stepped toward the engine room exit before turning to Vasquez. "I want you and Troll to, what does the FBI call it when they do it...toss? I want you two to toss Villa Dellacroix for that flash drive. And, if it's not there, then check Carol McAllister's car at the Vero Beach Police compound." He waited for Vasquez to nod in agreement and pointed a finger at his lieutenant. "I want those bank codes."

"Si, Padron."

***

Just after sunset the same day, Mark McAllister had the urge to hit the beach for a quick five miler. Looking south toward Port Fierce, as he liked to call it, he adjusted his tan and fuchsia Bora Bora cap and tightened the draw string on his black Nike shorts. After completing his stretch, he strained his eyes to make out the lights of South Hutchinson Island outlining the spit of land to the south. He was alone on the beach as a soft southeasterly breeze blew across the water and distant lights on the horizon grew brighter in the twilight. In the distance he could see the navigational buoys begin their interval blinking as pelicans and ospreys soared to a safe haven for the coming night. He closed his eyes and took a deep breath, inhaling the sweet sea air and listening to the sounds of the seashore; the softly-breaking surf and mournful cries of seagulls in flight.

The surf seemed to break in synchrony with his stride as he bolted from Villa Riomar and headed north up the beach.

It was high tide, which put him higher up on the beach where the sand was softer and the footing more difficult, but a better workout for him if he could avoid spraining an ankle on one of the abandoned sand castles along the way. The mating calls of the cicadas were becoming louder with the gathering gloom, a sound his late wife loved listening to. Ready to restart his life, he forced himself to delve deeper into his imaginary crystal ball as he focused on the latest bizarre events at the Wilde residence.

Passing Villa Dellacroix, the estate looked dark and foreboding with only the soft glow of security lights. With no one home, he figured Dan must still be in the hospital and Stella locked up at Chatahootchee; all in all, events far more bizarre than what he'd imagined when they moved in two months earlier. His thoughts turned to Stella, with her stunning green eyes that seemed to take everything in, missing nothing, eyes that drew him into another universe.

His breathing deepened by the time he reached Humiston Park, and his rhythm settled into a smooth and easy cadence. In the distance he saw a loggerhead turtle struggling to crawl her way up the beach to lay her eggs, early with her delivery. The loggerheads usually waited until mid-summer to unload their treasure of eggs, and as high up on the beach as they could climb. No worries, he thought. By 7 a.m. the Turtle Patrol would have the new nest staked out and cordoned off in brightly-colored tape to keep the tourists away from her future hatchlings.

"Mark! Up here!" The group of four Vero Beach lifeguards that were so popular with the ladies stood at the aluminum railing in front of their office. John was waving as Vince, Rokas and Sean held binoculars, studying something in the surf further out.

He shaded his eyes and gazed out to sea, wondering which senior citizen had lost his Depends in the surf today before bounding up the stairway to see what dire emergency had captured their attention.

"What's up, guys?"

Vince adjusted the focus as sea spray obscured the view. "Some nut case is out there in six-foot seas, way too far out." John hit the air horn three more times, Mark wincing from the ear-shattering noise, wondering if they could hear it in Utah. John blew it again, hoping they could get the swimmer's attention over the roar of the surf as Vince handed the binoculars to Mark for a peek at the drama unfolding. "What do you think he's doin' out there, anyway?" Vince asked.

Mark focused on the errant swimmer struggling to make headway in the heavy surf. "Umm…looks like the backstroke," handing the binoculars back to Vince with a smile.

The guards chuckled as Vince grabbed the binoculars. "Gimme those, wiseguy. Sean, take the paddleboard out there and bring him in."

Ready to keep moving, Mark couldn't help noticing the odd-looking, club-footed octogenarian with the hump on his back who always sat on the boardwalk bench closest to the stairway. There, he would sit and leer at the bikini-clad girls coming and going. The perv they called "Elmo" was the subject of at least two complaints from young girls each week. He had a perverse habit of sitting in his blue Honda Civic and pleasuring himself until someone would approach his car. "Is Elmo behaving himself today?" inquired Mark.

"You mean apart from running back and forth, flushing all the toilets, turning on the bathroom hand dryers ten times a day and leering at all the fifteen-year-olds?" replied Vince.

They all gave one last look at Elmo sitting on the bench, waiting for his next victim. "Sounds like you guys got this under control. See you in five miles," jumping down on the beach to finish the northern leg of his run.

Minutes later, he reached the Vero Beach Resort where the reggae music floated from the outside bar at Cobalt as the lights of the hotel illuminated couples roaming toward the beach looking to share an intimate moment. Next, he came upon the twin towers of Village Spires, the tallest structures in Vero, where he remembered playing tennis with a former girlfriend from Boca on the condo's clay courts many years earlier. Marianne Something, he recalled, and she'd really knocked his balls around on that trip. He remembered losing to her hugely on the courts with the intention of winning big in the bedroom. It was a fond memory of Marianne, and about the last time he could remember playing tennis with more than two fuzzy balls.

The next beachfront marvel along the way was a row of two-story Mediterranean-style McMansions with barrel-tile roofs and graceful arches supported by classical Ionic and Corinthian columns. The five McMansions were nestled near the purest example of neo-Frank Lloyd Wright architecture to be seen in Vero, a concrete behemoth of 8,000 sq. ft. With its glass front, right angles and straight clean lines, the monstrous home was an elegant fortress that looked like it could withstand anything Mother Nature could throw at it.

Finished running the eight sets of stairways at Jaycee Park, he hit the beach again, passing the Ocean Club series of condos, then the upscale four-story Caledon, with its rounded corners and graceful curves. Sea Quay followed next, the only condo in Vero with its very own iconic concrete pier where so many would pose for photos. Having reached his halfway point, Mark rounded the tall pre-cast concrete legs of the pier as he turned to head back. The night was encroaching, and he knew from experience that avoiding shells, sharp objects and holes dug by kids in the dark would become more difficult to avoid as the light faded.

It was two miles further south at Mulligan's when he heard the barking dog, a familiar bark, one he hadn't heard since getting shot in Boca during his encounter with the fugitive Tommy Tomlinson. But that was two years ago, and the chances of hooking up again with his favorite black Labrador seemed remote to him, especially in a city a hundred miles further north.

"Mark! Mark McAllister!" He recognized Megan's voice and looked around the beach. "Over here," shouted Megan, standing and waving from a beachside table at Mulligan's. Bailey was barking and straining at his leash, wanting to break free and romp with the man who saved his master years earlier. Mark trotted up the stairs and over to her table. Dressed in shorts and a low-cut blouse, the attractive former secretary at Nautilus Realty in Boca Beach gave him a huge hug, and Bailey jumped up to join in. "How are you? Haven't seen you in years. You look great!" she said.

"Walkin' and talkin', still on the right side of the grass, dear girl," smiling as he squatted to pet his favorite canine. Bailey yipped away, pawing him and licking his salty arm. "Watcha doin' in Vero?" he asked, scratching Bailey's chin.

"Meet my mom," gesturing to the well-dressed woman in her 70s waiting to be introduced. After apologizing for his appearance and sharing some chit-chat with Megan and her mother, he heard a voice from behind.

"Sir, I'm sorry," said the waitress, "...but you have to be wearing a shirt to be here."

"No worries," said Mark, turning to explain, "...just saying hello. I'll be gone in 60 seconds." He could tell Bailey was ready to hit the beach. The big black Lab shared a bond with Mark that words could never describe, and Mark was convinced they shared a kind of telepathic connection.

Megan said, "I've been reading about your trip around the world on *Dream Girl*. How's your latest novel coming?"

"It's developing," he said, not wanting to be too specific. Bailey kept pulling against his leash, anxious for a romp. "Hey, while you and your mom finish your blackened dolphin and pina coladas, mind if I take Bailey for a run? I can have him back to you in a half hour."

Megan smiled at the thought of reuniting the two heroes from her ordeal in Boca years earlier and handed him Bailey's leash. "Sure," she said. "Looks like he's ready. I haven't had a chance to walk him today." Bailey barked his approval and pawed him a high five.

"Be back in a half hour," taking his leash. "C'mon, boy." Bailey didn't need to be asked twice, and together they bounded down the steps and hit the beach running. About a quarter-mile down the beach, when he thought no one was looking, Mark unclipped Bailey's leash to let him run free. The frisky canine bolted, happily chasing down sandpipers through the surf and flying frisbees with equal enthusiasm before returning to Mark's side, panting loudly.

Villa Dellacroix loomed ahead, and as they approached the estate home, Bailey stopped, pointed and began barking loudly. From the dog's reaction, Mark could tell something wasn't right and followed Bailey up the dunes to take a peek, knowing the Lab had a nose for trouble. Under the dim security lights, Mark did a double take as he saw what appeared to be a bear run out the courtyard gate on two legs, then down the brick paver driveway. Refocusing, he realized it wasn't a bear, but a huge hairy man who was running toward the street. Unable to see the car that waited at the end of the driveway from the top of the dune, Mark yelled for Bailey to come back, fearing for the dog's safety. Then he heard a door slam and a car speed off to the south past Villa Riomar. What had Bailey gotten him into?

"Bailey, here boy." Bailey returned to his side, barking furiously as Mark held him and reattached his leash before he could bolt again. Then all hell broke loose as the audible phase of the burglar alarm went off and the security lights inside the home began flashing, the alarm siren wailing loudly. An eerie feeling came over him as he realized there'd been a break-in at his neighbor's house. The telltale wail of police sirens escalated from far off in the distance, and Mark was conflicted over whether to stay and help the cops or head next door to check and see if his own home at Villa Riomar had been broken into. Choosing to wait near the Wilde's pool for the inevitable arrival of the men in blue, he bent to pet the joyously oblivious black Lab standing at his side.

A commanding male voice shouted: "Freeze! Police! Put your hands on your head and kneel. Now!" Mark hesitated, uncomfortable with being treated like a criminal. The same voice, only closer; "On your knees NOW!"

Confused, Mark did as he was instructed, still holding Bailey's leash over his head. "Woah! Guys, lighten up. I'm an author, not a burglar!" pleaded Mark with his hands on his head. Bailey whined and laid down beside him as the dog covered his eyes with his paws. Not wanting to be shot by accident, Mark continued to explain. "Guys, I'm not the perp. I'm the next door neighbor." Amazed at their response time, "How'd you get here so fast?"

The responding officer circled Mark, squaring off with him, keeping his Glock pointed. "We got a tip. Don't move until we get this sorted out," he said. The muscle-bound young officer had closely-cropped hair, sergeant stripes and wore a badge that read "Sgt. Huddleston". Obviously experienced at responding to B & E calls, the sergeant seemed like a no-nonsense guy. A second officer approached from across the pool courtyard holding a computer tablet in one hand and a 9mm Beretta in the other.

"The place's been tossed, Chris," said the second officer as he joined them. "This is where that drug zombie stabbed her husband." He did a slow survey of the pool, grounds and courtyard. "Nice place." He gestured toward Mark with his gun. "Okay. Who are you?"

"Mark McAllister," he replied, looking first at the sergeant still pointing his .40 cal. Glock at him, then back to the second cop. "A friend of the drug zombie that stabbed her husband." The two officers continued to glare at him, skeptical of his answer. "I live next door at Villa Riomar," he continued. Eyeing his outfit, the second officer holstered his weapon and entered Mark's name into his tablet.

"You say you live on Ocean Boulevard?" asked the cop.

"Yessir."

"We'll get all this straightened out." After a moment studying the screen, he said, "Got his FDL photo here, Chris. 596 South Ocean Boulevard. Look's like he's telling the truth."

"Okay, stand up," said a slightly annoyed Sgt. Huddleston as he holstered his gun, obviously disappointed that he'd collared a neighbor instead of a perp. "What're you doing here, Mr. McAllister? Don't tell me you were monitoring your police radio," he added with a grimace.

Bailey uncovered his eyes and sat up at Mark's side, looking up to him for directions. "I was taking a run with Bailey here when he began barking," scratching Bailey's chin. "He's got a nose for trouble, so I followed him here." Sgt. Huddleston took out his pad and began making notations. "We got lucky and captured a serial killer together in Boca a coupla years back," added Mark as he gave his favorite canine a big hug. "This dog's got talent."

"Tommy Tomlinson," said the second officer reading his tablet, "…three years ago on South Boca Beach. It's all right here on Google," he said, holding up the device and reading the article. "Jeez, says here you got a $17 million reward?" The sergeant was incredulous.

"Yessir," said Mark, "…along with a bullet wound to the face."

"For $17 million, I'd take a bullet in the *balls*," said the officer.

"Well, I didn't exactly have a choice in the matter."

The second cop stepped up and introduced himself. "Sorry about the mistaken identity, Mr. McAllister," extending his hand with a smile. "Corporal Dave Murdock," handing the tablet off to Sgt. Huddleston. "Chris, check it out. We got us a real live hero here, buddy."

Mark shook his hand. "Not sure about the hero part, but getting shot again was not on my 'to do' list."

Sgt. Huddleston asked, "What did you see here, Mr. McAllister?"

"I caught a glimpse of what looked like a running bear, then realized it was probably the perp running to the getaway"-

"A bear?" questioned Huddleston. "Musta been pretty hairy."

"Well, it was from back there," pointing behind him, "...and I don't run with my best pair of glasses," he added apologetically. "I think you'll find Mr. Wilde at St. Mary's recovering from a stab wound, and Mrs. Wilde at a psych hospital in the panhandle."

"And all this time I thought this was a nice neighborhood," replied Huddleston with raised eyebrows.

Ignoring the sergeant's comment, Mark turned toward his home, wondering if Villa Riomar had also been broken into. "Would one of you guys be willing to accompany us over to my house to check on things?" looking at one officer, then the other. "I didn't leave the alarm on."

Finished with his update of the Tommy Tomlinson saga on Murdock's tablet, Huddleston handed it back to his corporal. "Go with him, Dave. Take the rest of his statement while you're over there. I'll handle the forensics here," said the sergeant as he head-ed back inside to meet the lab team that was on the way.

Officer Murdock turned to the author and said, "C'mon, Mr. McAllister. Stay behind me. We don't need any dead heroes. Let's go check on your house." Exiting the Wilde's pool courtyard, they headed next door to Villa Riomar with the officer in the lead. After a quick inspection of the home and determining it was safe, Murdock holstered his weapon. "You are one lucky man, Mr. McAllister. You could've been shot."

Mark thought about the officer's comment. "Or trampled by a runaway bear," he cracked. Indeed, he did feel lucky that his place hadn't been broken into but wondered why the burglars had tar-geted his neighbor's estate. They must have known there was an alarm system.

"Maybe I'll take advantage of my lucky streak and go skydiving tomorrow."

CHAPTER NINETEEN

The black Ford Taurus turned into the parking lot at Chatahootchee State Hospital and pulled into a space marked "LAW
ENFORCEMENT ONLY". It was a cloudy day in June as the three
clean-cut men dressed in dark suits with FBI badges exited the vehicle and strode briskly up the red-brick steps. The balding older
agent in charge pulled an envelope out of his coat pocket as he
surveyed the red brick building he was about to enter. Looking in-
distinguishable from so many other red brick buildings in the area,
he noticed the peeling eaves and fascia were badly in need of a coat
of paint as the three men entered the building and presented their
IDs to the rotund security guard waiting behind the counter.

"Special Agent Vasquez, here to move Stella Louise Wilde to
a new facility," holding up his FBI badge and writ. "These are my
orders signed by District Manager Greenberg to remand her."

The portly 50-ish guard wearing a brass badge with the name
"GREELEY" printed on it gave Vasquez a quizzical look. "Why are
you taking her?"

In a hurry to get back on the road, Vasquez had little patience with cop-wannabees. "She's no longer safe here," he stated flatly. The other two agents shifted their weight nervously, waiting to hear Greeley's response. "This is Agent Blake and Agent Sorvino," added Vasquez, the men quickly flashing their badges.

Feeling intimidated, Greeley became a little skittish, unaccustomed to such high-level attention to his turf. Convinced the employment application he submitted a month ago to the FBI was still under consideration, Greeley gave the badges a cursory glance before nodding his approval. "Harvey, go get Mrs. Wilde," he said to the orderly clad in a white uniform. "Help her gather her things, and tell her the FBI's here to move her to another facility. I'm sure she'll be happy to hear the news."

The matronly older receptionist with her hair in a bun brought up the patient file on her computer to assist with the transfer, adjusting her glasses to read the schedule. "Harvey, Mrs. Wilde should be in the rec room playing bingo with the Alzheimer patients," she said over her shoulder. To the agents, she shrugged and added, "She likes to win." Harvey nodded and headed through the double doors toward the rec room, already feeling sorry over losing his favorite patient. Eye candy at the institution was hard to come by.

Anxious to hit the road with Stella in custody, Vasquez intervened and took advantage of Greeley's agreeable attitude. "She won't need a thing, Officer," he said in a patronizing tone. "Would you tell Harvey just to bring Mrs. Wilde? We have her things in the car and we'll be taking care of everything else," he assured the guard.

"Right away, Agent Vasquez," said Greeley, happy to be a part of the team. He turned smartly in his patent leather shoes to track down Harvey and retrieve their most popular patient.

Moments later, Stella Wilde appeared at the counter, accompanied by Greeley and the orderly. Strawberry-blonde hair perfectly coiffured, she wore a teal-colored sundress with giant yellow flowers, her stunning green eyes dancing with joy at the thought of finally leaving Chatahootchee State Hospital after weeks of tortuous confinement. Still, she was cautious, given the hard lessons learned at the hands of law enforcement. To Agent Vasquez, she asked, "Did Special Agent Beretto call you?" remembering Morgan's promise to call Beretto on his way back to Vero. Her mistrust of federal agents was front and center, and she studied their faces carefully for clues about what kind of treatment was in store for her.

Vasquez had done some homework and knew about Hank Greenberg, but he had no idea who Beretto was. Thinking on his feet, he touched his forehead as if his name had just come to mind and went with the flow. "Ah...yeah, I think he was the one who spoke to my boss, District Manager Greenberg," hoping his comment would put her at ease. He reached for Stella as she stepped cautiously from behind the counter. "I'm Special Agent Vasquez," flashing his ID, "...and this is Agent Blake and Agent Sorvino." Stella was hesitant. Something seemed a little off. "Ma'am, if you'll please come with us, we need to get you out of here as quickly as possible." Blake and Sorvino took her arms to lead her out, but Stella stopped before reaching the front door.

"What's the rush?" she asked in her best dumb-blonde act.

"You're no longer safe here," said Vasquez. She waited for him to explain further. "We're taking you to a safe house." The two agents beside her tightened their grip on her arms as they continued to lead her out the door. Stella stopped them in the doorway.

"What safe house?" she wanted to know, straining against the grip on her arms. Vasquez winced at the question. "I have a right to know where we're going," she insisted.

Vasquez clarified their intentions. "Ma'am, for your protection," nodding toward the hospital staff standing by, "... we can't say until we're on the road." His answer was purposely vague, but it seemed logical, given the circumstances. And, it was the one answer that would persuade her it was safe to get in the car with the three men.

She slid into the back seat of the black Ford Taurus, wedged between Vasquez and Sorvino while Blake occupied the driver's seat. The three men were soon captivated by her good looks and sensual moves, and Stella was ebullient to finally be free of Chatahootchee as she proceeded to hold court. Soon, she had the three eating out of her hand as she joked about Crazy Larry always wacking off around her, and the stories of Aunt Veola running amuck, promising to divulge the whereabouts of her uncle Jimmy Hoffa's gravesite. After weeks of dealing with wackos, she allowed herself to relax with her FBI hosts, milking their attention by letting her dress ride up her taut thighs just enough to keep them interested and focused on fantasy instead of the facts that she intended to wring from them. There were details about the men that troubled her. She noticed the lamination peeling from Sorvino's badge as if it were artificially layered over something else, and it seemed odd to her. Obviously, they weren't cut from the same bolt of cloth as other Quantico graduates she'd met, so she continued to carefully draw them out. Maybe they were special ops. She intended to find out.

The strawberry-blonde beauty leaned close to Sorvino with her story; "When I was a girl growing up in Dallas, my daddy taught me how to shoot skeet and gave me a Walther PPK for personal protection. At the Dallas Gun Club. I took first place in my age group." Crossing her legs invitingly, she continued. "You know...a .380 auto, the gun James Bond liked to use."

Quietly amused, Sorvino looked at her and gave her a crooked smile. Behind the wheel, Blake watched her in the rear view mirror as he prepared to exit I-10 east onto I-75 south while Sorvino continued staring at her legs like a Neanderthal in heat. Giving his anatomical fantasy about her full reign, the only response he could muster was, "Really? First place, huh?"

"Yup. I took first place at the 4-H Pistol Competition when I was 16," she proudly informed him, hoping he would take the bait as Vasquez gazed out the window at the rows of potato plants flying by at 80 miles an hour. As the eldest of the three men, Vasquez felt it somewhat indignant to compete with a younger man for her attention.

To Sorvino she said, "It held eight rounds. You know it?"

Sorvino gave her the same crooked smile, unable to take his eyes from her as the Taurus hurtled down the road past farm after farm of planted soybeans and potato plants. "Yeah, I know it. I wear one on my ankle for back-up." Looking to impress her, he removed the stainless PPK from his ankle holster to show her. He popped the clip out and ejected the cartridge in the chamber before presenting it for her inspection, catching the bullet in mid-air.

"Like it?" he asked her. Oddly, she noticed the serial number had been filed off the automatic and the barrel threaded to accept a silencer. She wondered why an FBI agent would use an automatic with no serial number and fitted for a silencer. "Best-power-to-size ratio of any automatic made," he boasted, obviously proud of his back-up weapon. Sorvino smiled, replacing the clip by giving it an authoritative smack with the heel of his hand. It made her nervous to see him chamber a round before holstering it again on his ankle.

She gave him a forced smile. "Nice," was all she said as Sorvino nodded to her. Unsettled over the missing serial number and silencer threadings, she became sullen as she thought about her options. The men were beginning to seem more like mercenaries than Quantico grads.

Vasquez leaned forward in his seat and pointed ahead to the exit he directed Blake to take. "This is where we pick up the boss and drop off the rental," said Vasquez. "Security precaution," he explained to Stella who nodded hesitantly.

Taking the exit and crossing through the next intersection, Blake drove the Taurus to the far side of the car rental lot next to the Hardees before switching off the ignition. He placed the keys over the sun visor, then turned around to address the three passengers in the back seat. "Burger anyone?" Stella shook her head as she stared out the window, wondering about the black Humvee with the dark limousine tint parked two spaces over. She noticed a peculiar array of antennas on the roof that she'd never seen before; one short-wave radio, one corkscrew-type, and a miniature aerodynamic satellite receiver like the one on her family's sailboat. Very stealthy and high-tech, she thought, but it bothered her that the Humvee didn't resemble a law enforcement vehicle.

She continued to study the Humvee. "Is that our next ride?" she asked. She heard one of the men reply with a "yup." She really wanted to trust these guys but was feeling like she might be stuck with the "B" team.

Sorvino grabbed her arm to help her out as Vasquez stepped away from the car, talking with someone on his cell phone in a very hush-hush manner. "Let's go, honey. The boss is waiting," said Sorvino. Finished with his call, Vasquez held the door of the Humvee open for her as she climbed into the back seat, locking eyes with him for a second before the doors slammed shut. Blake flipped the lock button from the driver's seat, securing all the doors. Suddenly feeling trapped, she glanced behind her at a roll of duct tape and two black duffle bags in the cargo area.

Vasquez leaned forward and, to the man sitting up front in the passenger seat, he said, "Boss, do you remember the beautiful Stella Wilde?" The man who wore a black pork pie hat, Terminator-style sunglasses and blue jump suit turned to face his guest. To Stella, he looked vaguely familiar. She racked her brain to try and recall where she'd seen him before.

"Enchante, Mrs. Wilde. We met at Chatahootchee a while back," said the man she knew only as Gary. He tipped his hat in mock respect and gave her a twisted smile. "Through the glass window at the visitation booth, about a month ago." By the time it dawned on her, she was too late. Vasquez had already pulled out what looked like a flashlight with prongs from his coat pocket. Stella screamed and violently kicked the back of the seat as the men subdued her, her scream muffled by Sorvino's hand over her mouth as Vasquez stuck the stun gun into her bare armpit. She remembered biting his hand and screaming a second time before passing out as a hundred thousand volts coursed through her body and a million stars swirled in her head. Her last thought before she lost consciousness was why she ever trusted the FBI.

Vasquez and Sorvino took her limp body by the arms and legs and gently laid her out in the back of the Humvee's cargo area.

The men proceeded to cover her mouth and bind her wrists and ankles with duct tape as Salamonaca took a moment to look her over appreciatively. "Such a beautiful woman. The boss will be pleased that she is undamaged and free of bruises."

"Piece o'cake," said Vasquez, kneeling over her. "El Padron's favorite video is of *her*," he said to his crew boss, *"…gardening in the nude."* Entertaining his own fantasy about Stella, he brushed her strawberry-blonde hair away from her face as she lay unconscious. "He has it saved to his laptop," he added. Vasquez guessed her height at five-six, a perfect fit for the six-foot black duffle bag he picked up at Home Depot along with the buckets of QuikKrete. With Stella unconscious, bound and gagged in the back of the Humvee, his appetite had resurfaced.

"Now, who wants a burger before we hit the road for Bahia Mar?" he asked. "I'm buying."

***

On a sunny weekday morning, Mark was taking a break from scribing his new novel. Thankfully, his publisher hadn't given him a hard time about the pace of his work or the delays in returning texts and emails, apparently deciding to give him extra time to grieve. Though his home was untouched by the burglars who'd ransacked Villa Dellacroix, he felt genuinely creeped out by the burglary next door and needed a change of scenery. *Dream Girl* had always been a home away from home, his starship to other galaxies, his time machine that could always transport him to a better state of mind. So, he found himself driving to Pelican Yacht Club to spend a few days aboard her and catch up on his to-do list of light maintenance.

The author enjoyed tinkering with the mechanical and electrical systems on the boat, but he enjoyed sailing her even more, especially the episodes that only a female first mate can offer. But every experienced sailor knows a sailboat requires a bit more seamanship, and it was always advisable to have at least two seasoned sailors aboard, but not always easy to find available crew during the weekdays. Before the Wilde fiasco, Mark had entertained the idea of inviting the couple aboard for a day sail, but with the recent turn of events, that opportunity no longer seemed likely. Today, he busied himself with checking the sheets and standing rigging for signs of wear, and getting his boat organized for a day sail.

Rummaging about on deck, Mark heard the sound of street shoes stepping toward him on the dock as he coiled a line, giving each loop a perfect half-twist like he was taught in his first Coast Guard course twenty years ago. It was low tide, and he found himself shading his eyes and squinting up into the morning sun at a man wearing a dark suit standing next to the piling. "Mr. McAllister?" asked the stranger.

Given the recent crazy events of the past few weeks, Mark was cautious. "Depends on who's asking."

The man on the dock reached over and extended his hand. "Special Agent Dominic Beretto, FBI. I'm a big fan."

Mark hung the coil of Dacron line on a mast cleat, stepped to the port rail and reached to shake his hand. "Captain Mark McAllister of *Dream Girl.*" He figured if titles were getting thrown around today, he would offer one of his own.

Beretto gave him a polite mock salute. "May I come aboard, sir?"

Mark stared at his wingtips. "You'll need some deck shoes. Or just your socks." Curious about why the man had tracked him down at the yacht club, Mark remembered his name from his conversation with Stella and recalled that he was someone she trusted. He waved the man aboard. "Permission granted. Step on down, Agent Beretto."

Beretto reached down and respectfully untied his leather street shoes, setting them on the dock neatly next to the piling before stepping onto the fiberglass deck in his stocking feet. "Good morning. Will no shoes work, mon capitaine?" Mark liked his attitude.

"Bonjour. Bien sur," answered Mark. "Comment allez vous aujourd'hui?"

Beretto smiled. "Tres bien. Et vous?"

"They teach you French at Quantico?" asked Mark.

"No. Actually, that I learned as part of a classical education at Harvard Law."

"So, you came here all the way from Harvard Law to see me?"

"By way of Quantico."

Though Beretto was appreciating the banter, Mark continued to wonder about the reason for his visit. "Are you here as a fan or on official business, Agent Beretto?"

"I'll explain if you have a few minutes, Mr. McAllister." Beretto looked down at his stocking feet and wiggled his toes before looking up. "I have some unresolved accounting issues that I thought you might be able to help me with," he explained.

"Unresolved accounting issues, huh? Very cryptic, but for church and state, Agent Beretto, I have all the time you need. However, you should know that I'm often unable to account for myself, much less the issues of others, a bit short on patience and even shorter on money."

Beretto smiled and surveyed his surroundings. "Nice sailboat." Mark seemed unfazed with the flattery, so the agent added, "Nice yacht club, too."

"Home away from home," he said, regarding Beretto for a moment. A man in his 50s, he reminded Mark of Clint Eastwood, with his short-cropped salt-and-pepper hair, sallow face, hazel eyes, and a light-weight blue wool suit, with a nice shirt and tie. What seemed incongruous to Mark were the argyle socks that insulated the man's bare feet from the fiberglass deck. Apart from the argyles, he seemed like a no-nonsense guy, and worthy of an honest conversation.

"Are you comfortable talking out here?" he asked Mark.

"Depends on how long 'a few minutes' is."

"Give me an hour. If I bore you, I'll go away and leave you alone."

Sounds like a deal.

Mark considered spending an hour with the man, but dreading to be drawn into something he wasn't sure he wanted to be a part of. But, he was in need of a sailing crew, and the plot was thickening, as they say, and the drama with his neighbors at Villa Dellacroix was tugging on him with all the gravitational pull of a black hole. "Do you know how to sail?"

"Not really."

"Willing to learn?"

Beretto hesitated, sensing an opportunity to negotiate. "Quid pro quo?"

Mark smiled at the FBI agent. He could see the Harvard-lawyer side of his personality coming out. "Sure, why not." *Indeed, why knot?*

Beretto took a moment to remove his jacket and tie, uncovering a shoulder holster that held a .40 cal. Glock and spare clip which he also removed and placed on his neatly-folded jacket. "Where can I put this?" he asked.

"Down below," Mark pointing down the companionway. Beretto disappeared below deck, reappearing a minute later with his shirt and cuffs rolled up, looking like a new sailing apprentice and ready to be conscripted for his first lesson in nautical skills.

"Now what?" he asked.

Mark explained how to cast off, and the author and his FBI-guy trainee were underway in minutes, Mark with a crew member, he presumed, who was about to shed some light on a wild series of events that were sure to get even wackier. The sun had risen higher in the sky, and a strong tide was ebbing, helping to propel the 67-foot Baltic out the Port Fierce channel at a swift nine knots over the sandy bottom that was visible 30 feet below. With a quid pro quo arrangement in place, Mark began to mentally assemble a long list of sailing tips to barter with Beretto for what he hoped to learn.

Dream Girl headed northeast on a reach in the light southerly wind, out into the relatively-calm four-foot seas of the Atlantic Ocean. He kept the centerboard up so their course would fade them closer to shore as they headed for Vero Beach, sixteen miles north. Beretto learned fast, and inside a half-hour, he knew how to raise and lower the sails, trim the sheets, and learned the difference between the head and backstays, and standing vs. running rigging. The bit about the captain's brief relationship with his next-door neighbors he found nothing short of amusing.

Mark offered the wheel to his trainee as he prepared to go below and pour them both a cup of tea from his thermos. Tapping on the binnacle compass, Mark said, "Keep her heading at 195 degrees." Beretto nodded. Returning topside, he offered a cup to Beretto as he took the helm again. Standing at the binnacle in his washed-out jeans and Cabo Wabo T-shirt, he asked, "Are you enjoying yourself, Mr. Beretto?"

"Actually, yes I am, very similar to my day sail with Stella Wilde and her father several weeks ago on *Seaquel*. We had quite an interesting conversation." He looked at Mark like he'd just tossed a pot roast to a hungry lion, waiting for him to pounce with more questions.

"And, so, how is the Wilde couple faring?" he asked, continuing to steer the yacht as Beretto tended the sheets. "Getting along any better?" Mark had a great dumb blonde act, but Beretto got down to business and laid another card on the table, sidestepping the author's question.

"Mr. McAllister, we have you on a surveillance tape from Chatahootchee, so we know you had an extensive conversation with Stella. Let's put all our cards on the table. Agree?"

Mark looked at Beretto's cup of tea. "Would you like some honey? I'm out of milk."

"I'm good."

Mark thought about what he was about to say. He had a feeling it was time to be more direct with the Special Agent, but wanted to blow enough smoke to get Beretto to tell him everything would be okay, that it was being handled properly, that Stella would be safe.

But he stopped short, not quite there yet. "Well, since we've been sailing together, you might as well call me Mark."

"Okay. Call me Dom." A pained expression crossed his face. "In answer to your question about the Wildes, I'm taking a chance with you in sharing the details of an ongoing investigation by telling you they've both been abducted. By the same man, we think. You know who I'm talking about, don't you?"

"Emilio Rosa."

"Exactly right. They were abducted by men posing as hospital staff and federal law enforcement agents with fake IDs and FBI badges." Beretto waited for some form of disapproval from the author, but apart from a sad expression, it never came. "Why don't you start by telling me about your conversation with Stella? What did she tell you?"

Mark remembered everything that she'd said, and at the time, wasn't sure of how much of it he could believe. Now, he wrestled with how much of her personal information he should divulge to Beretto, but had no reason to mistrust the FBI agent. "She told me she felt her life was in danger...that, ah...through one of his thugs, Rosa was after her bank passcodes." Beretto was listening so intently he over trimmed the jib, so Mark steered up ten degrees to compensate. "She was pretty upset and in quite a funk. Said she had no one she could trust and she was taking anti-depressants."

"Anything else?"

"Yeah. She said you told her Dan had gone into the drug trafficking business with a new partner." Mark cocked his head. "Was she wearing your wire when she stabbed her husband in self-defense?"

Beretto nodded but stopped short of elaborating on his answer. "Look, Mark...you seem like a nice guy, and I know you care about Stella. We have surveillance tapes. But it's an open investigation, and I can't comment"-

"This was *your* idea as I recall, Dom. Are we gonna put all our cards on the table, or not?"

He thought it over before replying. "Quid pro quo. Do you know where her missing flash drive is?"

"We're playing the big cards first, huh?" Secretly, Mark liked the man's style. He wanted to help with her rescue, but with certain conditions of his own as he thought about the set of keys in his safe deposit box at Northern Trust. "Why? What's on the drive?"

Beretto set his cup on the cushioned seat next to him and stood up. "This is much bigger than you or me, Mark, and bigger than having a crush on some hot-looking gangster's wife."

Mark gave him a stern look. "Crush? You sure that doesn't describe us both?"

Beretto sidestepped his question. "This case is about taking out the leader of the Juarez cartel, arguably the most powerful cartel in North America, and that flash drive may contain important evidence that you can't just decide to withhold"-

"It's private property that her husband entrusted to my late wife," Mark admitted matter-of-factly, offering a different survey of the legal landscape, "…and neither of us really know what's on the drive." The agent acknowledged his point with a tilt of his head. "Do you have a warrant for it?" Beretto shook his head, and Mark continued. "Either we're a team, or my memory could get a little fuzzy. Why should I care what happens to the cartel?" Mark wasn't going to make it easy for him unless they both got what they wanted.

Beretto became emotional, and Mark noted it wasn't the greatest attribute for a police officer to allow his feelings to be read so easily. "Because they behead people and make snuff films with the headless bodies. They sell drugs to children, force innocent young girls to become prostitutes, extort money from hard-working American businessmen. They murder people. And now, this particular Mexican cartel is expanding into the southern U.S. and threatening the life of someone I *know* you care about." He paused to let that sink in.

Mark was defensive. "She's a married woman, Dom, and married to a gangster herself, as you pointed out. Does the FBI consider her expendable too?"

Beretto continued to study him, not replying and not buying into it. He softened his tone. "Look. I understand what you've been through with the loss of your wife," watching Mark wince. "While you may not admit you care about Stella, at least admit that the cartels are hurting our country and our children by pushing their drugs and organized crime. And we *are* winning the war against drugs and organized crime."

"Have you mentioned this to the Juarez cartel?"

Beretto gave him a tight smile. "Rosa already knows it, which is why he's continuously looking for legitimate businesses to launder his drug money. He knows it better than our own citizens who are fed nothing but the bad news that reporters spin and exaggerate to create their make-believe headlines, which in turn push ratings and ad revenue higher. You know how that works. You even wrote about it in your novel. I think the phrase you used was 'It's all about the money.'"

Mark sensed a wind shift, looking up at the tell tales as a fresh breeze filled the sails and *Dream Girl* heeled to port another few degrees. "And you know this how?" he asked, adjusting course fifteen degrees to port. "The Cliff Notes or reading a review?"

Beretto tailed the jib sheet perfectly before stepping to the starboard rail and staring out to sea. "I read your book. And, if you are as perceptive as you seem to be in your writing, then I hope you will agree to work with us."

Hiding his genuine surprised in learning that Beretto had time to read his novels, Mark reached down for the binoculars in the teak holder on the binnacle. Without replying to his overture, he handed them to the FBI agent. "If you look due west about a thousand yards," pointing toward shore, "...you'll see the Wilde's home, Villa Dellacroix. And the home next to it I shared with my late wife, Villa Riomar. You know about the break-in the other night?"

Beretto was busy scanning the beach with the binoculars. "Yes, I heard about it, along with your bear sighting." He lowered the binoculars and smiled before refocusing. "Beautiful homes." The FBI agent studied the estate homes through the glasses for a few moments, then handed the binoculars back to Mark. "A shame that a Mexican drug cartel is now doing business in Vero Beach. What will you do now?"

Mark glanced at his watch, "I'll show you how to tack," changing direction in more than one sense.

Beretto smiled at the irony. "No, I mean when this is over?"

"I suppose it depends on how all this plays out. Tell me, Dom, what were they looking for when they tossed the place?"

Beretto squinted at him. "You've got a great dumb blonde act. C'mon. The drive, what else?" Mark wasn't surprised. "With Stella out of the way and her bank passcodes compromised, do you have any idea what Rosa could do with $1.7 billion?"

"Buy a country?"

"He already owns one."

"And now he wants another."

His FBI crewman nodded. "Will you help us?"

"Yes. But I have some conditions. I can help you with her rescue, and I will encourage her to trust you enough to gather more evidence, but I'd like to be there every step of the way when you do." Beretto listened, and Mark continued with another incendiary little tidbit. "By the way, there are two flash drives, and the second one may prove to be far more valuable to your investigation."

Beretto leaned forward, anxious to hear more details. "Oh? Tell me about it."

Mark gave him an ambiguous smile. "Quid pro quo, remember?"

Beretto nodded. "I'll clear you with my boss, but he won't be happy letting a civilian in"-

Time for the takeaway, thought Mark. "Then let me know when it's all agreed."

The agent stroked his chin for a moment, considering his proposal, and what could be gained by his participation. "All right. We'll bring you in as a 'consultant'," making the air quotes with his fingers, "...but I gotta warn you, bullets may fly."

"Been there, done that. Give me an M-16 with a scope, and a NATO sidearm, and I'll be fine," Mark assured him. "I'm trained in the use of automatic weapons and an excellent marksman." Beretto looked askance at him, waiting for some clarification. Mark pointed out to sea."Out there, you can't dial 911. I was always prepared to defend my boat and crew from international pirates," Mark explained further, "...though I never had to shoot anyone."

Beretto seemed to regard him in a new light. "I feel so much better," with a hint of sarcasm. "You'll have to wear a Kevlar jacket."

"Under these conditions, wouldn't leave home without it."

So, with their new understanding, they reset the sails to head back to the yacht club, tacking through the breeze and running against the tide which was slowing its ebb. After tacking back and forth for half an hour and making slight headway, a tired Mr. Beretto asked, "Wouldn't we do better starting the engine?"

"No sport in that," replied Mark. "Sailing against the wind is a test of skill and patience. Tacking is a test of character."

"It's a waste of time," declared the apprentice. Beretto had made his way up to the bow rail, squatting under the jib, seeming to relish the feel of the wind on his face and the sound of the bow cutting through the sea, acquiescing to the captain's wishes. Mark could see his new apprentice was enjoying himself and handled both the main and jib sheets from the cockpit as his crew took a break, presumably to plan how they would rescue their girl Stella. Beretto looked back to the captain with a pleading look after several more tacks, and Mark knew what he wanted. Following a quick lesson on how to roller furl the jib, then the staysail and main sail, his FBI apprentice was relieved to hear Mark start the diesel engine, tired of having the jib slap him on the top of his head on every tack.

Rounding the tip of South Hutchison Island, Mark rationalized his decision to return to port under power by telling himself it was always best to power into port when in the company of an inexperienced crew in order to avoid an embarrassing outcome. Plowing into a dock or moored vessel with *Dream Girl* while fellow yachtsmen were having drinks on the clubhouse loggia would have proven a serious embarrassment, and an unsatisfactory ending to an otherwise enjoyable day sail.

The author and the FBI agent managed to secure the yacht alongside the pier and disappeared below to collect their gear.

After slipping back into his holstered Glock, Beretto stepped closer to pose a question as he tied his tie. "You're doing this for her, aren't you?" Mark raised his eyebrows and cocked his head but didn't reply. Beretto turned philosophical. "Who was it? Voltaire, I think, who said, 'God created woman to tame man.' Are we so in need of taming?" he asked, adjusting the fit of his holster. Preparing to depart, the two men found themselves back on deck as Mark continued to think about the question posed by his crew.

"Let me answer your question this way, Dom: 'I am not afraid of storms for I am learning to sail my ship.' Now, who would you suppose is the author of *that* famous quote?"

Beretto played along. "Christopher Columbus?" Mark shook his head. "Captain Ahab?" He shook it again.

"You see, that's the trap that men often find themselves in. It was a woman-Louisa May Alcott."

"I would not have guessed that." Beretto reached out and shook his hand appreciatively. "Thank you for the instruction and the ride, Mark. I took one of your business cards off the navigation table, and I *will* keep you in the loop. Remember our deal." He stepped off the boat and onto the dock to slip into his shoes as Mark plugged in the three 50-amp shore power cables and the fresh water supply before double-checking the spring line.

When he was finished, he called out to Beretto. "Emilio Rosa and Dan Wilde ought to be in the same cell together." The FBI agent waved to him as he added, "We should go sailing again."

CHAPTER TWENTY

D r. Katherine Tremelle tossed the two cherry Maalox tablets into her mouth, chewing them up thoughtfully as she examined the label on the bottle of Fiji water and wondered if it was really from Fiji. The label stated the company was headquartered in Los Angeles. For a moment, she considered the insanity of shipping bottled water half-way around the world just so she could use it to wash the cherry anti-acid tablets down. In her present state-of-mind, she would have preferred a double shot of chilled Casamigos since it *was* Friday and after five, but she had a rule about imbibing at her office that she refused to compromise.

After finishing the last of her research for the day, Dr. Tremelle made herself comfortable behind her desk, removing her high heels and propping her feet up on the leather hassock as she sorted through her mail and her feelings. Still incensed over Hirt's treachery, she was determined to figure out a way to quench her burning desire for justice. Eyeing her computer's electrical cord for a moment, she imagined what it would be like to strangle her former friend with it. There wasn't a jury in the land who would convict her, she thought, not with the evidence she would bring to light. Without a violent bone in her body, she dismissed the idea as rampant animal instinct, and certainly beneath her intellectual capabilities and moral code. She took a moment to appreciate her office surroundings, meticulously decorated in dark walnut and traditional décor, with a few original post-impressionist beach pastels by Howard Behrens. Her favorite was a striking beach scene titled "Yellow and Orange Sails", an original that hung on the wall opposite her desk. Losing herself in the details of the colorful beachside masterpiece, she imagined herself to be the young bikini-clad girl in the foreground with her hat draped over her knee, the daydream always helping to clear her mind.

As one of the preeminent psychiatrists in her field, and the Director of Clinical Research and Trials at Valiant Pharmaceutical, the outrage Dr. Tremelle was feeling over one of her fellow psychiatrists using highly-confidential information to make himself an egregious profit was literally making her sick to her stomach. As usual, the press didn't have the whole story, and hearing about Hirt's new Bentley and penthouse at Village Spires only added to her contempt for him. Then there was the criminal aspect of prescribing to the patient a drug known to be harmful, potentially a felony assault and battery case, and a crime particularly heinous in that a physician had intentionally violated the Hippocratic Oath in his pursuit of profit. Unlike her former friend, she took the oath quite seriously.

The fact that Dr. Hirt had betrayed her trust had infuriated her so much that she'd paid cash for a burner phone at Best Buy and called the FBI's tip line to leave an anonymous message. But that was a week ago, and she was mystified as to why they hadn't arrested him yet. Desperate for atonement, she knew what she had to do.

***

William Farley listened again in his Atlanta office to the recorded call of an anonymous tipster that the FBI had transferred to his workstation, hoping for a break in the case. For the past eight years, Farley had been the Regional Director of SEC Enforcement for the Southeastern U.S., but had never heard about an insider trading case quite as bizarre as this one. Without a witness to go on record, Farley doubted if he had enough evidence for probable cause. Even with Hirt's own physician assistant's testimony claiming he'd been coerced by Hirt into writing the prescription, he would need a warrant to connect the dots and make his case, especially after Hirt had lawyered up. In the absence of any public announcement of an arrest or press release concerning the anonymous information, he had a feeling that he'd hear from the tipster again. She sounded knowledgeable, well-educated and very motivated, even angry, and tipsters like that weren't likely to let it go until they were satisfied justice had been served. His confidence was vindicated by the call that came in on his office phone. His phone rang three times before he answered.

"William Farley."

A sultry female voice said, "Mr. Farley. I got your name from an online search of SEC personnel. You've got an enviable track record of convictions. I'm calling to help you with a high-profile case involving the so-called drug zombie stabbing."

"Who are you?"

"Forgive me, but I must remain anonymous. But, I am prepared to help you solve the case."

"Are you the tipster who called the FBI a week ago?"

After a moment she said, "Yes." The proverbial pregnant pause ensued before she continued. "Why hasn't anything been done?"

Farley tried to contain his glee in seeing that his profile of the tipster was accurate as he gestured frantically through the glass at his technical assistant to trace the call. "We didn't have enough evidence to act on your tip."

"Well, this time you will. The person who engineered these crimes is Dr. Christopher Hirt, a prominent Vero psychiatrist. And don't try to trace this call-I won't be on long enough."

"That's a shame. I was just beginning to enjoy our little chat." Farley smiled, looking for any way to keep her talking, trying to diminish the importance of her call. "How do you know it was Hirt? You work with him or something?"

"That's irrelevant. Now, do you want to hear what I have to say or not?"

Farley sensed her determination to follow her own script. "All right, you have my attention. God gave me two ears and one mouth, and I know when to use them in that proportion."

"What *does* matter now is that you know he probably used his own computer to hack into Valiant's website to plan this whole thing, so there will be a verifiable record of the hack and the information he retrieved that will help you prove intent."

"Anything else?" Farley was taking notes, impressed with the way her mind worked.

"He's already spent over a million dollars of the money he made when he shorted Valiant's stock."

"On what?" *C'mon, lay it out for me, sweet cakes.*

"Dr. Hirt paid cash for a penthouse at Village Spires, and a new Bentley convertible, both right after Valiant's stock got hammered." She paused to check her notes while Farley continued his own note taking, hoping she would stay on long enough to complete the trace. Without a shred of condescension, she said, "Let me break it down for you, Mr. Farley. Hirt has an account at Morgan Stanley here in Vero, which you have the authority to investigate, and most of these events I'm referencing are a matter of public record and easily verified with a little research, which I will leave to you."

Farley wondered if the anonymous caller was on a personal vendetta or an ex-lover that Hirt may have dumped. He pushed her a little harder. "Look, I appreciate your help, whoever you are, but if you really want to help us put this guy away, we need to have someone go on record. Will you go on record?"

"Mr. Farley, you don't need me to go on record. You have his receptionist's and P.A.'s testimony, and with the information I just gave you, you'll have all you need to get a Federal warrant and prove his guilt." She hesitated, then said, "God speed. Bring him to justice." Then, she was off the phone.

Farley knew she was right. If her information was accurate, and he had no reason to doubt her, he would have no problem getting a Federal warrant. They'd have everything except Hirt's DNA, and after it was over, they'd probably have that as well.

His next call was to his boss, the Assistant Director of SEC Enforcement, a call he was sure would be well-received.

***

Fresh from his day sail with McAllister, Special Agent Dominic Beretto made a stop at Bahia Mar's two-bedroom Ambassador's Suite to check on his stakeout team as they continued their 24/7 surveillance of *Bella Rosa*. It was late afternoon, and his men looked weary as he entered the room. Except for the empty pizza boxes, it looked like a high-tech war zone, with three laser microphones aimed at various decks on the yacht, two refractor telescopes with integrated digital cameras, three sets of high-power binoculars, two infrared cameras, and a myriad of computers, monitors, laptops and communication equipment sitting on folding tables, all wired together to maximize speed and effectiveness in processing the stream of surveillance data. The FBI stakeout team also had a few low-tech tricks up their sleeve, including a drug-sniffing canine team camouflaged as a middle-aged couple out walking their dog. Over the last ten days, they'd captured masses of photos, conversations and some coded planning aboard *Bella Rosa*, but so far nothing that would green light them for a full-scale bust of Rosa and his U.S. headquarters.

A few days earlier, the Bahia Mar manager was kind enough to extend their stay *gratis* for an indefinite period after discovering that the Bureau was in the middle of a search for a suitable resort to host their upcoming July conference. With dollar signs in his eyes, the manager was in such a hospitable mood that he even offered to send up some "dancers" along with their late-night room service orders to bolster their morale, an offer that Beretto dutifully but reluctantly declined. Pandering to Rosa and the cartel's members, party girls came and went like ten dollar hookers, along with cases of liquor and gourmet foods, up and down the gangplank at all hours of the day and night. Looking for ways to pass the time and entertain themselves, he'd heard Scott and Perez placing bets on which of the girls would successfully negotiate the tricky slope of the aluminum gangplank without removing their stilettos.

"How's it goin', guys?" asked Beretto, leaning over Scott and Perez for a view of the drug lord's mega yacht from their prime western exposure. "Keeping yourselves entertained by our favorite gangster?" He knew there were a lot of distractions to filter out. Their seventh-floor perch was surrounded by dozens of downtown nightclubs at the epicenter of "party central", the busiest section of Lauderdale's intracoastal waterway. *They didn't call it Snort Liquordale for nothin'.*

Scott pointed at the monitors. "Rosa's got two drones covering the yacht, boss. They've buzzed our area a few times, but I doubt they can see us through the mirror coating."

"Where are they now?" asked Beretto.

Scott rechecked his computer monitors. "One is directly above the hotel, and the other moves up and down the intracoastal over the center of boat traffic, guarding *Bella Rosa* from anyone approaching from the waterway."

Beretto looked over Scott's shoulder at the monitors. "Uh-huh. You think they have infrared capabilities?"

"Doubtful, boss. Line-of-sight and low-light optics, I would say," answered Scott.

"How long can they stay aloft?" Beretto wanted to know.

"About three hours with high-capacity lithium," answered Scott, "...or indefinitely with fresh battery packs, which is more likely the case. They've been aloft almost constantly." The tech agent added, "Ya know, Dom, with those drones, it'll be impossible to sneak up on them."

"Thanks Captain Obvious. Trust me, we're not going to sneak up on them," assured Beretto. "When we have what we need, we're gonna hit them right between the eyes with a knockout punch. Wham!" smacking a fist into his hand. "Have there been any sightings of Wilde?"

"No, boss," answered Perez. "If he's aboard *Bella Rosa,* they're keeping him below deck. I'm guessing they're using him for leverage after unloading him from a boat on the far side a few nights ago."

Scott asked, "Why don't we get our own drones up?"

Beretto rubbed his chin. "So far, they don't seem to have a clue that we're here. We put drones up, maybe they get more cautious. No, they'll slip up. We need something solid. What we need is indisputable probable cause before we unzip our fly."

Perez moved closer to the window, excited about something. "Guys, check this out. Looks like a Baha Grille delivery van backing in." The agent was momentarily distracted by a large chartered ketch-rigged Morgan motoring in toward an empty berth with a dozen bikini-clad sorority girls on deck. He reached over and activated the video recorder, refocusing his binoculars as Beretto and Scott grabbed theirs to focus on the van. The men watched two burly security guards tramping down *Bella Rosa's* gangplank while talking into their radios, presumably to assist with the delivery as the van's driver unlocked the rear doors and waved them over. "Looks like those two goons, Blake and Sorvino again. Wonder why Troll's not with them."

"Troll must be with RatMan," said Beretto. His instincts told him something big was up as he scowled at Scott and Perez. "That truck's dirty," he declared. They watched as Rosa's men stacked boxes labeled as black beans, flour and corn tortillas, salsa, and chicken with rice onto a hand truck and began dragging it up the gangplank like they were provisioning the yacht's pantry. But Beretto wasn't buying it. He turned to Scott and Perez. "What's your take on this, guys?"

Perez spoke first. "If you're a billionaire with expensive tastes, why do you drop a steady gourmet diet for the past ten days to slum it up with Mexican fast food?"

Beretto cocked his head. "Yeah, good point, Epi. What do you think, Lenny?"

Scott chimed in. "I'm thinkin' either drugs or cash in those boxes, boss." The agents watched one of the drones hover over the van protectively as Rosa's men began to make a second trip up the gangway with a stack of sealed boxes. They noticed two more heavily-armed guards appear at the top of the gangplank as they unloaded the van.

"Somethin's up." Beretto picked up his radio and pushed the talk button to speak with their undercover canine handlers sitting in the unmarked van on the other side of the hotel. "McNeal? You there?"

The three heard several seconds of static. Then, "I'm here, Dom."

"You're up. I want you to walk Cody past that Baha Grille delivery van on the dock. Hurry up before they close the doors. You got eyes on it?"

"Yeah, Dom. Let me put my Topsiders on and grab my 'Mrs.' Be there in a coupla minutes."

"Roger that. Make it snappy."

Scott was busy fine-tuning the audio and video feeds as Perez stepped hastily toward one of the two bathrooms to relieve himself. "Gotta drain my lizard, guys."

"T.M.I., buddy," quipped Beretto without lowering his binoculars. Walking into view was a middle-aged man wearing cargo shorts, a floral shirt and a baseball cap accompanied by a woman wearing a khaki cover-up and straw fedora. The woman had a male German shepherd tugging at his leash. "I can see McNeal and Suarez making their way toward the van. Let's see how Cody reacts when they make their pass."

Perez returned to the window and grabbed his binoculars. "What I miss?" he asked.

"The apocalypse," cracked Scott. The three agents watched Blake and Sorvino carefully unload a black duffle bag from the van. Through their binoculars, they could see something inside the black bag was wiggling. In a tense moment, the agents watched Cody stop and fixate on the duffle bag, his ears perking up before McNeal and Suarez pulled him away with the leash, but the drug-sniffing canine gave no signs that indicated the presence of drugs.

"That bag look like it's moving around to you guys?" asked Perez.

"There it goes again. Something movin' inside," said Scott.

Beretto continued to focus on the bag being lifted up the gangplank. "Yeah, somethin' definitely wrong about that duffle bag. *Someone's* being smuggled aboard." He lowered his binoculars. "Story is Rosa's smuggled illegal immigrants and young women before, but why would he bring them aboard his yacht?"

Beretto said, "It'd be a thin beef without knowing for sure. Could be an exotic dancer...or a bag of pythons-who knows?"

"Or Stella Wilde," added Perez.

***

Special Agent Dominic Beretto was having an off-color dream. In his dream, he was being artfully fellated by the government's star witness, Stella Wilde, her strawberry-blonde hair spilling deliciously over his lap. He woke up clutching his groin, realizing that he'd dozed off in the back seat. Surprised by the tumescent effect of his fantasy, ordinarily it would have been okay except for the fact that he was sitting next to the SEC Regional Director William Farley who was also catnapping during the two-hour trip to Vero Beach. Embarrassed, Beretto grabbed one of the case file folders from the seat between them and slid it over his lap to hide the bulge in his pants. SEC Agent Allison Farrington looked back from the front seat to give him a smile and a knowing wink before returning to her tablet.

Streaking past the Jensen Beach Boulevard exit, the black Chevy Suburban headed north on I-95 with the four Federal agents, two from the FBI and two from the SEC. Beretto had picked up the SEC Regional Director from the Palm Beach International Airport after Farley flew in on a direct flight from Atlanta. Once both men were awake, the two went back to work reviewing the details of the five-page arrest warrant, sifting through a raft of supporting evidence for clues as to what additional physical evidence they would gather during the arrest. FBI Agent Joe Pearson handled the driving, while Farley's technical assistant Allison Farrington of the SEC's Atlanta office took care of the navigation and familiarized the task force with digital photos of the medical office's staff. Just two days after receiving a second anonymous tip, the multi-jurisdictional task force was on its way to serve a three-count warrant on a person they all agreed deserved to be in jail.

Caught up in all the fine print for the past hour, the men had lost track of the time. Farley checked his watch. "Dom, it's almost four o'clock. We gotta step on it if we want to get there before they close." Beretto nodded and leaned forward to talk to the driver.

"Joe, hit the lights and kick it up a notch. We gotta move it."

"You got it, Dom." Pearson reached down and planted the blue light on the dash, activating the rotating beacon and hit the gas, bringing the Suburban's speed up to 95. Agent Pearson turned out to be a better driver than a conversationalist as he zipped in and out of the irate South Florida drivers trying to beat the rush hour traffic. Most of them rarely had the courtesy to wave with all five fingers as they begrudgingly allowed the Suburban to pass.

Farley turned to his FBI colleague. "I had my assistant call a coupla TV stations, including the local affiliate WPEC and let them know what we're doing. The world needs to know this guy's a real cockroach." Beretto nodded. "We'll let the media help us out," he suggested with a big smile. He expected to see armored vehicles, helicopters, SWAT teams, and likely enough uniformed officers from city and county to make it look like everyone's getting a piece of the action.

Beretto rolled with it. "Think we have enough gas masks to handle the tear gas, Bill?" joked Beretto. That was good for a snicker from the SEC Director.

Forty minutes later, they turned north onto Indian River Boulevard, only a few minutes from the Medical Center where Dan Wilde had been abducted a few days before. "How's Danny boy doing, Dom?"

"We don't know. He could be sleeping with the fishes for all we know."

"Fishes?" replied Farley with a wry smile. "You mean tacos, don't you?"

At a quarter to five, Pearson parked the Suburban on the grass in front of the medical building, the other thirty-one parking spaces already taken by reporters, police officers, TV vans with satellite antennas, and one armored SWAT vehicle that was likely just for show. Farrington and Pearson got busy unloading the hand trucks they would use to load the computers and hard-copy files as Hirt's attorney pulled in next to the FBI's black Suburban.

"Martin Shkreli, attorney for Dr. Hirt," announced the fat balding man who reminded them of Bernie Madoff as he handed Beretto and Farley his card.

To Shkreli, Farley said, "Well, since you're here, you can read Hirt his rights." As the three headed inside, the throng of reporters closed in around them with a myriad of questions, one on top of the other. The reporters reminded Beretto of a bunch of piranhas devouring a side of beef. To the uniformed officers, he said, "Keep everyone outside except attorneys and law enforcement personnel."

"I'd like to read the arrest warrant," said Shkreli.

Farley pointed at the office doors. "You'll get your chance inside."

Alerted by the media circus and dozens of policemen that had gathered outside his office, Hirt had phoned his attorney twenty minutes earlier. He stood waiting between the two fake marble pillars in front of the reception desk, leaning casually on the granite counter as the four agents and his attorney stormed his office.

Farley spoke first. "Dr. Christopher Hirt," holding up the documents, "William Farley, District Supervisor, Securities and Exchange Commission. I have a Federal warrant for your arrest, including any and all files, computers and recording devices." Reading from the charge sheet, he added, "You are under arrest for insider trading, felony assault and battery, and felony cyber hacking."

Angry over the entire charade, Hirt faced off with the agents. "Screw you and all the rest of your Keystone Cops!" he shouted, thrusting his index finger into Farley's chest.

In a move to protect his SEC cohort, Beretto stepped between them to shield Farley and gestured toward Shkreli. "Your attorney will now read you your Miranda rights, Dr. Hirt," said Beretto as he handed the paperwork to Shkreli. "You can keep those, counselor. I made extra copies," pulling out the handcuffs.

As Shkreli read a very distraught Hirt his rights, the psychiatrist lost his temper again, venting his resentment. "You guys are making a big mistake. I'll sue you, the SEC, the FBI"-

Shkreli interrupted him. "Chris, shut up for God's sake. Do you understand your rights?" Hirt nodded as he made eye contact with his receptionist and physician assistant who'd been standing calmly in front of the reception desk with their hands clasped as if part of a church choir.

"Face up against the pillar, doc, and put your hands behind you," said Beretto, placing his hands in the cuffs and squeezing them tight. "We got a real nice cell waitin' for you at the Federal Courthouse in West Palm. Coupla headcases you might recognize, maybe even a few of your own patients," Beretto getting right in his face, "...and I'm sure they're just *dying* to see you, doc." Hirt winced at the reference to harming his patients.

Farley pointedly looked at his watch and smirked at Hirt. "Well, whaddya know, doc. Friday, five o'clock. Courthouse just closed. Guess you'll have to wait 'til Monday for your arraignment and bond hearing. No worries. You'll love your new digs." Shkreli shrugged and remained silent while Hirt gave him a disgusted look. Farley grabbed one arm and Beretto the other as they led Hirt outside to face the media circus.

Outside in the parking lot, the horde of reporters encircled the four men, directing all sorts of incendiary questions to Hirt. "Is it true you sold Valiant stock short before it collapsed? Did you know the Seraquim would cause your patient to react violently? Hey doc, who's gonna drive your new Bentley when you're in prison?" asked three reporters in rapid-fire succession. Ready to lose his temper again, Hirt struggled to hold his contempt in check while Shkreli flatly replied "no comment" to all three questions.

Steps from the FBI's waiting SUV, a WPEC-TV reporter managed to get his microphone right under Hirt's nose and asked, "Is it true that you work for the Mexican cartel and planned this to get rid of Daniel Wilde?"

Hirt's face contorted in anger. "That's the most absurd"-

Shkreli grabbed Hirt's shoulder, stepping between his client and the reporter. "We have no comment." And so it went until Beretto opened the Suburban's rear door and held Hirt's head down to ensure he didn't hit the SUV's door frame.

Looking the sleazy psychiatrist in the eye, Beretto said, "Stella Wilde says 'hi'."

CHAPTER TWENTY-ONE

S itting beside Stella in one of the guest staterooms aboard *Bella Rosa*, Blake watched her come around. "Take it easy," he cautioned her, readjusting the hand towel on her forehead that he'd soaked in the ice bucket beside the bed.

"Where am I?" asked Stella, still woozy from the high-voltage charge from the stun gun. She tried to rub her eyes but her wrists were still bound with duct tape, making her movements awkward. After she was drugged, rendered unconscious and stuffed into a duffle bag for the ride to Ft. Lauderdale, Blake was expecting some gratitude from her. For now, he kept his desires a secret.

"You're safe aboard *Bella Rosa*," he reassured her.

She recognized the man's voice from her ordeal in the Humvee. The familiar smell of teak oil and stainless steel cleaner, along with the unmistakable sounds of bells and horns from passing boats confirmed she was captive on a waterfront yacht. "Whose boat am I on?" she asked.

"You could hardly call it a boat," corrected Blake. "You're on a 90-meter Feadship."

"Okay, whose Feadship am I on then?"

"Your husband's new business partner, Emilio Rosa. Try to lay still, Mrs. Wilde. You have a bruise on your head." After what she'd heard about Rosa, she shuddered at the thought of what he might have in store for her. Her vision of being keelhauled and fed to the sharks was not her idea of a fun day on the water.

Stretched out on the queen-size bed over a soft Donna Karan bedspread, she wore the same teal-colored sundress with big yellow flowers she'd slipped into back at the psyche hospital. She could still feel the documents folded up inside her panties as she tried to open her eyes, but her eyelids felt like they were glued together. "Can't see a damn thing. What's wrong with my eyes?"

Sitting astride a foot stool beside her bed, Blake leaned over her. "There may have been some tear gas inside that duffle bag you rode in." He shrugged. "A previous occupant," he explained. Earlier, Troll had come by to drop off a cocktail dress, high heels and a pair of panties for her to change into, her clothing that he collected from the burglary at Villa Dellacroix days earlier. A habitual panty sniffer from the age of six, Troll was still secretly enjoying his only trophy from the Villa Dellacroix burglary-her other pair of panties. Sadly, he was forced to leave behind the real prize-her fishnet stockings-after they got caught in the door when the alarm went off.

Blake opened a drawer on the teak cabinet and withdrew a bottle of Visine. "Hold your head still." Applying the soothing liquid to her eyes, he said, "The stewards have provisioned the stateroom for you, Mrs. Wilde. Don Rosa wants you to feel at home since you may be here for a while."

The drops made her eyes feel better, and she was able to open one eye. Stella recognized Blake as the driver of the Humvee and wondered why he was being so nice. He didn't seem as mean as the other psychos on Vasquez's crew, but then again, Stella wasn't always good at getting first impressions right-especially when it came to men. "And where is *here?*" she wanted to know.

"Bahia Mar. I have toiletries, cosmetics, and some of your clothes"-

"How'd you get my clothes?"

"From the gym bag we brought from Chatahootchee," he lied, not wanting her to know Rosa had Salamonaca and Troll burglarize her home. The eye drops were working, and Stella was able to open both eyes as he handed her a bottle of Gatorade. She chugged half the bottle as a mean-looking guard with a scarred face stepped back into view outside the stateroom. The guard cupped his hand to shade his eyes, peering into the large porthole to check on them before turning around.

"I heard the other men call you Blake," she said between gulps. He nodded. "So, obviously, you guys aren't with the FBI. Who do you work for?" eyeing him suspiciously as she gulped down the rest of the Gatorade and noticed the .45 automatic stuck in the back of his jeans.

Blake hesitated, afraid the truth might make him less likable, but wanting her to trust him. "Your husband's business partner, don Rosa. But don't let that bother you. He takes good care of his business associates, makes them a lot of money." She handed him the empty bottle, looking at him skeptically. "Contrary to what others may say about him, he's first and foremost a businessman, Mrs. Wilde."

"Who kidnaps his business partner's wife at gun point? C'mon, Blake, he's a ruthless drug lord." To work her magic, she cocked her head and gave him an alluring smile, lifting one knee higher as she let her dress slide down her thigh.

"Tell me about yourself. How'd you get mixed up with these guys? I can keep a secret," her green eyes searching his for some measure of compassion.

He snuck a peek at her legs before taking a seat on the edge of her bed, and she imagined how quickly she could grab the cell phone from his back pocket before dismissing it as a bad idea. "The don took me in when the Durango cartel murdered my mother when I was only five." Meeting her gaze, he added, "Mr. Rosa's been like a father to me, raised me like his own son, even paid for my education." He scooted his stool closer to his patient. "How do your eyes feel?"

She smiled again, pleased that her magic was working. "Better. Thanks for the eye drops. Please, call me Stella. So, okay, maybe your boss isn't *completely* ruthless. Tell me, why am I here, Blake?"

He found her directness sexy, and her emerald green eyes seemed to look right through him. "My boss has a business proposition for you."

"What, he couldn't just call or text me?" she asked.

"Not with the FBI intercepting all your messages," he reminded her. She gave him a questioning look. "Why do you think it took so long for your attorney to respond to your calls?" For a moment she considered that he could be telling her the truth, recalling what Morgan had told her about the cartel's cell towers. There was an unreadable silence in the stateroom before he stood and spoke again. "We have a day or two before don Rosa returns from his meeting with the other dons in Mexico. It would be much to your advantage to look as presentable as possible." Sensing his affection for her, she held up her wrists, still uncomfortably bound with duct tape.

Stella asked, "How am I supposed to"-

Blake pulled a hunting knife from a leather sheath under his shirt. Suddenly fearful, she searched his eyes to gauge his intentions. "So, what's it gonna be?" he asked. "You gonna be a good girl," flipping the knife over in his hand and catching it like it was a magic trick, "...or a bad girl?" Stella lowered her hands without a reply. "Bad girls get put back into the duffle bag; good girls get to bathe themselves and freshen up, maybe even order room service on the house phone," pointing with the knife.

She held out her bound hands to him and gave him a sweet puppy-dog look in a plea to have them free again. When he hesitated, she said. "I'll be a good girl, Blake," with as much sincerity as she could muster. She glanced at the tape around her wrists, then up at him.

He cut through the tape in one easy slice. "You make me look bad, or try to escape," tilting his head toward the guard outside,

"…they *will shoot you*, Stella. *And* your husband." She was surprised by his remark, and Blake realized he may have said too much.

"Dan's here?" she asked incredulously, her eyes widening as she tried to sit up on the bed, but the pain in her arm held her back. She'd become the expert on fading relationships, burdened by the suffocating hollowness that plagued her since stabbing her double-dealing husband in self-defense. "What Dan did," waving her hand, "…it's just unbelievable. You have no idea," drawing on her acting skills.

Yeah, I probably do, thought Blake, letting her vent and hiding his feelings, knowing he was on dangerous ground with this stunning woman.

Stella continued her rant. "It's like my whole life comes down to this one place, this"—sweeping her arm in indignation—"rotten situation. Five weeks in an insane asylum with a bunch of fruitcakes after my husband tries to choke me to death, and now I'm a prisoner on a drug lord's yacht."

Blake could feel her pain, seeing she was alone and terrified, just trying to survive. But he had his orders and violating them carried deadly consequences. He gave her a nod before he stood to depart. "You'll see him soon enough…together…when the don returns." Holding up a key that hung from a gold chain around his neck, he added, "I'm gonna lock you in now. Don't try to escape, Stella." Blake took a step toward her. "You have your whole life ahead of you, and you don't want it to end by doing something stupid." Tapping his head, "Be smart."

He exited her stateroom and she listened to him lock the door, then a short profane conversation in Spanish between Blake and the guard outside. She sat up on the edge of the bed and turned her attention back to the clothes and toiletries, thankful for the opportunity to clean herself up. A hot bath and a glass of cabernet was what she craved after that nightmare of a ride stuffed inside a duffle bag.

Instinctively, Stella knew her future hinged on her meeting with Rosa. With the heels of her hands on the edge of the bed, she took a deep breath, reaching down inside herself, drawing upon every shred of strength and composure she could muster. For the first time since her incarceration, she began to feel cogent and sharp. Though she knew little of Rosa's plans for her, she continued to listen to her intuition that reminded her he was a man with a man's weaknesses, and she'd have her shot at bending him to her will.

She retrieved the two folded pages from her panties that would save her life. Surveying the room for a safe hiding place, she slipped them under the mattress, then scanned the room again to make sure it was free of security cameras. Surrounding her was an opulent décor, but the teak bulkheads accented with gold lame molding seemed a little glitzy. The intricate teak parquet floor looked like it was hand-cut and was reminiscent of the workmanship on her family's yacht. Curious to see if the pattern continued throughout the stateroom, she peered under the bed where she spotted a cell phone. Blake must have dropped it on his way out, she thought. Her heart raced as she reached under the bed to retrieve it before noticing the guard outside turning to check on her. She quickly laid the phone on the bed in front of her, blocking his view as she stood with her back to him, knowing the guard would hear if she called anyone.

The guard continued to glare at her through the porthole as she pretended to prepare herself for a bath. The trick worked, the guard turning away as she continued to slip out of her sundress. Her mind frozen with fear, the only number she could remember was Mark's, so she texted him as fast as her thumbs could move. She got off a partial message before she heard footsteps outside her door and quickly pushed the phone back under the bed after hitting the send button.

Mark,

It's Stella. Need your help. I'm being held hostage on Bella

She could hear the key turning in the door lock. "Stella, it's Blake," as he entered the stateroom. "Forgot my phone." Saying nothing to him, she demurely slipped her sundress back over her head as Blake searched the room, relieved to find it under her bed. Pocketing his phone, he said, "You get cleaned up now. Don Rosa is arriving in the morning. Be ready for your breakfast meeting at eight." Then he shut and locked her door again.

Once she was alone, she picked up the house phone to order room service, hoping they would have a cabernet that would bring her taste buds back to life after five long weeks of being denied so many things she loved.

She thought about Mark, wondering if he got her message.

***

Special Agent Dominic Beretto stood beside the eight-by-ten-foot laminate story board covered with color photos of Rosa's fifteen-man crew on *Bella Rosa*. To his task force, he described who was in the photos, along with the lines connecting the photos and the functions normally assigned to each of his crew. There was Roberto deCespedes, their crackerjack IT guy, who'd made it possible for Rosa to hack into certain FBI files; "RatMan" Ramone Salamonaca, their explosives expert, who handled the really tricky dirty work like assassinations and kidnappings; Vasquez, Blake, Sorvino and Mendoza, the muscle men who handled the more mundane stuff. Then there was Troll, the hairiest thug that Rosa's money could buy. Near the top of the story board was a photo of their new general counsel, Victor Hernandez, whose appointment was made necessary by the demise of Damon Morgan.

Beretto went on to explain how the involvement of Daniel Wilde and his Baja Grille franchise, along with the car bombing of their former general counsel Damon Morgan, were complicating things over the past few weeks. The timeline had become more difficult to piece together, which left some of the events open to speculation. Though the arrest of Dr. Hirt wasn't central to the investigation, his participation in the plot to eliminate Stella Wilde and the additional crimes committed by the psychiatrist provided a new twist to the possible testimony of their star witness. Beretto identified several pieces of missing key information, but the mounting evidence was making it easier to connect the dots. He went on to describe the five gruesome homicides stretching from the Texas panhandle to Chatahootchee, Vero and South Florida that linked the Juarez cartel and provided more evidence of the group's growing footprint.

Present at the meeting, and surrounded by a myriad of laptops, PCs and tablets supporting their presentation, were Agents Leonard Scott and Epifanio Perez, along with Regional Director Hank Greenberg who sat at the head of the table. The Director was in from Miami for a firsthand review of the FBI's case against Emilio Rosa. Greenberg needed something to hang his hat on, hoping to hear something solid from his West Palm office. With an upcoming budget meeting in Atlanta next week, he was under pressure to justify the expense of weeks of surveillance by his agents and prove to his bosses they were making progress in their prosecution of the drug lord.

Following Beretto's summary, Greenberg needed to clarify a few things and began by tossing out a few key questions. "So, what do we have linking Rosa to Morgan's car bomb?"

Scott replied, "Our lab indicates the explosive identified at the scene was a variant of the type of C-4 used by the Juarez cartel in several other bombings." He brought up the chromatography on one of the monitors and turned it toward Greenberg. "It's a perfect match."

Perez stepped up with more evidence. "CCTV footage from retail locations along the route suggests the presence of Rosa's men-Salamonaca, Vasquez, Blake and Sorvino-at three different points on the day in question. Not exactly a co-inkydink." Greenberg nodded, waiting to hear more.

Beretto pointed to the storyboard. "Our surveillance indicated Morgan was going rogue when Rosa's men caught up with him after his visit with Stella Wilde. That speaks to motive. Also, we now know he slipped a package to her while he was at Chatahootchee." Greenberg waited for him to explain. "We think it included some kind of insurance, likely a second flash drive. We've searched everywhere, but so far"-

"Okay," said Greenberg, to Beretto. "You mentioned something about this author guy, ah…McAllister, referencing *two* flash drives. How does he know this, and do we know what's on either of them?"

It was Scott's turn to answer. "We're pretty sure Mrs. Wilde's bank account passcodes are encoded on the first, the one Rosa sent RatMan to intercept"-

"RatMan?" queried Greenberg.

"Ramone Salamonaca," clarified Beretto. "And we think this information comes by way of Mrs. Wilde, who, as you know, was abducted from Chatahootchee by men posing as our guys." Thank God the media hadn't gotten hold of *that* story, he thought. "And we have good reason to believe she may now be held hostage aboard Rosa's yacht as we speak. But, we have no proof."

"I guess I missed the memo on the wife swapping party," cracked Greenberg. "We got Mrs. McAllister doing Mr. Wilde, then we have Mr. McAllister doing Mrs. Wilde?"

Beretto got defensive on the reference to his crush. "Actually, we're not really sure about what's going on between the author and Mrs. Wilde, but he *has* promised to produce one of the flash drives."

"*He* has it?" asked Greenberg.

"That's what he claims. After he insisted that he be allowed to help in her rescue, I made him a deal to bring him on as an *ad hoc* consultant," Beretto making the air quotes with his fingers, "...if he agrees to hand it over to us for analysis." He shrugged. "Maybe he thinks it'll make a good story, I dunno. I *do* think he knows more than he's telling us." Beretto waited for Greenberg to rubber stamp his arrangement.

The Director rubbed his neck and leaned his head back, trying to ease the tension. The investigation was giving him a headache, and with the added risks of bringing a civilian into their crew, he needed more convincing. "What else can McAllister give us?" he asked Beretto.

Beretto joined his crew at the table and took a seat across from his boss. "He and his late wife knew the Wildes pretty well...dinners, drinks, the same country clubs-that sort of thing. They've been neighbors for months, and he's witnessed some of Rosa's men in action." He leaned forward with his elbows on the table. "I want him with us, Hank. He's in good with our star witness, and she trusts him." Greenberg looked at him blankly. "Something else to consider. McAllister has a history of solving crimes and he could bring us some good press."

Greenberg relented, waving his hand in the air. "All right, Dom. Have him sign a waiver and don't get him in over his head. Make sure he wears a vest. He'll be *your* responsibility." Beretto nodded, relieved that at least one of the flash drives would be in his hands shortly, along with one more ally in his quest for FBI stardom.

Greenberg pointed at the storyboard. "I see photos of Baja Grille semis and vans. What've we got on them?"

Scott offered an update. "We witnessed a delivery the other day. May have been boxes of cash, but no drugs. Wilde signed over a majority interest in Baja Grille to Rosa as a cover for land-based cocaine shipments in exchange for a partnership turned train-wreck." He looked around the table. "Now, Rosa wants all of it."

Greenberg looked confused. "Why do you suppose he did that?"

Scott looked at his boss, and Beretto nodded for him to continue. "Baja Grille was never making the kind of money Wilde claimed it was. Right before he made plans to take it public in an IPO, he hired a crooked CPA to cook the books. Then he had a major cash-flow problem with Barclays and the IRS. Rosa found out Wilde needed a bailout and used Morgan to float the idea of using the business as a front for something *far* more profitable."

"Okay," said Greenberg, "...so why didn't Wilde just go to his wife for"-

Perez pointed at the story board. "She cut him off, Hank. His wife had already fronted him $30 million in play money when he invested with Barclays. The word on the street was he had a T-bond portfolio leveraged twenty-two to one. *That* resulted in a $28 million margin call, along with pending criminal tax fraud charges at the IRS."

Greenberg raised his eyebrows and looked away in disbelief. "Jeez. This guy Wilde's a piece'a work. And now you guys think Rosa's holding them *both* hostage?" Beretto nodded. "What proof do we have?" asked the Director.

It was Scott's turn to elucidate. "They were both abducted on different days from their hospitals...by professionals, I might"-

Perez interrupted. "And someone was wiggling inside a duffle bag when"-

"C'mon, guys," said Greenberg, his hands flat on the table. "With what I know about Rosa, probably a stripper or something. Not enough for a warrant. What's our surveillance telling us? We still got eyes and ears on his yacht?"

It was Beretto's turn to be the bearer of bad news. "They must've figured out they were under surveillance. They're using high-frequency signals from the drones to jam our microphones." He looked at Greenberg apologetically. "For the last 24 hours, we've been deaf as a post." He pointed at Scott. "So, except for the two internet video cameras still in the room-Lenny, check the feed-we took a break from our surveillance. We're here to figure out our next move."

"Russian made jammers," clarified Scott. "You can buy just about any of this stuff on the black market." Glancing at the video feed of *Bella Rosa's* real time image on the monitor, Scott failed to notice the fresh plume of diesel exhaust coming from the yacht's smokestack.

Greenberg was incredulous. "Flying drones with jamming equipment? Who are these guys?"

Beretto explained, "Rosa's now one of the three biggest traffickers in the world, Hank. His revenues exceed those of many third-world countries." Greenberg's eyebrows went up.

Hearing footsteps, the men looked over to see their office manager step into the room with a U.S. Postal Service courier. "Sorry to interrupt, but this just came in for you," said Lillian. The four agents regarded the courier cautiously as he stepped forward with a cardboard delivery envelope zippered inside a plastic covering. Greenberg reached for it, but the postman said it was addressed to Beretto.

"How'd you get inside?" asked Perez.

"The door was unlocked," said the courier defensively as Greenberg scowled at the man.

Correcting the apparent breakdown in office security, Lillian explained further. "It's okay, Director Greenberg. I vetted him before I brought him back here," giving the courier a reassuring look. "He insisted on hand-delivering it."

"Will you sign here, please?" asked the courier, holding up an electronic tablet. Curious about the package, Beretto quickly scribbled his name before eyeing the Chatahoochee postmark and tearing open the envelope. Inside was a thick stack of letter-size documents filled with printed material, along with a flash drive that slid out onto the table top. The men eyed the contents suspiciously.

Greenberg cracked, "What's that? Mrs. Wilde's last will and testament?" Completely absorbed in reading the documents, Beretto was indifferent to his boss's question.

"What the hell is it, Dom?" asked Greenberg again in a more serious tone.

Beretto continued to speed read the documents, shuffling through the pages. "Well I'll be a son-of-a"- He looked around the table. "You guys are *not* gonna believe this."

Greenberg raised his voice, insisting on an answer from Beretto. "Dominic, don't force me to"-

Beretto stood up slowly, and in a solemn tone he said, "It's everything we need. Gentlemen," looking at each man individually, "…you wanted a miracle." Gesturing at the contents on the table, "I give you Stella Wilde."

His curiosity boiling over, Greenberg reached across the table for the papers. A surprised look crossed his face as he began to grasp the significance of the information that described the cartel's operations detailed in the 154 pages in his hands. After scanning twenty pages, he looked up at the group. "This is...*unbelievable.*" To Agent Perez he said, "Epi, you and Lenny get on your phones and computers. I need you to verify as much of this information as you can in the next 24 hours. Do it quietly, and use a cover."

Distracted by the package's arrival, Scott rechecked *Bella Rosa's* image on the video monitor. Alarmed by the pictures of the crew casting off lines as the yacht began to pull away from the dock, he leaned over the table to get a better view of the monitor. "Dom, Hank, look at this. She's setting sail."

Beretto leaned across the table for confirmation, glaring at the screen. "This is significant. Rosa's yacht hasn't been away from Bahia Mar in a while. He's up to something." Looking up at his boss, he locked eyes with Greenberg. "You thinkin' what I'm thinkin', Hank?"

Nodding in agreement and holding the contents of the package up like it was manna from heaven, Greenberg said, "With *this* evidence, are you kidding? Make the call, Dom."

Scott fixed his attention on the video image of *Bella Rosa* turning away from the dock as she headed into the intracoastal, while Perez was already comparing the data from the documents with information in the FBI database.

Beretto stepped briskly to his desk and dialed his office manager. He was guessing Rosa's yacht was likely headed south, then around the Keys and into the Gulf of Mexico. "Lillian, drop what you're doing and get me the Coast Guard Commandant on the phone...the Key West station. Pronto." Beretto stared at the documents in his hand, still amazed that Stella had been able to get them out to him. "Then, I need you to make some highly-confidential copies for me."

CHAPTER TWENTY-TWO

Stella was having a dream she was baking in the sun, stretched out on a chaise lounge on the second floor master terrace at Villa Dellacroix when she heard the buzzing of a drone high overhead. Sprawled out in the nude, she could hear the drone getting closer as it descended toward her, sounding like a giant male mosquito. Then she could see it, hovering over the pool at a height exactly even with her chaise lounge a hundred feet from her as it slowly came closer. Apprehensive about what its intentions were or who controlled it, she watched it through the openings in the wrought-iron frame of the railing as it approached her.

In her dream, the drone hovered eerily, now only twenty feet away, invading her privacy like a one-eyed robot with sinister intentions. She felt vulnerable, but not completely defenseless. She stepped through the glass sliding doors and into the master bedroom she once shared with her husband. Stella reached inside her walk-in closet to retrieve the stainless steel twelve-gauge Mossberg pump hanging on the wall, and by its weight, she could tell it was loaded. Positioning herself in a shooting stance on the terrace, she pumped it once and chambered a round, took aim and fired as if she were shooting skeet back at the Dallas Gun Club. The buckshot blew the drone into a hundred pieces as she watched the remnants scatter, littering the pool deck and her garden of tomato, basil and pepper plants below. At last, the annoying buzz of the drone's motors that had plagued her *au naturel* summer gardening was silenced once and for all. Satisfied with her shot, she propped the twelve gauge against the terrace wall and went inside to take a nap.

In her dream, the empty bed was left unmade, and from the way the pillows were arranged, it looked as if her husband had just gotten out of it. Laying down in the bed, she gazed up at the spinning ceiling fan directly above her head as she took deep measured breaths, burying her face in the pillow that smelled of Yardley English lavender, her husband's soap. She mordantly wondered if he was lying in the same spot when he decided to kill her, collect her life insurance, and take control of her family trust. How long had she been asleep beside him and clueless about his intentions?

Restless and unable to nap, she went into the family room and hit the play button for the *Best of Tantra Lounge* on her i-Pod, a deeply sensual piece that she and Dan used to make love to. The tantra put her in a randy mood as she took a seat on the suede sofa and prepared to pleasure herself when she noticed Dan had left some papers on the onyx coffee table. Recognizing what looked like her signature on the top page, she scrutinized the wording and realized it was a forged application to double her life insurance. Beneath that lay a three-page will with her forged signature appearing at the bottom. The yellow smiley-faced emoticons were dancing around on the page like a video game, and taunting her with their vulgarity were the carefully-crafted paragraphs bequeathing Stella's entire fortune to Dan. She was madder than a gay lover with tonsillitis on Valentine's Day.

The psycho. Why couldn't she have married a man with a good heart and high moral fiber?

Furious, she snatched the bogus documents and took them outside on the terrace where she'd just dispatched the drone with a single shot. Holding them up for a final inspection, she stooped down and set the fake papers against the vertical splines of the wrought-iron railing with the offending language facing her. She hoisted her twelve gauge and aimed it at the documents, firing twice at point blank range. The shots went straight through the metal railing and blew the disgusting documents into hundreds of bits of confetti-size paper. Supremely satisfied, she watched the tiny pieces drift around aimlessly in the slight ocean breeze. Slowly, the confetti fell to the ground as the cloud of materiel settled over the garden and courtyard like a fresh layer of snow.

Stella awoke from her dream to the sound of shotgun blasts coming from somewhere above her on the ship, and from the gentle rolling motion, she realized *Bella Rosa* was now underway. In her panties and bra, and still woozy from several glasses of Camus, she got up and looked out her porthole just in time to see Blake scurrying toward her stateroom on the deck outside. He was accompanied by the biggest, hairiest guy she'd ever laid eyes on. Knowing what was expected of her, she quickly grabbed the black sequined party dress from the hanger and stepped into it as Blake turned his key in the lock.

"Stella, wake up," banging on the door and calling out as he entered, "The don is ready to see you." Troll stood in the open doorway scratching his back against the doorjamb like a big hairy bear as he watched Stella zip up her dress. She jumped at the sound of two more shotgun blasts.

"Who's shooting?" she asked.

"Don Rosa enjoys shooting skeet after breakfast," explained Blake. "No worries. Let's get you freshened up. You are to meet him in the Grande Salon in ten minutes." He checked his watch and gestured toward the huge hairy guy with the strange pattern of shaved areas on his shirtless chest that lurked in the doorway- whose parents, she was certain, had mated with a Kodiak bear. "Troll will keep you company until I return," he announced as Troll dragged a chair across the parquet floor and parked his mas- sive frame in it while gnawing on a Slim Jim and chasing it with gulps from a 32 oz. bottle of Mountain Dew.

"You look like you're in pain, Mr. Troll," she said in an attempt to be pleasant.

"Still gotta .30 caliber…stuck in the crack o'…my butt," he com- plained between swallows of soda, "…but I feel a lot better…with you here," leering at her. Done with his beef jerky and Mountain Dew, he licked his fingers and thought about having his way with her, if only the don would turn him loose.

She was strangely curious about the huge hairy brute, but his response creeped her out. Stella excused herself, shutting the door to the head and locking herself in to make her final improve- ments, deciding to keep it locked until Blake returned. She hoped it was bear-proof. Gathering her cosmetics together on the marble countertop, she began to apply her make-up in the mirror as she thought again about her partial text message to Mark, stopping for a moment to say a quick prayer that she'd still be alive by the time he responded.

Finished with her makeup, she heard Blake's voice again. "Stella, time to go. Don Rosa is waiting." She unlocked the door, and together, the three of them made their way down the companionway to her meeting with her husband's new business partner.

Flanked by his two favorite thugs Salamonaca and Vasquez, Rosa stood as she entered *Bella Rosa's* opulent Grande Salon. She noticed that Rosa was a big man, with hair plugs, cold black eyes and skin as brown as the smoking Cohiba he held. Dressed casually, he wore tan Dockers and a beige short-sleeve Cuban shirt that showed off the deep tan he acquired from the many hours of golf at Doral. With Troll and Blake standing beside her, she extended her hand politely, and Rosa took the opportunity to kiss it. The drug lord said, "I've been enjoying your gardening videos for months, Stella. First time I saw your videos, I forgot how to breathe."

Embarrassed by his remark, she continued to look boldly into his cold black eyes without flinching. She'd heard all the horrible stories, and holding his gaze was one of the most difficult things she had to do in her life-and-death poker game with the notorious drug lord. "How do you do, Mr. Rosa," she said, withdrawing her hand from his grasp.

"Please," he said, gesturing toward the facing leather armchair,"...won't you have a seat. We have much to discuss." She crossed her legs slowly to invite his stare, her allure not going unnoticed. Troll and Blake remained standing behind her chair. "Would you like something to drink, some champagne, perhaps?" offered Rosa as he took a long pull from his cigar.

Surveying the glitzy gold lame and marble interior surrounding her, Stella gave him a forced smile and said, "A mimosa sounds good. By the way, where are we heading?"

Rosa snapped his fingers as the steward disappeared to bring their drinks. "For a cruise, dear girl. After all, we are a pleasure yacht, yes?"

Not expecting a straight answer, she smiled again, then a look of concern crossed her face. "I heard gunshots earlier."

"I enjoy shooting skeet after breakfast," aiming his finger and thumb into the air, "...and sharpening my marksmanship," he replied. "You never know when your shooting skills will be tested, wouldn't you agree, Stella?"

Refusing to be intimidated, she asked, "Please tell me where is my husband is, Mr. Rosa. Is he onboard?"

Rosa was impressed by her boldness but pressed his own agenda. In a paternal tone, he said, "You better start worrying about yourself, Stella."

"He's here, isn't he?" she asked again.

Rosa looked at Blake and Troll standing over her and shook his head at them. "As long as you cooperate with us, dear girl, your husband will live." He noticed her wince at the threat. "Very simply, you have something I want, and I have something you want." He took a step closer and continued to elaborate. "The information Morgan stole from us and gave to you will cause our cartel a lot of grief." Rosa's eyes narrowed, his brow furrowing. "Now, *you* have something that doesn't belong to you. Where is it?"

Stella had anticipated this moment and laid out the deal she'd been rehearsing since her abduction; "If anything happens to Dan, or if I disappear, all that information about your operations will be handed over to the FBI, the DEA, other cartels, Federales and CNN…and *The New York Times*." She shrugged helplessly, watching his face contort with skepticism as she held up her empty palms. "It's out of my hands, Mr. Rosa."

Salamonaca spoke up. "I don't think she gave it to anybody, boss. I think she's just trying to save her own"-

Rosa held up his hand to silence him. Restraining his annoyance with her, he eyed the Cohiba, rolling it between his thumb and forefinger as he gathered his thoughts. "I had heard you're a reasonable woman, Stella." Disappointed, he cocked his head. "I was really hoping you'd be more reasonable about this." Stella continued to give him a determined look as he sat forward in the leather chair. "Here is what we're going to do, pretty lady. I'm going to give you one day to think about this. Then, well… Danny boy may have to go for a swim." Sensing she didn't quite understand what a sleazeball her husband had been, he continued to elaborate on his misdeeds. "I took him in, trusted him as my new partner and gave him $40 million to pay his bills-*your* bills also, as I understand-as a token of my good faith. Instead, he went behind my back and spent the money on his own drug deal with my Columbian suppliers." He waited for her response, but Stella's failure to agree annoyed him. "Your husband's a piece of crap, and he owes me $40 million," bleakly intoning her culpability.

Stella had always known her husband was a snake when it came to business and that he'd faced the scrutiny of society on several occasions. But why should he be forced to face the judgment of a drug lord, a man who had no moral or legal right to end *anybody's* life? Wisely, she kept her thoughts to herself. "And now you want to kill him," she calmly surmised.

With a calm but implacable demeanor, Rosa answered her in a vernacular worthy of a Supreme Court judge; "He is fully blame-worthy and must be punished in accordance with the punitive pur-poses of the cartel. You may be able to save yourself, Stella, but you may *not* be able to save your husband."

Stella reached inside the top of her dress and pulled out the two printed pages, holding them out for Salamonaca's inspection. "Mr. Rosa, I understand that Dan wronged you, and I'm prepared to do whatever I can, financially, to make things right." She took a deep breath. "But I will do whatever it takes to protect us. Here are two pages from the 154 that will go public if I don't return to Vero with my husband."

Nodding to confirm their validity, Ramone handed the papers to his boss, whose face soured like he was reading his own obitu-ary. When he was finished, he looked up at her. "And the $40 mil-lion in cocaine?" asked Rosa.

"When I find it, I'll have it returned to you. Believe me, I want nothing to do with the cocaine business."

Rosa smirked dismissively. "And what do I get in return for let-ting you live?"

"My eternal silence, my enduring respect, the return of all your sensitive documents, and the $40 million in coke," said Stella calm-ly. "And, I am no longer your hostage and want my husband's busi-ness back. And to be left alone."

Rosa raised his eyebrows at her bravado, drawing deeply on his Cohiba before exhaling a cloud of smoke. "That's a long list of demands from someone in such a poor bargaining position."

She searched for a handle on the moment. "Are you familiar with the acronym MAD in nuclear warfare?" she asked him.

"Mutually assured destruction," interjected Vasquez, frowning at her. She was on a roll, but Rosa seemed skeptical. After all, it was his show, his money, his muscle, his ship, his guns, and he knew it.

From her conniving husband, Stella had learned a thing or two about the tools of the trade. Watching the drug lord puff away on his high-dollar smoke, she offered to him what she thought he would best understand. "Once we part company, I have nothing to profit from your demise, Mr. Rosa." They studied each other meaningfully for a few moments as something mystical stirred inside her, something that was urging her to stand up to this man with every fiber of her being.

When it came to women, Rosa learned years ago it was best to be patient. Part of him was secretly enjoying her company, testing himself to see how long he could resist her rationale and her charms. After all, it was only money, and there was a river of it out there. One thing clearly emerging through the cigar smoke was his decision that such a beautiful woman should indeed be exempt from torture. But others may not.

Weighing his options, Rosa looked up at his hostage sternly, locking eyes with her and taking another step closer. "If I don't have the name of the person you gave it to by tomorrow after dinner, it's because there isn't one. I have to make a choice, Stella. But now it's your turn." He nodded at Blake and Troll. "Take her back to her stateroom," waving his cigar. "Let her think it over."

With her unsettling dismissal, Stella remained defiant but cooperative, standing with her captors before they took her by the arms and led her from El Padron's courtroom. Plunged into the dark and ugly world that now seemed ready to claim her husband's life, she was trying to claw her way out but felt immersed in quicksand and sinking deeper.

She wondered if her nightmare would ever end.

CHAPTER TWENTY-THREE

I n the southeastern sky behind the approaching Coast Guard cutter, blue-grey storm clouds billowed up on the horizon ominously. A light rain began to fall with the storm's advance, and the wind picked up and shifted to the southeast with whitecaps forming on the water. Dispatched on a search and rescue mission nine hours earlier by Area Commands from her home port of Key West, the U.S. Coast Guard Cutter *Mohawk* had cruised to a point fifteen miles east-southeast of Fowey Rock Light. Waiting for her prey just out of radar range, the 210-foot medium endurance cutter (WMEC) slowed to nine knots as she continued on her course to intercept *Bella Rosa*. Equipped with the latest anti-radar stealth electronics, which reduced the ship's radar profile to that of a sport fisherman, she also carried a reconnaissance chopper and a five-inch gun with two 50 cal. rapid-fire deck guns mounted fore and aft.

The sun had dropped below the horizon ten minutes earlier, and in the approaching twilight and advancing foul weather, the two port-side lookouts standing watch on *Mohawk* could just barely make out the sweep of Fowey's white light through their binoculars. Keeping watch over the building wind and seas, the famous cast-iron lighthouse off *Mohawk's* port quarter was located seven miles southeast of Cape Florida on Key Biscayne. As the weather worsened, the lookouts shifted their watch positions inside, just aft of the cutter's command center.

Their cutter *Mohawk* was named after the Algonquin tribe of Iroquoian Indians who inhabited the Mohawk valley of New York, most notably during the 18th century. The tribe became famous for their camaraderie, their special skills, ingenuity and determination in battle. One of the last of the 210-foot "Famous" class cutters to be built, the ship held its place in history as the third United States vessel to bear this name. It was the intention of Captain Daniel C. Hightower and his crew to continue to emulate the strength and skill of those early native-American warriors, even if only on a search-and-rescue interdiction of a pleasure craft owned by a Mexican drug lord. The cutter had executed numerous search and boarding operations flawlessly, without loss of life, and the captain took his pledge to enforce U.S. laws on the high seas with the utmost gravity.

To compensate for his own limited combat experience, Captain Hightower tended to surround himself with more experienced officers who were well-versed in interdiction and combat tactics. Dressed informally in the traditional blue Coast Guard garb, his short grey hair, weathered face and crow's feet spoke to his maturity as a leader of men. From his command chair on the bridge, the captain searched the horizon for *Bella Rosa* through his binoculars as a steady eighteen-knot wind whipped the seas into a light froth. Concerned with the deteriorating visibility and his timetable, he turned to his executive officer.

"How we doin' with the SEAL team, Mark?"

Standing just behind the helmsman, Senior Chief Petty Officer Steinberg checked his watch and addressed the captain. "Sir, they're gearing up in the second-deck staging area and should be ready to deploy in about fifteen minutes."

"All right. Good." What's the ETA on our chopper with the FBI team?"

"They should be arriving any minute now, sir. They report that *Bella Rosa* has ignored all attempts to hail her."

Hightower lifted his cap and smoothed his hair back. "Guess we shouldn't be surprised, since they've ignored all our attempts over the last hour."

"No sir, guess not." Steinberg thought about another detail. "One thing that does concern me, sir. The FBI intel reports the vessel may be equipped with Stinger surface-to-air missiles."

"No worries, Mark. We'll keep the chopper out of harm's way and use our stand-off capability-just in case they want to try and shoot it out."

"Yes, sir, I concur," said Steinberg. A seaman appeared on the bridge with a tray of coffee. "Coffee, sir?" he asked, handing the skipper a cup of java.

Hightower sipped the brew and squinted at the open ocean that lay ahead. "One way or another, we're gonna put an end to their trafficking, and the intolerable murdering and kidnapping of U.S. citizens."

Sipping his coffee, SCPO Steinberg was in full agreement with his skipper. "It's outrageous, sir. According to my police sources, this guy Rosa's been operating like he's got diplomatic immunity."

Hightower set his coffee down on the bridge window ledge. "Well, that bullshit will be ending soon. Have the FBI task force report to me as soon as they arrive."

"Yes, sir," said Steinberg.

Petty Officer Second Class Sloan rang the captain on the intercom. "Skipper, sir, flight ops reports our Jayhawk on final approach three miles out."

"Roger that," responded Hightower, clicking off the intercom. Checking first the apparent wind indicator, "Helmsman, come about to heading one-four-five degrees and reduce speed to five knots. Let's make it easy for them."

"Yes, sir, heading one-four-five, reducing speed to five knots," repeated the helmsman.

***

Looking down from the Sikorsky Jayhawk in the darkening drizzle as it descended from five hundred feet, Mark McAllister could see the cutter turning into the wind as they approached from astern. At the advice of Beretto, he had worn his black low-visibility foul weather gear and left the high-vis yellow behind. Surrounding him aboard the HH-60 turbo chopper were Special Agents Beretto, Perez, and Scott, along with the pilot and co-pilot, Airmen Jennings and Thomas. Their flight from the top of the Brickell Plaza Federal Building in Miami to the cutter *Mohawk* had

341

been shorter but somewhat bumpier than the earlier 35-minute flight in the FBI chopper from Vero to the Miami Coast Guard headquarters.

Mark felt honored to be a part of the rescue team, and true to his word, he retrieved the flash drive from his safe deposit box at Northern Trust in Vero Beach earlier in the day, handing it over to Beretto for analysis along with the keys to Dan Wilde's home and Bentley. One of the few more puzzling items in his late wife's possession before she died, he was actually glad to rid himself of the keychain, relieved that the drive hadn't fallen into Rosa's hands. Mark had shared Stella's partial text with Beretto at the Vero FBI office, and though the two men hoped for the best, they were prepared for the worst. "Clever as the devil, and twice as pretty," was Beretto's comment to ease his concern over her safety.

Still, Mark's thoughts were of Stella. "I wish I could let her know her bank passcodes are secure," he shouted to Beretto through the chopper's headset over the whine of the twin turbos. "She was pretty worried that Rosa would spirit away her family's trust. It might give her a bit more confidence in the way she deals with him."

Beretto thought it through with less emotion. "As long as Rosa's uncertain about her access to her $1.7 billion and the cartel's files, he may keep her alive. Dan may not be so lucky. Rosa's murdered men for lesser reasons. I think he's using her husband for leverage."

Feeling some unexpected turbulence on their final approach, Mark held the overhead bar tighter to steady himself. "You might be right, Dom. With a maniac like Rosa, who knows?"

Tapping his finger against his temple, Beretto held on tightly and replied, "Better to be thinking with your big head, buddy."

With the light rain and moderate wind pelting the chopper's aluminum frame, Mark and the FBI task force watched through the windows as the chopper hovered over the cutter's helipad, then dropped the final two feet onto the deck with a jolt. Airman Thomas turned in the co-pilot's seat to give them a reassuring grin and a thumbs up, then unbuckled to slide open the passenger doors.

On the helipad outside, a crewmember rushed up, ducking his head to clear the still-rotating blades. "Captain Hightower wants to see you guys right away," he shouted over the noise of the decelerating turbines. "I'll take you to the command center. Follow me."

***

Stella Wilde was wondering how she came to be controlled by two very different crime bosses so totally at odds with each other; her husband, and Emilio Rosa. Nightfall had brought more rain, and her captors had kept her sequestered in her stateroom for the past 24 hours with little indication of their plans for her. She wondered if she would ever see Dan again. And if she did, what would she say? Needing some closure, she struggled with the list of his imbecilic screw-ups, but all she really wanted from him, besides his endless remorse, was knowing the answers to her three simple questions:

(1) What made you choose me as your wife?
(2) How much money do we need to be happy?
(3) Why did you try to strangle me?

After her five weeks in the psyche ward, and now held hostage by a power-crazed drug lord, Stella not only yearned for her freedom, but for some answers to her life's questions. If she was to survive, she felt ready to be born again and instinctively knew it was time to recreate herself. Yesterday, she was clever and wanted to change the world, but today, she was wiser and wanted to change herself.

She remembered the heavy cross-wakes inside Port Everglades and thought about their passage from Bahia Mar, unable to remember if she'd dreamt about sailing through the port, or if she'd been watching the parade of tugs and containerships from the windows in her starboard stateroom. Until now, the weather for the ocean leg of the passage had been mild, but she knew that was about to change.

Stella noticed the indicator in the brass barometer on her stateroom wall begin to fall precipitously around dinner time when she heard heavy footsteps in the passageway outside. The anxiety over her predicament weighed on her appetite, and she'd forced herself to finish the tuna salad sandwich the steward brought her earlier, washing it down with half a bottle of Camus to buoy her resolve.

She was ready when the men entered her room. "Where we goin'?" she asked Blake and Troll when they appeared in her doorway. Though they gave her appreciative looks in her tight-fitting black cocktail dress, neither had bothered to reply. Each held one of Stella's arms as they led her down the lighted companionway along the stainless steel railing toward *Bella Rosa's* stern. Having no idea of what Rosa had in store for her, she and her captors took the stairway up toward the aft salon on the second deck, a tricky feat in the Jimmy Choo high-heels she wore. She wondered which of his personalities she would be facing tonight; the old-school Spanish gentleman, or the murderous drug lord. Would she find redemption, or would she embrace destruction?

Entering the brightly-lit aft salon with her two taciturn escorts, she gasped at the sight of her half-conscious, bruised and bloodied husband standing with his hands tie-wrapped to a stainless steel grab rail over his head. Her heart sank as she realized he'd been tortured and could barely stand up, his mouth duct taped shut. The surgical scrubs he wore were stained by an open wound above his eye, and a trickle of blood ran down his face and neck. A large galvanized tub sat empty next to his bare feet, as if suggesting another round of yet unknown barbaric abuse lay ahead.

Overcome with pain and unable to speak, Wilde could only moan when their eyes met. Wanting to embrace her husband, she started toward him, but Blake and Troll held her back. Rosa, Salamonaca and Sorvino stood behind a folding metal work table laid out with a set of vise grips, an ice pick, claw hammer, and a large bowl of pure cocaine. As if there were some unexplained secret tribunal underway, the three were all dressed in black with Salamonaca holding a Beretta at his side that he pointed at the floor.

"What have you done to him?" she demanded of the men.

With a sanctimonious air, Rosa replied, "As I've said, I had to make a difficult decision. Now it's your turn, Stella. For the last time, where are my files?"

Fresh out of ideas, she blurted, "Spread all over the world if you don't let us go!"

Disgusted with her answer, Rosa turned to his bloodied captive, his patience at an end. "Mr. Wilde, since you like Colombian cocaine so much, Javier and Ramone have prepared a special treat for you." On Rosa's que, Sorvino held Wilde's head back, while Salamonaca held the gun to his temple and a tablespoon of uncut cocaine to his nostrils. "*You're* a party animal. Let's see you party, cowboy." Salamonaca cocked the gun and pressed it harder against Wilde's head, forcing him to inhale a huge helping of the pure narcotic. From the bowl of coke on the table, Salamonaca refilled the spoon and forced Wilde to snort another generous helping as his eyes grew larger with fear.

Holding her arms tightly, Troll held Stella back from the grotesque display as Blake pulled his .45 automatic and held it to her head. Pleading for mercy, she said, "Mr. Rosa, please…I'm begging you. Let us go and your information will be safe. I promise," a tear running down her cheek.

Rosa gestured for another spoonful, ignoring Stella's plea. "Ramone, give him some more. He wants to be a cocaine cowboy, so let him ride with it. *Again*, Mr. Wilde." With the gun pressed to his temple, Wilde was forced to snort another sickening dose of the powder, his body beginning to writhe from the rush as he twisted violently to free himself. Feeling he was about to have a heart attack, his eyes widened with terror and his heart began to pound uncontrollably as another huge dose of uncut cocaine coursed through his veins.

Stella knew his heart would burst if they kept it up. "Please, Mr. Rosa. Stop."

Rosa gave her a demonic look. "Give me a *name* and *location*, Stella." She hung her head, exasperated over his unwillingness to believe her before looking up at her husband.

"Dan, how did you get us into this?" she implored him. "We were the consummate couple. How'd we come apart like this?" she pleaded. "We let it slip away over money. Now, we say goodbye like this? Why, Dan?"

"Again," demanded Rosa, ignoring the banter. Wilde's pupils were so dilated from the powerful drug that his eyes looked completely black. With ten times more than a normal dose of coke in his system, Wilde began to convulse from the overdose, straining against the tie wraps binding his wrists to the overhead grab rail. Rosa snapped his fingers, and Sorvino disappeared, then returned with two bags of QuikKrete, a trowel, and a five-gallon container of water. Placing Wilde's feet inside the metal tub, he began mixing the powder and water around Wilde's feet.

Rosa locked eyes with Stella. "Hardens in under four minutes," he gloated. At Rosa's bidding, they slid Wilde and the tub of KwikKrete across the floor further down the grab rail, positioning him at the starboard-side door adjacent to the deck outside. The men watched as Wilde continued to convulse uncontrollably for a few more minutes before Salamonaca stepped into the drizzle outside to swing open the stainless steel gate. He peered over the side of the moving yacht to make sure there were no obstacles protruding from the hull below to impede the traitor's fall.

To Stella, Rosa said, "He can't redeem himself, but he can redeem you." All she could do was turn her head away, and in the absence of a reply, Rosa checked his watch. "Ramone, it's time. Push him to the edge." Pulling out a survival knife, Salamonaca cut Wilde loose from the grab rail and the two men moved him out the door, setting Wilde on the edge of the ship's railing. The tub teetered on the edge, balanced only by Salamonaca's hold on his victim's arm.

Realizing what they were about to do, Stella screamed. "NNNOOOOOOOO!! Please!" struggling to break free from their grasp.

Rosa gave her a dark look as he stepped toward her husband teetering on the rail. "To understand everything is to forgive everything," enunciating his words to her from across the salon. Without taking his eyes off Stella, Rosa reached outside into the darkness for her husband's shoulder and pushed him overboard, watching him splash with the bucket of QuikKrete into the black void of the Atlantic Ocean below.

"You are forgiven," he pronounced, his eyes fixed again on Stella through the stateroom window. Overcome with grief, Stella fell to her knees, then on all fours, retching at the sight of her husband going overboard. One of his trump cards now played, Rosa stepped back inside the Grande Salon to see if she was ready to change her story.

Nauseated by her husband's drowning, her stomach heaved several more times before she slowly picked herself up off the floor. Standing solemn faced, her arms held by Blake and Troll, she was overcome with a resolute calmness, her fear of death seeming to evaporate as she stood to face the man responsible for murdering her husband in cold blood, her resolve hardened by his savagery.

To Emilio Rosa, she said, "Someone will be punished. Instead of spilling anymore blood, I have faith in God that, in some way, my husband's death will be avenged by a power higher than me."

CHAPTER TWENTY-FOUR

M atching speed at nine knots, *Mohawk* trailed 500 yards astern of *Bella Rosa*, the cutter's radar-evading electronics making her appear like a 50-foot sportfish on the Feadship's Furuno radar system. Captain Hightower was pleased it was a moonless night, and in an additional effort to avoid detection, she was underway with her stealth lighting configuration activated, making her hard to spot in the dark drizzly night. To avoid the possibility of losing the lives of hostages or his own men in a full-scale assault, Hightower had been reluctant to order the boarding of the vessel until the odds were more in his favor.

Denied permission to engage their targets, the frustrated four-man SEAL fire team positioned on *Mohawk*'s bow watched the drama unfold through their scopes. The snipers were horrified to witness what looked like Rosa pushing one of his two hostages overboard with a galvanized tub attached to his feet, but from their angle they couldn't be sure when a rogue wave broke over the cutter's bow. The interior lighting inside *Bella Rosa's* salon made it easier to identify targets through the sliding glass doors, but keeping the scopes on their Barrett sniper rifles dry and focused in the rain was tricky with the ship's rolling bow action.

Chief Petty Officer Pinnell adjusted the dial on the top of his scope ever so slightly, sharpening the crosshairs that pinpointed a mole on the bridge of Rosa's nose. Gently, the team leader chambered a round in his .50 cal. Barrett, still focused on the drug lord as he glanced quickly at the other three men in his team to check their targeting. With Petty Officer First Class Murphy sighted in on RatMan, and PO2 Healy and Bennett sighted on Sorvino and Blake, each of his men had any man that held a weapon squarely in their crosshairs.

Pinnell was proud of his SEAL team. Under his command, the team had earned two unit citations for Meritorious Conduct in the past eighteen months; one during their interdiction of Somali pirates off the African coast, and the other when they prevented terrorists from taking over a large refinery in Kuwait. He pressed the talk button on his headset. "Roger that last, Captain. I say again, one hostage overboard, and I have eyes on Mrs. Wilde who is still at gunpoint. Permission to engage, sir."

On the bridge overlooking the SEAL team, Captain Hightower replied, "Negative on your request at this time, Chief. Stand by." Pinnell overheard some background chatter over his headset before Hightower continued. "My XO suggests launching the inflatable for search and rescue."

"Sir, may I suggest that launching the Avon may be a waste of time. My men say the victim may have had weights attached to him. He dropped like a set of Olympic barbells, sir." Distressed over his inability to prevent the victim from being thrown overboard, Pinnell worried about any further loss of life. There were drawbacks to their stand-off tactics. The difficulty of keeping his men focused on their targets in the drizzle and from the bow of a moving vessel meant that engaging them at precisely the perfect moment wasn't always possible.

"Roger that. We're showing depth of 650 feet here. He's on the bottom by now," said Captain Hightower.

"Yes, sir, I'm afraid so," replied Pinnell reluctantly.

Hightower thought a moment. "If any further loss of life looks imminent, you have my permission to engage, Chief. Use your best judgment. I'd like to get at least one of them out of there alive."

"Yes, sir. I'd like that, too. Sorry we couldn't save Mr. Wilde," said Pinnell. "We lost sight of him when that rogue wave broke over the bow."

What the Captain said next didn't make him feel any better. "You did the best you could, Chief." Hightower glanced over at the FBI team of Beretto, Scott and Perez, accompanied by a civilian as the group joined him on the bridge. "Got a feeling he was considered expendable," added the Captain.

"If you say so, sir," replied Pinnell.

When informed of the incident, Mark was saddened to learn they'd lost Dan Wilde overboard minutes earlier. "Dom, we can't lose Stella." The FBI agent nodded in agreement.

Beretto approached the Captain as Scott and Perez stood by. "Sir, Mrs. Wilde is the key witness in this entire investigation. We really need to ensure her safety."

Hightower regarded the FBI agent and his men. "I have a primary duty to protect my crew, Agent Beretto." After Beretto nodded in understanding, Hightower added, "What did you have in mind?"

"What about a boarding using Coast Guard marksmen?" asked Mark. "That would give us stand-off capabilities, even if it's just a diversionary boarding to draw their attention away from Stella."

The Captain raised his eyebrows at the two younger men. "You sure you guys don't have some personal feelings for this woman?" he asked, looking at Beretto, then at Mark.

Beretto was first to deny the Captain's intuition. "Purely professional," he suggested, meeting Mark's eyes. The author looked away, unwilling to confirm or deny what he knew was untrue.

At that moment, PO2 Gilchrist stepped forward to the bridge from the logistics room to speak with his skipper. "Sir, weather radar suggests the wind and rain may be diminishing for the next hour or so."

A look of relief crossed the Captain's face. "Thank you, Gilchrist." Turning to the group of men, he said, "Well, gentlemen, you may get your wish." He keyed the overhead intercom to speak with his XO who was already busy preparing a boarding party. "Chief Steinberg?"

A moment passed before Steinberg replied. Watching the faces of the men surrounding him on the bridge waiting to hear his orders, Hightower said, "I want you to prepare two boarding parties with five men each, two sharpshooters in each boat. Stealth tactics. I'm sending Agents Beretto, Scott and Perez with you. You may launch as soon as you're geared up. Weather maybe clearing."

"Yes, sir, we can deploy in five minutes," acknowledged Steinberg.

"Roger that. I will inform the SEAL team."

"Yessir."

Mark stepped up to speak with the Captain. "Sir, I'm a qualified marksman with an M-16 and a nine millimeter. I'd like to go with them."

Hightower was skeptical. "Mr. McAllister, you're a non-combatant. You're lucky to be here at all."

Using all his power of persuasion, Mark said, "Sir, Stella trusts me, and those Avons can handle up to eight men. Also, I know the layout of that Feadship. I want to help, sir, and I understand the risks."

While Hightower hesitated, Beretto chimed in. "Sir, that was the deal we made. Mr. McAllister has given us vital information, and he'll be my responsibility. We could always use an extra marksman."

Reluctantly, Hightower relented. "All right, McAllister. Go with them." He turned to Beretto and leveled an index finger at him. "He's *your* responsibility! God speed the both of ya!"

***

Somewhere east of the Alligator Reef Lighthouse that marked the outer reef off Islamorada, *Bella Rosa* continued on a southerly course at nine knots with *Mohawk* in close pursuit. Navigating in the pitch-black sea with clearing skies, the group leader in the lead Avon stayed focused on the lights of Rosa's Feadship now only 90 yards ahead. The stealth electronics was working perfectly, and so far, the Coast Guard cutter had gone undetected by Rosa's men.

The two fully-loaded Avons had launched from the cutter's stern, and with the state-of-the-art sound shielding, continued to motor quietly toward *Bella Rosa* with the four-man SEAL team still positioned on *Mohawk's* bow. Hoping to remain undetected until they boarded her, the plan was to overwhelm Rosa's men with an assault from the stern using the yacht's swim platform to gain access. The fifteen heavily-armed men included two Coast Guard sharpshooters in each boat with the FBI team in the lead inflatable. The seas had settled down, minimizing the bow spray and making it easier for Mark to keep a sharp eye out for lookouts that might suddenly appear on *Bella Rosa's* fantail. So far, the element of surprise was still on their side. He wondered how long their luck would hold.

His heart pounding fiercely, Mark nodded at Beretto sitting next to him in the lead Avon, the adrenaline coursing through his veins as he held the M-16 and hoped like hell he wouldn't have to use it. Part of him was already regretting volunteering for the mission. He rechecked the rest of the gear the quartermaster had given him; Kevlar vest, flashlight, survival knife, EPIRB, and four extra 40-round clips. Everything was going according to plan until he looked back and noticed the trailing Avon stopped dead in the water by a lobster trap that had fouled their prop with a polypropylene line. Their own boat slowed to a crawl as he and Beretto watched one of the men jump overboard with his survival knife to free the prop. In less than a minute, the man had cut the line free and signaled for both boats to continue as his crew pulled him back into the Avon. Ahead, Mark could see *Bella Rosa's* swim platform glistening in the dark as they motored to within thirty feet of their target.

Suddenly, he heard men shouting in Spanish and saw a man appear at the stern rail holding a Scorpion .30 cal. automatic rifle. As the man spotted the boarding party from a distance of twenty feet, he was quickly joined on the fantail by a second guard also equipped with a Scorpion. Rosa's men chambered rounds and took aim at his Avon.

"U.S. Coast Guard! Lower your weapons!" shouted the team leader as Rosa's men raised their weapons and prepared to fire. The guards ignored the order, leaned back and took aim. Shots rang out, the noise deafening as both guards were struck by .50 caliber bullets fired from *Mohawk* before Mark and his group could open fire, and both guards went down just as his crew reached the swim platform. With Beretto, Scott, Perez and three other team members, they leaped onto the swim platform and frantically ran up the steps to the stern, crouching behind the bulkhead where the two guards now lay motionless. More shots rang out and he felt a bullet whiz by his head. He looked behind him and could see that a Guardsman was down, sprawled out on the floor of the Avon, in pain and gasping for air. As Mark started toward him to render first aid, he met Mark's eyes, gave him the "OK" sign and pointed at his vest.

"Targets are down!" yelled one of the snipers into his headset. "One of them ran forward. I think it was Rosa."

From their crouching position behind the stern rail, the three remaining Guardsmen split from his group, one heading down the port rail toward the bow and two more moving to starboard. Mark and his FBI team crouched at the stern rail as the second Avon pulled up to unload five more Guardsmen. In close quarters, Beretto signaled for his men to switch to their nine millimeters, and the four slung their rifles over their shoulders as the second group of men made their way up the stairway. Mark peeked over the top of the bulkhead and pointed his Beretta toward the shattered glass sliders to identify more targets and scan the area for Stella.

What he saw next almost stopped his heart. With three of Rosa's men lying motionless on the blood-stained salon floor, he was horrified to see Salamonaca put a gun to Stella's head and drag her toward the stern, screaming obscenities and using her body to shield his own from the SEAL team on *Mohawk's* bow.

"Back off or she dies," yelled Rosa's number one assassin as he jammed his gun to her temple. With tears rolling down her cheeks, Stella was undoubtedly thinking this had to be the end of the road. The sight of Stella with a gun to her head drove him to action.

With RatMan using her body to shield his, Mark knew the SEAL team wouldn't have a shot from *Mohawk's* bow. It was truly a Mexican standoff, he thought, as the desperate assassin held her in front of him and screamed his demands a second time. Thirty feet from where Mark crouched, they hadn't spotted him yet as he squatted behind the bulkhead. Fear was the mind-killer, he kept telling himself, struggling to shrug off his panic, remembering what it was like to get shot. He had an idea. With two fingers, he signaled to Beretto through the smoke that he was heading forward along the port side railing to improve his angle. Crawling forward quickly under the salon windows, Mark stopped at a section that was blown out from the earlier round of gunfire. Very carefully, he set his M-16 down on the deck strewn with glass shards and raised his head to see over the shattered window ledge. Crouched twenty feet from RatMan and Stella, at a right angle and slightly behind them, Mark could see that he was the only one who had a shot at stopping RatMan. He thought about all the hours he'd spent at pistol training and prayed to God his aim would be true as he raised the Beretta, his palms sweating, hoping to save her. Lucky, lucky, lucky he thought as he took aim.

"Mark, look out!" yelled Stella. Out of the corner of his eye, RatMan had spotted Mark crouched at the demolished window and quickly turned to aim, his head only inches from Stella's when he fired twice. One bullet shattered the double-cased aluminum window frame just below Mark's chin and lodged in the casing without penetrating, the other in the metal bulkhead. Taking aim again with his Beretta, he pointed it at RatMan's chest and squeezed the trigger. The shot hit him just under the armpit, and he heard Stella scream again as RatMan staggered backward from the impact, releasing his hostage as he fired two more stray shots into the yacht's headliner over his head. Stella hit the floor panic-stricken and frantically crawled away on all fours as she peered up at Mark, her eyes pleading for him to end it. Realizing this would be his last opportunity, Mark stood, and as RatMan brought his gun to bear again, Mark fired two more rounds at his attacker. Both bullets hit home as RatMan screamed in pain, falling on his back, coming to a final rest on the floor beside Blake, Sorvino and Troll.

With four of Rosa's best men down along with two of his guards, Beretto yelled directions at Scott and Perez as they picked their way through the shattered glass doors of the salon, backed up by the five Guardsmen from the second Avon. Two more of Rosa's security guards stepped into the salon with their hands raised as two Guardsmen quickly placed them in handcuffs. Side arms pointing ahead, the remaining men from the second Avon scampered along the port and starboard decks and moved toward the bow in the search for Rosa.

Breathing heavily in relief, his face lightly streaked with blood from flying glass and aluminum shards, Mark holstered his gun and walked to Stella with outstretched arms. Grasping her shoulders, he looked her in the eye and said, "I'm sorry we couldn't save your husband, Stella."

"I'm not sure anyone could save him," she replied, still stunned by all that had happened. She gave him a hug, looking around the smoke-filled salon, then back up at him. "Look at you," brushing off the debris and wiping his face, "...dress you up but can't take you anywhere."

The two were joined by Beretto in the center of the salon floor as he holstered his weapon and leaned in to give his star witness a hug. To Mark, he said, "Nice shootin', Tex," with a pat on the back. "Didn't think you had it in you."

"It was either me or him. You got a murderer shooting at you, you gotta"-

"No worries, Mark. You did the right thing," replied Beretto. "You saved our girl," nodding at Stella, "...and rid the world of RatMan. Trust me, the world's a better place without him."

Agent Scott joined the three in the middle of the demolished room, stepping over the bodies of Rosa's men. To Beretto, he said, "Hightower's sending over a third Avon to assist with the clean-up."

Pointing toward the bow with his gun, he added, "Gonna go find Rosa," and headed down the starboard deck with Perez and the rest of the men.

"Dominic, you got my package, right?" she asked. Beretto nodded. "Can I assume that, with those files, I'm off your list of co-conspirators now?"

"Yes ma'am, you may. And anytime you need an able-bodied crew for your sailboat, just want you to know that I'm now a graduate of Capt. McAllister's School of Apprentice Seamen," nodding at Mark. With a sweep of his arms he said, "And now, we've got some cleaning up to do."

Before anyone could move, the three were shocked to see a blood-covered Emilio Rosa lunge toward them from the spiral staircase at the far end of the salon. With two .30 caliber Scorpions slung over his shoulders pointing at them and ready to fire, he yelled, "Everybody! Drop your weapons and face away! I'm taking"-

On *Mohawk's* bow fifty yards from *Bella Rosa's* stern, Chief Petty Officer Pinnell was ready. Finally, he had the shot he'd waited hours for and the prize was in his sights. "You're not taking nobody nowhere," said Pinnell outloud as he quickly lined up a shot that had to be threaded between a panic-stricken Stella Wilde and a surprised Agent Beretto. Without hesitation, he squeezed the trigger and the Barrett fired, sending a single .50 caliber projectile traveling at 3,340 feet per second right through the center of Rosa's chest. With his fingers still on the triggers, the drug lord fell backwards from the impact, haphazardly firing a dozen rounds into the headliner above as he dropped like a three-hundred-pound sack of cocaine. After the shooting stopped, Stella, Mark and Dominic surveyed the room in disbelief, finding themselves on the floor once again and lucky to be alive as pieces of the ceiling continued to fall around them.

Stella waited for the smoke to clear before picking herself up, the last gunshots still ringing in her ears. Rosa lay motionless on the floor as the men watched her slowly pick herself off the floor and walk across the room like she was in a trance. She walked to where the drug lord lay in a pool of blood and taking his last few breaths. Standing over her tormentor, she crossed herself and focused her full attention on the man at her feet.

Unable to move, Rosa watched her lips begin to form the last words he would ever hear. In a trance-like state, Stella said, "It would do all our hearts...a world of good...to see you in...a box of wood." She thought of Dan, and the vision forever etched in her brain of Rosa pushing him overboard as the immortal lines of Dylan Thomas echoed in her head;

Where blew a flower may a flower no more, lift its head to the blows of the rain.

For the last time, she looked him in the eye. "Now, you too, are forgiven." With his final breath, he reached up for her hand, wanting to feel comforted by her, to feel her warmth and softness, to feel her forgiveness, but the grief she felt kept her hands firmly at her sides.

There had been a time she remembered, not that long ago as a young girl, when she believed in the future, a future she couldn't wait to embrace. But now she wanted to slow the world down, the future looking more and more like someplace she didn't want to be. She hadn't planned to bring down the murdering leader of the drug trafficking ring that held her captive and murdered her husband, but deep down inside, she knew the world was better off.

She watched Rosa's cold black eyes close for the last time, his hand dropping limply to the floor as she turned to look at the group of men who waited to hear what she would say next.

Returning to her rescuers, with a regal air she asked, "Gentlemen, can I go home now?"

Mark felt the tugging on his heartstrings, like millions of stars were lining up for this one moment in time, a moment he'd yearned for since the beginning of time. To her he said, "You once asked me if I would take you there. Remember?" She nodded demurely. "Come with me," he said.

They walked hand-in-hand along the dimly-lit deck all the way to the very front of *Bella Rosa* without saying a word. Alone with her at the bow, he turned to her with his hands on her hips. "So, Stella, what are you serving your guests these days on your private dining terrace?"

She took a moment to wipe a tear from her eye, fondly remembering the question from six weeks earlier as they kissed for the first time, a kiss that defined timeless.

Managing a weak smile, she looked into his eyes and replied, "Maybe some coffee, maybe some tea...........maybe a little bit of me."

CHAPTER TWENTY-FIVE

Three months had passed since the shootout with Rosa and his men aboard *Bella Rosa* off Islamorada. Soulfully in need of a change in scenery, Mark and Stella had embarked on a colorful sailing trip on *Dream Girl,* sailing the 67-foot Baltic 5,993 miles through the Panama Canal all the way to the Tahitian Islands. For the author and his new first mate, it was the added experiences you have when you are in danger of losing your life that create the longest-lasting memories, and it was those same violent memories that the couple wanted to vanquish during their exploration of the South Pacific. After being held against her will in a psyche ward for five hellish weeks, then kidnapped and almost murdered by a homicidal Mexican drug lord, Stella was long overdue for the vacation of vacations. True to his word, Mark was taking her to his promised sanctuaries, the vibrant worlds she'd never before seen.

He enjoyed sitting back in the cockpit and steering the yacht with his feet on the big stainless steel wheel when conditions permitted. The mild weather summoned a reflection on the years he spent in Vero Beach, a town where etiquette and social protocol still mattered. His reverie prompted him to wonder what Abigail Van Buren would have to say about their situation. In a humorous mood, he imagined the letter he might write would read:

"Dear Abby, my wife was screwing the mobster next door before he was stabbed by his own wife, who was then locked up in the loony bin by the FBI. Then the mobster was kidnapped by a Mexican drug lord and dropped overboard in a bucket of concrete. After losing my own wife in a tragic accident with a dump truck, the drug lord kidnapped the mobster's wife, whom I helped rescue, and we are now married. My new wife and I still own homes next door to each other, so should I bake her brownies and continue boning her, or serve her enchiladas and live separately? Signed, Confused in Vero Beach."

Abby might well reply, "Dear CIVB, A gentleman neighbor should always phone or write ahead, married or not, but make sure she's gotten rid of that knife and takes her meds! Watch a few of her favorite movies (but not *Fatal Attraction*), and don't stay overnight unless she wants to have sex with you. Signed, Abigail Van Buren."

Then he decided that he was being silly and never wrote the letter. Having sailed 6,000 miles west from Vero to explore the cultural differences that set Tahitian etiquette apart from that of Vero Beach, he was certain the Polynesian chieftains would find the story just as wacky as Abigail Van Buren would.

It had been a day of weather extremes on the main island of Tahiti, alternating between sunny skies and purplish-blue-hued cloudbursts that refreshed the lush tropical foliage and only made Mark and Stella appreciate the setting all the more. The newlyweds had spent the morning basking in the private recesses and warm, crystal-clear turquoise waters of the Maraa Grotto. There, they listened to warblers, cuckoos and blue lorikeets singing the praises of two back-to-back rainbows as the sun re-emerged from its temporary hiding place in the clouds. It was this incredibly alluring tropical paradise so far removed from Vero Beach that evoked the possibility of a radical change in lifestyle, a spiritual rebirth for them both.

They'd been sailing for almost two months in French Polynesia, and after cruising the out islands of Marquesas and Tuamotus, it was nice to make it back to civilization for a change-if Tahiti could even be thought of that way. Mark joked to Stella that if he ordered dinner in French he would likely be served a toilet and the left front fender of a '59 Renault. But since honing their French language skills over the last three months, the couple no longer had any qualms about conducting business in the world's most beautiful language, or whispering it during endearing moments of passion. They especially looked forward to visiting the Bonne Marche on the largest island in the French Polynesian chain. It was a place where they had real supermarkets, liquor stores, internet, people, even traffic, and sometimes they were in disbelief over having missed all that. But before they sailed into the harbour at Papeete, they had some sites to see first.

Continuing their sojourn, the couple's wanderlust was far from satiated, even with the more unpredictable weather of summer coming on and a bit of sea fatigue in their bones. The weather in the Tahitian Islands was never boring, often changeable at the drop of a hat. After enjoying the incredible magic and mystery of Maraa Grotto with its unique rock formations, they gunkholed the boat in and out of anchorages on the way to Taravao. There, they dropped anchor and burned two tanks of Nitrox while diving for black pearls among a grouping of rainbow-lipped oysters that the natives called Concha Nacar. Stella surfaced the lucky diver, opening her third and seventh oysters with her stainless blade to discover two stunning black pearls they would later have crafted into earrings by an artisan at the Bonne Marche in Papeete.

Also on their bucket list for the island of Tahiti was the beach at Teahupoo, where the famous Billabong Pro surf competition was held at the end of the south coast road in Tahiti Iti. On the beach, the couple met a guy named Phillipe who happened to be the editor of Polynesian Radio One. Completely taken with Stella in her black Brazilian thong, Phillipe had the idea to interview Mark after discovering he was a best-selling author, but they both suspected it was really Stella he wanted to please. Knowing what his publisher would say about free publicity, Mark went along with it. So, Phillipe had his crew set up a mobile studio for the interview right on the beach at Teahupoo and include a simulcast on the radio web site, and it turned out to be a lot of fun for everyone.

Even more fun was on tap when a reporter from the largest newspaper in Tahiti, *La Depeche de Tahiti*, came upon the simulcast scene on his scooter and offered to write an article about their adventures that would include some scenes from the apprehension of Emilio Rosa. Later, when they read the article, they were both quite taken with the reporter's comparison of Stella to the beauty of "the island's sunsets that set fire to boundless horizons and endless coral reefs far too breathtaking to describe in words alone." For Mark, it was true; her strawberry-blonde hair and sparkling emerald-green eyes did have a way of setting fire to endless horizons of island sunsets. For the next week they spent their time simply enjoying Tahitian life, drinking Hinano beer and eating coconuts and fresh crab with some of the most endearing people on the planet.

Three days had passed since their return sail from Papeete, and Mark and Stella were sitting at a four-top in the Grande Dining Hall at Sofitel with a beautiful view of the surrounding lagoon as the sun was about to set. The casually-dressed newly-weds had booked the honeymoon suite at the Sofitel Private Island Resort in Bora Bora, a French-built boutique property that is nestled on its own motu and surrounded by the crystal clear turquoise waters of the Bora Bora Lagoon. From their table they had a view of *Dream Girl*, moored stern-to at the private dock that offered double 220-volt hookups that could accommodate the yacht's air conditioners. Their favored resort for those times when they wanted to really stretch their legs on land, Sofitel offered incredible views looking back toward the main island, and the cuisine and service were consistently five-star.

Speaking softly between themselves, they voiced the praises of an elegant European-style twenty-room bed and breakfast they'd discovered on their sail around the tip of Bora Bora. Built of solid marble, exclusive Eternelle Resort was nestled on the secluded southern-most tip of Matira Beach at Matira Point. The finest stretch of pink-sand beach in all of Bora Bora began at Matira Point, and through Stella's new well-connected banker at Credit Suisse, they'd found out that the beautiful B&B was for sale and came with the added bonus of a four-year backlog of guest bookings. Clinking champagne glasses, Mark could tell what she was thinking.

"Know where we could pick up a spare $42 million?" he asked Stella.

"You know the money is irrelevant, mon cherie," she replied with a knowing smile.

Grinning, he supposed if your maiden surname was Dodge, then maybe what she said was true. One of the benefits of the super-rich, *and* being on the right side of the grass, was the ability to make acquisitions and write a bank cheque without having to worry about arranging financing. Although he didn't consider himself super-rich, he appreciated the convenience of having a wife who was.

"*How* irrelevant?" he asked playfully, reaching under her sheer black cover-up to squeeze her bare thigh under the table. She squirmed agreeably at his touch and kicked off her Jimmy Choo wedges, softly planting a bare foot into his manhood.

"We'll find out tomorrow morning when we meet with Devon," she whispered. He could feel her toes burrowing inside the leg of his Polo cargo shorts before noticing that a distinguished Japanese couple at the next table was quite amused with Stella's antics. Smiling politely at the couple, Mark rearranged his Guy Harvey shirt to cover her probing foot while she continued with her mischievous gymnastics and jiggled her bikini-clad breasts from across the table to tease him.

In Bora Bora, most resorts offer special romantic sunset dinners. At the Sofitel Private Island resort, they have a very unique experience, quite different than any other resort. What Stella and Mark especially liked were the incredibly romantic beach dinners, the two part evening affairs. Starting their night at the top of the motu with breathtaking views of Bora Bora, at sunset the staff popped open champagne and seated them at a waterfront table to enjoy a cold glass of bubbly and canapes with the incredible sunset views.

After the sun sank below the horizon, the staff guided them down the lighted tiki-torch path to the beach where they sat at candlelit tables for two and could dig their toes in the sand, and when they were alone, each other's privates. While the stars and moon twinkled in the Polynesian sky above, they were served a delicious gourmet meal accompanied by native dancers who spouted fire while twirling flaming batons and providing enough flames to sear the imagination.

Later, they set fire to their evening with two hours of love making that was too hot for words. Afterword, Mark showed her a list of some key questions on his tablet prepared for Devon Rousseaux, their new banker from Credit Suisse. Though his credentials seemed impeccable, he enjoyed doing his own vetting. The ubiquitous Credit Suisse ATMs that dispensed cash in either French francs or American dollars were a real convenience for them both, and Stella nodded her approval of his list before pulling him down on her for more dessert. It was one of those evenings that they would look back on fondly and remember many years down the road.

***

The next day was Monday, October 9, Columbus Day in the U.S., and the holiday always reminded him of the wild and woolly Columbus Day Regattas of past years. It had rained on the island of Bora Bora last night, as predicted, and the winds were indeed from the southwest, blowing over Mount Otemanu, the highest point on the eighteen-square mile island. Together with Mount Pahia, Otemanu formed the remnants of an extinct volcano that once existed in the center of the island, and today its craggy remnants still towered over the island. Together, the two pinnacles were legendary, giving the exotic island the distinctive skyline recognized throughout the world.

Following their amorous evening together in the third-floor honeymoon suite at Sofitel, Mark had risen at dawn, dressed, and left Stella snoozing peacefully in bed. The rainstorm that sounded like a freight train passing in the night was on his mind, and he wanted to check on *Dream Girl's* mooring as he quietly shut the gold-lame door and headed down the marbled hallway to the docks along the lagoon. Waiting for the elevator, he thought about their nine a.m. meeting with Devon Rousseaux. Though they both agreed he was well-qualified to manage their affairs, he noticed she had an inclination for choosing trust attorneys who looked like they'd just stepped off a GQ runway. Of course, looks didn't always guarantee success. Just ask Damon Morgan.

Finding that *Dream Girl* had ridden the storm out flawlessly like the staid lady that she was, Mark returned to their suite after sharing a brief "bonjour" and pleasantries with a few of the hotel staff and stopping to pick a fresh papaya and a pink hibiscus for his bride. A half-hour later, the couple found themselves seated in Sofitel's five-star Bamboo Room restaurant overlooking the crystal-clear turquoise waters of the lagoon, waiting on Devon Rousseaux to make his appearance. Hotel guests were commenting on how ravishing Stella looked with the pink hibiscus behind her ear, and minutes after Mark and Stella ordered a Norwegian smoked salmon platter with fresh mango, coconut, and papaya with two triple Kopi luwak expressos, in walked Monsieur Devon Rousseaux, Managing Director of Wealth Management at Credit Suisse. Dressed in a dark blue pinstripe Brioni suit with a pink dress shirt and matching Hermes tie, and a black leather satchel over his shoulder, Rousseaux looked head-to-toe like the proverbial Swiss banker as he meandered his way to their waterfront table.

"Enchante," said Rousseaux, kissing Stella's hand and shaking Mark's. "What a view! Mr. and Mrs. McAllister, I have some excellent news. May I join you?"

"Of course," replied Mark as they sat. "Please...it's Mark and Stella. What would you like, Devon?"

"Oui. Bien sur. Italian expresso for me," he replied, setting his satchel of files and laptop in the seat next to him.

Stella smiled and offered a suggestion. "You should try the Kopi luwak, Devon. If you're an expresso aficionado, you'll like it."

"On your recommendation then, Stella," Rousseaux nodding to the young Polynesian waitress. "A triple, please."

Mark took a moment to evaluate the attorney/banker sitting across the table. From their last meeting in Vero Beach, he knew Rousseaux to be a graduate of Harvard Business School and Harvard Law, with an M.B.A. from Tufts University. A well-dressed man with a European flair, Rousseaux appeared to be in his late forties, with kind blue eyes, silver hair and a smile that must have set him back a cool fifty grand in dental work. He was a likable guy, and they relied on Stella's inscrutable sense of intuition to give him a seat at their table.

As the waitress served their expressos, salmon and fruit, they politely asked for some privacy. Stella set her cup down and leaned forward. "So, Devon," she began, "...what's the good news?"

Reaching inside his satchel, Rousseaux pulled out a thick file and spread it open on the table. "In their infinite wisdom," he began, "...the Florida Secretary of State rejected your former late husband's stock transfer of Baja Grille shares to Mr. Rosa, citing 'irregularities' in the documents." She waited for him to explain further as Mark gave him a questioning look. Rousseaux shrugged and added, "Our bank used to deal with one or two regulators, but now it's five or six." Mark nodded his understanding. "Therefore, with the survivorship clause now executed, the entire company is bequeathed to you, Stella," he said, beaming and folding his hands on the table.

Mark put his hand up. "Okay, Devon," he said. "Before we go any further, we spoke of a negotiated management fee of 50 basis points. Will you and Credit Suisse agree to that?"

The banker smiled at his question. "Oui, monsieur, if we can have the whole enchilada, pun intended."

He liked his sense of humor and looked at his wife for her answer. "I'll move the family trust to Credit Suisse," said Stella with a wave of her hand. "I'm through with Barclays."

Hearing her say this was music to his ears and Rousseaux produced a transfer authorization from his satchel. "Let me collect your signature right here please, Stella," pointing with his index finger. After she signed as trustee, he continued. "Obviously, with the demise of Emilio Rosa, we were all spared the expense of a trial, and, with that, the avoidance of negative publicity that would have devalued Baja Grille company stock. Because of the history there, I had a feeling you'd want out, so I had our bankers shop the company and find a potential buyer."

She looked at Mark, then at Devon. "Very intuitive, Devon. Who and how much?" she asked.

"Pepsi-Cola. Normally, they insist on a CAGR of ten percent, but because they anticipate large synergies from the merger by folding it into their subsidiary Taco Bell, they were flexible in their offer of $78 million. Rousseaux watched her wince at the price.

"Because the price was a little under market, I encouraged them to offer you a special convertible preferred stock with a six percent quarterly dividend. If you want it."

She looked at Mark. "Do I?"

Mark replied, "I think you do," doing a check of Pepsi's metrics on his tablet. "Pepsi has a fortress balance sheet and should continue to grow at a CAGR of nine percent, and with the six percent dividend, you'd have an annual total return of about fifteen percent." He looked at Devon. "Unless they could up their offer."

Rousseaux shook his head. "They started with an offer of $65 million in common stock a week ago, so..."

"Do it, Devon," said Stella. She gave Mark a big smile and hooked her arm around his. "Put $42 million of it into a joint marital account in both our names and the balance into my family trust account. Offer the owners of Eternelle their full asking price of $42 million, they pay all closing costs."

Impressed with the elegance and directness of her response, Rousseaux cocked his head and raised his eyebrows. "Of course," he replied, typing the notes into his laptop as he looked up at her. "No one can forecast the economy with complete certainty, but I believe your husband's expectations will prove to be conservative." When he finished with the notes in his laptop, he remembered something else. "Oh, almost forgot. We discovered an extra $28 million in Baja's cash account," lowering his voice and leaning forward in his chair, "...with an entry specified as 'sale of certain commodities'." The banker gave them both a knowing wink.

Rousseaux was not expecting her to be prepared with plans for large amounts of unforeseen cash balances, but Stella was ready to roll with it. "Let's set up a charitable remainder trust with those funds," looking at her husband who was nodding in approval. "Mark and I have a list of charities we would like to add as beneficiaries. We want to spend our lives on good things that will outlast us," she explained.

Wow, he thought. "Ah...okay then. I'll set it up." The banker had a feeling he was going to enjoy his new clients. "Oh, and there's this, Stella," showing her a written settlement offer from Valiant Pharmaceutical. "After sending them a demand letter on your behalf, I negotiated a cash settlement of $63 million from Valiant with the stipulation that we accept a private *undisclosed* payment, avoid talking to the press, and agree to dismiss our suit with prejudice." He saw that the settlement amount was a surprise to her and continued to explain. "In our pre-discovery research into the clinical trials, we uncovered some rather gruesome facts about the side effects of the drugs you were prescribed that would be impossible for a jury to overlook. Because of what we discovered, there is a punitive element to the settlement that exceeds actual damages. Congratulations, Stella." He slid the settlement agreement across the table for her signature.

She looked away, out over Bora Bora's beautiful lagoon, at *Dream Girl*, at the people coming and going on the beach, searching for the right words and the right answer. With a slight wince she lowered her head and thought for a moment about all the hurt that the drugs had actually caused. In retrospect, she couldn't hold Valiant responsible for destroying a marriage that was already destined for destruction. Stella thought about Dan. *Our souls are made from the love we share, undimmed by time.*

She thought about three possible heavenly surprises; those expecting to see certain souls that were missing; those surprised to see others they didn't expect to see; and those surprised to see *her*. Every now and then, she thought, we do find it within our hearts to forgive others, and it cost nothing to forgive, except perhaps a loss of face or pride. So let it go. *Thank you for guiding me past the obstacles along the way, and for keeping me strong when all seemed lost.*

She thought about what Mark said to her almost five months ago, whispering the words softly to herself. "Every winter that ever descended has ended." It would take her longer than a winter to heal, but at least this settlement would bring her some measure of closure and perhaps some joy to others.

Turning back to the two men at her table waiting patiently for her answer, she said, "Fine," looking up at Mark as he gave her a hug. To Rousseaux, she said, "I'll agree to their terms. I'm ready to move on. Put the entire settlement into the charitable trust. I will let you know how we want to allocate the funds in a few days."

"I'll take care of it," said Rousseaux confidently, looking at Stella in a whole new light. She seemed to have an aura surrounding her that he hadn't noticed earlier. "Will there be anything else?"

"I think we're good, Devon. Merci beaucoup, monsieur," she replied with a smile, then turned her gaze out over the Bora Bora lagoon at the boats anchored in the harbor. The "Pearl of the Pacific", she searched for the words, but could find none to describe the unforgettable natural beauty of the island accented with all the incredible varieties of turquoise water.

Rousseaux put the cap back on his Mount Blanc pen, closed his laptop, sat back and looked at her thoughtfully. The beautiful girl could herself be held captive to a world of beauty. Instinctively, he knew she wasn't going anywhere.

"When Cortez arrived in the Americas, he burned his ships. Welcome to the New World, Stella."

***

Reconciling the past with the present was never easy for him. Most of the professionals Mark knew that were still living in New York told him the nightmare of 9/11 was the catalyst for a re-examination of their lives and led them to a whole new set of priorities. He considered that a good plan for the future, but it didn't do much to change the past. Deep within his subconscious, he juggled the images, past and present, trying to get them to make sense.

To everyone on the plane, from six thousand feet the skyline of Manhattan was a stunning sight. He was returning to Vero Beach from New York. Villa Riomar, the place he once called home, was now only a place where vines grew over the masonry walls and the years had eroded from his mind. Gone were the good memories he once had, with only the empty beach and flinty jagged edges of sullied seduction, disappointments and the unforeseen betrayals that remained, the pieces of a bygone era. In his dream, he heard the doorbell ring.

The gate house at Villa Riomar was constructed inside the outer wall of the estate so no one was able to appear at his door without first passing through the automated wrought iron gates that faced Ocean Boulevard, which he always kept closed during the night. To open them, you needed a code, or the remote control that was sitting on his foyer table. Not hearing a car or seeing approaching headlights, he concluded his doorbell had to have been rung by someone arriving on foot from the adjoining estate, all the more mysterious because Villa Dellacroix continued to be shrouded in darkness.

Could it be Hector stopping by to pay him a social visit, or was it the live-in housekeeper from Villa Dellacroix?

Alone in his living room, he set his Armagnac down on the onyx coffee table and walked to the main entry foyer. As the door-bell rang a second time, he stopped to make himself more pre-sentable, straightening his Polo shirt and smoothing his hair in the mirror. Then, without flipping on the outside light or gaping through the peephole to see who was ringing his doorbell, he un-locked the door and swung it open.

Standing in the shadows, staring at Mark with his cold black lifeless eyes, was the ghost of Emilio Rosa.